The Works of Kurt Weill:
Transformations and Reconfigurations in 20th-Century Music

Contemporary Composers

General Editors
Massimiliano Locanto
Massimiliano Sala

Volume 5

Publications of the Centro Studi Opera Omnia Luigi Boccherini
Pubblicazioni del Centro Studi Opera Omnia Luigi Boccherini
Publications du Centro Studi Opera Omnia Luigi Boccherini
Veröffentlichungen des Centro Studi Opera Omnia Luigi Boccherini
Publicaciones del Centro Studi Opera Omnia Luigi Boccherini
Lucca

The Works of Kurt Weill

Transformations and Reconfigurations in 20th-Century Music

EDITED BY
NAOMI GRABER AND MARIDA RIZZUTI

BREPOLS
TURNHOUT
MMXXIII

© BREPOLS 2023

All rights reserved. No part of this publication may be reproduced,
stored in a retrieval system, or transmitted, in any form or by any means,
electronic, mechanical, photocopying, recording, or otherwise, without
the prior permission of the publisher.

D/2023/0095/152

ISBN 978-2-503-60674-3

Printed in Italy

Contents

Naomi Graber, with Marida Rizzuti
    Preface   vii

Transformations

Stephen Hinton
    Weill's Cinematic Imagination: Reality and Fantasy   3

Francesco Finocchiaro
    Kurt Weill and the Principle of 'Concertante Music'   21

William A. Everett
    Kurt Weill and the American Operetta Tradition:
    The Firebrand of Florence and *Where Do We Go from Here*?   37

Naomi Graber,
    «Steel Veins»: *Railroads on Parade*
    and the Industrial Folk   57

Marida Rizzuti
    Shared Authorship and Compositional Process in 1940s Hollywood:
    One Touch of Venus by Kurt Weill and Ann Ronell   79

Arianne Johnson Quinn
    Musical Language, Censorship, and Theatrical Identity
    in Kurt Weill's London Works (1930-1935)   99

TIM CARTER
 Kurt Weill's 'Song of the Free' (1942): A «United Nations Anthem»?   117

RECONFIGURATIONS

NILS GROSCH
 How Many Weills? Rethinking a Musician's Identity   147

LEO IZZO
 Changes in Kurt Weill's Music: Cross Cultural
 Reception between Jazz and Avant-garde   163

MISAKO OHTA
 Die Dreigroschenoper in Japan:
 The 'Threepenny Fever' in Its Early Days   185

TOBIAS FASSHAUER
 «Hard to Distinguish from Cole Porter»:
 On the Deeper Truth of an Invective by Adorno   209

REBECCA SCHMID
 Street Scenes   225

KIM H. KOWALKE
 Whats Makes Weill Weill?   247

ABSTRACTS AND BIOGRAPHIES   263

INDEX OF NAMES   271

Preface

On 21 February 1947, Kurt Weill sent a note to *Life* magazine to correct a recent article:

> I have a gentle beef about one of your phrases. Although I was born in Germany, I do not consider myself a «German composer». The Nazis obviously did not consider me as such either, and I left their country (an arrangement which suited both me and my rulers admirably) in 1933. I am an American citizen and during my dozen years in this country have composed exclusively for the American stage, writing the scores for *Johnny Johnson, Knickerbocker Holiday, Lady in the Dark, One Touch of Venus, The Firebrand of Florence* (ouch!) and *Street Scene*[1].

Kurt Weill's self-positioning emerges clearly from these brief lines: having composed exclusively for American audiences for over a decade, he considered himself a full citizen both legally and ideologically, and one who no longer maintained any loyalty to his former homeland.

This statement has appeared in scholarly accounts of Kurt Weill since his death in 1950, sometimes as evidence of a true split between his European and American careers, and sometimes as an opening for a more nuanced exploration of Weill's transnational career. Jürgen Schebera cites this passage as evidence of the composer's «determination not only to apply for citizenship but to become an American in thought, feeling, and speech»[2]. However, Kim Kowalke uses Weill's words as the starting point to explore Weill's entire career, noting that America — and its German counterpart, «Amerika» — was a constant for the composer on both sides of the Atlantic[3]. Stephen Hinton goes one step further, observing that scholarly interpretations of Weill's «gentle beef» raise issues beyond a single individual's biography, issues «concerning the extent to which national history, collective guilt, political significance, and aesthetic judgement are separated and separable»[4].

---

[1]. Weill 1947.

[2]. Schebera 1995, p. 296.

[3]. Kowalke 2000, pp. 76, 78-81. Kowalke notes that Weill's lifelong engagement with America/Amerika was ambivalent in both Germany and the United States. In the former, it represented a heady mix modernity, primitivism, and capitalist danger, while in the latter it was «fundamentally decent», yet still in need of «cautionary tales».

[4]. Hinton 2012, p. 197. Hinton goes on to posit a new vision of exile studies that allows for a more nuanced account of Weill's American career.

Preface

Yet this was not the first time Weill hoped to leverage an identity position to gain favor with audiences and institutions. Both before and after his immigration, Weill made numerous claims about his various aesthetic and national identities. To the organizers of a 1922 festival of chamber music in Donaueschingen, he emphasized his connection with his teacher Ferrucio Busoni and (somewhat dubiously) claimed to be from Freiburg[5]. In early 1941, an (almost certainly fictional) account of a conversation with playwright Moss Hart in the souvenir program for *Lady in the Dark* had Weill emphasizing his connections with German operatic and modernist culture alongside his desire to revolutionize American theatre:

> I started my career in music by writing chamber music, symphonies, sonatas and so forth. Then I began to write operas. There were about 120 opera houses in Germany at that time and it was a great field for a composer. It also brought me into contact with theatre. I had a feeling for the theatre, that I wanted to compose for it rather than for the concert hall. Here again, I found that opera was too formalized. I looked about for something which would provide me with greater freedom. It was then that I met George [*sic*] Kaiser, author of *Gas*, and other great plays. He occupied the same position in Germany in those days as Eugene O'Neill does in America[6].

Though Weill likely never spoke those exact words, his willingness to highlight his European past speaks to the desire of *Lady in the Dark*'s production team to accentuate Weill's operatic credentials in order to portray the show as something more sophisticated than the average Broadway musical.

On a practical level, Weill's ability to know which facets of his biography to underline at any given time shows a composer with an acute business sense, and keen insights into the relationship between audience and artist[7]. Weill was never untruthful about his identities. After all, 'identity' encompasses a wide range of meanings and analytical categories, all of which are negotiations between an individual and their cultural surroundings. Even after his death, Weill's identities continued to multiply. For mid-century Broadway creatives, he became a symbol of the Weimar Republic that he claimed to have left behind; in the *Washington Post*, critic Richard L. Coe called John Kander, Fred Ebbs, and Bob Fosse's *Chicago* (1975) «the sort of musical Brecht and Weill might have written in *St. Joan of the Stockyards* had they

---

[5]. Though Weill was born in Dessau, his family had roots in Freiburg. See GROSCH 2023, p. 149.

[6]. Souvenir Program for *Lady in the Dark*, available in the production files of *Lady in the Dark* at the Weill-Lenya Research Center in New York, NY.

[7]. Stephen Hinton, drawing psychologist David Reisman, considers this latter aspect of Weill's career to be a fundamental part of the composer's psychology, calling him an «other-directed» composer (HINTON 1999). Similarly, Kim Kowalke notes that these insights are a significant continuity in his career, noting that his style is essentially *Offentlich*, that is, public-facing (KOWALKE 1995).

Preface

been raised on American vaudeville»[8]. For some German critics attending the production of *Der Weg der Verheißung* in 1999, Weill was emblematic of a generation who was forced to abandon their German identities for Jewish ones, despite the composer's claims that the work was «universal»[9]. In this light, it is not just Weill who creates his identities. Rather, 'Weill' is a co-creation of the composer and his audiences, interpreters, and biographers, all working — sometimes in tandem, sometimes at cross-purposes — to understand the complexities of his life, career, and music[10].

The essays in this volume attempt to capture those complexities of Weill's career by bringing together a group of scholars as international as the composer himself to engage in a shared reflection on some foundational themes in research on the composer. 'Transformations' addresses aspects of Weill's aesthetics, career, and biography, exploring his dramaturgy, and how he positioned himself within the various artistic communities of Germany, the United States and beyond. In 'Reconfigurations', the authors investigate aspects of Weill's reception and legacy beyond his sphere of influence, including how he has been misunderstood in relation to his contemporaries, how his music has been reinterpreted, and how new theoretical approaches to musical theatre can elucidate his vast influence.

'Transformations' opens with discussions of Weill's extensive but little-known writings on film. Drawing on the work of Walter Benjamin, Wolfgang Ette, and Berthold Hoeckner, Stephen Hinton shows how Weill's thoughts on multimedial music chart a course between Brechtian detachment and emotional engagement, drawing on music's capacity to create a kind of 'magic'. Francesco Finocchiaro picks up the thread of Weill's thoughts on music and movies, putting into context the composer's desire for a 'concertante' film music. The author situates Weill's thinking within the German debates about the relationship between music and image in the early days of film, analyzing Weill's unique definition of audio-visual 'montage'. William A. Everett continues the reflection of Weill's interest genre dialogue on stage and on film by addressing Weill's engagement with the idea of 'operetta', specifically, the American variety, showing how two works, *The Firebrand of Florence* and the film *Where Do We Go from Here?* (both 1945) engage with and subvert the conventions of American operetta for comic and dramatic effect.

The next four essays all address Weill's working methods and his relationship to audiences. Naomi Graber situates *Railroads on Parade* (1939, rev. 1940) within the broader context of the 1939-1940 New York World's Fair, showing how Weill's folksong-laden score participates in broader industrial public-relations campaigns in the wake of the New Deal. Marida Rizzuti investigates the topic of the unusual relationship between arranger and composer in the studio

---

[8]. COE 1975.
[9]. LEVITZ 2000, pp. 98-99.
[10]. As Claire Taylor-Jay notes, this formulation of a composer's 'identity' owes much to Roland Barthes and Michel Foucault's deconstruction of the 'author'. See TAYLOR-JAY 2009, pp. 89-91.

Preface

system era through the case study of the partnership between Kurt Weill and Ann Ronell during the production of the film of *One Touch of Venus* (1948). The following essays take up the issue of nationalism and government. Arianne Johnson Quinn focuses on Weill's London period, which preceded his final departure from Europe. Using the British productions of *Anna-Anna* (as *Die sieben Todsünden* [1933] was retitled) and *A Kingdom for a Cow* (1935), she shows that Weill's ambivalent reception in London resulted from a combination of shifting cultural winds and governmental policy. Those same forces were at work during World War II, as Tim Carter demonstrates, though Weill was better positioned to navigate them as he sought to support the allied troupes in a variety of efforts, culminating in the radio broadcast of his 'Song of the Free' in 1942.

Nils Grosch initiates the second part of the volume, 'Reconfigurations', by addressing Weill's identity from the perspective of image construction. Drawing on ideas of cultural mobility, Grosch shows that the idea of a unified identity is chimerical, and that Weill transformed and reconfigured himself throughout his life, as most artists do. Leo Izzo continues the discussion of Weill's reception with his analyses of jazz artists' interpretations and reinterpretations of the composer's music. He shows that Weill's music continued to have a transnational appeal long after the composer's death, with artists as disparate as pop singer Bobby Darin and Italian avant-gardist Bruno Maderna adapting Weill's songs for a variety of contexts and audiences. The issue of Weill's reception beyond his immediate sphere is taken up by Misako Ohta in her account of the reception of *Die Dreigroschenoper* in Japan of the 1920s and 1930s. She notes that the Japanese 'Threepenny Fever' reflected a number of trends in Japanese theatre and culture, even as the work itself underwent significant transformations for its stage debut.

The next two essays situate Weill's music specifically within American musical theatre, both in his lifetime and after. Picking up on Theodor Adorno's comment that Weill's American music was «hard to distinguish from Cole Porter», Tobias Fasshauer shows that, *pace* Adorno, Porter's music is nuanced and sophisticated. Fasshauer notes significant similarities between Weill and Porter's musical syntax and poetics, showing how skilled composers can forge paths of originality even within standardized genres. Rebecca Schmid investigates similar parallels between Weill and Leonard Bernstein. She notes that the latter's *West Side Story* (1957) draws on the harmonic and dramaturgical example of *Street Scene* (1947), especially in the construction of the central romantic pairings of both works. Both shows blur the boundaries between 'musical' and 'opera', a project of vital importance Weill and Bernstein throughout their Broadway careers.

The volume ends with Weill's own reflections on his career. Using Weill's obituaries, as well as his own words, Kim H. Kowalke addresses a long-standing issue in Weill studies: the bifurcation of the composer's career and person into two distinct entities: one German, the second American. To counter this, Kowalke notes several prominent continuities in the composer's practices.

Preface

Throughout this volume, Weill's continuous efforts to speak to his audiences on their own terms — German, British, American, and beyond — emerges, alongside his constant efforts at experimentation and innovation across the media landscape. In turn, Weill adapted to and was adopted by myriad musical cultures, sometimes with difficulty, sometimes successfully, but always revealing facets of both the composer and the circumstances surrounding his music. No single volume could hope to cover the entire life and impact of such a composer, and many deserving subjects remain unaddressed here, including Weill's complex and lifelong relationship with Jews and Judaism, and his unique approach to issues of race and ethnicity more broadly. Rather, we hope to continue the conversation.

***

The origin of this volume is rooted in the international conference *Music, Cinema, and Modernism: The Works and Heritage of Kurt Weill between Europe and America*, held at the University of Turin in virtual mode on 20 and 21 May 2021, organized by the Department of Humanistic Studies at Unito in collaboration with the Centro Studi Opera Omnia Luigi Boccherini, with the support of The Kurt Weill Foundation for Music. The critical reflections and lively debate sparked during those days, despite the online mode, were the starting point for this book.

The most challenging part of a book to write are the acknowledgements: we thank the Board of Trustees of the Kurt Weill Foundation, specifically Brady Sansone for supporting the organizational and administrative phases of the Turin Conference, Dave Stein, archivist of Weill-Lenya Research Center, for his unconditional commitment to everything related to primary sources on Kurt Weill. We would like to thank the contributors who have made this valuable, thought-provoking book such a forum for sharing knowledge about a pivotal twentieth-century composer. Sincere thanks go to Massimiliano Sala for being the first person with whom we started to say that «we should do something about Weill», and Roberto Illiano for his constant and supportive work during the book's processing stages. Last but not least we'd like to thank Giulia Carluccio, who since the first presentation of the Weill project has warmly, enthusiastically, and wholeheartedly welcomed the idea, supporting it and making its realization possible.

Naomi Graber, with Marida Rizzuti

This publication is funded in part by the Kurt Weill Foundation for Music, Inc., New York, NY and the Dipartimento di Studi Umanistici, Università degli Studi di Torino. Available for any rights holders who could not be reached.

Preface

Bibliography

Coe 1975
Coe, Richard L. 'American Musical Dazzlers', in: *Washington Post*, 13 July 1975, p. 142.

Grosch 2023
Grosch, Nils. 'How Many Weills? Rethinking a Musician's Identity', in: *The Works of Kurt Weill: Transformations and Reconfigurations in 20th-Century Music*, edited by Naomi Graber and Marida Rizzuti, Turnhout, Brepols, 2023 (Contemporary Composers, 5), pp. 147-161.

Hinton 1999
Hinton, Stephen. 'Hindemith and Weill: Cases of 'Inner' and 'Other' Direction', in: *Driven Into Paradise: The Musical Migration from Nazi Germany to the United States*, edited by Reinhold Brinkmann and Christoph Wolff, Berkeley-Los Angeles, University of California Press, 1999, pp. 261-278.

Hinton 2012
Id. *Weill's Musical Theatre: Stages of Reform*, Berkeley-Los Angeles, University of California Press, 2012.

Kowalke 1995
Kowalke, Kim H. 'Kurt Weill, Modernism, and Popular Culture: *Öffentlichkeit als Stil*', in: *Modernism/Modernity*, II/1 (1995), pp. 27-69.

Kowalke 2000
Id. 'Kurt Weill's American Dreams', in: *Theater*, XXX/3 (2000), pp. 76-81.

Levitz 2000
Levitz, Tamara. 'Either a German or a Jew: The German Reception of Kurt Weill's *Der Weg der Verheißung*', in: *Theater*, XXX/3 (2000), pp. 97-105.

Schebera 1995
Schebera, Jürgen. *Kurt Weill: An Illustrated Life*, translated by Caroline Murphy, New Haven (CT), Yale University Press, 1995.

Taylor-Jay 2009
Taylor-Jay, Claire. 'The Composer's Voice? Compositional Style and the Criteria of Value in Weill, Krenek and Stravinsky', in: *Journal of the Royal Music Association*, CXXXIV/1 (2009), pp. 85-111.

Weill 1947
Weill, Kurt. 'Letters to the Editor: Gentle Beef', in *Life*, XX/11 (17 March 1917), p. 17, <https://www.kwf.org/kurt-weill/recommended/gentle-beef/>, accessed May 2023.

Transformations

Weill's Cinematic Imagination:
Reality and Fantasy

Stephen Hinton
(Stanford University)

I

STRADDLING THE WORLDS of reality and fantasy, Weill's cinematic imagination permeates his creative work as a galvanizing affinity between the media of stage and screen. It refers principally to the fact that his compositions for the stage were substantially influenced by the cinema as that medium emerged in the first half of the twentieth century. Nor was his film output insubstantial, overshadowed though it tends to be by the much better-known and more numerous works for the musical theatre[1].

Moving to less concrete matters, composing for films is something that Weill speculated about, producing numerous published and unpublished texts on the topic, and which he also fantasized about with projects of various kinds that either remained unfinished or on some level were finished in such a way that left his artistic imagination unsatisfied. The creative imaginings Weill brought to bear from his life in the theatre bumped up against the hard realities of the film industry.

Fantasy is relevant in another critical respect, too. Just as Weill's teacher Busoni had considered music's proper roles on stage and decisively influenced his disciple's own thinking on the matter, so Weill sought to reassess those roles for the cinema. To be considered, then, is how the composer's musical aesthetics for the stage and screen can be situated in the broader discourse about Walter Benjamin's concept of «aura» and its putative disappearance in the age of art's technological reproducibility — and, as discussed below, how this discourse has been both reassessed and developed in some recent writings about music.

---

[1]. This essay draws in part on material from the chapter 'Stage vs. Screen' in: HINTON 2012, pp. 323-359.

Weill's perhaps biggest fantasy involved combining film, the emerging artistic medium of his time, and opera, his «real domain», as he called it in later life, to produce an envisaged «film opera», to use his own generic coinage. In order to demonstrate that film opera was not just an unrealized ideal, however, even if it was largely that, mention should be made of *Where Do We Go from Here?*, a movie that realized, at least in one notable segment, the kind of thing he seems to have been aiming at with this concept. Released in 1945, the movie's «film opera» segment comes some 15 years after he first used the term in an article that reads like an artistic manifesto.

II

Published in the *Frankfurter Zeitung* on 24 May 1930, just as Weill was signing a contract for G. W. Pabst's film version of his own *Dreigroschenoper* (1928, film released as *3 Groschen-Oper* in 1931), 'Tonfilm, Opernfilm, Filmoper' addresses the very matter of reality versus fantasy at the outset: «There is no denying that sound film or talkies [*Tonfilm*] lags far behind the possibilities that our imagination [*Phantasie*] uncovered as this new technology began to emerge»[2]. He goes on in the article to distinguish between the medium of sound film generally and two subgenres in which he declares a special interest. «Opera-film» (*Opernfilm*) is the term he uses to describe a film version of a preexisting opera — *3 Groschen-Oper* would fall under this category in spite of the radical changes made to the original. The term «film-opera» (*Filmoper*) he reserves for original sound films conceived from the outset in terms of musical principles. If his own involvement in film began in the former category, his creative ambitions tended more toward the latter — «tended» being the operative word for the reasons indicated already.

Like Benjamin's vastly better-known and more consequential essay of five years later, 'Das Kunstwerk im Zeitalter seiner technischen Reproduzierbarkeit', an early version of which was published in French in the *Zeitschrift für Sozialforschung* in 1936, Weill's film article belongs to a sizable corpus of theoretical writings from the period — Benjamin's *Zeitalter* or age — that may be read as early contributions to media theory: before, that is, the discipline of «Media Theory» established itself somewhat later in the century and certainly long before our own digital multimedia revolution relocated mass media to the virtual world of cyberspace. Those early texts were responding to, as well as shaping, the *first* multimedia revolution — a revolution that Weill was inclined neither to ignore nor to resist[3]. The central issue that informed

---

[2]. WEILL 1930, quoted here from WEILL 2000, p. 110: «Es ist nicht zu leugnen, dass der Tonfilm noch sehr weit zurück ist gegenüber den Möglichkeiten, die unsere Phantasie bei dem Heraufkommen dieser neuen Technik entdeckte».

[3]. Benjamin's essay exists in several versions. Written between autumn 1935 and February 1936, the first version appeared in a slightly abridged French translation in the *Zeitschrift für Sozialforschung* in 1936 (BENJAMIN 1936). The revised and expanded second version that appeared posthumously in German in the *Gesammelte*

Benjamin's essay — that art and its reception were undergoing a substantial change because of the new media, especially through 1) the possibility of mass reproduction, 2) the transformed representation of reality, and 3) a transformed collective perception — concerned Weill, too, and was prompted above all by the medium of film and the even more recent one of radio.

III

Weill's formation as a composer for the musical theatre was intimately bound up with his experience of these new media. Even though he professed a 'Commitment to Opera', to cite the title of a manifesto of his from 1925, he understood the relationship between musical theatre and the new media to be reciprocal[4]. For some five years he wrote regular columns for *Der deutsche Rundfunk* — a German forerunner of the British *The Radio Times* — as one of that journal's music critics. His contributions ranged from perfunctory reports on operas broadcast on the radio to think-pieces with titles such as 'Möglichkeiten absoluter Radiokunst' ('On the Possibilities of Radio Art') in which he speculatively transferred to the new medium an essentially Busonian aesthetic of self-sufficient or 'absolute' music[5]. As a composer, then, he was keen to explore working in radio and film just as he acknowledged how these media, especially film, left their mark on his works for the stage. It was a two-way street: as a composer for the stage he wanted to bring his experience in opera houses and the theatre to bear on music composed expressly for the radio and the cinema. But those media, especially cinema, also affected what he wrote for the theatre. These are questions of poietics, of course, pertaining to the whole business of authorship and how composers for the musical theatre write in the age of technological revolution. They are also questions of aesthetics in the etymological sense of the term, pertaining to the arena of reception, located somewhere in the involved and sometimes quite arcane discourse surrounding Benjamin's concept of «aura». They are questions, in short, that remain as relevant today as Benjamin's essay continues to be, albeit with significant caveats.

IV

An initial and quite obvious instance of creative cross-pollination is the inclusion of a cinematic sequence in the 1925 one-act opera *Royal Palace*, for which the surrealist poet Iwan Goll wrote the libretto. The first of three ballet-like interludes, the film is set in motion by

---

Schriften (BENJAMIN 1989) forms the basis of the English translation quoted here (BENJAMIN 2006). A third version appeared in German as BENJAMIN 1980 and in English as BENJAMIN 2003. For a comparison of the various versions, see HANSEN 2004. See also the texts on *Medientheorie* published in KÜMMEL – LÖFFLER 2002.

[4]. WEILL 1926.

[5]. A complete catalogue of Weill's contributions to *Der deutsche Rundfunk* along with a representative selection of the edited texts is included in WEILL 2000.

the three men in the life of Dejanira, a figure transplanted from classical myth. Although the film has unfortunately been lost, the piano-vocal score describes the sequence as showing «all contemporary delectations: Dejanira in Nizza, in the sleeping car *en route* to Constantinople, a ball, Russian ballet, flight to the North Pole, etc.», all of which is accompanied in the orchestra pit by a raucous foxtrot.

A perhaps less obvious instance of cross-pollination are the quintessentially epic elements of the scene titles deployed in works such as *Die Dreigroschenoper*, which suggest the kind of narrative guideposts used in silent movies. Reflecting the work's neoclassical aesthetic, the 'epic' projections supply narrative summaries of the plot and emphasize how the 'play with music' works with separate and separable elements. The result is a form of radical, de-familiarizing montage that informed both how the work was written and how it was staged, with the barebones set design, the makeshift white half-curtain with the work's title emblazoned on it by hand, and the instrumentalists positioned visibly on stage rather than hidden in the orchestra pit. Some of the work's elements, in particular ballads such as the 'Barbara-Song', 'Seeräuberjenny' and 'Solomonsong', seem separable also in the sense that they provide the opportunity for the actors to step out of their role and narrate stories not immediately connected to the plot. It was thus possible, for example, for 'Seeräuberjenny' to be reassigned from Polly (in the premiere) to Jenny in Brecht's revised version for the collected *Versuche* edition of his works in 1931 and also in Pabst's film *3 Groschen-Oper* from the same year. This modular conception made it a mere formality for individual numbers to be transmitted separately, as occurred with the various sheet music editions and recordings.

Much later, in his American opera *Street Scene* (1947) and the college opera *Down in the Valley* (1948), Weill would underscore spoken dialogue in the manner of cinematic melodramas. Quintessentially film-like moments also occur in *Street Scene* where the music accompanying the dialogue alludes to other parts of the score — melodrama, that is, with motifs of reminiscence crafted in an undeniably Wagnerian fashion. *Down in the Valley* is similarly cinematic, not only in its use of underscored dialogue, but also in its overall narrative organization based on temporal flashbacks.

«It is quite evident», the composer wrote in the programmatically titled article 'Verschiebungen in der musikalischen Produktion' ('Shifts in Musical Production') from 1927, «that the development of music [in contemporary opera] is receiving new impulses from theatre produced for the cinema»[6]. He also added that «it has proved to be quite possible, working closely with representatives of equal stature in the sister arts, to set about creating the kind of music theatre that can provide an untopical, unique and definitive representation of our age», mentioning in particular his *Mahagonny-Songspiel* (1927) as an exemplar of a «new

---

[6]. WEILL 1927, p. 63: «Auf diesen und auf anderen Gebieten der neuen Oper zeigt sich deutlich, dass die musikalische Entwicklung vom Theaterfilm eine neue Befruchtung erlangt».

epic form» that «makes it possible to give opera a structure that is absolutely musical, even instrumental [*konzertante*]».

As well as being creatively receptive to «new impulses from theatre produced for the cinema», Weill was no less sensitive to distinguishing between music produced for the stage and that for the screen. In the 1930 article he emphasized the need «to examine what possibilities there are to show a singing person in sound film». He viewed film as quite different from theatre in this regard. «It seems almost out of the question that a person would stand there and sing in a sound film as on the operatic stage»[7]. But he did not rule out duets, «especially if they contain elements of the plot or of movement». He also entertained what he calls «new possibilities of presenting song in motion». The example he cites is the «singing chauffeur» in *Liebeswalzer* (1929). Another option is «disconnecting a song from the camera by showing its effect on the listener»; here he refers to Marlene Dietrich's song in *Der blaue Engel (1930)*[8]. Both examples belong to what film theorists would nowadays call «source» or «diegetic» music — music that forms an integral part of the narrative as opposed to being merely a means of narration or representation; represented music, in other words, as opposed to the music of representation.

v

Expressing his enthusiasm for Mickey Mouse and other Disney films, Weill described them as «rhythmically fixed animated films that establish a thoroughly new and original form of *film ballet*».

> Everything dissolves itself in movement but finds itself again in rhythm. A skeleton plays xylophone with its lower leg on the ribs of a neighboring skeleton, a locomotive strenuously drags itself up a mountain, and the jaw of a predator suddenly becomes the gentlest of all glockenspiels[9].

---

[7]. WEILL 1930, p. 111: «Es wäre zunächst zu untersuchen, welche Möglichkeiten es gibt, den singenden Menschen im Tonfilm zu zeigen. Es erscheint fast ausgeschlossen, dass im Tonfilm sich ein Mensch wie auf der Opernbühne hinstellt und singt».

[8]. *Ibidem*: «Eher denkbar sind bereits Duettwirkungen, besonders wenn sie Handlungs- oder Bewegungselemente enthalten. Wir erkennen aber auch bereits neuartige Möglichkeiten, einen Gesang in der Bewegung zu zeigen (wie etwa das Lied eines fahrenden Chauffeurs im *Liebeswalzer*) oder einen Gesang von der Kamera her aufzulösen, indem man während des Gesanges zugleich die Wirkung auf den Hörer zeigt (wie bei dem Lied der Marlene Dietrich im *Blauen Engel*)».

[9]. *Ibidem*, p. 112: «Diese nach rein musikalischen Gesetzen gezeichneten, rhythmisch fixierten Bewegungsfilme, die eine durchaus neue und originale Form des "Filmballetts" begründen, zeigen gewissermaßen die Relativität aller Erscheinungen [...] In der Bewegung löst sich alles auf, aber im Rhythmus findet sich alles wieder. Ein Skelett spielt mit seinem Unterschenkel auf den Rippen seines Nachbarskeletts Xylophon, eine

Ill. 1: *Silly Symphony: The Skeleton Dance.*

He is referring here to the Disney films called *Silly Symphonies*, specifically to the first of the series made in 1929 and titled *The Skeleton Dance*[10] (Ill. 1). The music was composed by Carl W. Stalling, perhaps best known for 'Looney Tunes' and 'Merrie Melodies'. It was Stalling, in fact, who approached Disney about creating the series of animated short films, and who created the music first, thus echoing Weill's own Busonian idea about self-sufficient instrumental music (*konzertante Musik*, as he called it) for the stage. The animation followed the composition, not the other way around, created as it was expressly to match the already existing music — a procedure later carried out on a much larger scale with preexisting classical music in Disney's 1940 movie *Fantasia*.

If the music for *The Skeleton Dance* sounds familiar to Weillians, it is likely because its rhythmic gestures reemerge in the 'Dance of the Tumblers', with the ballet of the bones fleshed out, so to speak, for acrobats at Liza's circus in *Lady in the Dark* (1941); it also casts a furtive 'self-borrowing' glance back to the Chaplinesque banana dance in *Der Silbersee* (1933). Here again, the intermedial crosspollination of cinema and theatre.

But for Weill «opera, whose impact depends on the unmediated contact of the singer with the audience, seems the least suited of all forms of theatre simply to be captured on

Lokomotive schleppt sich in mühseliger Gymnastik einen Berg hinauf, und das Gebiss eines Raubtiers wird rasch zum lieblichsten aller Glockenspiele».

[10]. *Silly Symphony: The Skeleton Dance* is available on YouTube at: <https://www.youtube.com/watch?v=vOGhAV-84iI>, accessed April 2023.

film»[11]. The solution would be «to produce a sound film so removed from the original that it amounted to a new creation». «More important than such experiments is the creation of original sound films», namely «film-operas». That is Weill's priority: «Only when one has clearly established the basic formal tenets concerning the musical possibilities of sound film can one begin to think about transforming a classic opera into an "opera-film"»[12]. Also worth bearing in mind here is that many of Weill's musical theatre works do not depend solely on the unmediated contact of the singer with the audience, but involve all manner of mediation or «epic» interventions.

But opportunities for new creations — whether opera-films or film-operas — were few and far between. Pabst's movie adaptation ended in a lawsuit, which Weill won (because he wasn't properly consulted) and Brecht lost (because he failed to hold up his end of the bargain)[13]. It also inspired Brecht's *Dreigroschenprozess*, a substantial tract on the perils of the commodification of art that no doubt influenced Benjamin as he prepared his artwork essay[14].

VI

Not until Weill came to Hollywood in 1938 would he be able to test his aesthetic ideals again against the reality of the studio system with *You and Me*, a morally didactic film noir directed by Fritz Lang (Ill. 2). As well introducing experiments with the musicalization of inanimate objects à la Micky Mouse, something more fully described in Weill's notes on *You and Me* than realized in the film, just as the film overall reduced the musical content envisaged by the composer, including the excision of a theme song that was supposed to recur throughout as a leitmotif, Weill did seize the opportunity to insert a torch song[15]. Here the reformed or at least reforming gangsters (played by Silvia Sidney and George Raft) are seen reacting to a nightclub diseuse as she performs a soulful ballad about a guy who may be good-for-nothing but is nonetheless «right», a throwback to the pipe-smoking 'Surabaya Johnny' from *Happy End* (1929) and also redolent of Kern and Wodehouse's 'Bill' from *Showboat* (1927) — perhaps a composite, or hybrid, of the two.

---

[11]. WEILL 1930, p. 113: «Gerade die Oper, deren Wirkung vom unmittelbaren Kontakt des Sängers mit dem Publikum abhängig ist, scheint von allen Theaterformen am wenigsten geeignet, einfach abfotografiert zu werden».

[12]. «Es lässt sich allenfalls denken, dass man [...] einen Tonfilm herstellt, der sich allerdings so weit von seinem Vorbild enterfernen würde, dass er beinahe einer Neuschöpfung gleichkäme. [...] Erst wenn man so über die musikalischen Möglichkeiten und die formalen Grundgesetze des Tonfilms Klarheit gewonnen hat, kann man daran denken, eine klassische Oper zu einem "Opernfilm" umzugestalten».

[13]. See HINTON 2012, pp. 328-332.

[14]. BRECHT 1931.

[15]. Weill's typescript notes 'About the music for *You and Me*' (dated 24 May 1937) are housed in the Weill-Lenya Archive at Yale University, New Haven, USA. They are published in WEILL 1990, pp. 120-123.

ILL. 2: Billboard poster for *You and Me*, directed by Fritz Lang.

Weill's Cinematic Imagination: Reality and Fantasy

A formal analogy of 'The Right Guy for Me' suggests itself for Weillians not only with 'Surabaya Johnny' but also with 'Seeräuberjenny', where the song functions diegetically, just as Weill prescribed, as the main possibility for showing a singing person in sound film. In that sense, *Die Dreigroschenoper* was part of Weill's film aesthetic *avant la lettre*, as it were.

VII

The last movie example comes from *Where Do We Go from Here?*, which was directed by Gregory Ratoff and released in 1945. It is the story of a young man called Bill frustrated by his failure for health reasons to enlist in the armed forces. He manages, however, to transport himself back to several key moments in American history with the help of a genie. The key scene from a musical perspective is the one in which the central character, played by Fred MacMurray, finds himself in the midst of a mutiny on one of Columbus's ships in 1492 (a scene based in historical fact), whereupon he lends support to the celebrated explorer of the New World by inviting the disaffected sailors to «imagine what happens to posterity without Columbus» (Ill. 3). The libretto by Ira Gershwin makes no secret of the lyricist's fondness for Gilbert and Sullivan, as illustrated by the following excerpt from the concluding song of the sequence. Published posthumously as 'The Nina, the Pinta, the Santa Maria', the number incorporates four stanzas, the first two preceded by an introduction and the second by a «Recitativo (Free)». Here are the third and the fourth:

> No automat nickels
> No Heinz and his pickles
> No land of the brave and the freeah,
> Just think what you're losing
> If you don't keep cruising
> the Nina, the Pinta, the Santa Maria.
> No Radio City
> And who'll feed the kitty
> At Belmont Park and Hialeah!
> But you'll be unveiling
> A new world by sailing
> the Nina, the Pinta, the Santa Maria.

As with the Gilbert and Sullivan Savoy operas, this is opera about opera. The hapless Bill has been transported not only in time, but also into a foreign genre, and he seems both surprised and pleased with himself when he realizes that his vocal performance is going better than he might otherwise have reason to expect.

Ill. 3: Fortunio Bonanova as Christopher Columbus in the movie *Where Do We Go from Here?* (1945).

That a comic movie would contain a Savoy opera segment lasting a full nine minutes is remarkable. And Weill, too, seemed quite proud of his «regular little comic opera», as he described it[16]. Writing to his agent, he heralded «the great acclaim which the score for *Where do we go from here* got» as «an indication of the vast new possibilities for music in pictures». He was «convinced», he wrote, «that someday somebody will write a "film-opera" which will start a new trend in musical pictures — and I hope it will be me»[17].

Weill himself described *Where Do We Go from Here?* as «a sort of humorous fantasy» with which he was «on the whole very pleased». If the movie gave him faith in starting «a new trend in musical pictures» that he could participate in, its quintessentially cinematic «time travel» structure is something that had been prefigured in *Lady in the Dark* and which would reappear as the fundamental narrative conceit of the vaudeville *Love Life* (1948).

---

[16]. Weill 1946, p. 400.

[17]. Letter to Irving Lazar, dated 28 November 1946; copy in Weill-Lenya Research Center, Kurt Weill Foundation, New York.

But the nine-minute opera travesty was as far as he got in his quest, and a real film-opera would remain a pipe-dream for him. The reasons are probably several. On the production or poietic side, there's the fact that even in the theatre, Weill gravitated toward mixed genres rather than pure opera. Many of his works are variants of the Mozartian singspiel. His creative leanings may have taken him closer, if anything, to a film musical, not a film opera. And then there's the whole matter of the composer's role in Hollywood, about which he complained bitterly, likening himself on occasion to a sex worker to excuse his acquiescence (a trope also used by Hanns Eisler, incidentally)[18]. The home for a musician working with «artists of equal stature in the sister arts»[19] was not cinema, but the theatre.

Poietics become aesthetics with regard to singing: «It seems almost out of the question», he had written earlier, «that a person would stand there and sing in a sound film as on the operatic stage». The point is that they wouldn't or, if they did, that the effect would be quite different. This is where the issues that Benjamin was attempting to address with his concept of aura come into play. In his aesthetics of film music, more anecdotal than systematic, Weill frequently acknowledged a fundamental difference between live music and canned music. At the same time, he emphasized music's special role, in an almost Schopenhauerian way, on account of its ability to convey «inner song» and embody a «rarer level of truth»[20]. His relationship to the romantic heritage seems to have been as ambivalent as Benjamin's was to the concept of aura, an attitude which Miriam Hansen has characterized as «being torn between the extremes of revolutionary avant-gardism and elegiac mourning for beautiful semblance»[21]. Like Benjamin, Weill too was grappling with «the possibility of experience in mass-mediated modernity»[22].

For all of his commitment to epic forms of theatre — no doubt influenced in their form, if not entirely in their spirit, by the mass medium of the cinema — it can be argued that Weill never entirely eschewed a taste for the sublime. It is a taste nurtured by his youthful exposure to Wagner, and one that resurfaced in his later works for the musical stage. If Wagner was invoked in the collaborations with Brecht primarily to convey brash cynicism about love and eros in the modern world, Wagnerian intonations in works such as *The Firebrand of Florence* (1945) and *One Touch of Venus* (1943) sentimentally hanker after the emotional authenticity of

---

[18]. On 5 March 1937, Weill wrote to Group Theatre director Cheryl Crawford: «Don't worry, Hollywood will not get to me. A whore never loves the man who pays her, she wants to get rid of him as soon as she has rendered her services. That is my relation to Hollywood. (I am the whore.) Most people try to mix the whore-business with ‹love› — that's why they don't get away». Copy of letter in Weill-Lenya Research Center.

[19]. Weill 1927, p. 63.

[20]. Weill stated in 1936, «The stage has a reason for existence today only if it aspires to a rarer level of truth». Weill 1936.

[21]. Hansen 2008, p. 338.

[22]. *Ibidem*, p. 375.

a distant and irretrievable past[23]. Overall, the lingering spirit of Wagner reflects a fundamental ambivalence toward the romantic aesthetics of the sublime. And as Mika Elo and several others have observed, it is this transcendental aesthetic category that plays a constitutive, defining role for Benjamin's aura, too[24].

VIII

Continuing in this vein, I should like to offer some concluding reflections on the cinematic imagination that go beyond Benjamin's theories about the posited disappearance of aura in artworks in the age of mechanical reproduction, above all in cinema. Benjamin's perennially relevant and challenging text invites, indeed has invited, notable attempts at revision and qualification. Of particular note is *Film, Music, Memory* by Berthold Hoeckner, published in 2019, in which the author seeks to «show how music can be evocative of cinematic experience»[25]. Hoeckner's principal aim is to transform Benjamin's concept of the «optical unconscious» for musical purposes into the «optical-acoustic unconscious» of the film score, based on the intuition that music «seems to possess a magic force that makes us see and remember otherwise, for it breathes life into the memory image, making it move»[26]. «In the soundtrack of life, music endows events with meanings that linger as memories»[27].

Other notable contributions include Wolfgang Ette's 'Benjamins Reproduktionsaufsatz und die Musik' in the 2013 essay collection *Klang und Musik bei Walter Benjamin*[28]. Comparison of Ette's and Hoeckner's extension of Benjamin's ideas illustrates not only the suggestive, labile nature of these ideas, but also a variety of options for critical engagement.

Hoeckner's book is a challenging read in a twofold sense: it is challenging in its theoretical sophistication (Benjamin and Adorno in all of their similarities and differences are just two of the many philosophically oriented authors invoked and cited); and it is challenging, too, in laying down a marker for film studies, an appeal to appreciate the terms in which what the author calls that «magic force» of cinematic music «helps to ‹liberate› spectatorial consciousness so that it can experience cinematic emotion»[29]. The word «magic» occurs frequently throughout the book. At stake is nothing less than establishing in Benjaminian terms a specifically «cinematic aura» for music in the age of its technological reproducibility — something that Hoeckner undertakes with both intellectual acuity and stylistic aplomb.

---

[23]. See HINTON 2009.
[24]. ELO 2005.
[25]. HOECKNER 2019, p. 231.
[26]. *Ibidem*, p. 12.
[27]. *Ibidem*, p. 117.
[28]. ETTE 2013.
[29]. *Ibidem*, p. 55.

Weill's Cinematic Imagination: Reality and Fantasy

It will be recalled that Benjamin adapted Freud's unconscious to account for the kind of distracted attention that cinema affords through optical means. Acknowledging an affinity with Dadaism and its defamiliarizing achievements in painting and literature, Benjamin posited that the public was seeking comparable effects in film. «The distracting element in film is also primarily tactile», he wrote, «being based on successive changes of scene and focus which have a percussive effect on the spectator»[30]. But the addition of music changes all that, of course. With music in the mix, with his optical-musical unconscious, Hoeckner is aiming to capture a quite different mode of cinematic reception, one in which the spectator is not so much distracted as drawn in in an intensely absorbing and personally subjective way by music's «magic».

Ette, by contrast, although he also focuses on song, in particular on pop music, draws musical consequences from the three versions of Benjamin's visually oriented text quite different from those drawn by Hoeckner. Acknowledging the broad significance of Benjamin's media theory or «aesthetics», as Benjamin himself calls his ideas about the distracted reception of art, Ette argues that modern-day music reception corresponds especially well with Benjamin's distraction paradigm for art in the age of mechanical reproduction. Indeed, he claims that it is in music, far more than in film, that this kind of reception has unfolded in the century since Benjamin formulated those ideas.

Here Ette touches on a central difference between Benjamin, on the one hand, who entertains a positive concept of distraction, and Adorno, on the other, who dismissed «atomized listening» from a position of resistance to the culture industry in favor of immersive structural listening[31]. Where Adorno diagnoses distracted listeners as displaying regressive behavior, Benjamin sees them as potentially productive, as *Produzenten*, effectively blurring the line between the author and the public.

At the time he was writing, Benjamin's reception aesthetics had intensely political connotations, which emerge at the end of his text in terms of the critical distinction, much debated and contested, between the aestheticization of politics and the politicization of aesthetics, the latter being facilitated by progressive art and productive distraction, the former by the totalizing monumentality of fascist propaganda[32]. In this spirit, albeit under very different cultural conditions, Ette criticizes most films — with very few exceptions — as partaking of what Brecht would call «aristotelean unity». Conventional film music doubtless plays a decisive and constitutive role in stitching together such unity from the perspective of the viewer/listener — something that Benjamin could hardly foresee from his visually biased standpoint. Ette's interest, in other words, is in the theoretical precepts of epic theatre, whose tenets have dominated the reception of Weill's musical theatre and which I discussed elsewhere

---

[30]. Benjamin 2006, p. 30.
[31]. Adorno 1938.
[32]. See Sontag 1975.

with respect to the important distinction in thinking about the role of music, that is, between epic structures (as in number form) and reception, that is, how much music transforms how we experience theatre, not just epic theatre[33].

IX

The gap between reality and fantasy that plays itself out on several levels in Weill's cinematic imagination serves as a reminder that his identity as an artist derives from collaborative projects, in film even more so than in theatre. In film one might even go so far as to say that his theory was more consistent and constitutive for that identity than his motley practice. At the heart of that theory and practice is the central contribution of the performed musical number, the diegetic song, something already key to his experiments in epic theatre. In its conception and reception, depending on a variety of factors, that song may or may not promote the kind of distracted listening that both Benjamin and, later, Ette championed. Conversely, whether on stage or on screen, the discrete song may bristle with the kind of magic, a cinematic aura, if you like, that Hoeckner theorizes in *Film, Music, Memory*. Even Adorno's evident nostalgia for Weill's music of the 1920s celebrated in the essay 'Nach einem Vierteljahrhundert' ('After a Quarter of a Century'), a time in which «an entire generation loved according to the intonations of *The Threepenny Opera*»[34] seems susceptible to that analysis, albeit caught between the narrative threads of memory and the critical gaze of a negative dialectician. «The longing for Weill's music today», Adorno continues, «that is nothing but the longing for anarchic, shabby, stolen happiness at the expense of the administered world in the moment of the latter's evident irresistibility»[35]. The reception of Weill's music is, in short, a complicated matter caught between magic and defamiliarization.

To return in conclusion to *You and Me*: like the Columbus scene in *Where Do We Go from Here?* the music is emphatically music about music. If the Gilbert and Sullivan parody in the latter aesthetically sanctions a comic re-enactment of American history in the form of an extended operatic scene, in the former — whether through Lang's or Weill's inspiration — the reception of song is thematized through twofold mediation. The song is doubly diegetic: it is performed music, cinematically illustrated just as the foxtrot in *Royal Palace* underscored an exotic trip around the world; it is also deployed to illustrate how music can conjure up personal longing and desire («showing its effect on the listener», as Weill put it in 1930 apropos *Der*

---

[33]. HINTON 1988.
[34]. ADORNO 1955; quoted from *Gesammelte Schriften*, p. 549.
[35]. *Ibidem*, «Vielleicht gibt davon die beste Vorstellung, dass man sagt, es habe eine ganze Generation nach dem Tonfall der Dreigroschenoper geliebt. [...] Die Sehnsucht aber nach Weills Musik heute — das ist nichts anderes als die nach anarchischem, schäbigem, gestohlenem Glück auf Kosten der verwalteten Welt noch im Augenblick ihrer offenbaren Unwiderstehlichkeit».

blaue Engel). As embedded in Lang's movie, Weill's cinematic song combines the reflective detachment of epic theatre with the subjective, emotional potential of music's magic.

Bibliography

Adorno 1938
Adorno, Theodor Wiesengrund. 'Über den Fetischcharakter in der Musik und die Regression des Hörens', in: *Zeitschrift für Sozialforschung*, VII (1938), pp. 321-356.

Adorno 1955
Id. 'Nach einem Vierteljahrhundert', in: *Programmheft der Städtischen Bühnen Düsseldorf (1955-56)*, No. 6, pp. 131-140; reprinted in Id. *Gesammelte Schriften. 18: Musikalische Schriften. V*, edited by Rolf Tiedemann and Klaus Schultz, Frankfurt, Suhrkamp Verlag, 1984, pp. 548-551.

Benjamin 1936
Benjamin, Walter. 'L'œuvre d'art à l'époque de sa reproduction mécanisée', translated by Pierre Klossowski, in: *Zeitschrift für Sozialforschung*, V (1936), pp. 40-63.

Benjamin 1980
Id. 'Das Kunstwerk im Zeitalter seiner technischen Reproduzierbarkeit' [second version], in: Id. *Gesammelte Schriften*, I/2, edited by Rolf Tiedemann and Hermann Schweppenhauser, Frankfurt, Suhrkamp Verlag, 1980, pp. 471-508.

Benjamin 1989
Id. 'Das Kunstwerk im Zeitalter seiner technischen Reproduzierbarkeit' [third version], in: Id. *Gesammelte Schriften. 7*, edited by Rolf Tiedemann and Hermann Schweppenhauser, Frankfurt, Suhrkamp-Verlag, 1989, pp. 350-384.

Benjamin 2003
Id. 'The Work of Art in the Age of Its Technological Reproducibility: Third Version', in: Id. *Selected Writings. 4: 1938-1940*, edited by Howard Eiland and Michael W. Jennings, Cambridge (MA), Harvard University Press, 2003, pp. 251-283.

Benjamin 2006
Id. 'The Work of Art in the Age of Its Technological Reproducibility: Second Version', in: *The Work of Art in the Age of Its Technological Reproducibility, and Other Writings on Media*, edited by Michael W. Jennings, Brigid Doherty and Thomas Y. Levin, translated by Edmund Jephcott, Rodney Livingstone, Howard Eiland, *et al.*, Cambridge (MA), The Belknap Press of Harvard University Press, 2006, pp. 19-55.

Brecht 1931
Brecht, Bertolt. 'Der Dreigroschenprozess: Ein soziologisches Experiment', in: Id. *Versuche. 3*, Berlin, Kiepenheuer, 1931.

Elo 2005
Elo, Mika. 'Die Wiederkehr der Aura', in: *Walter Benjamins Medientheorie*, edited by Christian Schulte, Konstanz, UVK-Verlag, 2005, pp. 117-135.

Ette 2013
Ette, Wolfgang. 'Benjamins Reproduktionsaufsatz und die Musik', in: *Klang und Musik bei Walter Benjamin*, edited by Tobias Robert Klein, Munich, Wilhelm Fink, 2013, pp. 143-148.

Hansen 2004
Hansen, Miriam. 'Room-for-Play: Benjamin's Gamble with Cinema', in: *October*, xix (2004), pp. 3-45.

Hansen 2008
Ead. 'Benjamin's Aura', in: *Critical Inquiry*, xxxiv/2 (2008), pp. 336-375.

Hinton 1988
Hinton, Stephen. 'The Concept of Epic Opera: Theoretical Anomalies in the Brecht-Weill Partnership', in: *Festschrift Carl Dahlhaus*, edited by Hermann Danuser, Helga de la Motte, Silke Leopold and Norbert Miller, Laaber, Laaber-Verlag, 1988, pp. 283-294.

Hinton 2009
Id. 'Weill Contra Wagner: Aspects of Ambivalence', in «...*dass alles hätte anders kommen können»: Beiträge zur Musikgeschichte des 20. Jahrhunderts*, edited by Susanne Schaal, Luitgard Schader and Hans-Jürgen Winkler, Frankfurt, Schott, 2009 (Frankfurter Studien, 12), pp. 155-174.

Hinton 2012
Id. *Weill's Musical Theater: Stages of Reform*, Berkeley-Los Angeles, University of California Press, 2012.

Hoeckner 2019
Hoeckner, Berthold. *Film, Music, Memory*, Chicago, University of Chicago Press, 2019.

Kümmel – Löffler 2002
Medientheorie 1888-1933, edited by Albert Kümmel and Petra Löffler, Frankfurt, Suhrkamp Verlag, 2002.

Sontag 1975
Sontag, Susan. 'Fascinating Fascism', in: *The New York Review of Books*, xxii (6 February 1975), <https://www.nybooks.com/articles/1975/02/06/fascinating-fascism/>, accessed April 2023.

Weill 1926
Weill, Kurt. 'Bekenntnis zur Oper', in: *Blätter der Staatsoper Dresden*, no. 131 (April 1926), pp. 97-99; reprinted in Weill 2000, pp. 45-47.

Weill 1927
Id. 'Verschiebungen in der musikalischen Produktion', in: *Berliner Tageblatt*, 1 October 1927; reprinted in Weill 2000, pp. 61-64.

Weill 1930
Id. 'Tonfilm, Opernfilm, Filmoper', in: *Frankfurter Zeitung*, 24 May 1930; reprinted in Weill 2000, pp. 109-114.

Weill 1936
Id. 'The Alchemy of Music', in: *Stage*, xiv/2 (1936), pp. 63-64.

Weill 1946
Id. 'Music in the Movies', in: *Harper's Bazaar*, lxxx/9 (1946), pp. 257, 398, 400.

Weill 1990
Id. *Musik und Theater: Gesammelte Schriften*, edited by Stephen Hinton and Jürgen Schebera, Berlin, Henschelverlag, 1990.

Weill 2000
Id. *Musik und musikalisches Theater: Gesammelte Schriften*, edited by Stephen Hinton and Jürgen Schebera with Elmar Juchem, Mainz, Schott, 2000.

Kurt Weill and the Principle of 'Concertante Music'*

Francesco Finocchiaro
(Università Statale di Milano)

Beyond Illustration

In an interview with Lotte Eisner published in *Film-Kurier* on 13 October 1927 with regard to the question of 'Musikalische Illustration oder Filmmusik?' Kurt Weill declared:

> Film music only needs to appropriate the inner formal laws of film, that is, it must now turn away, like all other arts are doing, from naturalism and symbolism, and strive for absolute creation[1].

Lotte Eisner then asked him:

> [L. E.] Do you mean that you are against any kind of illustration?
> [K. W.] Yes, I do, because musical illustration only apparently corresponds to the scenic events. Actually, it breaks down the movie. Music should not work with literary means, nor should it slavishly follow the plot, or come to the fore through the use of special effects. It doesn't need to support what is already clearly visible. It should interpret in its own way the hidden meaning lying behind the film[2].

---

[*]. The present essay elaborates on the contents of my monograph *Musical Modernism and German Cinema from 1913 to 1933*, Basingstoke, Palgrave Macmillan, 2017. I would like to thank Springer Publishing for giving permission to reproduce some parts of it.

[1]. Weill-Eisner 1927, p. 437.

[2]. *Ibidem*.

According to the composer, film music had to move away from the age-old principle of 'musical illustration' and revert to absolute music[3]. This radical change, which (according to Weill) was already under way in other genres such as opera, theatre, pantomime etc., was meant to foster the emancipation of film music from the subordinate role of the orchestral component to stage action. In cinema, just like in the opera, the orchestra should not simply illustrate the events that take place onstage, but should have a «purely musical shaping»[4], a formal and structural integrity of its own. Music, Weill continued, should claim a «concertante» role[5], which means that it should interact on an equal footing with the other elements of the drama instead of merely doubling them.

After this reflection, Weill strongly criticized Edmund Meisel's music and the latter's principle of *Lautbarmachung* ('acoustic manifestation')[6], which in Weill's view would never be able to provide «a solution to the problem of film music»[7]. Meisel's cinematic scores for films like *Panzerkreuzer Potemkin* (1925), *Oktober* (1928), *Berlin* (1927), could be described as «visual sound»[8]. Meisel's 'sonorizations' intentionally aimed at mirroring the moving images, becoming an antisubjective, hyper-realistic voice of the visual sphere. In the name of an «exact conformity»[9] between music and film, Meisel set out to musically illustrate film images down to the smallest detail. Indeed, what guided his compositional work was the idea of film as a sum of two entities, the visual and the sonic spheres, which should be perfectly identical and superimposable.

On the contrary, according to Weill the long-awaited solution to the film music problem, i.e., the issue of its identity and dramaturgical role in cinema, was to be achieved through an «objective, almost concertante film music». In the composer's view, music should be an independent component that stands in a dialectical relationship with the staged

---

[3]. «Absolute music became the goal of young composers. They gave up any external or internal "programs", deliberately avoided large orchestral sets, limited their means of expression, directing them towards the enhancement of inner expression, unconsciously reconnected to the style of the masters of a cappella music and of the pre-classical era, and finally developed an almost fanatical penchant for chamber music — these are the main features of this evolution». WEILL 1926, pp. 42-43.

[4]. WEILL 1927A, p. 55.

[5]. WEILL 1927B, p. 60.

[6]. So Edmund Meisel said in his concert program for the premiere of *Hoppla, wir leben!*, which took place on 3 September 1927, at the Theater am Nollendorfplatz: «Modern music for the masses! Off with the throwback bourgeois, painstakingly built music that is only written for individuals! Give the masses an acoustic manifestation [*Lautbarmachung*] of reality in the spirit of our time». The original concert program is archived at the Piscator collection in Berlin's Akademie der Künste.

[7]. WEILL-EISNER 1927, p. 438.

[8]. HUNTER 1932, p. 53.

[9]. MEISEL 1927, p. 53.

events. Through this 'concertante' quality, music can become an essential part of the «epic attitude» of the work of art[10].

Weill explained the link between the 'concertante' quality of music and epic theatre — a much-discussed topic in the composer's writings — in an article titled 'Zeitoper', which appeared in 1928 in the magazine *Melos*:

> The new musical theatre that is emerging today has epic qualities. Its purpose is not to illustrate, but to report. It does not aim at structuring its narrative according to peaks of tension, it wants to talk about the human being, his actions and what motivates him to carry out these actions. Music in this new musical theatre gives up the function of boosting the plot from the inside, embellishing transitions, providing a background to processes, and firing up passions. It goes down its own broad, calm way, enters only in the static moments of the plot, and can therefore (when associated with the right theme) show its absolute, concertante character[11].

The function of music in epic theatre can be summarized as an element of estrangement. Through the tension that it establishes with the action, or visual sphere — for instance by providing an antiphrastic counterpoint to it, or by interrupting its flow — music unmasks the illusion of realism of the narrative fiction. This use of music prevents spectators from passively identifying with fiction, instead pushing them to actively search for nuances of meaning that hide behind outer behaviors. In this respect, 'concertante music' has a radically anti-Romantic nature:

> For "Romantic" art deactivates thinking, it works with narcotic devices — it only shows individuals in a state of exception, and at its climax (in Wagner) it even gives up any representation of the human being. […] In the opera of the nineteenth century and of the beginning of the twentieth century, the task of music consisted in creating atmospheres, illustrating situations, and emphasizing dramatic moments[12].

According to Weill, music should not express the inner feelings of the characters in the play, since the aim of the new musical theatre is not to represent the exceptional fate of individuals. Epic theatre, on the contrary, aims to abstract the general from the individual, to objectivize private ideas and emotions, so as to arrive at an exemplary representation of the human.

---

[10]. WEILL-EISNER 1927, p. 438.
[11]. WEILL 1928, p. 66.
[12]. WEILL 1929, p. 84.

Francesco Finocchiaro

Around Weill

Weill's writings of the years 1927-1928 constitute one of the first attempts to theorize, for cinematic music, a relationship that is not merely illustrative of the visual sphere. His notion of 'concertante music' laid the foundations for a conception of music that, by establishing a dialectical tension with the scenic events, prevents spectators' empathic identification and encourages an attitude of critical distancing.

At the turn of the 1920s and 1930s, such claims for the definitive emancipation of music from illustration became more and more frequent on the part of German-language composers as well as film directors. Journalistic comments on Paul Dessau's score for Władysław Starewicz's *Der verzauberte Wald* (1927) in the *Film-Kurier* of September 1928 are an example:

> Although Dessau largely follows the film, his music indeed proceeds its own way. Basically, he does not "illustrate" at all, but musically transports us, in a free and joyful way, into a fairytale atmosphere, just like the one we see represented above, on the screen[13].

Significantly, the author of the article (known only as 'Dr. K.') presents this choice as a contribution to a critical discussion on the «Problem of cinematic illustration» and Dessau himself as an «exponent of a future of film music». Using similar words, in July 1929, Hans Feld describes Schmidt-Boelcke's music for Dziga Vertov's *Man with a Movie Camera* (1929) as «making music against the film»[14]. The criticisms expressed two years later again by Weill and then by Eisler are in the same vein. The first reiterates how «any generic background music in the sound film has nothing to do with the essence of the music»[15]. The second one defines the «uninterrupted musical accompaniment of a film» as «meaningless»[16].

One of the most interesting documents of this new concept is Walter Ruttmann's 'Tonfilmregie', published in *Anbruch* in April 1929. The director criticized the use of sound in cinema, in particular the case in which the use of sound was limited to simple synchronization with visual details. In the film industry's most basic products, sound is used in a realistic way, creating the illusion of people chatting or of objects producing audible sounds: an erroneous idea having its roots «in that mentality that regards silent film as the evolution of photography and figures out that this evolution must continue in the direction of a color, three-dimensional, talking cinema and so on»[17]. On the contrary, Ruttmann argues, sound could be an artistic

---

[13]. DR. K. 1928.
[14]. FELD 1929, p. 2.
[15]. WEILL 1931.
[16]. S.N. 1931, p. 2.
[17]. RUTTMANN 1929, pp. 176-177.

resource if it were conceived as montage material, as opposed to the visual sphere. For it to be considered montage material, the acoustic component (voice, diegetic sounds, and music) should not merely duplicate what is already represented in the visuals, but should strive for a dissociation from the images. The method of composition of sound cinema should be inspired by the principle of 'counterpoint':

> This to say that the image cannot be enhanced by a sound played parallelly to it. This would undoubtedly be a weakening, just like a statement repeated twice, or as a weak excuse that one tries to corroborate with two different arguments. A counterpoint to the audiovisual configuration would instead be an intentional contrast between the means of expression of the image and sound, mutually correlated to enhance the meaning[18].

As evident, the first theoretical attempts towards overcoming the illustration of the visuals, in favor of an acoustic component that aims at putting itself in dialectical tension with the scenic events, have their roots in the silent era and in the years of the problematic transition to recorded sound. The metaphor of 'counterpoint', actually a variant of Weill's one about 'concertante music', alludes to a refined non-coincidence between audio and visual spheres. Both metaphors hint at the semantic potential of the film seen as a syncretic text: one whose meaning effects are not the product of mere addition, but of the dialectical interaction, and sometimes even the contrast, among literary, theatrical, and musical components, along with properly iconic and gestural codes.

Almost one year earlier than Ruttmann's essay 'Tonfilmregie', the metaphor of 'counterpoint' had actually appeared in Meisel's article titled 'Der Tonfilm hat eigene Gesetze', published in *Film-Kurier*[19]. It is noteworthy that, by interrogating in an entirely abstract way the laws of the newborn sound cinema, Meisel distanced himself from the use of sound as a mere acoustic manifestation of reality. Correlating image and sound on the basis of a principle of exact correspondence, he claims, is a method that can work best for newsreels or naturalistic documentaries, not for *Tonspielfilm*, i.e. sound cinema in the proper sense of the word. It is possible to see in this position a self-criticism towards the principle of *Lautbarmachung*, forcefully proclaimed years earlier. Rather than the principle of 'exact conformity', of an image made audible so to speak, the notion of montage now emerges, explicitly referring to its models in the ambiance of Soviet cinema. According to Meisel, the real novelty of recorded-sound cinema would consist in integrating the sound band into the editing process, making it an equal component to the visual sphere. In order to explain what is meant by the use of sound as montage material, the author of *Potemkin*'s music makes use of another musical metaphor, that

---

[18]. *Ibidem*.
[19]. MEISEL 1928.

of the 'score', conceived as a space-time diagram in which the «contrapuntal composition» among the several components of the cinematic text becomes intelligible.

The analogy between audiovisual montage and polyphonic writing is of surprising modernity. All the more so because such a change of paradigm was embraced by the theorist of *Lautbarmachung* himself. Meisel, who resided in Moscow earlier that year to discuss the music for *Oktober* with Eisenstein, may have benefited from the exchange with the Russian director and with the ideas on sound cinema developed in the circle of Soviet filmmakers. It is noteworthy that the metaphors of 'counterpoint' and 'score-like composition' (*partiturnyj tip kompozicii*) would play a large role in Eisenstein's subsequent writings on montage theory[20].

Metaphors such 'counterpoint', 'polyphony', 'concerto' etc. therefore seemed to provide, around the 1930s, a conceptual model for developing a conception of music, or simply of sound (as it is in the 'Manifesto of Asynchronism'), that goes beyond the old-fashioned principle of illustration. The pervasive occurrence of these metaphors in the writings of directors (Eisenstein, Ruttmann), film critics (Bronstein, Kracauer), as well as composers (Weill, Hindemith, to say nothing of Adorno and Eisler) could lead us to infer conceptual influences and derivations, which in truth are quite difficult to outline. Suffice it to think that Weill's notion of concertante music alluded to a principle of separation among the components of the show, while Eisenstein's notion of vertical montage, also conveyed by the same metaphorical tropes, rooted in Russian director's original conception of an inner link between visual and sonic spheres, by means of refined audiovisual correspondences.

This should be enough to warn us: at the same age, various authors used similar metaphors to mean quite different things, and the resemblances between their discourses could be only apparent.

Asynchronism

Musically inspired metaphors such as 'concertante music' (Weill), 'counterpoint' (Ruttmann), and 'score-like composition' (Meisel) are therefore at the basis of the first theoretical elaborations aimed at a cinematic mediatization of sound. Such expressions recur pervasively in the aesthetic discourse on cinema and function as a model for a properly syncretic conception of the cinematic text. They all allude to a non-coincidence between soundtrack and video: music and sound should not pursue the trivial purpose of illustrating what is happening in the visuals but should lead a life of their own.

Metaphors of 'concertante music' or 'counterpoint', however, point to different procedures that directly affect the musical component. One of these is what we can categorize

---

[20]. Eisenstein 1948, pp. 216-396.

as 'formal asynchronism', that is, a lack of coincidence between the visual and sonic spheres achieved through the apparent misalignment of images and sounds, or of montage cuts and rhythmic accents — a procedure we can see at work in Hans Richter's cinema.

Alles dreht sich, alles bewegt sich is the last film Richter created for Baden-Baden (1929). The work is conceived as a documentary on the Berlin carnival. Its running time was originally about fifteen minutes, but today we only have the final segment, which is three minutes long. The structure of the film can, however, be inferred, in broad outline, from Walter Gronostay's autograph score. A close look at it reveals that the film originally had six parts, as well as an initial introduction, and included twenty-seven musical numbers[21]:

No. 1 Titles

Part I – no. 2 *Stage photo*, no. 3 *Movement (moving photo)*, no. 4 *Sync sound: «Pleased to meet you!»*

Part II – n. 5 *Otto delivers a bunch of flowers, Max is disappointed, receives a rose, looks for Emilia, Max searches, crowd, young athletes, the boxing booth*, no. 6 *Sync sound (crier)*

Part III – no. 7 *Max, crowd, pendulum clock, prizes, pendulum clock, legs, Max's legs*, no. 8 *Sync sound: Cuckoo three times*, no. 9 *(Allegro)*, no. 10 *Sync sound (crier, lottery, prizes, number 14, number 13)*

Part IV – no. 11 *Otto has won the clock*, no. 12 *Target shooting*, no. 13 [missing], nos. 14-17 *Otto has won the clock, Carsten lets it slip under the counter, Max sits down on it*

Part V – no. 18 *Fairground, sound of voices*, no. 19 *Sync sound: cuckoo four times*, no. 20 *Sound of voices throughout, crier (with loudspeaker): «Here you will be able to see a natural female, see the breast that once enchanted the Great Master Begas»*, no. 21 [missing], no. 22 *The magician stands up*, no. 23 [missing], no. 24 *The arena fills up*, no. 25 *Number of athletes*, no. 26 *They walk face-downwards on the roof – sync sound follows: «Bravo!»*

Part VI – no. 27 *Fistfight, end.*

Though the film was conceived as a documentary, the way in which live scenes are represented has nothing realistic or factual about it; on the contrary, the exterior narration is only the by-product of a scenic composition, which centers on movement and visual rhythm. This can also clearly be seen in the surviving fragment, which corresponds to nos. 24 to 27. In it, we can recognize an underlying plot: we see live action from a circus show, in which an athlete performs acrobatic exercises and juggles in front of the public; this scene is followed by a brawl among the bystanders, on which the film closes.

---

21. This rough shot list can be inferred from the autograph score of Walter Gronostay, which is kept at the Archive of Berlin's Akademie der Künste, under the shelf mark 'GRONOSTAY 190'. The score does not mention numbers 13, 19-21, and 23.

Richter's cinematic language, here, takes into account the visual experiments of his earlier abstractionist period. The visual sphere represents absurd, unreal movements; it exploits optical effects: color inversion, slow motion, zooming, unusual perspectives, retrograde motion, accelerations contrasted with static images, and splitting or multiplying figures that morph into abstract motives.

The film uses a composite soundtrack, comprising both extradiegetic music and live-recorded noises and voices (the *Synchronaufnahmen* in nos. 4, 6, 8, 10, and 26). What is evident is the intention to connect noise, spoken word, and music in a relationship with the visual sphere that is not obvious or trivially illustrative, but anti-realistic and 'contrapuntal'. As Heinirch Strobel wrote in his review for *Melos*, Richter and Gronostay's film was the only one in the session to «seriously exploit the potential of the recorded soundtrack» thanks to a «well-contrived interaction between visual montage, music, and rhythmic declamation»[22]. Richter's use of sound openly opposed the obvious illustrative-naturalist approach which, in his eyes, was destined to mark the return of cinematic art to the naiveté and candor of its early days.

Gronostay's music, on the other hand, has its own line of development; it does not literally mirror the events reproduced in the visuals, but refers to them indirectly. It reproduces the effect of a frenzied montage by rapidly juxtaposing motivic units that are highly differentiated in their rhythmic-melodic contour and key (E minor; G minor; A-flat major), and in the group of instruments for which they are intended (piccolo, mandolin, and banjo; cornet and harmonium; oboe, mandolin, and banjo; cornet and harmonium). The musical discourse advances through a collage of musical hints that parody circus music in both their shape and instrumentation. The collage structure and the discontinuity of the musical discourse allude to — but do not slavishly mirror — the extremely fragmentary montage. In this way, the musical and the visual montage create, excepting a few synchronized points that clearly perform a demarcating function, a sophisticated polyrhythmic interplay.

This analogy between the forms of representation in their respective syntagmatic continuum, ostensibly unconcerned with the paradigmatic relation between music and referential content, is the point of arrival of an artistic research experience that was common to both the musical and cinematic avant-garde circles. At the same time, in this subtle, yet remote correspondence lies a sophisticated solution to the problem of music illustration in cinema: the final attainment of a formal asynchronism that would be highly consequential for cinematic music in the following years[23].

---

[22]. STROBEL 1929, p. 398.

[23]. Similar procedures were applied, by way of example, in *Simfonija Donbassa* (Donbass Symphony) (1931) by Dziga Vertov. The film aims to achieve a temporal asynchronization that prevents any spontaneous blending between visual and acoustic events.

Kurt Weill and the Principle of 'Concertante Music'

Counterpoint

A strong stance against illustration and in favor of a 'contrapuntal' relationship between acoustic component and the visual sphere is expressed in a noteworthy article titled 'Musikalische «Illustration»' by Kurt Schröder, published in *Film-Kurier* in 1934:

> This happens very often when reading the announcement of a film producer: "The musical illustration (or accompaniment) of the film [...] was provided by Mr. x.y."
>
> But what should the musician have to illustrate or accompany? Should he perhaps illustrate or paint images (which the film consists of)? I would say this is the director's job! Or does he have to illustrate something again that the director has already illustrated once?!
>
> I think that with this unfortunate term and the even more unfortunate practice of "illustrating" we have taken a completely wrong path. [...] I think that, in cinematic music, the composer's task must consist in tracing the inner plots of the visual action and writing his score by condensing this inner intertwining. [...] Thus, the music can be sometimes in direct opposition to the image present at that moment, and yet it turns on a light, like a flash, on the deeper meaning (and therefore on what is really important) that is hidden behind or below visual events.
>
> In my opinion, this strategy for film composition is the only one that guarantees the musician to play an artistic role in the creation of the film[24].

Schröder alludes here to a different type of audiovisual dissonance: we will define it as a 'semantic counterpoint', as it originates from a misalignment between the meaning contents conveyed separately by music and images. The disjunction between the acoustic and visual components of the filmic text can be described in rhetorical terms as antiphrasis. The idea of an antiphrastic musical accompaniment, based on the tension between two opposing emotional registers and introduced simultaneously in the images and music, took on different labels in film music theory. In Siegfried Kracauer's *Theory of Film*[25], and in Adorno and Eisler's *Composing for the Films*[26], the notion of an antiphrastic musical accompaniment is rephrased as 'dramaturgical counterpoint' — a variation on the original metaphor — which describes a type of music that stands in opposition to the emotional content of the images, so that the overall meaning of the narration is the product of a dialectical interaction between the visual and sonic spheres.

The principle of dramaturgical counterpoint was widely applied in Weill's musical theatre, from the music for Bertolt Brecht's *Dreigroschenoper* to the opera *Aufstieg und Fall der*

---

[24]. Schröder 1934.
[25]. Kracauer 1960.
[26]. Adorno – Eisler 1947.

Stadt Mahagonny, but also in many scores for German cinema of the early 1930s by art-music composers and film-music specialists such as Paul Dessau, Hanns Eisler, and Weill himself.

A basic, tentative principle of counterpoint is employed in the filmic adaptation of Brecht's *Dreigroschenoper*, which Weill created in collaboration with Georg Wilhelm Pabst in 1931. With the title *Die 3 Groschen-Oper*, the film remained closely tied to the aesthetic of opera as to renounce specifically cinematic features, which makes it, in effect, a sort of film-opera. Weill's songs are introduced one by one, in an almost identical fashion to those of the stage version, only adapted for diegetic use as asides to the narration. Only in the film's ending, which corresponds with the three new verses of 'Die Moritat von Mackie Messer', does music enhance the meaning of the visual images in the manner of semantic counterpoint. The first two verses accompany the signing of the contract between Peachum and Mackie before Polly and the Police Chief, while the third verse accompanies the image of the beggars, with the sign 'Ende' appearing during the instrumental closing. This is the only point where the musical accompaniment can be said to have an added value: «the free meditation on social critique»[27] contained in the famous last words of the 'Moritat' — «Denn die einen sind im Dunkeln / und die andern sind im Licht / Und man siehet die im Lichte / die im Dunkeln sieht man nicht» ('For there are some who are in darkness / and the others are in light / And you see the ones in light / while the ones in darkness cannot be seen') — is given a visual translation in the chiaroscuro image of the beggars' silhouettes gradually fading into darkness.

Die 3 Groschen-Oper was produced by Tobis Film with a sound recording system derived from the Triergon that did not yet allow for the mixing of music, spoken word, and live-recorded noise — meaning that music and dialogue were mutually exclusive. This technical limitation, however, became a resource for an aesthetic feature for this film, and what could have been considered a problem «turned into an aesthetic virtue»[28]. Indeed, we can ascribe to Brecht and Weill's ideal of an epic theatre the choice to develop the plot through a regular alternating succession of dialogue scenes and separate musical numbers designed as closed musical forms. In this approach, we can recognize a principle of *horizontal montage*: the alternating occurrence of dialogue scenes and musical numbers interrupts the narrative development, introducing reflective musical pauses in the plot that disrupt the illusion of reality. The self-contained, coherent forms of the musical structure, as well as the rejection of any mechanical illustration of the visuals, are aimed at alienating the deceptive appearance of a realistic whole. In Adorno and Eisler's *Composing for the Films* there is a passage that, read in this light, acquires a particular meaning:

> Aesthetic models of genuine motion-picture music are to be found in the incidental music written for dramas or the topical songs and production numbers

---

[27]. Mücke 2008, p. 123.
[28]. Fasshauer 2008, p. 85.

in musical comedies. These may be of little musical merit, but they have never served to create the illusion of a unity of the two media or to camouflage the illusionary character of the whole, but functioned as stimulants because they were foreign elements, which interrupted the dramatic context, or tended to raise this context from the realm of literal immediacy into that of meaning[29].

An estrangement that reveals the deceptive immediacy of filmic narration would, therefore, be achieved first of all by means of a horizontal montage — conceived as a disruption in the linear progression of narrative events.

Clearly, this principle is what also inspired the conception of Eisler's music for *Niemandsland* (1931), a film by Russian director Victor Trivas. A review of the premiere written by Herbert Ihering for the *Berliner Börsen-Courier* on 10 December 1931 mentions the composer's post-scriptum — uncovered by Tobias Fasshauer — which reveals important details about his conception of the score:

> This is what composer Hanns Eisler has to say about the film *Niemandsland*: "Following the cuts that were requested on account of the current, complex situation, two music pieces — 'Das Lied vom Krieg' and 'Die Hochzeit' — underwent substantial changes. This is all the more deplorable as it destroys the principle of construction through self-contained musical numbers. As a consequence of this cut, a self-contained musical number has been reduced to nothing more than incoherent musical illustration, not subject to any strictly musical law; something which the composer rejects as a principle"[30].

These few lines, which comment on the cuts made to the score for *Niemandsland*, are «the very first documented stance taken by Eisler on the theory and aesthetics of film music»[31]. The dramaturgic-musical principle described in these few lines harkens back to Weill's ideal of 'concertante music', which, whether applied to theatre or cinema, preserves music's formal integrity and avoids any simple illustrative uses.

In fact, Eisler's music of *Niemandsland* goes well beyond the horizontal montage principle that, as we have just seen, is at work in Pabst and Weill's *3 Groschen-Oper*. The processes of audiovisual montage utilized in Trivas's film rather refers, as Fasshauer observed[32], to Brecht's principle of separation among the components of epic theatre: in other words, music in film aspires to become an autonomous component in a syncretic, plurimedial text.

---

[29]. ADORNO – EISLER 1947, p. 49.
[30]. Herbert Ihering, 'Niemandsland', in: *Berliner Börsen-Courier*, 10 December 1931. Quoted in FASSHAUER 2008, p. 63.
[31]. FASSHAUER 2008, p. 63.
[32]. *Ibidem*, p. 64.

The Russian director's film, set during WWI and carrying a deeply felt pacifist message[33], exploits the contrast between disparate situations and introduces symbolic motifs in the narrative flow so as to encourage critical detachment on the part of spectators. This alienating montage extends to recorded-sound, spoken word, and music. The film's acoustic component is treated like any other 'montage material', according to a principle of separation among the components of the cinematic text.

In the film, at least three different processes allow us to talk about a 'concertante' principle in the sound and music sphere. The first of these can be viewed as an advanced development of the horizontal montage principle. This montage procedure is realized now as not just an alternation of dialogical and musical scenes, but as the building of the narrative through juxtaposing closed scenic-musical units. This construction is especially evident in the first part of the film, which shows fragments from the everyday life of the five main characters — the Englishman, the Frenchman, the German, the Jew, and 'the Negro' — in their respective lands before the outbreak of the war. After a 'Vorspiel', which will be discussed later, the first and second acts comprise three musical numbers, each corresponding to as many macro-scenes:

1. the 'Arbeitslied' accompanies four scenes that show workers in a factory, and the German carpenter in his workshop;

2. the 'Jüdische Hochzeit' (Jewish marriage) consists of two marches (with an inevitable parody of Mendelssohn's wedding march) and a classic *klezmer* song by the father of the bride ('Der rebe hot geheysn freylekh any'), which opens the dance;

3. the 'Niggerlied', a shimmy based on the alternation of a verse and a refrain, which accompanies the dance number of Smile, the black variety artist.

In addition to this horizontal montage of self-contained filmic-musical *tableaux*, a process of *vertical montage* is also evident, which introduces a contrast between visual and acoustic representations within the very same scenic-musical unit. The 'Vorspiel' music — a nervous, disturbing, uninterrupted pulsation in shimmy rhythm (two semiquavers and a quaver), against a minor harmonic background — accompanies the calm, idyllic opening scenes titled 'Meer' (Sea) and 'Landschaft bei Morgendämmerung' (Landscape at dawn). This is a typical instance of antiphrastic accompaniment: music does not empathize with the mood in the scene, but instead expresses opposing emotional content and thereby suggests to spectators the possibility of *another* meaning[34]. Antiphrastic musical accompaniment is the clearest example of what we have defined above as 'dramaturgical counterpoint'.

---

[33]. The film was banned in Germany on 22 April 1933. Few copies of it have survived, all of which differ in length, frames sequences, and soundtrack. Eisler's music has survived almost entirely in the autograph score, and can be accessed at the Archive of Akademie der Künste in Berlin.

[34]. The sequence is missing in the surviving U.S. version, where music functions as a commentary to the opening titles, but it is described in the certificate issued by German censors.

Kurt Weill and the Principle of 'Concertante Music'

The third and last process related to 'concertante music' is the blurring of the line between diegetic and extradiegetic music. Note, for example, how the alarm call at the end of the second act stretches the perceptual conventions of sound cinema. The alarm call in the brass section, which announces the outbreak of the war, acts as a clearly extradiegetic link between the scenes, each featuring one of three protagonists — Brown the Englishman, Durand the Frenchman, and Smile 'the Negro'. The characters, however, seem to distinctly hear the call, and react to it as if it were a diegetic sound that is effectively present in the film's simulated reality.

An equal and opposite course, from diegetic to extradiegetic, forms the basis for the scene of the 'Lied des Unterstands' — the most significant musical intervention in the entire second part of the film. The five protagonists meet as missing, injured, or defectors at the bottom of a trench in 'no man's land'. The moving 'Lied des Unterstands' begins in a clearly diegetic mode: to the sound of Smile's mouth harmonica, the Englishman, the German, and the Frenchman each sing one verse in their respective languages, addressed to the loved one who is waiting for them back in their homeland[35]. As the song goes on we see, as a result of a spatial ellipsis, first the soldiers' trenches, then the clouds in the night sky, except that now music has an evident, unmistakable, extradiegetic position with respect to the scene. The song flows into an *Andante* characterized by a polyphonic texture[36], which is introduced as the natural continuation of the harmonica motif. While we finally see the women of the missing soldiers — the German's wife rocking the cradle of an infant child, the Englishman's wife keeping vigil at her son's bedside, the Jew's wife in a refugee barrack, the Frenchman's lover in a print house — the *Andante* closes with a reprise of the opening harmonica motif, accomplishing an A-B-A$_1$ form that stretches across the ellipses of the montage and thereby restores unity between the diegetic (in part A) and extradiegetic (in B and A$_1$) parts.

Conclusion

In summary, the notion of 'concertante music' is at the core of at least four distinct montage processes that involve both sound and visual components:

1. formal asynchronism, that is, a lack of coincidence between the visual and sonic spheres achieved through the temporal misalignment of images and sounds;

---

[35]. According to Fasshauer, the piece is not Eisler's. At any rate, it is missing in the autograph score for *Niemandsland*. See Fasshauer 2008, p. 83.

[36]. The *Andante*, which is missing in the autograph score, was later woven into the third movement of the Suite for Orchestra Op. 24 No. 2, along with three other numbers from this score: the 'Vorspiel', the *klezmer* dance of the 'Jüdische Hochzeit', and the 'Schlußmarsch'.

2. horizontal montage of film-musical *tableaux* in the manner of a closed-number construction;

3. vertical montage of a musical commentary that has an antiphrastic value with respect to the meaning of the images;

4. permeability of the perceptual boundary between diegetic and extradiegetic music.

As said above, the notion of 'concertante music' represents one of the first theoretical elaborations aimed at deliberate cinematic mediatization of the acoustic component in film. It functions as an umbrella term, encompassing a variety of dramaturgic choices, all of which share two basic features: the first is the preservation of some degree of formal coherence in the music as a strategy to achieve dissociation from the image; the other is a tendency to view music and sound as self-standing components of the filmic text.

'Concertante music' is the keyword for a program of emancipation of film music, which insists on the need to overcome any slavish mirroring of the narrated events and strives for non-conventional forms of interaction with the visual sphere. Establishing a dialectical tension with the stage events, by means of an autonomous text with its own formal coherence and semantic density, is the most important legacy film music received from Weill's principle of 'concertante music'. That conception of cinematic music as an autonomous component, emancipated from any subordination to the image, will ultimately lead to an awareness of the syncretic effects inherent in the film seen as a plurimedial, multicomponential text.

BIBLIOGRAPHY

ADORNO – EISLER 1947
ADORNO, Theodor Wiesengrund – EISLER, Hanns. *Composing for the Films*, London-New York, Continuum, 1947 [new edition with an Introduction by Graham McCann, London, Continuum, 2007].

DR. K. 1928
DR. K. 'Paul Dessau als Exponent einer Filmmusik-Zukunft. Bemerkungen zum Problem: «Film-Illustration»', in: *Film-Kurier*, x/227 (22 September 1928), supplement *die Film-Musik*.

EISENSTEIN 1948
EISENSTEIN, Sergei. *Nonindifferent Nature*, (1948), edited by Herbert Marshall, Cambridge, Cambridge University Press, 1987.

FASSHAUER 2008
FASSHAUER, Tobias. 'Film – Musik – Montage. Beobachtungen in «Niemandsland»', in: *Kompositionen für den Film. Zu Theorie und Praxis von Hanns Eislers Filmmusik*, edited by Peter Schweinhardt, Wiesbaden, Breitkopf & Härtel, 2008, pp. 63-85.

FELD 1929
FELD, Hans. 'Die Filmmusik: Musikexperiment im Marmorhaus?', in: *Film-Kurier*, XI/156 (3 July 1929).

HUNTER 1932
HUNTER, William. *Scrutiny of Cinema*, London, Wishart, 1932.

KRACAUER 1960
KRACAUER, Siegfried. *Theory of Film: The Redemption of Physical Reality*, Oxford-New York, Oxford University Press, 1960.

MEISEL 1927
MEISEL, Edmund. 'Wie schreibt man Filmmusik?', (1927), in: *Der Stummfilmmusiker Edmund Meisel*, edited by Werner Sudendorf, Frankfurt, Deutsches Filmmuseum Frankfurt, 1984, pp. 58-60.

MEISEL 1928
ID. 'Der Tonfilm hat eigene Gesetze. Eine Mahnung', in: *Film-Kurier*, X/219 (13 September 1928), supplement *die Film-Musik*.

MÜCKE 2008
MÜCKE, Panja. *Musikalischer Film – musikalisches Theater. Medienwechsel und szenische Collage bei Kurt Weill*, Münster, Waxmann, 2008.

RUTTMANN 1929
RUTTMANN, Walter. 'Tonfilmregie', in: *Musikblätter des Anbruch*, XI/4 (April 1929), pp. 176-177.

SCHRÖDER 1934
SCHRÖDER, Kurt. 'Musikalische «Illustration»', in: *Film-Kurier*, XVI/227 (27 September 1934), supplement *die Film-Musik*.

S.N. 1931
S.N. 'Filmmusik, wie die Schaffenden sie sehen. Drei Kurz-Gespräche', in: *Film-Kurier*, XIII/174 (28 July 1931), p. 2.

STROBEL 1929
STROBEL, Heinrich. *Die Baden-Badener Kammermusik 1929*, in: *Melos*, VIII (1929), pp. 395-399.

WEILL 1926
WEILL, Kurt. *Die neue Oper*, (1926), in: ID. *Musik und musikalisches Theater. Gesammelte Schriften*, edited by Stephen Hinton and Jürgen Schebera, Mainz, Schott, 2000, pp. 42-45.

WEILL 1927A
ID. 'Busonis *Faust* und die Erneuerung der Opernform', (1927), in: *ibidem*, pp. 54-58.

WEILL 1927B
ID. 'Wie denken Sie über die zeitgemäße Weiterentwicklung der Oper?', (1927), in: *ibidem*, p. 60.

WEILL 1928
ID. 'Zeitoper', (1928), in: *ibidem*, pp. 64-67.

WEILL 1929
ID. 'Über den gestischen Charakter der Musik', (1929), in: *ibidem*, pp. 83-88.

WEILL 1931
ID. 'Los vom Naturalismus: Probleme der Tonfilmgestaltung', in: *Film-Kurier*, XIII/11 (14 January 1931), supplement *die Film-Musik*.

WEILL – EISNER 1927
ID. – EISNER, Lotte. 'Musikalische Illustration oder Filmmusik? Gespräch mit Lotte H. Eisner', (1927), in: ID. *Musik und musikalisches Theater. Gesammelte Schriften*, *op. cit.*, pp. 437-440.

Kurt Weill and the American Operetta Tradition: *The Firebrand of Florence* and *Where Do We Go from Here*?

William A. Everett
(University of Missouri-Kansas City, MO)

In 1941, Kurt Weill wrote Ira Gershwin to suggest that they create «a very entertaining opera comique on the Offenbach line». Nearly three years later, he told Lotte Lenya that for what would become *The Firebrand of Florence* (1945) he would «treat great parts of the score in real opera style»[1]. For in this, his fifth Broadway score, the émigré composer was keen to tap further into the operetta aesthetic, something he had already done with *Der Kuhhandel* (A Kingdom for a Cow) in the 1930s[2] along with *Johnny Johnson* (1936), *Knickerbocker Holiday* (1938), *Lady in the Dark* (1941), and *One Touch of Venus* (1943) on Broadway. As with his musical theatre works written in Germany, Weill wanted to open up new possibilities for the Broadway musical.

Like virtually any genre, it is nearly impossible to give a singular, finite definition for operetta. No set of qualifiers can be uniformly applied to works that have been dubbed operettas by creators, critics, audiences, or even academics. Except one. The centerpiece of a successful operetta is its wondrous musical score. Glamourous music spills forth from the finest operettas like bubbly champagne does from a crystal flute. Dance forms are regular features, especially waltzes, galops, and marches. Stories can be set in antiquity, in classical mythological realms, in the *Mitteleuropa* imaginary of Ruritania, in Imperial-infused Orientalist domains, or even

---

[1]. Kurt Weill to Ira Gershwin, letter dated 13 November 1941; Kurt Weill to Lotte Lenya, letter dated 14 July 1944; both quoted in Hinton 2012, p. 362.

[2]. Weill wrote *Der Kuhhandel* to a libretto by Robert Vambery in 1934. Unable to interest theatre managers in staging the work, in early 1935, Weill and Vambery worked with Reginald Arkell (book) and Desmond Carter (lyrics) to create an English-language version. *A Kingdom for a Cow* opened at London's Savoy Theatre on 28 June 1935, where it played for two weeks.

in the present day. Elements of satire, nevermore, and nostalgia and engagement of issues of gender, race, and social class are common occurrences that become intertwined with romantic tales of the boy-meets-girl, boy-loses-girl, boy-gets-girl (or girl-meets-boy, girl-loses-boy, girl-gets-boy) variety. Several geographical strands of what can be termed an operetta exist, each of which has its own sets of threads. These include the effervescent French *operette* of creators such as Jacques Offenbach and Charles Lecoq; the waltz-infused Viennese operettas of Franz von Suppé, Johann Strauss, Jr., and Franz Lehár; the Savoy Operas of Sir W. S. Gilbert and Sir Arthur Sullivan; and the early twentieth-century American works, sometimes called 'plays with music', by European immigrants Victor Herbert, Sigmund Romberg, and Rudolf Friml.

During the late 1930s and early 1940s, when Weill was contemplating writing a modern operetta for Broadway, the genre, at least in the United States, was neither completely dormant nor at the height of its popularity. While newer approaches to musical theatre by the likes of Cole Porter or Richard Rodgers and Oscar Hammerstein II were becoming increasingly popular, operetta on Broadway was being kept alive largely through a series of special or short-lived revivals, though a handful of these enjoyed more extended runs. Additionally, studio recordings of classic works, European and American, were appearing with greater frequency. Various summer theatre companies across the United States were also producing operettas in their large outdoor venues and drawing large crowds of adoring fans. Finally, operettas were being envisioned for the silver screen. These were either film adaptations of successful stage works or original works created expressly for the movies. In the 1940s, to be fair, the film operetta genre was experiencing a relative low point when compared to its popularity in the 1930s and again in the 1950s.

It is within such contexts that Kurt Weill created two works with especially overt operetta overtones, both of which appeared in 1945. First to be discussed is the Broadway musical *The Firebrand of Florence*, an adaptation of Edwin Justus Mayer's 1924 play about the Italian Renaissance sculptor Benvenuto Cellini that opened at the Alvin Theatre on 22 March. Many of the tropes associated with operetta are evoked in this work, oftentimes in a subversive fashion that lovingly mocks their venerated theatrical heritage. Second, the film *Where Do We Go from Here?* which Twentieth-Century Fox released on 23 May, includes two sequences that reflect two different approaches to operetta, one set in a Teutonic tavern and the other aboard Christopher Columbus's Santa Maria. A third musical sequence, cut from the film, echoed a third approach to operetta, one that referred to an exoticized and unapologetically racist depiction of Native Americans. Both *The Firebrand of Florence* and *Where Do We Go from Here?* have lyrics by Ira Gershwin, and both, despite their merits, have largely fallen into obscurity.

Before moving to Weill's operetta constructs, it will prove valuable to look in more detail at the state of operetta in the U.S. during the 1940s (see TABLE 1). English-language versions of

Viennese operettas had been gracing Broadway stages for decades[3]. The most successful of these, lasting an impressive 611 performances, was *Rosalinda* (1942), a revised version of Strauss's *Die Fledermaus* set in the 1890s and produced by the recently established New Opera Company[4]. *Rosalinda*'s success came in part because, as reviewer Arthur Pollock noted, it «aims to kid the old piece»[5]. This joyful reflexivity, when works cheerfully admit their own stock conventions, is often seen in so-called 'backstage' musicals, where a show-within-a show offers opportunities for such commentary, as in Cole Porter's *Kiss Me, Kate* (1948). Of central importance here, it is also a feature of both *The Firebrand of Florence* and *Where Do We Go from Here?* as will be discussed below, though Weill's treatment is often more subtle than in the works listed immediately above.

Table 1: Operettas Produced on Broadway in the 1940s

Adaptations of Viennese Works

Rosalinda (based on *Die Fledermaus*, music by Johann Strauss, Jr., American book by John Meehan, Jr. and Gottfried Reinhardt, lyrics by Paul Kerby)
- 28 October 1942, 44th Street Theatre (transferred to the Imperial Theatre, the 44th Street Theatre, and the 46th Street Theatre), 611 performances

The Merry Widow (music by Franz Lehár, book by Victor Leon and Leo Stein, English lyrics by Adrian Ross)
- 15 July 1942, Carnegie Hall, English lyrics by Adrian Ross, 39 performances
- 4 August 1943, Majestic Theatre, book adapted by Sidney Sheldon and Ben Roberts, lyrics by Adrian Ross, 322 performances; 7 October 1944, City Center (with additional music by Robert Stolz and lyrics by Edward Gilbert), 32 performances

The Gypsy Baron (music by Johann Strauss, Jr., adapted by George Mead)
- 14 November 1944, City Center, 11 performances by the New York City Opera
- 6 October 1945, in repertory at City Center, 4 performances

Adaptations of French Works

La Vie Parisienne (music by Jacques Offenbach, English book by Felix Brentano and Louis Verneuil, English lyrics by Marion Farquhar)
- 5 November 1941, 44th Street Theatre, 7 performances
- 10 November 1942, Broadway Theatre, 17 performances
- 12 January 1945, City Center, 37 performances

---

[3]. For more on this topic, see SCOTT 2019.
[4]. Yolanda Mero-Irian (1887-1963), a Hungarian-born pianist/impresario/philanthropist, founded the New Opera Company around 1941. Her company produced several operetta adaptations in Broadway theatres in the 1940s.
[5]. POLLOCK 1942.

Helen Goes to Troy (based on *La belle Hélène*, music by Offenbach, book by Gottfried Reinhardt and John Meehan, Jr., lyrics by Herbert Baker)
- 24 April 1944, Alvin Theatre, 97 performances

Revivals of Gilbert and Sullivan Works, All Performed in Repertory

The Gondoliers (7 performances), *The Mikado* (7 performances), and *The Pirates of Penzance* (6 performances), produced by the Lyric Opera Company
- 30 September to 19 October 1940, 44th Street Theatre

H.M.S. Pinafore (with the dance special *The Green Table*, 18 performances), *The Mikado* (with the ballet specials *The Big City* and *A Ball in Old Vienna*, 19 performances), *The Pirates of Penzance* (with the ballet special *The Prodigal Son*, 11 performances), *Iolanthe* (5 performances), *Trial by Jury* (7 performances), and *The Gondoliers* (3 performances), produced by the Messrs. Schubert
- 21 January to 14 March 1942, St. James Theatre

The Mikado (6 performances), *Trial by Jury* and *H.M.S. Pinafore* (7 performances), *Cox and Box* and *The Pirates of Penzance* (8 performances), *The Gondoliers* (4 performances), *Iolanthe* (6 performances), *Patience* (4 performances), *Ruddigore* (3 performances), and *The Yeoman of the Guard* (1 performance), produced by the Gilbert and Sullivan Opera Company
- 11 February to 26 March 1944, Ambassador Theatre

Revivals of American Operettas

The New Moon (music by Sigmund Romberg, book by Oscar Hammerstein II, Frank Mandel, and Laurence Schwab, lyrics by Hammerstein)
- 18 August 1942, Carnegie Hall, 24 performances
- May 17, 1944, City Center, 44 performances

The Student Prince in Heidelberg (music by Sigmund Romberg, book and lyrics by Dorothy Donnelly)
- 8 June 1943, Broadway Theatre, 153 performances

The Vagabond King (music by Rudolf Friml, book and lyrics by Russell Janney)
- 29 June 1943, Shubert Theatre, 56 performances

Blossom Time (music by Sigmund Romberg, book and lyrics by Dorothy Donnelly)
- 4 September 1943, Ambassador Theatre, 47 performances

The Red Mill (music by Victor Herbert, book and lyrics by Henry Blossom, additional lyrics by Forman Brown)
- 16 October 1945, Ziegfeld Theatre (transferred to the 46th Street Theatre and the Shubert Theatre), 531 performances

The Desert Song (music by Sigmund Romberg, with Otto Harbach, Oscar Hammerstein II, and Frank Mandel)
- January 8, 1946, City Center, 45 performances

Kurt Weill and the American Operetta Tradition

Two different productions of Lehár's international megahit *The Merry Widow* (Vienna, 1905 as *Die lustige Witwe*; London and New York, 1907) appeared on Broadway in the early 1940s. The first, which played at Carnegie Hall in 1942, was so popular that its two-week limited run was extended to just over a month in order to meet audience demand. The second, which opened at the Majestic Theatre in 1943, enjoyed a strong and lengthy run of 322 performances. Though it did not last as long as *Rosalinda*, it too was an unqualified commercial success. The production played a brief reprise at City Center after it closed at the Majestic. Part of this particular *Merry Widow*'s longevity may have to do with its French setting, which could have served as a reminder of life in Paris before the Nazi Occupation and therefore as a manifestation of one culture on whose behalf the Allies were fighting.

More typical at the time on Broadway were shorter runs of European works, some of which were performed in repertory. For example, Strauss's *The Gypsy Baron* had productions in 1944 and again the following year, while Offenbach's *La Vie Parisienne* was seen in 1941, 1942, and 1945. Substantially revised versions of continental works that followed the *Rosalinda* model (what nowadays may be called revivals) tended to play a bit longer. A prime example is *Helen Goes to Troy*, Erich Wolfgang Korngold's reworking of Offenbach's *La belle Hélène* that jettisoned large chunks of the original score and replaced them with interpolations from other Offenbach works. The show played 97 performances in 1944 at the Alvin Theatre, the same venue where *The Firebrand of Florence* would run the next year. In *Helen Goes to Troy*, the basic story of Paris wooing Helen is kept, but the action is augmented to incorporate Homeric characters and, as one critic noted, contemporary references to «peace, appeasement and what not — but nothing to get Lillian Hellman into a sweat»[6]. Three cycles of works by the team of Gilbert and Sullivan played in repertory on Broadway in the early 1940s. These were all limited-run offerings and included productions by the Lyric Opera Company at the 44th Street Theatre in 1940, the esteemed Messrs. Shubert at the St. James Theatre in 1942, and the Gilbert and Sullivan Opera Company at the Ambassador Theatre in 1944 (see TABLE 1 for a list of repertory included in each cycle).

Finally, American operettas from earlier in the century were making comebacks in the 1940s — this style of operetta is perhaps the one through which Weill's works were most vividly viewed by contemporary audiences. The decade of the 1920s was especially rich for the genre, and many of the works from that era retained their luster, often with a slightly nostalgic tinge, two decades later. All four of Sigmund Romberg's hits from the 1920s — *Blossom Time* (1921), *The Student Prince* (1924), *The Desert Song* (1926), and *The New Moon* (1928) — had

---

[6]. CHAPMAN 1944. Lillian Hellman (1905-1984) was a successful Broadway playwright known for her political activism and communist sympathies. She was the librettist for the original version of Leonard Bernstein's *Candide* (1958) and approached the composer-conductor with the idea to create the show.

Broadway revivals, albeit generally for limited runs. *The Student Prince* is the exception here, with its 153 performances at the Broadway Theatre in 1943. This is especially curious, for *The Student Prince* is a celebration of sorts of nineteenth-century Germany, which was seen in contemporary theatrical terms as a place wrapped in romantic love and beer-infused male comradery rather than as the antecedent of a present-day wartime enemy. By contrast, only one of Rudolf Friml's operettas, *The Vagabond King* (1925) returned to Broadway during the 1940s. *The Vagabond King* is set in medieval France and concerns the poet François Villon, who saves Paris from foreign invasion. Villon's heroic deeds on behalf of his people would have held especially significant resonance for audiences in 1945, when France was under Nazi occupation. None of Friml's other famous works, which include *The Firefly* (1912) and *Rose-Marie* (1924), had made it back to Broadway since 1931. Victor Herbert's *The Red Mill*, a hit in 1905, was again a hit in 1945. In the 'strangers-in-a-strange-land'-style plot, where recent arrivals do not understand the ways and customs of their new environments, two American vaudevillians travel to Holland. There, they disrupt various operetta-like scenarios with their comic antics, not completely unlike what Bill does while moving through American history in *Where Do We Go from Here?*

In the 1940s, audiences for operetta extended far beyond Broadway. Studio recordings of classic works were becoming increasingly popular during the decade, though the trend did not reach its heyday until the 1950s. Decca released selections from *The Merry Widow* in 1944 and *The Desert Song* in 1945, both in sets of 78-rpm records[7]. These recordings featured Kitty Carlisle, Wilbur Evans, and Felix Knight, all of whom would have been known to keen listeners at the time for their work on radio. Similarly, classic operettas continued to thrive in outdoor summer theatres as well as in productions by light opera companies across the United States. For example, the Los Angeles Civic Light Opera Association staged several classic operettas for week-long runs in the early 1940s. These included Herbert's *Naughty Marietta* in 1941 and Friml's *The Vagabond King* and Noël Coward's *Bitter Sweet* in two consecutive weeks in 1942[8].

Operetta certainly maintained a place in the changing musical theatre ecosystem of the 1940s. The genre's past glories were being kept alive through performance, live and on record, and — to a limited degree — on screen. Part of the modernist aesthetic was to look to styles and idioms of the past and refashion them in contemporary terms, sometimes in a direct fashion and other times with a sense of irony. This is where Kurt Weill enters the sphere of operetta in the United States.

---

[7]. *The Merry Widow*, Decca DA-364 (1944); *The Desert Song*, Decca DA-370 (1945).

[8]. *Naughty Marietta* played the week of 26 May 1941, *The Vagabond King* the week of 11 May 1942, and *Bitter Sweet* the week of 18 May 1942. Copies of playbills are in the author's collection.

Kurt Weill and the American Operetta Tradition

The Firebrand of Florence

The Firebrand of Florence opened at the Alvin Theatre on Broadway on 22 March 1945 to mixed reviews: the score was praised (as one would hope for a work dubbed an operetta by critics) while other aspects, including the performances of the four principals, were judged more harshly. Max Gordon, the producer, seeing how the show was losing money, closed it on 28 April, after just forty-three performances (seventy-one, when the out-of-town previews are included). This was a decidedly short run for a new musical on Broadway, but when viewed in the context of the myriad of operetta revivals that were being staged in the early 1940s, it was par for the course. The difference was that the revivals were budgeted for short runs, perhaps taking into account a modest audience demand, something that was not the case for *Firebrand*.

Weill's «new musical», as it was called on the playbill, was an adaptation of Edwin Justus Mayer's play *The Firebrand*. The play enjoyed a successful 261-performance run at the Morosco Theatre on Broadway in 1924 and 1925. After reading the script, Weill wrote enthusiastically to Gershwin, «it is a ready made libretto for the kind of smart, intelligent, intimate romantic-satirical operetta for the international market which we always talked about»[9]. Mayer's play consists of vignettes drawn from the autobiography of the Italian Renaissance goldsmith and sculptor Benvenuto Cellini. Cellini's various escapades include murdering four men, engaging in various sexual liaisons, challenging authority figures, and in general behaving as a rogue. The satire on mores and morality includes a requisite romance between Cellini and his model, the prostitute Angela, but in the end, Cellini cedes his affections to those of the Duke and plans his own antics with the Duchess.

Mayer himself prepared the play's adaptation into a musical libretto. Large portions of the original text were kept as dialogue scenes, but massive cuts were made to accommodate the musical numbers[10]. Importantly, the characterizations of the four principals — Benvenuto, Angela, the Duke, and the Duchess — were substantially altered. Benvenuto and Angela were romanticized and their rambunctiousness toned down, while the Duke and Duchess moved toward somewhat buffoon-like caricatures of their original selves. Benvenuto in particular was transformed to become a more conventional operetta hero, one who is ultimately honest and forthright in his love, as opposed to his rapscallion nature in 1924.

The plot of *The Firebrand of Florence*, to reduce it to its most essential elements, concerns Benvenuto Cellini and his amorous pursuit of Angela. The Duke and the Duchess provide foils for the lovelorn pair. To fulfill Broadway expectations and also to feature the dance ensemble, the musical's director, John Murray Anderson, insisted that a happy ending be added that

---

[9]. Hirsch 2002, p. 239.
[10]. Galand 2002, p. 25.

was not in the original play. Weill wrote to Gershwin that he wanted the story to end with a heartbroken Angela as Cellini leaves for France[11]. But instead, *The Firebrand of Florence*, as it played on Broadway, ends with Angela and Cellini together against the backdrop of a visual spectacle and narrative denouement set in Versailles.

Operetta mandates its own set of vocal expectations, many of which informed the idea of character-defining music in mid-century American musicals. Romantic leads typically inhabit music with long, legato lines and lush orchestral underpinning, which is infused with operatic elements such as coloratura. These roles require performers with classically trained (a.k.a. 'legitimate') voices. Comic characters, on the other hand, usually are given songs with shorter phrases in a somewhat speech-singing style that lie in lower vocal ranges. Their music often evokes the sound aesthetics associated with the likes of musical revue, cabaret, and music hall. This paradigm became one of the defining elements of American operettas of the 1920s. For example, in *Rose-Marie*, Rose-Marie and Jim are the romantic couple who sing imploringly to each other while Lady Jane and Herman become the comic one who make the audience giggle. Likewise, in *The Desert Song*, Margot and Pierre sing vaultingly spacious music as the lovelorn pair while Susan and Bennie offer fast-paced song-and-dance routines as the jokey one. This type of musical characterization continues in *The Firebrand of Florence*. Benvenuto and Angela, a baritone and a soprano, sing the unashamedly lyrical music, while the Duke and Duchess proffer more character-driven songs.

Weill, while maintaining this arrangement, also subverts it. Typically, the romantic couple is of a higher social status than the comic one, and hence their respective musical styles take on associations, broadly speaking, with social class. Weill inverts this norm. Following the class-based paradigm of American operettas such as *The New Moon*, the Duke and Duchess *should* sing flowing music with their legitimately trained voices while the more plebian Benvenuto and Angela *should* perform the score's more novelty-style songs. But the opposite is true here, for the trope of class-associated musical style is inverted and therefore subverted.

What is also distinctive — and problematic — about the paired couples in *The Firebrand of Florence* is the comic couple's romantic yearnings for their lyrical counterparts—the Duke wants Angela, and the Duchess covets Cellini. This models an all-too-familiar paradigm in which an authority figure makes inappropriate and unwanted sexual advances on a person in a subservient situation[12]. This #metoo scenario, all too familiar in so many opera, operetta, and musical plots, is, alas, evident here.

---

[11]. GALAND 1999, p. 338.
[12]. This also happens in *Knickerbocker Holiday*.

Most operettas end happily, with both principal couples being together[13]. *The Firebrand of Florence*, not surprisingly, also eschews this convention. While Anderson's forced addition of the Versailles scene makes this trope seem likely for Benvenuto and Angela, this is not the case when it comes to the Duke and the Duchess. But then the Duke and the Duchess are not the social subservients like the comic pairs in the American operettas with which the audience would have been familiar (e.g., *Rose-Marie*, *The Desert Song*, *The New Moon*), so their futures are less prescribed. The Duke has taken as his latest lover Benvenuto's servant Emilia, and certainly not feeling bereft, the Duchess is scheming to recapture what Sam Brookes adroitly calls in his adapted narration for a 2003 performance, «Cellini's chisel»[14].

One dimension of Viennese (and French) operetta that Weill, Gershwin, and Mayer do maintain in *The Firebrand of Florence* is sex. As operetta scholar Kevin Clarke has noted, sex was at the fore of many of the most successful Viennese works. Clarke cites the Viennese critic Felix Salten, who in his famous review of the premiere of *Die lustige Witwe* in 1905 described the music as «filled with carnal lust» so that «desire and sexual cravings fully break through»[15]. These undertones simmer throughout *The Firebrand of Florence*, and one place where they become explicit is in the final words of the Duchess's 'Sing Me Not a Ballad': «Spare me your advances — just, oh just make love». Furthermore, before becoming a model, Angela had been a prostitute. Her character has precedents on Broadway in the ethnically Othered women whose physical bodies take precedence over their singing voices in several American operettas from the 1920s. Examples include the Indigenous Canadian Wanda in *Rose-Marie* and the Moroccan Azuri in *The Desert Song*, both of which are fundamentally dancing roles and do not entail any solo songs. Weill does, however, thwart Broadway tradition by creating this type of role — a sexually promiscuous younger woman — for a performer who must have legitimate vocal training and be more a classical singer than a dancer. In doing so, he actually returns to the nineteenth-century Viennese model of Johann Strauss, Jr. in works such as *Die Fledermaus* and characters such as Adele, recalling of course that *Die Fledermaus* had enjoyed a recent Broadway revival.

Structurally, operettas consist of a mixture of individual songs, passages of spoken dialogue, and multi-sectional musical scenes. The musical scenes typically include one or more embedded songs, a variety of musical textures (e.g., solos, duets, choral numbers), dance sequences, passages that resemble recitative (of both dry and accompanied varieties) or arioso,

---

[13]. Notable exceptions include the works that Sigmund Romberg created with the Shuberts, including *Maytime* (1917), which has a compromise ending — the grandchildren of the romantic leads realize the love denied their grandparents; *Blossom Time* (1921), in which a fictionalized Franz Schubert dies on stage; and *The Student Prince* (1924), which ends with the title character and his beloved Kathie sing their farewells to a reprise of the operetta's principal love waltz, 'Deep in My Heart, Dear'.

[14]. BROOKES 2003, p. 127.

[15]. CLARKE 2019.

underscored dialogue, and usually some sort of dramatic plot twist. Such constructs often occur as act finales, especially for internal acts, though they can appear anywhere in an operetta. Three especially significant operetta-style musical scenes occur in *The Firebrand of Florence*: 1) the opening 'Execution Scene', 2) the act 1 finale, 3) and the act 2 'Trial Scene'. According to Galand, these passages contain forty percent of all the music in the show[16]. Forty percent! Nearly half the score is concentrated into these three musical scenes, all of which use music as an essential element in the storytelling.

From the very beginning, Weill informs his audience of the importance of the musical score — that fundamental feature of operetta — in *The Firebrand of Florence*. The extended twenty-minute musical sequence provides the audience with its first look into the work's aesthetic approach. With choral numbers featuring different groups, recitative and arioso sections, and a grand musical entrance for the title character, the number is in fact a self-contained cameo during which Cellini is brought to the gallows for a public hanging before a last-minute reprieve by the Duke. Importantly, the sequence introduces the tarantella as the musical topos that will underlie the entire work[17]. As the gallows builders gleefully celebrate their employment, they do so to a moderately paced tarantella. Gershwin's clever lyric «One man's death is another man's living» captures not only a bit of ironic black humor but also the association of the tarantella with the tarantula's fatal sting. A bit later, when the citizens of Florence sing the praises of their city, they take up what Galand calls «the rhythm of Offenbach's boleros»[18]. Certain sections alternate between 6/8 and 3/4, which hint at a Spanish jota and led Weill to call the chorus «a sort of Tarantella, italian [*sic*] and spanish [*sic*] at the same time»[19]. This 'sort of Tarentella' returns at the end of the scene, further establishing the prominence of tarantella in the score.

The opening scene also includes the entrance of the title character, and the audience's first aural impression of Benvenuto Cellini proves him to be first and foremost a romantic. Rich string-dominated orchestrations support his impassioned greetings to the assembled masses as the magistrate gives him three minutes to plead his case. The three-minute limit is not arbitrary, for the audience in 1945 would have recognized it as the time on one side of a 78-rpm disc and therefore a standard length for a popular song. This was their cue that a song destined to become one of the show's highlights was about to begin. 'Life, Love, and Laughter' is just that. The

---

[16]. GALAND 2002, p. 38.

[17]. The characteristic dance has a precedent in Mayer's play, where it is mentioned by name. Late in Act 1, Angela confesses to Cellini that the Duke had started romancing her before he heard that the Duchess had returned. Cellini responds, «Did he dance a tarantella at the news?». In his ambiguous reply, to which Angela answers «He ran to her» (MAYER 1926, p. 64), the reference to the dance could either refer ironically to its fatalist narrative or evoke a mock cause for celebration.

[18]. GALAND 2002, p. 39.

[19]. *Ibidem*.

soaring ballad returns throughout the score, including in the show's finale, though with slightly altered words as the story develops.

A commodification of entertainment underlies the opening number; the length of 'Life, Love, and Laughter' is but one example. Broadway was (and remains) very much a commercial enterprise, and this reality offers opportunities for meta-theatrical commentary. To offer another example, the vendors sing their memorable jingles to entice folks to buy food and souvenirs of what promises to be «the greatest hanging of the season». One must wonder if the vendors are hawking their wares only to the masses gathering on stage to watch an execution or if they are also calling to the audience in the theatre to buy their own intermission nibbles and mementos from their evening out. Then, after the audience hears the achingly beautiful 'Life, Love, and Laughter' and the Duke pardons Cellini, a vendor returns to proffer souvenirs for the «greatest pardon of the season», among which could be a record of Earl Wrightson (who created the title role) singing 'Life, Love, and Laughter'.

The second extended scene, the twelve-minute Act 1 finale, further affirms the central role of the tarantella in *The Firebrand of Florence*. It is even marked «finale alla Tarantella»[20]. As is typical of internal act finales in operettas, the music here combines reprises with new material. This finale begins with the celebratory Florentine tarantella from the opening scene, now with lyrics that emphasize nighttime lovemaking. After the Duke is asked to sign a death warrant for Benvenuto, Angela, Emilia, and the Duke suggest instead that everyone dance a «good hot tarantella», since that will be useful, according to Gershwin's lyrics, «for keeping an orgy advancing». An energetic, faster-paced tarantella thus ensues, after which the Duchess enters over an orchestral reprise of the more relaxed, yet still vigorous «Florence» tarantella.

At this point, Weill uses musical identifiers to accentuate the differences between the Duchess on one hand and the romantic coupling of Angela and Benvenuto on the other. As Benvenuto is trying to escape the Duke's clutches by hiding in the Duchess's bedchamber, she responds to his pleas for help with a reprise of her song 'Sing Me Not a Ballad', which she introduced earlier in the act. The shorter phrases of the song are ideal for this sort of musical moment, where they can be separated by Cellini's interjections. This is in stark relief to Angela and Benvenuto's duet version of 'Life, Love, and Laughter', which appears later in the sequence with its long, uninterrupted lines.

As often happens in internal act finales, some sort of dramatic turn occurs just before the curtain. Such suspenseful moments are plentiful in various strands of operettas and musicals. To give just a sampling, there is Katisha's 'stop the wedding' entrance in *The Mikado*, the dramatic confrontation and its aftermath between the countess and Tassilo in Emmerich Kálmán's *Gräfin Mariza* ('Countess Maritza', 1924), the title character's brother blackmailing her to marry a man she does not love in *Rose-Marie*, and the 'Dream Ballet' in Rodgers and

---

[20]. Hirsch 2002, p. 246.

Hammerstein's *Oklahoma!* (1943). Here, the Duke and Duchess each venture out onto their shared veranda with the intent of discovering the identity of their spouse's secret lover. Instead, they find each other. The spoken scene, set as melodrama, accentuates the difference between their relationship and that of Benvenuto and Angela. Simply put, the Duke and Duchess are incapable of singing a love duet, unlike their counterparts. The act ends with an orchestral reprise of 'Life, Love, and Laughter', a reminder of what Benvenuto and Angela have and the Duke and Duchess do not.

The third extended musical sequence in *The Firebrand of Florence* was to be the work's final scene, but became its penultimate one. The nineteen-minute 'Trial Scene' (Act 2, scene 5) features Cellini's trial, another pardon (echoing the opening 'Execution Scene') and, after an extended passage of dialogue, Benvenuto's departure to Paris[21]. If it would have been the final scene, its length, certain musical attributes, and overall dramatic function — conviction and pardon — would have balanced the opening sequence quite nicely. In the scene that precedes the trial, the vendors return to sell souvenirs, this time for «the greatest trial of the season». The reprise sets up the architectonic similarities between this scene and the opening one. As in the opening scene, here the magistrate tells Benvenuto that he has three minutes — the time it will take to fill one side of a 78-rpm record, perhaps a B side to 'Life, Love, and Laughter' — in which to tell his story. His response here is not a grand expansive ballad like before but rather a slightly faster-paced song that proffers the philosophical notion that people are destined to do what they do simply because of who they are. With its gently oscillating accompaniment, grace notes on off-beats, and interspersed *a cappella* segments, 'You Have to Do What You Do Do' bears a possible kinship with 'It Ain't Necessarily So' from the Gershwins' *Porgy and Bess* (1935). That song's biblical references are supplanted here with ones coming from astrology and classical antiquity. Rather than using the sources to question belief, as Sportin' Life does in 'It Ain't Necessarily So', Benvenuto (through Gershwin's clever lyrics) provides numerous examples to show one cannot be blamed for being oneself; for example, Plato could not be blamed for being Platonic.

The sequence also demonstrates a clever dramaturgical use of the waltz, the musical conduit for duets between the romantic leads in many Viennese and American operettas. Two waltzes occur in the sequence, one each for the Duke and Duchess. Unlike what happens in works such as *The Merry Widow* or *The Student Prince*, these waltzes are not duets. After hearing Benvenuto proclaim 'You Have to Do What You Do Do', the Duke expresses his elation in a joyous, carefree waltz, 'Nobody Is to Blame'. A bit later, the Countess sings her waltz, 'The Little Naked Boy', to Angela as she reveals the pain a young lover can bring, thinking of herself (and Benvenuto), while also warning Angela about such men. The Duke and the Duchess each

---

[21]. GALAND 1999, p. 338.

ILL. 1: Cellini (Earl Wrightson), Angela (Beverly Tyler), Duke (Melville Cooper), Duchess (Lotte Lenya) in the original Broadway production of *The Firebrand of Florence*, 1945.

reveal something about themselves through their respective waltzes, but the nature of their relationship prohibits them from singing a true waltz duet.

One reason that is often cited for the failure of *The Firebrand of Florence* concerns problems with the casting, namely that the individual performers' styles and abilities did not match either the music they were required to sing or the characters they were asked to play[22]. Neither Earl Wrightson as Benvenuto nor Beverly Tyler as Angela had voices that could sustain the enormity of Weill's vocal demands. Wrightson was known mostly for his studio recordings, including those of American operettas from the 1920s. Making a record is very different than

---

[22]. See, for example, SCRANTON TRIBUNE 1945.

singing eight performances every week, not to mention having to be able to act. Tyler at the time was a teenaged Hollywood starlet. She was cast because she was, according to Lys Symonette, «somebody's girlfriend, and she brought in money from MGM, which helped to get the show on»[23]. After *The Firebrand of Florence*, Tyler appeared in various B movies. While Wrightson and Tyler both had decent voices, the recurring vocal requirements of a vaulting operetta score did not match their specific talents[24].

In *The Firebrand of Florence*, Weill and his co-creators simultaneously emulated and subverted familiar operetta tropes, especially in the three extended musical scenes. These include aspects of musical characterization and the prominence of particular dances, namely tarantellas over waltzes. Fanciful evocations of distant times and places, another hallmark of operetta, are clearly evident in *The Firebrand of Florence*. Such musical imaginings are also present in the music for the film *Where Do We Go from Here?* which Weill was working on at the same time he was writing *The Firebrand of Florence*. It is to that film and its operetta evocations to which we shall now turn our attention.

Where Do We Go from Here?

In Morrie Ryskind and Sig Herzig's story, which formed the basis of Ryskind's screenplay for *Where Do We Go from Here?* Bill Morgan (played by Fred MacMurray) desperately wants to join the Army and serve in World War II in order to impress the flighty Lucilla (played by June Haver). He is classified as 4-F, which means he cannot serve due to a medical condition. He meets a genie named Ali (played by Gene Sheldon) whose magic timepiece is broken. When Ali asks Bill for his wish, Bill responds that he wishes to be in the military. Ali grants his request, but with a twist. Bill finds himself in George Washington's army at Valley Forge, where he is sent to gather information from the Germans. Just as the Germans prepare to execute Bill for being a spy, Ali appears and sends him to his next posting, this time in the navy. Bill now ends up being

---

[23]. HIRSCH 2002, p. 244.

[24]. The casting of the Duke and the Duchess reveal similar issues. Melville Cooper (1896-1973), who played the Duke, was a well-known British comic actor. Many in the theatre audience would have recognized him as the High Sheriff of Nottingham in *The Adventures of Robin Hood* (1938), where he appeared as the nemesis of Errol Flynn's character. Cooper's natural antics did not match the character of a voracious nobleman. Even though Weill fought to have his wife Lotta Lenya (1898-1981) play the Duchess, the general consensus was that she was miscast (see *ibidem*, pp. 240-242). Her character was less a tough yet vulnerable survivor and more in line with the sexually ravenous characters recently played by the actress Vivienne Segal, who was considered for the role (*ibidem*, p. 243). Segal's characters in the early 1940s included Vera in Rodgers and Hart's *Pal Joey* (1940), where she introduced 'Bewitched, Bothered, and Bewildered', and Queen Morgan le Fay in the same team's revival of *A Connecticut Yankee* (1943), in which she introduced the murder-happy song written expressly for her, 'To Keep My Love Alive'.

part of Christopher Columbus's expedition of 1492. But Bill isn't interested in going to Cuba with Columbus and instead leaves alone on a small dinghy for New York. There, he purchases Manhattan from Chief Badger (played by Anthony Quinn), a fictionalized Legape leader, in 1626, and later ends up in Nieuw Amsterdam. Ali returns Bill — and his friend-turned-love-interest, Sally (or more specifically her Dutch incarnation as Katrina, both played by Joan Leslie) — to the twentieth century. The genie magically stamps Bill's military application and the film ends with Bill marching in a victory parade, arm in arm with Sally.

When the film was shot in 1944, such a parade was something to be hoped for. On its 23 May 1945 opening day, VE Day (Victory in Europe Day, 8 May) was recent memory, while VJ Day (Victory over Japan Day, 15 August), which marked the end of the war in the Pacific, was still in the future. This final sequence, therefore, when the film was released and even more so when it made, was envisioned as morale-building home-front optimism in its depiction of an eventual Allied victory. *Where Do We Go from Here?* thus forms part of the home front propaganda that Hollywood studios were producing in the 1940s.

Operetta occupied a small part in this cinematic repertory. In 1943, *The Desert Song* was refitted as United States propaganda. Dennis Morgan plays Paul Hudson, an American pianist who helps the Riffs thwart Nazi attempts to build a railroad across North Africa. In *Where Do We Go from Here?* Bill, an ordinary guy with a knowledge of history, secures the future of his country at key moments in its past. His efforts echo those of his real-life counterparts in 1945.

Two extended operetta-influenced sequences and an unrealized third one feature in *Where Do We Go from Here?* The first takes place when Bill finds himself in 1776 and the second when he ends up in 1492. The unrealized sequence would have taken place when Bill prepares to purchase Manhattan from the Lenape.

After marching in Washington's regiment to 'Yankee Doodle', Bill visits the Valley Forge USO club, a conflation of a quintessential eighteenth-century operetta locale like could be found in Herbert's *Naughty Marietta* or Romberg's *The New Moon* (though both of those are set in Louisiana) and the popular World War II venues for military men away from home. This amalgamation of the artifice of operetta with the present day is also reflected in the music for this sequence. Centered on the duet 'If Love Remains', the music moves from an evocation of a stately minuet to a swing-inspired tap dance number. A front of curtain scene, in theatrical terms, provides a link between the Valley Forge USO setting and that which follows. Bill warns George Washington that Benedict Arnold is a traitor and goes to gather information about the size of the Hessian troops gathered in Trenton.

When the music resumes, Bill has arrived firmly in the realm of Teutonic fantasy. At the boisterous Trenton Bierstube, Hessian soldiers and their ladies offer a parody of the famous beer garden scenes from *The Student Prince*. They begin with a spirited rendition of the popular German song 'Ach, du lieber Augustin' played by a diegetic wind band, a soundworld in direct contrast to that of the small string ensemble seen at the Valley Forge USO. A new dissonant

Ill. 2: The Trenton Bierstube in *Where Do We Go from Here?*

melody appears as part of the song; its peppered metric and harmonic dissonances have no visible effect on the revelers[25]. The film characters seem unaware that their present and their future — that is, the audience's past and its present — have become conflated. The Hessian colonel, impeccably portrayed by noted character actor Herman Bing, implores the revelers to «Drink! Drink!» an overt reference to the famous 'Drinking Song' from *The Student Prince*. The dissonant melody returns to create musical unity between the two sections.

Next comes the 'Song of the Rhineland', led by Gretchen, a barmaid who is the incarnation of Lucilla (also played by Haver), the woman with whom Bill thinks he is in love. The number projects the exaggerated artifice and camp qualities that were becoming increasingly associated with operetta. The genre was moving along two divergent yet simultaneous paths in the 1940s, one toward increased lushness and a romanticized nostalgia — as in *The Firebrand of Florence* — and the other toward overt camp and self-aware artifice. In 'Song of the Rhineland', Weill and Gershwin merge the operettic past with the current political situation and use operetta itself as a way to make Nazi Germany the object of ridicule. This display is rife with blond wigs worn by everyone in the Bierstube, frequent direct glances to the camera, and mocking of the self-praise of the Germans. At one point, the Rhinelanders sing of their own superiority,

---

[25]. Such modernist treatment of the familiar song is not unique to Weill, for something similar happens when Arnold Schoenberg quotes it in the second movement of the Second String Quartet (1908), though it is the other parts in the polyphonic texture that provide the dissonance rather than a new melody.

with Gershwin's anachronistic lyrics telling the film audience that even their — that is, the eighteenth-century Rhinelanders' — «goose-step is goosier». The dissonant melody makes yet another appearance in the dance sequence that concludes the scene.

The temporal conflation of the eighteenth and twentieth centuries continues after the scene concludes when the German general, General Rahl (played by Otto Preminger) appears as a balding, monocled Nazi in fancy dress. His image provides unmistakably stark contrast to the stereotypical blond wigs and effervescent camp of the eighteenth-century Hessians. Reality has invaded the artifice of operetta.

The other operetta-inspired sequence resonates strongly with *The Firebrand of Florence*. The ten-minute sung-through musical scene, in two parts, takes place aboard Christopher Columbus's ship the Santa Maria. As in the 'Execution Scene' of *The Firebrand of Florence*, here a complete story is told. Columbus's crew is frustrated and threaten mutiny until Bill tells them of the future they will bring. Weill requires true operatic baritones for the characters of Columbus (played by Fortunio Bonanova) and Benito, the sailor who leads the mutiny (played by Carlos Ramirez). Dances such as the tarantella and bolero do a great deal to establish a specific Italian aural atmosphere with a Spanish flavor, which is enhanced though the on-screen appearance of a mandolin and a peppering of Italian words. Recitatives, declamatory duets, and *bel canto fioriture* (melodic embellishments associated with many nineteenth-century Italian operas) likewise feature prominently throughout the first part of the scene. Rather than echoing the Germanic operetta tradition, here Weill turns his attention more toward the realm of opera buffa and mixes it with elements from the American operetta tradition, namely the prominence of the male chorus. Weill called the passage «a little Italian opera»[26], thus acknowledging its roots and sung-through nature. Benito and Columbus both have solo sections in which they are joined by the rousing male chorus. Benito leads them as they sing of their nostalgic longing for home, especially food, while Columbus reminds them of their «loyalty to royalty» in the form of Queen Isabella. This questioning of loyalty could also have a meta-theatrical function, for is Columbus asking for their loyalty to *Ruritanian* royalty, the rulers in so many Viennese operettas, and by extension, to the tradition itself?

The second part of the scene shifts to Bill and likewise marks a direct contrast in vocal timbre from the trained operatic to that of a singing actor. Bill tells the crew of the futures that their encounter will bring in the joyful bolero 'The Nina, the Pinta, the Santa Maria' (marked «tarantella» in the score[27]). His music is much narrower in range, and many of his prophecies are declaimed on the same pitch in an almost recitative style. He is not from the realm of Columbus, where according to Weill's aural imaginary, everyone sings opera. Instead, he is an ordinary 1940s American guy who loves and wants to serve his country. He communicates with

---

[26]. Weill to Maurice Abravanel, 11 December 1943. Quoted in GALAND 2002, p. 19.
[27]. GRABER 2021, p. 163.

the crew not through opera, which would be insincere for him, but rather through a popular musical style associated with the Mediterranean world that he, as someone who went to dances, would know.

A third operetta-inspired scene was planned for the film, but was cut. It would have taken place during the Manhattan sequence when Bill purchases the island from Chief Badger. Weill and Gershwin wrote a song for the scene, 'Woo, Woo, Woo, Manhattan', which they recorded for a tryout album. The song, with its embarrassingly racist refrain that includes the act of repeatedly placing and removing one's hand over one's mouth, features standard Indianist tropes such as harmonically static repeated notes and melodies doubled in parallel thirds. It thus makes overt references to Friml's *Rose-Marie*, with its famous 'Indian Love Call' and infamous 'Totem Tom Tom'. Fortunately, this number was cut in editing[28].

To conclude, *The Firebrand of Florence* and *Where Do We Go from Here?* employ and subvert familiar operetta tropes that audiences in the 1940s would have known and recognized. Soaring baritone numbers exist alongside lively tarantellas and German-style drinking songs. Whereas temporal juxtapositions are central to the storytelling in *Where Do We Go from Here?* in a sense they also apply to the operetta audiences themselves in the 1940s. People living in whatever present, then or now, can imagine themselves transported to the past through these temporally escapist pieces. But the realities of the present time remain. Oftentimes such references are subtle, but as in the Trenton Bierstube scene, they can also be made explicit. Weill and his co-creators, through these two works from 1945, thus became part of the legacy of operetta in the United States, a story that moves deftly between Broadway and Hollywood and includes a confluence of social realities and musical artifice, of performers and performance styles, and of audience expectations and aesthetic goals.

Bibliography

Brookes 2003
Brookes, Sam. 'Script Adaptation and Narration', in: *The Firebrand of Florence*, booklet for Kurt Weill, *The Firebrand of Florence*, CD, Capriccio 60 091, 2003.

Chapman 1944
Chapman, John. 'Jarmila Novotna Bewitching in a Beautiful *Helen Goes to Troy*', in: *Daily News* (New York), 25 April 1944.

Clarke 2019
Clarke, Kevin. 'Music Filled with Carnal Lust, Bordering on Frenzy: Rediscovering the Original Glory of Operetta', in: *bachtrack*, 1 October 2019, <https://bachtrack.com/feature-not-quite-opera-month-operetta-research-center-september-2019>, accessed April 2023.

---

[28]. *Ibidem*, p. 158.

GALAND 1999
GALAND, Joel. 'Reconstructing a Broadway Operetta: The Case of Kurt Weill's *Firebrand of Florence*', in: *Notes: Quarterly Journal of the Music Library Association*, LVI/2 (1999), pp. 331-339.

GALAND 2002
ID. 'Introduction', in: *Kurt Weill Edition. I/18: «The Firebrand of Florence»*, edited by Joel Galand, New York, Kurt Weill Foundation for Music, in association with European American Music Corporation, 2002, pp. 13-54.

GRABER 2021
GRABER, Naomi. *Kurt Weill's America*, Oxford-New York, Oxford University Press, 2021.

HINTON 2012
HINTON, Stephen. *Weill's Musical Theater: Stages of Reform*, Berkeley-Los Angeles, University of California Press, 2012.

HIRSCH 2002
HIRSCH, Foster Hirsch. *Kurt Weill on Stage: From Berlin to Broadway*, New York, Knopf, 2002.

MAYER 1926
MAYER, Edwin Justus. *The Firebrand: A Comedy in the Romantic Spirit*, London, Ernest Been, 1926.

POLLOCK 1942
POLLOCK, Arthur. 'Dashing *Rosalinda* of New Opera Company is Short of Good Actors', in: *Brooklyn Daily Eagle*, 1 November 1942.

SCOTT 2019
SCOTT, Derek B. *German Operetta on Broadway and in the West End, 1900-1940*, Cambridge, Cambridge University Press, 2019.

SCRANTON TRIBUNE 1945
'Critics Voice Varied Views of *Firebrand*', in: *Scranton Tribune*, 24 March 1945.

«Steel Veins»: *Railroads on Parade* and the Industrial Folk

Naomi Graber
(The University of Georgia, GA)

> *Other fairs have been chiefly concerned with selling products;*
> *this one will be chiefly concerned with selling ideas.*
> (Bernard Lichtenberg, *Public Opinion Quarterly*, 1938)

A visitor to the 1939-1940 New York World's Fair encountered seemingly limitless possibilities for a techno-utopian future. From consumer goods like dishwashers and televisions to grand visions of electrified cities connected by a lacework of roads, this 'World of Tomorrow' promised the people of the United States a future of personal comfort and economic opportunity, all for the seventy-five-cent price of admission. To present the average consumer with this prospective future, industries drew on myriad forms of musical media, live, recorded, and everything in between[1]. In the Transportation Area alone, consumers were spoiled for choice. Fairgoers could rest their feet while watching *In Tune with Tomorrow*, a 3D stop-motion film that showed a brand new Plymouth car assembling itself, as if by magic. Or they might ride in «sound-chairs» through General Motors' *Futurama*, a «vast world of future cities and countryside»[2]. After that, they might stroll across the street to see the Eastern President's Railroad Conference production of *Railroads on Parade*, a «Pageant-Drama of Rail Transport» by Edward Hungerford that featured a cavalcade of locomotives accompanied by Kurt Weill's score of new and old Americana.

These spectacles served as the culmination of a decade-long public relations campaign in the private sector to convince the public that government regulation stifled innovation and

---

[1]. Grieveson 2018, pp. 313-319.
[2]. Official Guidebook 1939, inside cover.

economic recovery. As President Franklin Roosevelt's New Deal seemingly threatened industrial autonomy and labor disputes erupted in numerous sectors, the economic downturn in late 1937 reignited debates over the best way forward[3]. In a coordinated effort that included the World's Fair, industries sought to show that the path out of the Great Depression led through free-market capitalism rather than government regulation. These campaigns retold American history as the story of technological progress towards comfort, convenience, and luxury brought about by benevolent inventors and captains of industry. Emergent technology such as the electric microphone and constantly improving sound-film synchronization brought the vast scale of industry into sharp focus; boundless technological marvels made intimate by careful camera placement and crooning voices.

Railroads on Parade exemplifies these strategies. The pageant played at both the 1939 and the 1940 season of the fair, and though there were significant revisions in 1940, the basic outline remained the same. The first part depicted the history of the railroad as a story of men of genius inventing ever more efficient methods of overland transport, while politicians like Charles Carroll and Abraham Lincoln looked on from the sidelines. The second part focused on the railroad of the past fifty years and its increasing consumer comforts. The pageant portrayed the United States as a technological titan moving inexorably towards consumer luxury, propelled by far-seeing men of genius, assisted by cheerful, industrious workers while government officials merely applauded.

Weill's score supported these themes by including pastiches and quotations of U.S. folk genres such as work songs, hymns, and nineteenth-century popular music (see TABLE 1 for a complete list). These tunes accompanied an account of the history of the railroad, ending with a scene in a luxurious Pullman car, accompanied by a newly written modern popular song: 'Mile After Mile'. Accompanied by these tunes, the railroad appeared as an integral part of the United States, the «steel veins» of the living, breathing nation (as the program described it)[4]. Weill's score also participated in the broader public-relations movement to reclaim folklore for capitalism. While U.S. modernists were incorporating folk tunes into pieces with explicit ones such as Virgil Thomson's score for the government-sponsored documentary films (which also played at the fair), Weill differentiated his arrangements from theirs through his Broadway-style orchestrations, augmented in 1940 by the novachord. By uniting folk tunes, nineteenth-century songs and pastiches, and contemporary pop music with modernized orchestration, Weill supported the pageant's message that railroads were both traditional and modern, both historical treasures and *au courant* conveyances of luxury and elegance.

---

[3]. There was disagreement over the issues even within the Roosevelt administration. See KENNEDY 1999, pp. 350-356.

[4]. *BOOK OF THE PAGEANT* 1939.

«Steel Veins»: *Railroads on Parade* and the Industrial Folk

Table 1: Quotations and Contrafacts in *Railroads on Parade*
(songs are listed in the order they appear in the pageant)

1939 version	1940 version
'The British Grenadiers'	'Low Bridge'
'Low Bridge'	'Casey Jones' (appears twice)
'Casey Jones' (appears twice)	'John Henry'
'John Henry'	'She'll be Comin' 'Round the Moutain'
'She'll be Comin' 'Round the Mountain'	'Nancy Lee'
'Heave Away'	'Old Grey Mare'
'Whiskey Johnny'	'Old Bill'
'Old Grey Mare'	'Oh, California' (contrafact of 'Oh, Susanna', appears twice)
'This Train is Bound for Glory' (appears twice)	'Snagtoothed Sal'
'Oh, California' (contrafact of 'Oh, Susanna', appears twice)	'My Darling Clementine'
'I've been Working on the Railroad'	'Battle Hymn of the Republic'
'Auld Lang Syne'	'This Train is Bound for Glory'
'Old Bill'	'I've been Working on the Railroad'
'Snagtoothed Sal'	'Auld Lang Syne'
'My Darling Clementine'	'Two Little Girls in Blue'
'Battle Hymn of the Republic'	'Stars and Stripes Forever'

Railroads on Parade did not exist in a vacuum; the pageant was likely one of numerous spectacles any visitor to the fair saw that day, spectacles that may have communicated complementary or contradictory messages about the relationship between industry, labor, government, and the nation. Situating *Railroads on Parade* within the competing aesthetics and agendas of the 1939-1940 World's Fair brings into focus the contested ground of American folk music in the late 1930s, as well as the ways in which the railroad attempted to differentiate itself from other modes of transportation. While numerous scholars have explored the ways leftists of various stripes mobilized folk music, less attention has been paid to similar music from corporate America. *Railroads on Parade* exemplifies attempts by industry to borrow leftwing rhetoric, images, and sounds and reinterpret them. Yet *Railroads on Parade* was exceptional in the depth of its engagement with folklore, especially in music. The combination of folklore and technology in the libretto, staging, and music of *Railroads on Parade* helped to both situate the industry as one of many new and exciting paths to the future, yet also the only one with a glorious history that other industries lacked. That history, according to the pageant, was rooted in a combination of folk culture, ingenious engineering, Manifest Destiny, and visionary capitalism.

Naomi Graber

Folk Music and Leftwing Culture

With the onset of the Great Depression, numerous artists, musicians, writers, film-makers, and other creatives in the United States began to reexamine their cultural roots. The stock market crash of 1929 shattered both faith in the free market and the myth of the benevolent, civic-minded businessman that had infused the culture of the Gilded Age through the 1920s, and spurred the nation to search for new heroes and ideals, to construct new mythologies of America often emphasizing folkore[5]. But the ideas of 'the folk', 'folklore', and 'folk music' during the period were nebulous. They encompassed projects that focused on contemporary rural cultures such as the Federal Writers Project state guidebooks and John and Alan Lomax's folksong collections. Folklore cut across commercial and non-commercial realms, as well as 'art' and 'popular' circles. Academic enterprises such as the *Journal of American Folklore* published stories, tunes, and ethnographies while George Gershwin's 'folk opera' *Porgy and Bess* (1960) played on Broadway. The folksong 'Git Along Little Dogies' accompanied Aaron Copland's 'Street in a Frontier Town' in *Billy the Kid* (1938), while Gene Autry sang the same tune in a movie named after the song. Nineteenth-century popular songs became 'folk music' by the twentieth century, and there was often little distinction between historical folk music and newly composed songs in those styles[6].

Throughout these disparate strands, however, some common threads emerge. One is a search for something 'true' or 'real', especially given that in the early days of the Depression the government attempted to downplay the crisis[7]. William Stott calls this the «documentary impulse» of the era, the desire «to get the texture of reality, of America; to feel it and make it felt»[8]. This could usually be found in the more rural parts of the nation, where self-sufficiency, manual labor, and a symbiotic relationship with the natural world seemed to thrive. This impulse also manifested in a search for a «usable past», to use Van Wyck Brooks's term from 1910, as historical figures were reframed as folkloric everymen[9]. There was also a desire for something that represented 'the people' outside of the capitalist system[10]. Even in blatantly commercial enterprises such as Gene Autry's *Git Along Little Dogies* (1937), an anti-corporate ethos flourished; the film revolves around Autry's character preventing greedy oil tycoons from removing innocent ranchers from their land. In the world of politics, the left turned to folk culture to give the impression of harnessing the 'voice of the people', especially after the advent of the Popular Front in 1935[11]. Folkloric rhetoric also flourished in New Deal propaganda,

---

[5]. Kennedy 1999, pp. 10-13; Susman 1984, pp. 153-156.
[6]. Reuss 2000, pp. 19-20.
[7]. Stott 1973, pp. 67-73.
[8]. *Ibidem*, p. 128.
[9]. Jones 1971.
[10]. Reuss 2000, pp. 5-6, 128.
[11]. *Ibidem*, pp. 130-140, Cohen 2016, pp. 60-71.

including government sponsored films like Pare Lorentz's *The Plow that Broke the Plains* (1936) and *The River* (1938), with folksong-laden scores by Virgil Thomson[12].

Folklore and Capitalism

In response, the public-relations arms of the corporate world began to deploy a counter-offensive. Coordinated through the National Association of Manufacturers and new trade periodicals such as *Public Opinion Quarterly* (1937—) and *Business Screen* (1938-1973), large-scale cross-industry public-relations campaigns aimed at convincing the public that business promoted democracy, prosperity, and U.S. values, not just products[13]. The modern public-relations apparatus had grown significantly in the previous decades, with the birth of social psychology and innovations in technology and fueling a mix of corporate advertising and carefully orchestrated 'grassroots' events designed to sell products[14]. The entertainment industry was a crucial partner in these endeavors. Units like the Motion Picture Department of the Ford Motor Company or the Electrical Research Products Division of Western Electric released short documentaries for both commercial theatres and educational institutions in order to promote products or educate citizens «in new modes of 'productive' conduct and the new configuration of political economy mandated by monopoly capitalism»[15].

The World's Fair was part of these endeavors. The president, Grover Whalen, had briefly worked for the state government of New York, and became famous by making the ticker-tape parade a New York institution, beginning with the one for Charles Lindbergh in 1927. He was also former police commissioner known for his brutally anti-communist «Red Squads»[16]. Under his administration, most of the grounds were given over to private industrial exhibits, which showcased the wonders of the ostensible 'World of Tomorrow' and its consumer comforts. Gardner Ainsworth, a recent Princeton graduate analyzing the fair's promotional tactics for *Public Opinion Quarterly*, noted that the fair was supposed to «resurrect popular support» for industry, which recognized «the necessity of defending itself in the eyes of a hostile public». For this hostility, he blamed government propaganda: «It is as much the lack of confidence in capitalist democracy itself that must be overcome in the public mind, for it is on this abstract

---

[12]. COHEN 2016, pp. 71-74. The folkloric rhetoric inflected even President Roosevelt's famous 'fireside chats', which emphasized the the power of 'the people' (a watchword of the political left), and cultural rituals. EWEN 1996, pp. 260-262.

[13]. EWEN 1996, pp. 299-300.

[14]. These included events like *Light's Golden Jubilee* on 21 October 1929 to celebrate the fiftieth anniversary of the invention of the lightbulb. Although staged to appear spontaneous, it was carefully managed by General Electric and the National Electric Light Association. See *ibidem*, pp. 215-219.

[15]. GRIEVESON 2012, p. 108.

[16]. *NEW YORK TIMES* 1962.

emotional basis, backed up by a few damaging facts, that the masses can best be turned against business in general — and consequently, because the alliance is close today, against the Republican party»[17]. To counter this, the fair's public-relations director (and president of the Institute for Public Relations) Bernard Lichtenberg noted in the same journal that industry could «take a lesson in modern-day propaganda achievements. Just as the government is making use of such means as Pare Lorentz's *The River* on the screen and the Living Newspaper on the New York stage to get across a message in an entertaining way, so exhibitors at the New York Fair may be counted upon to stress the entertainment angle in presenting their story»[18].

These campaigns produced what James S. Miller calls an «industrial folk» aesthetic, which «sought throughout the 1930s to uncover — or more accurately, invent — the 'folk' history of industrial capitalism»[19]. Focusing on Henry Luce's *Fortune* magazine, Miller identifies two strategies. First, the magazine framed the folkloric 'everyman' figure as integral to the workings of modern industry rather than its antithesis. Homespun figures like the «mountaineer» farmers of the Tennessee Valley, while living in poverty, were nevertheless «incomparably American stock which produced such men as Lincoln and Chief Justice Marshall, and, for that matter, Cordell Hull»[20]. Miller also notes that *Fortune* drew on the folkloric ethos of the U.S. landscape, showing how technological progress blends seamlessly with the nation's natural beauty. On a flight on American Airlines, a passenger might see «The steel spins out across the prairies in its double lines. The checkered farming country opens. A glint of lack northward. The powerlines go marching through farms»[21]. As the epithet «mountaineer» makes clear, the line between the landscape and the 'folk' was often blurry; part of what defined a figure as part of the 'folk' was their harmonious relationship with the natural world, and their ability to cultivate its bounty.

This «industrial folk» aesthetic was often part of public relations campaigns to counter the news coverage of bloody labor disputes. For example, on 26 May 1937, men working for Ford beat labor organizer Walter Reuther and four others resulting in a serious publicity problem. Only a few days later on Memorial Day, police opened fire on a peaceful crowd of protesters who were marching to support the United Auto Workers in front of Republic Steel's South Chicago mill, killing ten (some shot in the back), and injuring thirty more[22]. Soon after, both Ford and Republic released 'educational' films that used this «industrial folk» aesthetic, both of which played at the fair. Republic Steel's thirty-five minute documentary called *Steel: Man's Servant* (1938), and embraced a «folksy» attitude towards the workers in the mills, depicting a group heating a coffee pot on a hot I-beam, and a woman checking her hair in a

---

[17]. AINSWORTH 1939, p. 695.
[18]. LICHTENBERG 1938, p. 315.
[19]. MILLER 2003, p. 87.
[20]. *Ibidem*, pp. 93-94.
[21]. *Ibidem*, p. 99.
[22]. KENNEDY 1999, pp. 316-318.

gleaming sheet of metal before returning to work[23]. Ford produced *Symphony in F*, which used stop-motion animation to bring to life the inscription on the exhibit wall: «From the earth comes the materials to be transformed for human service by men, management and machines». The film shows workers of all different colors (literally — they are plastic dolls) happily working together to extract natural resources and transform them into a Ford V8 engine. The portrayal of workers as compliant, happy, and industrious countered the terrible publicity both Ford and Republic Steel endured in the previous years. Other companies avoided showing contemporary labor altogether, and connected their products directly to the natural world, as in the case of the Du Pont Chemical Company's *The Wonder World of Chemistry* (1936), which sets a split-screen image of rayon thread being spun by a machine and slaves picking cotton on a historical plantation against the sound of Stephen Foster's 'The Old Folks at Home'[24].

The railroad industry shared a number of these concerns and strategies. From their inception until the 1920s, railroads experienced almost uninterrupted growth, but the interwar period saw a steep decline. Competition from automobiles and aviation began to pose a serious threat to the locomotive's virtual monopoly on overland transportation, but large-scale corruption and the threat of labor strife dating to the late nineteenth century also contributed[25]. World War I saw a break in these threats because the industry was nationalized, though they resumed in the early 1920s when control returned to private hands[26]. Consequently, the railroads were subject to several legislative acts aimed at mediating these disputes throughout the 1920s and 1930s. While the laws of the 1920s tended to favor employers, New Deal initiatives such as the 1934 amendments to the Railway Labor Act of 1926 and the Railroad Unemployment Insurance Act of 1938 strengthened the position of organized labor[27]. By the time of the World's Fair, the railroad industry needed to reassert the primacy of capital over labor, and establish that no further government interference was necessary.

As a long-time part of the railroad industry's public-relations apparatus, Hungerford was undoubtedly familiar with these trends. He had served as a press representative for the Brooklyn Rapid Transit Company and as an advertising manager for Wells Fargo[28]. His first foray into railroad pageantry was *Pageant of the Iron Horse* to celebrate the centennial of the Baltimore and Ohio Railroad in 1927, which was filmed for educational purposes. Although the film was silent, *Educational Screen* reported that for showings of the film, «The music has been selected from the available phonographic records as nearly as possible to correspond to

---

[23]. SULLIVAN 2013, pp. 36-38.
[24]. Du Pont Chemical also sponsored the radio program *Cavalcade of America*, which narrated episodes of U.S. history accompanied by folk music. See KUZNICK 1994, p. 355.
[25]. STOVER 1997, pp. 111-112, 169, 192-197.
[26]. *Ibidem*, pp. 179-181.
[27]. *Ibidem*, pp. 200-210, HIDY 2004, pp. 231-232.
[28]. SHAMPINE 2009.

that played by the Centenary band», who had accompanied the performance live, indicating that the pageant proceeded to the tune of familiar songs[29]. Hungerford was also responsible for other World's Fair pageants, including *Wings of a Century* at the 1933 World's Fair in Chicago. It was Hungerford's idea to accompany the pageant primarily with folk music; suggestions for songs are scattered throughout the draft of the libretto he gave to Weill to set[30]. Even though Weill refused many of the specific suggestions, he followed the general outline and ethos of what Hungerford had given him. As with many of Weill's early American works, the composer generally assented to his American-born collaborator's designs.

Folk Music as Nature

Along with the libretto, *Railroads on Parade* survives in several sources in the Papers of Kurt Weill and Lotte Lenya Yale University[31]. The full score transmits the instrumental parts for the 1939 and 1940 versions[32]. The vocal parts for the 1939 version may be found in Weill's piano vocal score, and some vocal parts for the 1940 version are in a notebook of Weill's sketches[33]. There is also a historical recording of the first half of the 1940 version that was discovered in 2008[34]. The dialogue in the recording mostly matches the extant libretto in places where the 1939 and 1940 versions align, so it is likely that few changes were made between Weill's copy and the final production.

While many of the industries at the fair used a touch of the «industrial folk», *Railroads on Parade* draws on it almost from beginning to end. Perhaps this because trains were already a well-established part of the U.S. folkloric tradition, especially in music. Weill's primary sources for the tunes in *Railroads on Parade* were John and Alan Lomax's seminal collection *American Folksongs and Ballads*, Carl Sandburg's *The American Songbag*, and Dorothy Scarborough's *On the Trail of Negro Folk-Songs*, all of which include a large selection of railroad songs. Hungerford leaned into the historical side of the industry for their flagship spectacle, rather than the production side, which dominated the Ford and Chrysler exhibit, or the futuristic side, as in the case of General Motors' *Futurama*. Much of the advertising for the pageant also leaned into the history of railroading, as historical engines were exhibited around the country to promote the

---

[29]. Educational Screen 1928.
[30]. 'The Papers of Kurt Weill and Lotte Lenya', MSS 30, Irving S. Gilmore Music Library, Yale University, Box 29 Folder 407. Unless otherwise noted, all archival materials come from this collection.
[31]. For a more complete account of the sources for this work, see Graber 2021, pp. 101, 105.
[32]. Box 28 Folders 405-406.
[33]. Box 29 Folder 411 and 409 respectively.
[34]. Kurt Weill's Lost Recording 2008.

pageant[35]. Given the broad interest in U.S. history and culture that gripped the public during the Great Depression, it was a canny strategy, especially since railroads were inferior in most other respects (convenience, speed, and reach) than cars and planes.

In its extensive use of folksong, the music in *Railroads on Parade* is in dialogue with New Deal aesthetics, especially those of documentary films like Virgil Thomson's *The Plow that Broke the Plains* and *The River*, both of which played at the fair in the Science and Education Building[36]. Both of Thomson's scores open with folk idioms, *The River* with the hymn 'How Firm a Foundation', which gives way to 'My Shepherd Will Supply My Need' as the narrator extolls the grandeur of the Mississippi. Similarly, *The Plow that Broke the Plains* opens with a somber prelude then moves to a pastoral section followed the Cowboy Song 'I Ride an Old Paint' as the narrator describes the unspoiled landscape of the plains and the benign presence of cattle ranchers before the dustbowl[37]. *Railroads on Parade* opens with a similar gesture, though quotations are absent. The opening is set in chorale-like texture, giving the impression of a somber hymn. This gives way to a wide-ranging melody that resembles a folk tune, though it is a pastiche rather than quotation. All three scores use religious and folk idioms to instill a sense of reverence, while drawing on visual, rhetorical, and musical references to the pastoral to give an impression of unspoiled nature.

However, while in Thomson's documentaries, quotations accompany natural landscapes or people who work in harmony with the land like cowboys, in *Railroads on Parade*, the folk tunes only appear alongside human transportation workers. The first quotation ('The British Grenadiers' in 1939, 'Low Bridge' in 1940) coincides with the opening of the Erie Canal. The presence of folk tunes at the moment of human intervention in the land naturalizes these industrial developments. In both *The River* and *The Plow that Broke the Plains*, technological intervention in the land is accompanied by harsh dissonances which seem to require narrative and musical resolution on through the herculean efforts of the government[38]. But in *Railroads on Parade*, technology evolves smoothly alongside U.S. popular music from folksong, to nineteenth-century popular song, and finally, to a modern day pop finale. This creates a «usable past» for

---

[35]. See for example *NEW YORK TIMES* 1939.

[36]. The Science and Education Building was one of the fair's disappointments. While much of the New York scientific community (including the science editor of the *New York Times*) publicly advocated for a stronger presence of non-industrial science at the fair, many of these individuals held strong leftwing views, and Whalen was reluctant to listen to their council. The Science and Education building was a compromise: the scientific community was given space, but no funding. In the end, the building was not even included on the Department of Science and Education's tours of the fair for school children. See KUZNICK 1994, pp. 356-359. This lack of funding may account for why relatively cheap government documentaries dominated the exhibit.

[37]. A great deal of Thomson's music for the prelude was cut, including a strange harmonization of the hymn 'Old Hundred'. See LERNER 1997, pp. 94-97.

[38]. *Ibidem*, pp. 98-123, 166-177.

the railroad, showing it developing alongside the natural world in harmony, reinforcing the idea that trains were fundamental to the national landscape just as *Fortune* helped naturalize the airplane. Anyone who attended the fair and saw both the pageant and the documentaries would be confronted with opposing messages about the relationship between industry and the landscape, but the musical rhetoric for both was similar.

THE NOVACHORD

Weill's orchestration also differs significantly from Thomson's. In the folkloric sections, Thomson employed transparent textures or grand symphonic sounds, while Weill's instrumentation resembles his theatre orchestras, with five wind players each doubling on two instruments (flute/piccolo, oboe/English horn, two alto sax/clarinet, tenor sax/bass clarinet), two trumpets, two trombones, a tuba, Hammond organ, guitar doubling on banjo, percussion, strings, and, in 1940, the novachord[39]. This timbral palette suggests a much more contemporary ethos. The combination of traditional tunes with modernized orchestration suggests a merging of the natural with the modern world.

This merging of nature and technology especially came through in the use of the voice. By the 1930s, electric microphone technology allowed for new styles of singing in which the performer sang softly into the microphone, which allowed that sound to be magnified above the instrumental ensemble. This created a sense of intimacy between the singer and the listener, leading to the rise of the crooning vocal star[40]. On the historical recording, the performers adopt this approach, especially in the solo sections, such as when the trains themselves sing in the 'Golden Spike' sequence (called 'The Wedding of the Rails' in 1940), as railroads from the four corners of the country join together. As the trains sang, the performer's organic human voice apparently emanated from a large piece of machinery. Although the trains do not sing folksongs quotations, they do sing in that style, unlike the narrators and historical figures, who mostly speak rather than sing. Their singing voices place the trains' in the world of the 'natural' with folksong-laden score, choruses, and solos rather than the 'real' historical world of the spoken sections.

In the 1940 version of the pageant, the combination of nature and technology was even more evident in the score with the addition the novachord. Invented in 1939 by Laurens Hammond of Hammond organ fame, the novachord was the first commercial polyphonic synthesizer. Players could modify the timbre by adjusting the attack, decay, tremolo, and timbral profile using a series of levers above the seventy-two key manual. According to *Nature*

---

[39]. The orchestration is most similar to Weill's *Knickerbocker Holiday* (1938).
[40]. KATZ 2004, p. 40.

magazine, several orchestral timbres were available, including passable evocations of brass, reeds, strings, harpsichord, clavichord, and Hawaiian guitar[41]. The instrument was an important part of the transportation area at the World's Fair. Its official debut took place just across the plaza at the Ford exhibit, where Ferde Grofé conducted a version of his *An American Biography: Henry Ford* arranged for the New World Orchestra, including four novachords and Hammond organ[42]. This short tone poem uses simple diatonic melodies and harmonies, highlighting the novachord's fidelity to more traditional musical materials and timbres rather than the strangeness that made it so popular in later science fiction and noir scores. The film version of General Motor's *Futurama* exhibit also employed a novachord for the sequences inside the ride. Weill may have also encountered the novachord at the movies; the interlude of Max Steiner's score for *Gone with the Wind* (1939) consists of Stephen Foster tunes rendered on novachord. This use of the novachord especially resembles Weill's first experiment with the instrument: an interlude for Elmer Rice's play *Two on an Island* (1939). Though the score is lost, Marc Blitzstein reported that it consisted of folk music arranged for the instrument[43].

The instrument is present in almost all of the revised sections of the 1940 *Railroads on Parade*, and features prominently in the 'Gold Rush' sequence[44]. First, it doubles the melody of 'Snag-toothed Sal', and a duet for novachord and Hammond organ accompanies the locomotive J.W. Bowker as it carries Collis P. Huntington, Leland Stanford, Charles Crocker, Mark Hopkins, and Theodore B. Judah across the Sacramento Valley in California's first railroad (Ex. 1)[45]. Although this duet is not a quotation (at least not one I could identify)[46], it borrows several gestures from turn-of-the-century Tin Pan Alley. The rhythmic profile resembles the refrain of Charles Graham, George Spaulding, and William B. Gray's 'Two Little Girls in Blue' (1893), which appears later in the pageant.

---

[41]. BROADHURST 2014.

[42]. The score resides in the Ferde Grofé Collection at the Library of Congress, Box 240 Folder 1. My thanks to Paul Sommerfeld for providing me with scores for this piece.

[43]. Drew 1987, p. 312.

[44]. Music for novachord only appears in the sources in the appendix to the main manuscript, which contains the inserts for the 1940 version, with one exception: the 'Overland Trail' sequence, but this is likely an archival error. The manuscript jumps from f. 84 to f. 85a (the beginning of the 'Overland Trail') and continues onto 85b and 85c before returning to f. 85. However, f. 85 largely repeats the material from f. 85a in a slightly different orchestration. The novachord only appears on the inserted pages (85a-c), and given that most of the 1940 inserts were marked similarly (i.e., numbered with letters according to the page number where they were inserted), these pages are most likely a 1940 insert that was not removed from the full manuscript before archiving.

[45]. Ex. 1 is taken from the full score. I have silently edited it to make articulation markings consistent and correct obvious errors.

[46]. The melody appears amongst Weill's sketches for the 1940 revisions, though it is not labeled. However, other quotations are labeled, indicating that this melody is probably original.

Ex. 1: *Railroads on Parade* (1940), duet for novachord and Hammond organ.

«Steel Veins»: *Railroads on Parade* and the Industrial Folk

Naomi Graber

«Steel Veins»: *Railroads on Parade* and the Industrial Folk

Like the amplified music more generally, the choice of novachord was likely practical. While contemporary critics noted that it was easily distinguishable from acoustic instruments, *Newsweek* reported that the sound was very similar to a piano over the radio, indicating that technological mediation (such as the microphones used in *Railroads on Parade*) attenuated the differences. Furthermore, the fact that the instrument produced sound through loudspeakers rather than a vibrating acoustic body made amplification easier, making it ideal for such electronically mediated settings like *Railroads on Parade*. The variety of timbres may have also appealed to Weill. While on the larger side for a theatre orchestra, the scale of *Railroads on Parade* and its outdoor setting would indicate something closer to Weill's other pageant, *The Eternal Road* (1937), which included all the instruments in *Railroads on Parade* as well as four French horns and four additional woodwind parts, including a bassoon. In the 1939 version, Weill often has the Hammond organ use the bassoon stop, indicating he may have felt the absence of a broader orchestral palette. While the novachord settings are not indicated in the surviving materials, the recording indicates he made use of multiple timbres, some meant to imitate acoustic sounds, other clearly electronic. On the recording's rendition of Ex. 1, mm. 20-27 use a brassier timbre than the surrounding sections, indicating a probable readjustment to the controls.

The presence of the novachord's electronic timbres within the electronically mediated sound-world of the pageant likely had an effect quite different from the instrument's later use as a signifier of strangeness. Unlike the Hammond organ, the novachord sounds clearly electronic as it plays Ex. 1, a sound audience's might recognize from futuristic sounds of *Futurama* and *An American Biography* from the General Motors and Ford exhibits respectively. Yet it also blends into the landscape of mediated acoustic timbres just as the trains seem to naturally arise naturally out of humanity's interaction with the landscape of the United States. Weill treats the instrument like a member of the ensemble, alternatively playing a supporting and featured role, and sharing melodic material. For example, the saxophones smoothly take over the Tin Pan Alley pastiche tune of Ex. 1, smoothly transitioning from electronic to acoustic sound, just as the folksongs smoothly transition into more modern style. The electronic mediation of the other instruments likely helped the novachord sound less strange, further blurring the aural lines between the acoustic and the electronic. Accompanied by sounds that were technologically mediated yet safe and familiar, the trains took on this Janus-faced aspect of the novachord, a technologically enhanced product emerging from and seamlessly blending into the nation's landscape to carry her people into a bright and comfortable future.

Folk Music as Music of the Folk

This parallel development of locomotives and music also shows that the railroads are in harmony with people — the 'folk' — as well as nature. The choice of folksongs in the score supported this. For all that railroads are part of the U.S. folksong lexicon, there are curiously few «railroad» folksongs in in *Railroads on Parade*. Weill only used four of the over thirty railroad songs in the collections he consulted: 'I've Been Working on the Railroad', 'She'll Be Coming 'Round the Mountain', 'John Henry' and 'Casey Jones', and the last three as instrumental rather than choral numbers[47]. In addition, the connection between 'She'll be Coming Round the Mountain' and trains is tenuous; despite the fact that it appears in the «railroad» portion of *The American Songbag*, the lyrics are unrelated to railroading. The only other 'train' song is 'This Train is Bound for Glory' from *American Ballads and Folksongs*, which is listed as a spiritual, and in which the train is purely metaphorical. There are work songs, but they come from waterways: 'Low Bridge' for the Erie Canal scene and the sea shanties 'Whisky Johnny' and 'Heave Away'. Other songs in *Railroads on Parade* include work-animal songs ('Snag-Toothed Sal' and 'Old Grey Mare' for example) or patriotic numbers ('Battle Hymn of the Republic').

This was probably a wise choice given the typical tenor of railroad folksongs, many of which deal in misery, either at the hands of the industry or the technology. For example, the Lomax lyrics to 'Paddy Works on the Erie' (which Hungerford suggested be included in *Railroads on Parade*) includes the verse

> Our contractor's name it was Tom King,
> He kept a store to rob the men,
> A Yankee clerk with in and pen,
> To cheat Pat on the railroad[48].

Many other songs detail railroad disasters or the deaths of workers, including 'Casey Jones' and 'John Henry', which is probably why those songs appear without lyrics in *Railroads on Parade*. Though train wrecks decreased significantly in the twentieth century, they still occurred, and were often caught on film and shown as part of newsreels. To state the obvious, reminding the audience of these incidents was not in the interests of the industry. The other category of railroad song common in the collections Weill consulted was the hobo song, which also went again went against the image of luxury the pageant was trying to communicate. By using folksongs — though not necessarily railroad folksongs — Weill maintained the folkloric aura of the railroad without reminding audiences of the industry's troubled history. Furthermore, the non-railroad folksongs broaden the mythology of the railroad, embedding it in the vast folkloric world of the United States.

---

[47]. LOMAX – LOMAX 1934 includes seventeen railroad songs, SANDBURG 1927 has twenty-four (including 'Hobo Songs'), and SCARBOROUGH 1925 has lyrics for seventeen, but only five tunes. There are three overlaps between the collections.

[48]. LOMAX – LOMAX 1934, pp. 21-22. The song also appears in SANDBURG 1927 p. 356 as 'Poor Paddy Works on the Railway'. Like the Lomax version, it is not complimentary towards the industry, though it is not as explicit about the hardships and corruption.

«Steel Veins»: *Railroads on Parade* and the Industrial Folk

Overall, the score tells the story of the laboring masses working in harmony to connect the vast expanse of the nation, and speed up the transfer of goods and services. Just like *Fortune* magazine's «mountaineer», the workers are both part of the 'folk' (they sing folksongs after all), and yet are crucial to the capitalist enterprise. The fact that the pageant was live rather than a film buttressed this facet of the production. Most films, including documentaries, rarely included choral singing, save possibly at the beginning or the end, but stage productions often included large choruses. While the episodic construction and 'march of time' narrative borrows from the aesthetics of documentary film and newsreels, the choral singing is much more characteristic of stage productions. It allows the workers to both work *and sing* in harmony as they smooth the passage of people and goods across the nation.

The masses of happily singing workers might also remind audiences of the workers choruses that arose during this period. Many of the songbooks for these choruses were published in the 1930s and consisted of a large number of folksongs and contrafacts of folksongs, though the political implications of these selections were sometimes at odds with productions like *Railroads on Parade*[49]. By singing ostensibly collectively-authored music that arose from a putative autochthonous 'people's culture', these choruses hoped to send a message that they were independent from corporate culture, and to show solidarity with each other, rather than the industry that employed them. In the pageant, the folksong choruses depict a labor force happily building infrastructure and working in the transportation industry. The pageant seems to unite folklore and industry through music, and reframing the phenomenon as intimately connected to corporate capitalist endeavors. Thus corporate capitalism and folksong become two sides of the same coin, rather than opposing forces.

Two Representative Examples: 'Casey Jones' and 'John Henry'

The presence of 'Casey Jones' and 'John Henry' play an important role in this facet of the production. Both songs come from black communities, and neither paints the railroad in a positive light. During the 1930s, 'Casey Jones' circulated with several different sets of lyrics. Weill's version most likely came from Dorothy Scarborough's *On the Trail of Negro Folk-Songs*, but it appears in the Lomax and Sandburg collections in the traditional version, which tells the story of an engineer who dies in a fiery wreck. All three sources include an introduction explaining the song's history. Scarborough and the Lomaxes place the song's origin in black communities, where the figure merged with other folkloric characters, both

---

[49]. Cantwell 1996, pp. 89-90, 93-94.

black and white[50]. Leftist activist Joe Hill published a revised lyric in 1912 in which the title character is a scab who dies because his engine has been badly repaired by non-union engineers, a version which circulated widely in workers' movements[51].

John Henry was a more nebulous figure, but still associated with the New Deal. In the Lomax version (which Weill used), 'John Henry' tells the story of black railroad laborer working himself to death in an effort to beat a steam drill's efficiency[52]. The song's portrayal of the dehumanizing nature of technology made the title character iconic, though its bleak outlook on the relationship between technological and human progress was antithetical to broader themes of the fair. The character had also appeared in other media, including in John Becker's woodcuts and prints made under the auspices of the Federal Art Project, some of which were displayed in the lobby of the Federal Theatre Project's all-black production of *Macbeth* in 1936[53].

It is unclear how much Weill knew about the leftist implications of either tune, though their ostensible roots in black culture may have appealed to him; work on *Railroads on Parade* coincided with work on *Ulysses Africanus*, an unfinished musical that has clear anti-racist goals, albeit somewhat naïvely and paternalistically realized[54]. The inclusion of what Weill thought of as a black version of 'I've Been Working on the Railroad' from *On the Trail of Negro Folk-Songs* supports the idea that Weill may have thought of these songs as a gesture of racial inclusion (albeit a naïve one). But in the context of the World's Fair with its white-washed industrial folklore, those implications (if they were meant at all) were likely lost on the audience. Rather, in context, with the inclusion of 'John Henry' and 'Casey Jones' without their tragic or anti-corporate lyrics, *Railroads on Parade* seems to reclaim these tunes for the industry's preferred history of locomotion. Especially given the prevalence of corporate folklore and folksong at the fair, consumers might make new associations with these songs, and take those associations into the wider world. The next time an audience member heard 'Casey Jones', 'John Henry', or any of the other tunes in this pageant and others, it might provoke warm and fuzzy feelings of patriotism and thoughts consumer comforts rather than solidarity with the laboring masses or fear of human obsolescence. By including tunes (though not lyrics) associated with the labor

---

[50]. SCARBOROUGH 1925, pp. 248-250, LOMAX – LOMAX 1934, pp. 35-39. On the real Casey Jones, see COHEN 2000, pp. 134-37.

[51]. ANDERSON 1942.

[52]. SANDBURG 1927 includes a short variation on the 'John Henry' song tradition called 'Ever Since Uncle John Henry Been Dead'.

[53]. GREEN 1993, pp. 64-66.

[54]. During the late 1930s, Weill's consciousness of racial inequality in the U.S. was growing, although he had yet to grasp the subtleties. This comes out especially in Weill's dealings with Paul and Eslanda Robeson in regards to *Ulysses Africanus*, which Weill (and librettist Maxwell Anderson) saw as an anti-racist project, but which Eslanda Robeson saw as deeply problematic. See GRABER 2021, pp. 333-335.

movement, *Railroads on Parade* does not just add new meaning to the songs, but displaces associations that were unfavorable to the industry.

***

The presence of folksong at the 1939-1940 World's Fair supported a number of competing messages. For Virgil Thomson and Pare Lorentz, it indicated a prelapsarian paradise that New Deal programs might be able to restore. But in the Transportation Area and elsewhere, folk music harmonized the technological and the natural without the need for government intervention. By participating in the invention of an «industrial folk», *Railroads on Parade* created a new «usable past» for the railroad industry, one in which labor and capital enjoyed a peaceful collaboration which benefited the entire nation as politicians merely got out of the way.

Bibliography

Ainsworth 1939
Ainsworth, Gardner. 'The New York Fair: Adventure in Promotion', in: *Public Opinion Quarterly*, III/4 (1939), pp. 694-704.

Anderson 1942
Anderson, William. 'On the Wobbly 'Casey Jones' and Other Songs', in: *California Folklore Quarterly*, I/4 (1942), pp. 373-376.

Book of the Pageant 1939
Railroads on Parade: Book of the Pageant, author's private collection, 1939.

Broadhurst 2014
Broadhurst, Sarah. 'Forerunner of the Moog', in: *Professional Engineering*, XXVII/2 (2014), p. 64.

Cantwell 1996
Cantwell, Robert. *When We Were Good: The Folk Revival*, Cambridge (MA), Harvard University Press, 1996.

Cohen 2000
Cohen, Norm. *Long Steel Rail: The Railroad in American Folksong*, Urbana, University of Illinois Press, ²2000.

Cohen 2016
Cohen, Ronald D. *Depression Folk: Grassroots Music and Left-Wing Politics in 1930s America*, Chapel Hill, University of North Carolina Press, 2016.

Drew 1987
Drew, David. *Kurt Weill: A Handbook*, Berkeley-Los Angeles, University of California Press, 1987.

Educational Screen 1928
'Centenary Pageant on Tour', in: *Educational Screen*, VII/1 (1928), available online at <https://archive.org/stream/educationalscree07chicrich/educationalscree07chicrich_djvu.txt>, accessed April 2023.

Ewen 1996
Ewen, Stuart. *PR!: A Social History of Spin*, New York, Basic, 1996.

Graber 2021
Graber, Naomi. *Kurt Weill's America*, Oxford-New York, Oxford University Press, 2021.

Green 1993
Green, Archie. *Wobblies, Pile Butts, and Other Heroes: Laborlore Explorations*, Urbana, University of Illinois Press, 1993.

Grieveson 2012
Grieveson, Lee. 'Visualizing Industrial Citizenship', in: *Learning with the Lights Off: Educational Film in the United States*, edited by Devin Orgeron, Marsha Orgeron and Dan Streible, Oxford-New York, Oxford University Press, 2012, pp. 107-132.

Grieveson 2018
Id. *Cinema and the Wealth of Nations: Media, Capital, and the Liberal World System*, Berkeley-Los Angeles, University of California Press, 2018.

Hidy 2004
Hidy, Ralph W. *The Great Northern: A History*, Minneapolis, University of Minnesota Press, 2004.

Jones 1971
Jones, Alfred Haworth. 'The Search for a Usable American Past in the New Deal Era', in: *American Quarterly*, XXIII/5 (1971), pp. 710-724.

Katz 2004
Katz, Mark. *Capturing Sound: How Technology Changed Music*, Berkeley-Los Angeles, University of California Press, 2004.

Kennedy 1999
Kennedy, David M. *Freedom From Fear: The American People in Depression and War, 1929-1945*, Oxford-New York, Oxford University Press, 1999.

Kurt Weill's Lost Recording 2008
Kurt Weill's Lost Recording: Railroads on Parade, transcription records, 2008.

Kuznick 1994
Kuznick, Peter J. 'Losing the World of Tomorrow: The Battle over the Presentation of Science at the 1939 New York World's Fair', in: *American Quarterly*, XLVI/3 (1994), pp. 341-373.

Lerner 1997
Lerner, Neil. *The Classical Documentary Score in American Films of Persuasion: Contexts and Case Studies, 1936-1945*, unpublished Ph.D. Diss., Durham, Duke University, 1997.

Lichtenberg 1938
Lichtenberg, Bernard. 'Business Backs New York World Fair to Meet New Deal Propaganda', in: *Public Opinion Quarterly*, II/2 (1938), pp. 314-320.

Lomax – Lomax 1934
Lomax, John A. – Lomax, Alan. *American Ballads and Folk Songs*, New York, Macmillan, 1934.

Miller 2003
Miller, James S. 'White-Collar Excavations: *Fortune* Magazine and the Invention of the Industrial Folk', in: *American Periodicals*, XIII (2003), pp. 84-104.

New York Times 1939
'Old Train «Speeds» on 16-Mile Trip', in: *New York Times*, 1 April 1939, p. 21.

New York Times 1962
'Grover A. Whalen Dies at 75; Made City's Welcome Famous', in: *New York Times*, 21 April 1962, pp. 1, 19.

Official Guidebook 1939
Official Guidebook of the New York World's Fair, Second Edition, New York, Exposition Publications, 1939.

Reuss 2000
Reuss, Richard A. with JoAnne C. Reuss. *American Folk Music and Left-Wing Politics, 1927-1957*, Lanham, (MD), Scarecrow, 2000.

Sandburg 1927
Sandburg, Carl. *The American Songbag*, New York, Harcourt, Brace, 1927.

Scarborough 1925
Scarborough, Dorothy. *On the Trail of Negro Folk-Songs*, Cambridge (MA), Harvard University Press, 1925.

Shampine 2009
Shampine, Dave. 'My Greatest Hobby is the Railroad', in: *Watertown Daily Times*, 5 July 2009, available online at <https://www.nny360.com/magazines/nnybusiness/uncategorized/january-2016-business-history-the-railroad-writer/article_91cd3776-1c85-5a95-9365-807090cfeff4.html>, accessed April 2023.

STOTT 1973
STOTT, William. *Documentary Expression and Thirties America*, Oxford-New York, Oxford University Press, 1973.

STOVER 1997
STOVER, John F. *American Railroads*, Chicago, University of Chicago Press, ²1997.

SULLIVAN 2013
SULLIVAN, Sara. 'Corporate Discourse of Sponsored Films of Steel Production in the United States, 1936-1956', in: *Velvet Life Trap*, no. 72 (2013), pp. 33-43.

SUSMAN 1984
SUSMAN, Warren. *Culture as History: The Transformation of American Society in the Twentieth Century*, New York, Pantheon, 1984.

Shared Authorship and Compositional Process in 1940s Hollywood: *One Touch of Venus* by Kurt Weill and Ann Ronell

Marida Rizzuti
(Università degli Studi di Torino)

The relationship between composer and arranger in the Hollywood production system during the 1940s, at a time when the era referred to as the 'golden age' (1920-1960) of classic cinema was taking shape, assumed a decisive role in the creation of soundtracks in the film production process. This study will reflect critically on the distinctions of function and contractual obligations between the two roles in circumstances where the composer engaged in an external collaboration with the studio, while the arranger was an employee of the studio's music department. This essay addresses the relationship established between Kurt Weill and Ann Ronell in the production of the soundtrack for the musical film *One Touch of Venus* (1948). This investigation is part of a larger project that aims to examine the nature of the delicate relationship between composers and arrangers in the studio era.

In the Hollywood studio era, the duties of the arranger significantly overlapped with those of the orchestrator. Even in the literature there remains some areas of ambiguity in the definition of 'who makes what' during the composition of music for the film. In *Scoring the Score*, Ian Sapiro[1] accurately profiles the extensive literature on 'orchestrator vs arranger' from the studio era, echoing what Kathryn Kalynak pointed out in *Settling the Score*: «the terms

---

[1]. Sapiro 2017, pp. 13-66. My heartfelt thanks to Naomi Graber for her valuable suggestions and appreciation of my research, and for her remarkable work toward 'Weill Trasformations': working four-handedly for the book I learned a lot from her. This contribution is an initial critical reflection on the relationship between composer and arranger in the Hollywood production process in the 1940s. The beginning of the research, the study of Kurt Weill and Ann Ronell's primary sources, was made possible by a Research and Travel Grant of The Kurt Weill Foundation, made in 2015. My research is far from over.

"orchestrator" and "arranger" were used fairly interchangeably in Hollywood in the studio era»[2]. To unravel such ambiguities, production studies can be used to study those aspects that, on the surface, are remote from a composer's compositional process (such as employment contracts), paying particular attention to the clauses inherent in the types of intervention in music production made by music professionals hired for specific films or employed in the studios' music departments.

By the 1940s, the transition from stage to screen for musicals was beginning to become established as a practice, especially in the re-presentation of the dramaturgical-musical structure adapted for the cinema[3], so a common process was acquiring the rights to make the stage musical into a film musical. The following is a table of the screen adaptations of Weill's musicals made during the 1940s, which gives a sense of the smooth interaction between the two production systems of Broadway and Hollywood, and the distinctiveness of Kurt Weill's relationship with Hollywood:

TABLE 1: WEILL'S MUSICALS FROM STAGE TO SCREEN (1941-1950)

Works	Broadway (unless otherwise noted)	Hollywood
Lady in the Dark	1941	1944 Paramount
One Touch of Venus	1943	1948 Universal International
Knickerbocker Holiday	1938	1944 United Artists
Where Do We Go From Here?		1945 Twentieth Century Fox
Down in the Valley	1948 Indiana University	1950 Television adaptation for NBC

In 1943, the musical *One Touch of Venus* was so successful on Broadway that, less than three weeks after its premiere, Kurt Weill received an offer to make a film adaptation: «[h]e signed a contract to have a movie made of *One Touch of Venus*, though he was reluctant, afraid his music would be mangled by Hollywood. To avoid that, he negotiated a contract that no other songs other than his could be included in the score. [...] From a composer's standpoint, Hollywood was not like Broadway. [...] There was little artistic control over how the music would be used, who might sing it, and if it would even be used»[4]. In the specific case of *One Touch of Venus*, Ronell was assigned the role of musical director of the movie: «this left Ronell in the lion's den of a Hollywood music department, again having to fend for herself and Weill's music»[5].

---

[2]. KALINAK 1992, p. 73.
[3]. See BROOMFIELD-MCHUGH 2019.
[4]. ZIMMERS 2009, p. 92.
[5]. *Ibidem*, p. 93.

Shared Authorship and Compositional Process in 1940s Hollywood

Kurt Weill in Hollywood

Kurt Weill's relations with the Hollywood film industry[6] developed even before the time of his arrival in the United States in 1935 (he was invited to work in Hollywood as early as 1934), and proceeded in parallel with his activities of composing and writing essays and articles. In this regard, some articles and interviews that appeared in magazines and newspapers between 1936 and 1946 assume particular prominence. They include the article 'The Alchemy of Music' in *Stage: The Magazine of After-dark Entertainment* (November 1936)[7], an interview titled 'National Music, Opera and the Movies. An Interview with Kurt Weill' in *Pacific Coast Musician* (3 July 1937)[8], and the article 'Music in the Movies' in *Harper's Bazaar* (September 1946)[9].

In the 1937 interview, the composer emphasised the decisive role of cinema as a new art form: «I believe the new musical art-form, a kind of opera, will come out of the movies, [...]. To put it exactly, opera must be effective theater, which is also required of a good film. I am interested in both, because I am convinced that the future of music depends much on its thought-moulding part in relation to modern society»[10]; along with the peculiarities of film music and the American film industry:

> [...] the difficulty with American film music, in contrast to that written abroad, is that American producers and directors are afraid that originality, even if mildly modern — that is to say music of the year 1900 — might frighten their audiences. Film music need only speak simple, clear, direct language, just as opera must effect once more a union with the theater on the same basis[11].

This article was published while Weill was in Los Angeles and during his collaboration with Fritz Lang on the film *You and Me* (1938).

'Music in the Movies' was significant because it appeared in a non-specialist but best-selling magazine in the United States at a time when Weill was at the peak of his success on Broadway. It thus testifies to how composition for the film medium was a central issue in Weill's contemporary aesthetic. In the article, Kurt Weill presented his personal view of the Hollywood production system, including suggestions for how to enhance certain relationships (director-composer-screenwriter) to improve the connection between images and music:

---

[6]. See Graber 2021.
[7]. Weill 1936.
[8]. Weill 1937a.
[9]. Weill 1946.
[10]. Weill 1937a.
[11]. *Ibidem*.

> The American movie audience is getting music-conscious. [...] The recording firms release albums of music from outstanding pictures; composers write orchestral suites base on their picture scores; symphonic arrangements of themes from their scores are played over the radio. [...] Can it be that the movies, after having given a terrific boost to the art of popular songwriting, are now beginning to popularize the work of contemporary composers? [...] Today, in a more democratic world, music has become a powerful medium in the hands of those who provide entertainment for the masses. [...]
>
> At the same time, the producers and directors of dramatic, non-musical pictures realized that a good underscoring job contributed a great deal to the success of a picture and that the right soundtrack mixture of spoken dialogue, music and sound effects was an integral part of its production. This opened a new field for the composer, and soon the big movie centers of the world created a new species of musician, the motion-picture composer. [...] The motion-picture is a perfect medium for an original musico-dramatic creation on the same level as the different forms of the musical theater: musical comedy, operetta, musical play and opera. If we want to develop an art form (or a form of entertainment) in which music has an integral part, we have to allow the composer to collaborate with the writer and director to the same extent as he collaborates in the musical theater[12].

He also commented on the social spillover of the film industry, and showed awareness of the potential of cinema as a new mass art form: «in the field of the film-musical itself, which is generally identified with a sort of glorified amplification of the musical comedy format, there have been quite a number of very successful attempts at interweaving music and action into a satisfying unity»[13]. He identified three genres of films in which greater participation by the composer could give greater benefit to the treatment of music and the film itself: the documentary, animated films and musical comedy.

Through an awareness of his own role and the potential associated with this new type of musician (the film composer), Weill builds a dramaturgical view of the functions of film music:

> In my *Dreigroschenoper* film, I tried to translate the form of the musical play into the medium of motion picture. In the Fritz Lang film *You and Me*, I tried out a new technique by using songs as a part of the background music, expressing the "inner voice" of the characters, and in the picture *Where Do We Go from Here*, Ira Gershwin and I wrote a regular little comic opera for the scene on Columbus' ship. It is a pretty safe bet that eventually something like a "film-opera" will grow out of all

---

[12]. WEILL 1946.
[13]. *Ibidem*.

this, and it is quite possible that the much-talked-about "American opera" will come
out of the most popular American form of entertainment — the motion picture[14].

In the case of *One Touch of Venus*, this included limited power over the score with the primary purpose of avoiding the kind of dissatisfaction he had previously experienced at seeing the treatment given to his music, as had happened with *Lady in the Dark*. In 1943-1944 the composer had experimented with the transition from stage to screen but had suffered a failure, not so much in terms of the music itself but in the way that the dramaturgical function that the songs had in the musical had been disrupted by the way they were employed in the film. Therefore, from the moment he received a proposal for a screen transposition of the musical, Weill had every intention to protect his work, and especially his role, through legal avenues.

Upon receiving the proposal to make *One Touch of Venus* on the screen, Weill took steps through his lawyer, Leah Salisbury, and his agent in Hollywood, Irving Paul Lazar, to protect his music by making his demands clear to the studio Universal, in the person of producer Lester Cowan:

> 1. All songs in the film must be from the original performance, and the accompaniment to the film must be based on themes from the original score.
> 2. The moving picture company has to call on me for the following services: a) to write any new songs or musical material as might be necessary for the moving picture treatment of the original show, b) to select and place the original songs for the requirements of the movie script and make necessary changes, c) to select themes and material from the original score for underscoring purposes. [...]
> 3. If I am to do the special service job as outlined above, I would have to get another frame with the text "Music by Kurt Weill", because I would be responsible for the entire music in the picture[15].

He also fought so that he could retain copyright of his music and have oversight over the newly developed versions, especially in terms of maintaining control over the stylistic features of the soundtrack. The music of *One Touch of Venus* in its Broadway version had its own specificity and distinctiveness, which the composer ensured through legal means would remain intact in the film version[16]. In later correspondence with both Salisbury and Ronell, the composer always

---

[14]. *Ibidem*.

[15]. Kurt Weill to Leah Salisbury, Typewritten letter (photocopy), 4 September 1944, Correspondence Ser. 40, The Kurt Weill Foundation for Music, Weill-Lenya Research Center, original Leah Salisbury papers, Columbia University, New York.

[16]. At the present state of my research I cannot refer to the contract between the parties, I refer to the correspondence between Weill and Salisbury, in particular four telegrams dated between 20 and 23 September

stressed the relevance of the «non-interpolation clause, [...] which means that they would have to call on me again if and when they need different songs from the ones I'm writing now and that they are not allowed to interpolate any numbers and that the underscoring has to be based on my music»[17]. The intent was to avoid the treatment that *Lady in the Dark* had suffered in the transition from stage to screen.

Who Was Ann Ronell, the Tin Pan Alley Girl?

These requests were accepted, and the studio paired the composer with the arranger Ann Ronell for the soundtrack for the film version of *One Touch of Venus*. Ronell, née Rosenblatt, was born in Omaha, Nebraska and studied at Radcliffe College with Walter Piston where she found herself at the center of a lively cultural and musical environment. In interviews, she often recalled the intellectual effervescence of that period: «in this way I was very lucky, because I had three lifelong friends from that job of mine at college. George Gershwin, Sigmund Romberg and Aaron Copland»[18]. After graduation, she moved to New York, where she worked as a piano accompanist and songwriter. Settling in Hollywood in the 1930s, thanks to the success of one of her songs *Willow Weep for Me* (1932) she began working for Disney in 1933 with *Three Little Pigs*. In the Hollywood milieu she frequently encountered many émigré composers, musicians and intellectuals. Through Ernst Toch she met Weill in 1937, with whom she established a lasting friendship; she also collaborated on the English translation of *Die Dreigroschenoper*, as well as writing lyrics for 'Soldier's Song' and 'The River is Blue' for a score Weill wrote for a film in 1938 that went unused, and, in California, continuing the work of arranging music for Weill after his return from there to New York[19].

For the production of the film *One Touch of Venus*, Weill and Ronell worked closely together in the creative process of the soundtrack and on the songs; it is possible to reconstruct

---

1944, in which Weill defined the terms of the contract, with the greatest emphasis on underscoring: «I insist that underscoring must be based on material from original show, because otherwise new underscoring music could overshadow music from show as in *Lady in the Dark*». Kurt Weill to Leah Salisbury, telegram (photocopy), 21 September 1944, Correspondence Ser. 40, The Kurt Weill Foundation for Music, Weill-Lenya Research Center, original Leah Salisbury papers, Columbia University, New York.

[17]. Kurt Weill to Leah Salisbury, Typewritten letter (photocopy), 12 May 1945, Correspondence Ser. 40, The Kurt Weill Foundation for Music, Weill-Lenya Research Center, original Leah Salisbury papers, Columbia University, New York.

[18]. Ann Ronell, An Oral History Interview with Kim Kowalke and Lys Symonette for the Kurt Weill Foundation for Music, Weill-Lenya Research Center, Series 60, 23 June 1988, p. 2.

[19]. See ZIMMERS 2009, pp. 92-99.

their methodology through their direct correspondence and also through the indirect correspondence that both Weill and Ronell had with others regarding this film.

The film *One Touch of Venus* was not merely a cinematic version of the hit Broadway musical: *One Touch of Venus* is a musical film, meaning by that definition a narrative use is made of song, which like dialogue performs a dramaturgical function. The most noticeable change occurs in the use of the songs from the musical and the function assigned to them. In the film, the presence of music has three well-defined roles: source music (that is, music which the characters can hear), underscoring, and musical numbers. The musical numbers that are reproduced from the stage musical are 'Speak Low' and 'That's Him'; all the other musical numbers in the musical were reworked and developed in the underscoring, and similarly the music for the ballet 'Bacchanale', which represents the turning point or climax in the musical, was arranged anew in the film whilst retaining the same dramaturgical function.

The plot concerns the vicissitudes of Eddie and Venus. Eddie accidentally awakens the statue of Venus with a kiss, only to be pursued by the art gallery owner Savory, who believes Eddie has stolen his statue. Eventually, Eddie and Venus fall in love, and he shows her the beauties of life on Earth, all the while on the run from Savory. Venus having come to life, the effects of the presence of the goddess of love begin to become apparent in New York City with a general and widespread falling in love among the city's population and with a noticeable increase in marriage licenses. The other characters in the story are not immune to the effects of Venus: Savory falls in love with Molly, his secretary who loved him before; Joe, roommate of Eddie, and Gloria, Eddie's girlfriend, fall in love with each other. Venus returns to being a statue; Eddie does not arrive in time to greet her. However, there is a happy ending, because a new saleswoman arrives in the Savory Department to work with Eddie and she has the same appearance as Venus.

The characters are grouped by pairs: Eddie and Venus, Joe and Gloria, Savory and Molly. Each pair is a step in the social hierarchy: Eddie is the hero, although he has a humble social position — he is a window dresser. Savory is the rival; he has a high, powerful social position, because he owns the department store and art gallery. Venus is the heroine; she has a high social position, so she should fall in love with Savory, but instead she falls in love with Eddie: this is the trigger of the plot. Molly is the supporting role for Venus, and has the same social position as Eddie; she is Savory's secretary, with whom she has always been in love. Joe and Gloria are comprimarios; they are in the same social position as Eddie.

Presented below is the list of the musical numbers from the Conductor Vocal Score, in the copy sent by Ronell to Weill on which on the first sheet is the dedication «For Kurtsky A Labor of Love, Ann 1947-1948»[20]:

---

[20]. Ann Ronell, Film music for *One Touch of Venus*, Ser. 10/06/27, Weill-Lenya Research Center, New York.

Table 2: *One Touch of Venus*, Conductor Vocal Score (WLRC)

Film Music for *One Touch of Venus*				
Conductor Vocal Score		*One Touch of Venus*	1570	Chappel & Co, Inc.
Main Title From themes of 'Speak Low' and 'Trouble with Women' — Weill + Nash and — 'Don't Look Now' and 'My Week' by Kurt Weill and Ann Ronell			Developed by Ann Ronell	
1 Main Title	20574	Lyric by Ann Ronell		
2 The Party	20575	'Trouble with Women' and 'My Week'	by Ann Ronell and Kurt Weill	
3 Statue Awakens (A)	20576		by Ann Ronell	
4+5 Statue Awakens (B)	20577	From 'Speak Low' by Kurt Weill	Developed by Ann Ronell	
6 Eight Seven Years	20579	From Theme 'Stranger Here Myself' by Kurt Weill	Developed by Ann Ronell	
8 Breaking into Savory's	20581	From Theme 'Stranger Here Myself' by Kurt Weill	Developed by Ann Ronell	
9+10 Intro to 'Speak Low'	20582		by Ann Ronell	
9+10 'Speak Low'	20583	by Kurt Weill and Ogden Nash	Additional music and Routine by Ann Ronell	Orch. by Leo Arnaud
11 Eviction Notice	20584	From 'Speak Low' by Kurt Weill and 'Don't Look Now' by Ann Ronell and Kurt Weill	Developed by Ann Ronell	
12 + 13 Sneaking Out		From Theme 'How Much I Love You' by Kurt Weill	Developed by Ann Ronell	
14 That's Him	20586	Music by Kurt Weill, Lyric by Ogden Nash	Addition Music and Lyric by Ann Ronell	
15 Getting Romeo	20587		by Ann Ronell	
16 Peek -a-Boo	20588		by Ann Ronell	
17 Call Me Whitfield	20588	from 'My Week'	by Ann Ronell and Kurt Weill	
18 Owl Effect	20589		by Ann Ronell	
19 Not Time Yet	20590	From 3 Themes: 'Stranger Here Myself', 'Speak Low', 'That's Him' by Kurt Weill	Developed by Ann Ronell	
Piano Vocal Score *One Touch of Venus*		'(Don't Look Now, but) My Heart Is Showing', Words by Ann Ronell, Music by Kurt Weill	Arrangement by Ann Ronell	
20 (Don't Look Now, but) My Heart Is Showing	20591	Lyric by Ann Ronell, Music by Kurt Weill and Ann Ronell		

21 Love Scene	20592		by Ann Ronell	
22+23 Pop Corn (pt. 1)	20593		by Ann Ronell	
24 Pop Corn (pt. 2)	20594	From Ballet 'Forty Minutes for Lunch' by Kurt Weill	Adapted by Ann Ronell	
25 Savory Savors Venus	20595	From 2 Themes: 'Speak Low', 'That's Him' by Kurt Weill	Developed by Ann Ronell	
26 Eager	20596	From 'My Week' by Kurt Weill and Ann Ronell	Developed by Ann Ronell	
27 Lights Out	20597		by Ann Ronell	
28 Departure of Venus	20598		by Ann Ronell	
29 Jupiter, Not Now	20599	From Ballet 'Bacchanale' by Kurt Weill	Adapted by Ann Ronell	
30 To the Hospital and Speak Low - Reprise	20600	From 'Speak Low' by Kurt Weill and Ogden Nash	Developed by Ann Ronell	
31 End Title	20601	From 'Speak Low' by Kurt Weill and 'Don't Look Now' by Kurt Weill and Ann Ronell	Developed by Ann Ronell	
32 End Cast	20602	from 'Speak Low' by Kurt Weill	Developed by Ann Ronell	

The Conductor Vocal Score supplies valuable information about the film score, especially concerning the collaboration between Weill and Ronell, as most of the musical material has its roots in the Broadway musical and underwent extensive adaptation work by Ronell so that it would be appropriate for the needs of the filmic narrative. See, for example, No. 6 'Eight Seven Years' and No. 8 'Breaking into Savory's': the underscoring is based on the musical theme 'I'm a Stranger Here Myself', which in the musical was the introduction to Venus and her own awareness of being 'Venus, Goddess of Love' on Earth for some strange reason. The use of that specific theme at that moment in the film fulfills a similar dramaturgical function in the musical: it represents Venus's awareness of her own role (Goddess of Love on Earth), it serves as an introduction to 'Speak Low', the first song in the film. No. 19 'Not Time Yet' is a second interesting example: to better define the relationship between the musical and film versions of *One Touch of Venus*, Ronell reworked dramaturgical-musical material, and in this case No. 19 is based on the reworking of three central musical motifs:

Stranger Here Myself	Theme of Venus	Underscore
Speak Low	Love theme	Song + underscore
That's Him	Love awareness theme 'That's Him, The Right One!'	Song + underscore

It is used to comment on a twist in the plot: Eddie falls in love with Venus, intending to show her the beauties of the city and life on Earth. This narrative twist occurs during a sequence on an elevator ride featuring only Eddie and Venus, so the three musical motifs represent the emotional state of the characters: Eddie whistles 'Speak Low', which then becomes the underscore; when the shot is on Venus looking at Eddie we hear 'That's Him', and when the shot is on both the motif is 'Stranger Here Myself'.

This is similar to what happens from a dramaturgical point of view in the use of 'Speak Low' (Nos. 9+10), that is, it is introduced by the use of underscoring using the motif of 'Stranger Here Myself' (Nos. 6, 8) as developed by Ronell; again No. 19 'Not Time Yet' is the preparation for No. 20 '(Don't Look Now, but) My Heart Is Showing'. No. 20 '(Don't Look Now, but) My Heart Is Showing' is the third song sung integrally in the film: it has the role of representing the effect of Venus on Earth, and thus a general falling in love. The lyrics of the '(Don't Look Now, but) My Heart Is Showing' are attributed to Ronell, with the music by Weill and Ronell, as the music is a rearrangement of 'Foolish Heart'.

To understand fully the path taken by *One Touch of Venus* from stage to screen, in the specifics of this song it is necessary to refer to two other sets of correspondence from the composer: one exchanged with Lazar, the second with Ronell. The two series of correspondences cover a period of time very close together, and because of the dynamics established within the production, the letters under consideration become useful tools for understanding the Hollywood production system.

Between the fall of 1947 and the spring of 1948, Lazar wrote almost weekly to Weill updating him on progress and especially on the obstacles that arose during the production. The impresario played an important mediating role between the composer and the producer, Cowan, acting as a guarantor of the contractual terms demanded by the composer. It also emerges that Cowan was convinced of the advantage of having the composer involved in the production, so that he could guarantee a consistency in the score that could not have been maintained otherwise. There is a precise moment when the two correspondences show perceptible points of contact: on 3 November 1947, Lazar informs Weill of Cowan's decision to entrust the writing of a new melody for the film to Ann Ronell and a ballad to him: «it seems to simmer down to the fact that he is only going to have three new musical numbers in the picture; a novelty tune which he contends Ann Ronell has written after I told him you would not be interested in interpolating; a ballad which he would like for you to write...»[21]. The novelty tune is likely to be 'Don't Look Now', while the ballad is not certain to have been composed, because of the effort made in ensuring compliance with the non-interpolation

---

[21]. Irving Paul Lazar to Kurt Weill, 3 November 1947, typescript (photocopy), Weill-Lenya Research Center, New York.

clause. On 11 November, Lazar informs him of the lawsuit filed by Bella Spewack against Kurnitz[22], Cowan and the entire production[23].

The decisive letters are those of 2 and 12 December 1947, in which reference is made in the former to the contract and the non-interpolation clause, and to the new melody ('Don't Look Now') composed by Ann Ronell; in the latter the arrival of the manuscript score and the photostatic reproduction of *One Touch of Venus* is confirmed. At the same time, the dense correspondence between Ronell and Weill took place between late 1947 and March 1948, by which time Weill had already reviewed most of the music for the film and the production was about to launch.

Table 3: Ronell-Weill Correspondence on *One Touch of Venus*, December 1947-April 1948

18/12/1947	Ann Ronell to Kurt Weill	
22/1/1948	Ann Ronell to Kurt Weill	
04/02/1948	Kurt Weill to Ann Ronell	Congratulations on a job well done
06/02/1948	Ann Ronell to Lester Cowan (producer) and William Seiter (director)	
29/01/1948	Ann Ronell to Kurt Weill	
01/03/1948	Ann Ronell to Kurt Weill	
22/03/1948	Ann Ronell to Kurt Weill	
02/04/1948	Ann Ronell to Kurt Weill	

In this correspondence with the composer, the arranger solicits comments and opinions on her work in adapting musical numbers to suit the score, showing particular attention to Weill's compositional wishes; his response, in his letter of 4 February 1948, in which he praises his colleague-friend's work in preserving the original musical material, is central: «I know you are putting up a very brave fight to keep my material, as far as it is being used, intact, and I appreciate very much the fine integrity which characterizes your fight in defense of the work

---

[22]. Harry Kurnitz was the screenwriter hired to write the script for *One Touch of Venus*. Bella Spewack was the first scriptwriter of the subject for *One Touch of Venus* on the stage. There was a dense correspondence between Spewack and Kurnitz between November 1947 and February 1948: Spewack accused Cowan of plagiarism for illicit use by Kurnitz of source material for her first Venus stage script. Spewack claimed that Kurnitz's script completely infringed on the protected material when it was sold in 1943; on the other hand, Kurnitz claimed that he never saw the earlier script and that he was the sole author. The production of the film suffered significant delays and the final script deep revisions.

[23]. The genesis of *One Touch of Venus* film was long and laborious, marked by a lawsuit at the script-writing stage. Again Kurt Weill's correspondence with his most trusted collaborators produces interesting and exciting information; in this case in his letter of 5 April 1943 to Ira Gershwin the composer entrusts his friend with an outburst («I had terrible troubles with the "Venus" show»). I refer to an analysis of Kurnitz's script and its implications for the musical dramaturgy of *One Touch of Venus* in Rizzuti 2015, pp. 122-133.

of a fellow artist and a friend»[24]. Above all, he is grateful to his friend for understanding his concerns about the process of transforming it from a stage musical to a film musical; despite fearing a total distortion of the essence of his music, Ronell was able to preserve the functions that characterized the music of *One Touch of Venus* stage, thus preserving Weill's ideas about the function of music in film, of dialogue with images and not just comment.

'Don't Look Now' presents itself as a 'new song', but it is a reworking of 'Foolish Heart', from *One Touch of Venus* stage which I will return to later. In general, the accompanying music in the film does not present a particularly daring orchestral approach. There is instead a more careful work on the settings, such as on character construction: Savory is the persona of the successful man, and Eddie is the persona of the resigned window dresser and Savory's succubus, Molly is the antagonist of Venus who ultimately benefits from the presence of the goddess of love on Earth, and in particular Venus's disorientation and her adaptation to the bourgeois conventions that regulate the heterosexual relationship. Weill always strongly emphasises the need to draw on the original material of the musical even for the underscoring parts, and does not identify a difference in dramaturgical function between songs and accompanying music. In a similar way to the musical, the characterisation of the characters in the film also occurs through musical motifs; in the film, musical motifs lose their number-related specificity, becoming recurring elements that distinguish sequences.

'(Don't Look Now, but) My Heart Is Showing' is used as the musical opening of the film, along with other motifs from *One Touch of Venus*. For this song, too, there was no easy genesis, the culmination of which was detailed a letter dated 4 February 1948, in which the composer complimented the arranger/composer on a job well done. He argued that the arrangement work on such important numbers as 'I'm a Stranger Here Myself' and 'Speak Low' mirrored the compositional choices made for the musical, and although he did not always agree with the choices made by Ronell, he found in them a stringent logic and consistency of which he approved:

> I liked very much what you have done with "I'm stranger", especially the way you have treated the punch lines at the end. I think the new lines at the top of page three could stand a little clarifications. "Speak low" is fine as long as it stays with Venus, but I'm not so sure of the effect when it switches to the other characters. The "Heart Song" scene can be effective and the new lyrics are very AnnRonell-ish. The new ending seems alright for the different character you want to give the song, but I wrote on the music sheet a suggestion for a change of the last bars. – According to your letter, these seem to be the only songs to be used in the picture. Do you think that is enough? I don't. But, who are we[25]?

---

[24]. Kurt Weill to Ann Ronell, 4 February 1948, Typescript (photocopy), Weill-Lenya Research Center, New York.

[25]. *Ibidem*.

Shared Authorship and Compositional Process in 1940s Hollywood

This song assumes a central role in the film's production — abstracting the discourse, it is useful to analyse '(Don't look now, but) My Heart is Showing' as a case study of possible production models in classical cinema, as it represents an example of multiple authorship in the soundtrack of *One Touch of Venus*.

'My Heart is Showing' shares much of the musical material from 'Foolish Heart', a song from the stage version of *One Touch of Venus* that was rejected by the Motion Picture Association of America censors because of some inappropriate aspects in the lyrics. Ronell, therefore, rewrote the lyrics of 'Foolish Heart' with some modifications and changed the title to '(Don't Look Now, but) My Heart Is Showing'.

Ex. 1: *One Touch of Venus* (1943), 'Foolish Heart' motif.

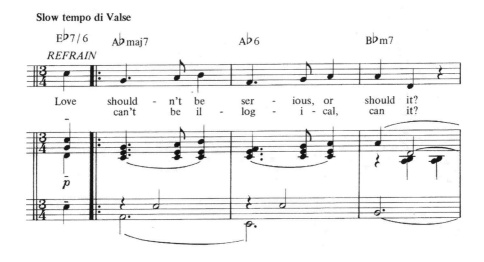

Ex. 2: *One Touch of Venus* (1948), 'My Heart Is Showing' motif.

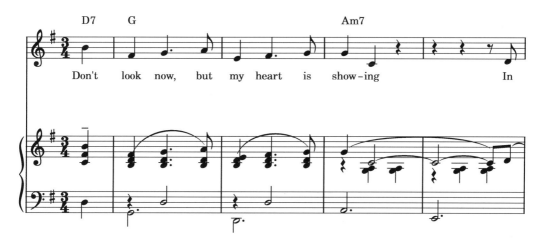

What characterised the subject of *One Touch of Venus* on stage were the elements of satire, the themes of social critique of urban alienation and one-dimensional domestic life in the suburbs entrusted to Venus's 'other' gaze, but these were toned down in the film version, which was more of a sophisticated romance. Yet Weill's reaction resulted in a close collaboration with Ronell that found form in the inclusion of 'Foolish Heart' disguised as 'My Heart is Showing'.

Ann Ronell composed following Weill's expressive stylistic devices: there is a clear similarity between '(Don't Look Now, but) My Heart is Showing' and 'Speak Low'[26] not only in structure, but especially in dramaturgical function; 'Speak Low' and 'My Heart Is Showing' have the function of the operatic love duet. The lead pair, Venus and Eddie, and the comprimarios pair, Gloria and Joe, alternately sing both songs at the two dramatic junctures of the plot: in the first case, in the department store sequence (Nos. 9+10) Venus sings 'Speak Low' for Eddie, and in an alternate montage Joe also is singing 'Speak Low' for Gloria. In the second case, in the park sequence (No. 20) Eddie sings 'Don't Look Now' for Venus, followed by Gloria singing for Joe.

Ex. 3: *One Touch of Venus* (1948), 'My Heart Is Showing' motif.

---

[26]. For a more in-depth analysis of 'Speak Low' and its dramaturgical function in the Broadway musical, see Rizzuti 2015, pp. 95-99.

Ex. 4: *One Touch of Venus* (1943), 'Speak Low' motif.

Ronell was faced with a twofold challenge: on the one hand to disguise the connections with 'Foolish Heart', and on the other to compose 'original' music that sounded à la manière de Weill, but with a character of its own that the composer called «very Ann Ronell-ish».

'My Heart Is Showing' is the running theme of the film: if 'Speak Low' is the pivot song of the Broadway version, in the film version the function of the love duet is performed by both 'Speak Low' and Ronell's song, approved by Weill. In the film, 'My Heart Is Showing' is sung by each couple (Venus and Eddie, Joe and Gloria) formed during Venus's time on Earth. Weill and Ronell chose to construct the soundtrack by differentiating between underscoring and songs with a narrative function, right from the first construction of the musical material. Referring to the summary of the Conductor Vocal Score, one can see the progressive numerical indication of the roles associated with the musical numbers and underscoring. For example, the No. 3 'Venus Awakens (A)' is followed by the Nos. 4+5 'Venus Awakens (B)': No. 3 is underscoring newly composed by Ronell, No. 4 is new development of Weill's original theme, in this specific case 'Stranger Here Myself'. Both are associated with the moment of Venus's transformation from statue to person; what is for the purposes of the discourse relevant here is the distinction between original composition, derivation and development of themes. In the underscoring parts, the musical themes are drawn from the numbers of the theatrical musical and subjected to a reworking that flows into a new arrangement, in some cases even using new orchestration, by Ronell. Their correspondence makes clear how close the nature of their collaboration was, especially with regard to the way that they defined, then experimented with, a shared authorial process[27].

Codetta

A similar collaboration between a freelance composer and an arranger/composer employed by one of the five majors during the years of the Hollywood studio system may be seen in the case of Stefan Wolpe[28] and Trude Rittmann[29], who in 1941 collaborated on the music for a propaganda documentary *Palestine at War*, commissioned by Palestine Labor Commission. The similarities here are pertinent to the Weill/Ronell partnership: Kurt Weill arrived in New York in 1935, Trude Rittmann in 1937, Stefan Wolpe in 1938; all three found themselves in the late 1930s and early 1940s experiencing various avenues of assimilation into the cultural, musical and theatrical life of New York and Los Angeles. Rittmann intended the documentary *Palestine at War* to be a launching opportunity for her colleague Wolpe into the film industry; unfortunately, the collaboration was a one-off, with Wolpe orienting his activities in the 1940s

---

[27]. I refer again to the letter of 4 February 1948 because along with the letter is a typescript sheet of the script in which the lyrics are by Ronell, and there are some handwritten notes by Weill concerning the musical structure of the song.

[28]. Stefan Wolpe, like Weill, was an immigrant who collaborated early on with the film production system, although Wolpe's experience differed in his process of assimilation into U.S. society.

[29]. Trude Rittmann was involved in the production of the most important musicals of the period between Broadway and Hollywood, working closely with Richard Rodgers from 1945 on *Carousel*, making arrangements for the films of *South Pacific* (1958), *The King and I* (1956), and *The Sound of Music* (1965), for which she expanded the song 'Do-Re-Mi'. As an orchestrator she worked on *Finian's Rainbow* (1968), *Gentlemen Prefer Blondes* (1953), and *Peter Pan* (1950). Between the 1950s and 1960s she worked on *Paint Your Wagon* (1969), *My Fair Lady* (1964), and *Camelot* (1967). She was also connected with the stage production of *One Touch of Venus* as rehearsal pianist of the music for Agnes de Mille's ballet choreography.

toward the Abstract Expressionist circuit of painters, and in the 1950s central he worked as director of the music department at Black Mountain College.

Both in the Weill/Ronell case and with Wolpe/Rittmann what emerges powerfully is the mediating role of female arrangers/composers in balancing a relationship between the composers' authorial demands and the production demands of the studios. In relation to this role, a question arises: in the age of the studio system, did female film music composers succeed only as arrangers? In an interview Ronell gave to columnist Marjory Fisher of the *San Francisco Chronicle* in 1949, Fisher described in the composer's own words the Hollywood environment: «[f]or all the big bad wolfs (or wolves, if you must!) around Hollywood, none are so fearsome as the organized group of males who long expended tremendous efforts to keep determined ladies out of the music writing departments of the film industry»[30].

The field of inquiry is open, beginning with Leslie Anderson's reflection, «Where do women fall within the spectrum of film music composition? Although women have been somewhat successful in the world of film as directors, writers and producers, as composers their impact has been minor. Unfortunately, women film and Tv composers of today still fall victim to the exclusionary "all-boy" network in operation within the film business»[31].

Conclusion

In the case of the Weill-Ronell collaboration, the shared authorship and compositional process are the result of two specific skills: on the one hand there is Weill, a musical theatre composer, and on the other Ronell, the Tin Pan Alley Girl, an in-house composer and arranger in Universal's Music Department. The musical film *One Touch of Venus* is for all intents and purposes an unusual vehicle for this type of combination, not so much because of the nature of the soundtrack (the clear division between background and songs), or because of the use of songs with a narrative function, for film musicals of the time these were fairly common features; but mainly because of the creative and production peculiarities that characterised it. The result of the collaboration between Weill and the Hollywood film industry, despite Ann Ronell's mediating work, was not the best, because the horizon of expectation of the two parties was different: Weill intended to assert and claim an awareness and control over music typical of a composer firmly convinced of his role in society. Such a vision conflicted with the productive nature of the Hollywood film industry. For *One Touch of Venus* Weill exerted control over every note in the film, as evidenced by his close correspondence with Salisbury and his close work with Ronell, with whom he had previously collaborated. Through tortuous mediation

---

[30]. Fisher 1949, cited in Zimmers 2009, p. 36.
[31]. Anderson 1991, p. 353.

between attorneys for the respective parties and through Ronell's reworking, the composer was satisfied with how the change of *One Touch of Venus* from the stage to the screen occurred, with the end result being a musical film. Besides, Weill had already shown foresight and his pioneering nature in 1937 in his article 'The Future of Opera in America', which appeared in *Modern Music* identifying films as the new all-inclusive art form: «[...] Composers also wrote works for radio, operas for schools, scenic choral pieces for mass meetings, and began to tackle the problem of musical films. [...] In America the new musical art work may after all develop from the medium of the movies. For nowhere else has the film attained that technical perfection and popularity which can smooth the way for a new art form»[32].

Bibliography

ANDERSON 1991
ANDERSON, Laura. 'Women Film and Television Composers in the United States', in: *The Musical Woman: An International Perspective: 1986-1990*, edited by Judith Lang Zaimont, Westport (CT), Greenwood Press, 1991, pp. 353-370.

BROOMFIELD-MCHUGH 2019
The Oxford Handbook of Musical Theatre Screen Adaptations, edited by Dominic Broomfield-McHugh, Oxford-New York, Oxford University Press, 2019.

FISHER 1949
FISHER, Marjory M. 'She's Not Afraid of 'Big Bad Wolf': She Wrote It', in: *San Francisco Chronicle*, 14 October 1949.

GRABER 2021
GRABER, Naomi. *Kurt Weill's America*, Oxford-New York, Oxford University Press, 2021.

KALINAK 1992
KALINAK, Kathryn. *Settling the Score: Music and the Classical Hollywood Film*, Madison (WI), University of Wisconsin Press, 1992.

RIZZUTI 2015
RIZZUTI, Marida. *Kurt Weill e Frederick Loewe. Pigmalione fra la 42° e il Covent Garden. Percorsi e prospettive di «One Touch of Venus» e «My Fair Lady» fra letteratura, teatro musicale e cinema*, Saarbrücken, Edizioni Accademiche Italiane, 2015.

SAPIRO 2017
SAPIRO, Ian. *Scoring the Score: The Role of the Orchestrator in the Contemporary Film Industry*, Abingdon-New York, Routledge, 2017.

---

[32]. WEILL 1937B.

WEILL 1936
WEILL, Kurt. 'The Alchemy of Music', in: *Stage: The Magazine of After-dark Entertainment*, XIV/2 (November 1936), pp. 63-64, available online at <https://www.kwf.org/kurt-weill/recommended/the-alchemy-of-music/>, accessed May 2023.

WEILL 1937A
ID. 'National Music, Opera and The Movies: An Interview with Kurt Weill', in: *Pacific Coast Musician*, XXVI/13 (3 July 1937), pp. 12-13, available online at <https://www.kwf.org/kurt-weill/recommended/national-music-opera-and-the-movies/>, accessed May 2023.

WEILL 1937B
ID. 'The Future of Opera in America', in: *Modern Music*, XIV/4 (May-June 1937), pp. 183-188, available online at <https://www.kwf.org/kurt-weill/recommended/the-future-of-opera-in-america/>, accessed May 2023.

WEILL 1946
ID. 'Music in the Movies', in: *Harper's Bazaar*, LXXX/9 (September 1946), pp. 257, 398, 400, available online at <https://www.kwf.org/kurt-weill/recommended/music-in-the-movies/>, accessed May 2023.

ZIMMERS 2009
ZIMMERS, Tighe E. *Tin Pan Alley Girl: A Biography of Ann Ronell*, Jefferson (NC), Mc Farland & Company, 2009.

Musical Language, Censorship, and Theatrical Identity in Kurt Weill's London Works (1930-1935)

Arianne Johnson Quinn
(College of Music, Florida State University)

"You wrote something about my exploiting jazz idioms the other week", he said, with a note of the gentlest possible reproach in his voice [...] but don't let us draw too rigid a distinction between "serious" music and "light" music. Music is not necessarily good because it is solemn. Take *Figaro* again; it is nearly all "light" music, yet who would say that it will not last for ever [*sic*]? — or, at least, as long as *Tristan*, which is "serious"[1].

Ever in defiance of his critics, Weill shot back at members of the London press who argued that his theatrical works contained a muddled blend of modernism, jazz, and light music, comparing himself to both W. A. Mozart and Richard Wagner. Weill's response highlights the curious position which he occupied in the world of London musical theatre; a position which was complicated by both the perception of his works and clouded by his German-Jewish identity. His London reputation was largely based on knowledge of his earlier German works, particularly those created in collaboration with Bertolt Brecht, raising the ire of the British intellectual and theatre communities in the 1940s. Although Weill's music was dismissed by the BBC (British Broadcasting Corporation) and other critical forces on artistic grounds, the fact remained that this dismissal occurred because he was both German and Jewish in an era of complex identity politics on the global stage.

This chapter re-evaluates Weill's place in London musical theatre, reframing this time of musical exile between his German and American careers as a period of creative experimentation and cultural assimilation through the lens of critical reception. His German and American periods are well known by scholars, practitioners, and theatre audiences. However, there is

---

[1]. Williams 1935a.

much to learn from Weill's London exile, which began in 1933 and served as a stopover between France and the United States[2]. This chapter explores Weill's London period within the context of the reception history for works such as *Der sieben Todsünden* (1933) (retitled *Anna-Anna*) and *A Kingdom for a Cow* (1935), and the ways in which these works collided with the opinions of the British cultural establishment. Through an exploration of the reception history of Weill's London works, we learn about the intermingled forces of critical opinion, governmental policy, and their effect on the rapidly changing theatre industry in London's West End.

Although in some ways, Weill arrived in London as a stranger, his work had been heard as early as 1930, and was broadcast several times by the BBC. These broadcasts included French and German language versions of *Der Lindberghflug* (1930), *Die Dreigroschenoper* (1930 and 1932), *Der Jasager* (1933), and *Die Bürgschaft* (1932)[3]. Other works were arranged and presented as instrumental concert arrangements, including a suite from *Die Dreigroschenoper*, and selections from *Aufstieg und Fall der Stadt Mahagonny* arranged by Eric White were given a lunchtime concert performance by the Bristol Women's Club in 1934[4]. *Die Dreigroschenoper* and the English reworking of *Die sieben Todsünden*, or *Anna-Anna* in particular received a great deal of critical attention. *The Threepenny Opera* (as it was titled in London), presented as a concert performance for the BBC rather than fully staged production, was billed as: «one of the most successful works of the brilliant young German, Kurt Weill»[5]. According to an account of this performance by a correspondent for *The Jewish Chronicle*: «The first performance of his version of *The Beggar's Opera* at the last of the series of BBC concerts of contemporary music brought the well-known German Jewish composer, Kurt Weill to London, and offered an excellent opportunity for discussing with this very interesting musician questions pertaining to his own work [...]. Weill is no more a stranger to the British public [...]»[6]; his interview notes both Weill's place in the contemporary music world and his notoriety for London audiences, whether in person or over the airwaves.

In addition to mixed views of Weill's musical works by the critical press in the prewar period, academic criticism of Weill seeped into the commercial press in pre-World War II Britain. Musicologist Alfred Einstein provided an astute analysis of the 1933 broadcast of *The Threepenny Opera* in which he stated: «England is probably the only country where it can at any rate still be broadcast», and further noted as a point of derision that, of the 69 melodies in the

---

[2]. Hirsch 2002 and Hinton 2012.

[3]. Sheffield Daily Telegraph 1930; The Scotsman 1930; The Scotsman 1932; The Stage 1933; The Scotsman 1933; The Era 1931; and The Era 1930. All dates here refer to the British broadcast dates. All other dates throughout the article refer to the theatrical premieres unless otherwise noted.

[4]. The Daily Independent 1933b; Western Daily Press 1934.

[5]. The Daily Independent 1933a.

[6]. The Jewish Chronicle 1935.

original *Beggar's Opera* Weill only used one[7]. Einstein's criticism of the work hinged on what he perceived as its stylistic muddle that was both between the original English work and the style of German art music. For British audiences, though the subject matter was interesting because it stemmed from British sources, it was nevertheless difficult to contextualize in an era of light musical theatre.

The response to Weill demonstrated that musical theatre was but one part of a much larger cultural wave of anti-German and anti-Jewish sentiment that was reflected in both musical production and broadcasting during this period. Weill's arrival collided with two significant moments: firstly, Hitler's announcement of rearmament, and secondly, the first wave of Jewish immigrants, including the 177 academics who had found a place in British university life. Each of these factors, from immigration to musical style, would determine whether or not Weill would be able to make a place for himself in London. Although other German operettas were indeed regularly performed during this period that immediately preceded the war, Weill brought with him the political baggage of «leftist» Weimar, his Jewish identity, and the «decadence» of its musical style[8].

Critical reviews of the 1930s hint at an undercurrent of something deeper, spurred by the political discourse brewing around the rise of Nazi Germany in 1933. The myriad of musical theatre works, including operetta, revue, musical comedy, and ballets that competed for the attention of audiences in the West End, created an artistic problem for Weill. Furthermore, his presence in London raised the ire of the establishment, who controlled everything from the press to government censorship. Nevertheless, Weill attempted to assimilate into London theatre life. His *The Threepenny Opera*, broadcasts of *Aufstieg und Fall der Stadt Mahagonny*, performances of *Der Sieben Todsünden* as *Anna-Anna*, and *A Kingdom for a Cow* received a mixed response, demonstrating that the perception of Weill's works reflected deeper political sentiments, rather than a rejection on artistic grounds. Other German works from this period were not performed in Britain until after the war, including *Happy End*, which only appeared in Edinburgh in 1965[9].

The Musical Stage in Interwar Britain

The commercial perception of Weill's works, though complicated, was a separate issue from his place in London cultural life as a German-Jewish composer. From the perspective of critics and audiences in the period from the 1930s-1950s, Weill's works were a curious mixture

---

[7]. Einstein n.d.
[8]. Overy 2009, p. 280.
[9]. Marriot 1965.

of German modernism and musical comedy pastiche. In particular, his English reworking of *Der Kuhhandel* that became *A Kingdom for a Cow* was in conflict with the public's demand for the light operettas such as Ivor Novello's with their lush melodies, Ruritanian and exotic themes or revivals of works such as *The Quaker Girl* (1910) or Lehár's *The Merry Widow* (1905)[10]. It was also vastly different from the style of other musical comedies by 'outsiders' such as Cole Porter's *Anything Goes* (1934)[11].

Typical examples of the musical comedy by British creators that were popular in the 1930s included revivals of Sidney Jones' *A Gaiety Girl* (1893) and Frederick Norton and Oscar Asche's *Chu Chin Chow* (1916), which William Everett notes was the then-longest running musical in the West End, drawing people from outside London by train, sparking the idea of train tours for London theatre, a practice that continued well into the 1960s[12]. Further, several successful musical comedies by American composers were staged by British producers such as Charles B. Cochran, including Cole Porter's *Nymph Errant* (1933), which only played in London[13]. Other influences on British musical theatre include the English operetta from the 1920s-mid 1940s and American shows that were imported in the post-World War I period beginning in 1918, such as *Show Boat* (London, 1928) and American operetta composers, including Rudolf Friml's *Rose-Marie* (1924) and Sigmund Romberg's *The Student Prince* (1924).

Artistically, Weill's works that were produced on the London stage blurred the boundaries between comic opera, operetta, and musical comedy. The style and cultural significance of the English operetta in the twentieth century, which was largely a continuation of the Gilbert and Sullivan generation, is a key piece in the reception history of Weill and works of other German émigrés[14]. Weill's stylistic blurring situated his works within the style of other stage works of the period; for instance, the musical language and performance style of English operetta resided between the worlds of opera and musical comedy, constituting an aesthetic middle ground.

Weill in London: Artistic Exile

Weill's time in London began as an extension of his Paris exile, as he sought work and safety outside Germany. Like many other artists and musicians, he was never able to fully integrate, although it is clear that he and Lenya considered settling permanently in London[15]. Critics noted his arrival as one of many displaced German Jews, and as one critic stated: «a

---

[10]. The Referee 1935.
[11]. The Daily Mail 1935.
[12]. Everett 2008, pp. 72-88.
[13]. Wright 2012, p. 6.
[14]. Purser 1955 and Martin 1981.
[15]. Symonette – Kowalke 1996, p. 162.

young man, thirty-five, German, with a Puckish Pickwickian face and a decided niche in the music of our time [...] Weill's arrival in England was voluntary, up to a point. In January 1933 seven German theatres had simultaneous first nights of *Der Silbersee* by Weill and Georg Kaiser. The next morning the production was banned — equally simultaneously. The *Reichskanzler* had arrived; Weill left and went to live in Paris»[16]. Weill initially considered Paris to be his new home, stating: «I know that here new battles await me, battles that at home are already old hat but still have to be waged here, and I feel I'll be able to do some good [...] In my heart of hearts I have never left Germany»[17]. Work opportunities were few in Paris, but the few that were to be found did allow him to foster connections with the theatrical establishment in London.

While he was in London, Weill met with impresario Edward James, who introduced him to Charles B. Cochran, along with other members of the British theatrical elite. Although London was potentially a stopgap measure until he could find a permanent residence in Europe or the United States, Weill tried his best to find work. In between periods of activity in Paris, he was in and out of London; his letters to Lenya indicate that he was hoping to settle in London on a more permanent basis. This was unlikely from an immigration standpoint however, as he was only granted a temporary visa on 22 January 1934, which specified that he would stay for one month only without pursuing employment[18]. However, once he arrived in London, he worked a series of odd jobs, indicating his need for economic survival, including as a rehearsal pianist for the Kurt Jooss Ballet[19].

As further proof of Weill's earnest search for work in London, including working as a ballet rehearsal accompanist, he received several offers, including from British theatre and film manager Basil Dean regarding a film version of *A Kingdom for a Cow*, and a tantalizing offer for a theatre of his own from British producer John Sutro[20]. Weill quickly became frustrated, and complained bitterly to Lenya: «Last week I was practically ready to give up doing anything over here, because there's no way to get ahead with the English»[21]. Through these encounters, it is clear that Weill made a serious attempt to adapt to both the style and expectations of British theatre, a culture in which performers, songwriters and producers held multiple roles at once.

«Anna-Anna» in London

In April of 1933, while Weill was still in France, the composer was in conversation with English producer and patron Edward James to discuss the possibility of a score for the

---

[16]. HUGHES 1935.
[17]. SYMONETTE – KOWALKE 1996, p. 79.
[18]. *Ibidem*, p. 148
[19]. THE STAR 1935.
[20]. SYMONETTE – KOWALKE 1996, p. 150.
[21]. *Ibidem*, p. 148.

ballet troupe Les Ballets 1933 which would feature James' wife Tilly Losch along with Lotte Lenya. Weill and Brecht's *Die sieben Todsünden*, as the work was entitled, opened first in Paris at the Théâtre des Champs-Élysées on 7 June 1933. It was later staged in London with both Losch and Lenya at the Savoy Theatre as *Anna-Anna*, opening in 1933, produced by James and choreographed by George Balanchine. The work, which Weill called a «ballet chanté», centered on the double personality of 'Anna', who sings (Anna I), while her counterpart (Anna II) dances. The dancing Anna moves through the 'seven deadly sins', each of which is portrayed in a different American city. Meanwhile her family, sung by two tenors, a bass and a baritone, acts as interlocuter from the side. The work was a blatant commentary on capitalist greed and avarice and provided a window in the end of the leftist culture of the Weimar era.

Despite auspicious beginnings, the London production of *Anna-Anna* ran for a mere two weeks. It was, however, received with critical interest because of its alignment with the feverish demand for ballet in London in the mid-1930s. Although the run was brief, *Anna-Anna* was also portrayed as Losch's triumph, thanks to the influence of her husband Edward James. As an anonymous critic for the *Western Morning News and Daily Gazette* noted: «Ballet is very much in the air at present. The latest group is Mr. Edward James' *Ballets of 1933* at the Savoy. The keynote here is intense modernity, and two of the three ballets in the opening are brilliant successful. *Anna-Anna* composed by Herr Kurt Weill and produced by M. Georges Balanchine, deals with the Siamese sisters that exist indissolubly linked in the nature of very woman [...] An interesting conception finely executed»[22]. It is telling that critical opinion centered on Weill and Balanchine with no mention of Brecht. A critic for *The Tatler* followed this with a direct comparison between Losch and ballerina Anna Pavlova, who was well known on the London stage. This critic also wrote: «Tilly Losch danced the Jekyll-Anna, while Lotte Lenja [*sic*] chanted in nasal American-German to Kurt Weill's music, the vicious Hyde-Anna. It was exciting but long-drawn». He also argued that the dance itself was the most exciting aspect of the production, though he had very little to say about the musical style[23]. As this critic noted, ballet was synonymous with 'modernity' and progress, especially for a Britain that longed to demonstrate just how cosmopolitan it was in the 1930s while still maintaining a strong identity in national culture.

«*A Kingdom for a Cow*»

A Kingdom for a Cow opened at the Savoy Theatre on 28 June 1935. The cast of *A Kingdom for a Cow* included notable British performers along with the Austro-German exotic dancer Henriette Margareta Niederauer who called herself 'La Jana' and who was one of several

---

[22]. THE WESTERN MORNING NEWS 1933.
[23]. THE TATLER 1933.

sensual exotic dancers onstage in the West End in the period[24]. The cast also included Jacqueline Francell as Juanita and Webster Booth as Juan. Because individual theatres were known for certain types of productions (for instance the Theatre Royal, Drury Lane was known for spectacle operettas, the London Coliseum housed pantomimes and the Adelphi housed revues), *A Kingdom for a Cow* was not specifically designated as any particular genre. Still, because of the venue (the Savoy), London audiences arrived at *A Kingdom for a Cow* with set expectations regarding the style of light opera.

In January of 1935, Weill traveled to London and began working on the production. He wrote: «I'm very curious to see how things will go in London and [how] these insular people will react»[25]. Although details are sparse, Weill's reworking of *Der Kuhhandel* with librettists Robert Vambery and Desmond Carter was set to be produced in the Savoy — famed home of the D'Oyly Carte Opera[26]. Early letters indicate that Weill pitched a translation of *Der Kuhhandel* to impresario Charles B. Cochran, thanks to an introduction by James. He wrote enthusiastically to Lenya stating: «[James] was very nice; he thought I would be tremendously well-liked in London and that I was exactly the man Cochran needs right now. For the time being he wants me to make sure that Cochran commissions two or three scenes from me for a big revue he will probably start in the fall [...]»[27]. Sir Charles Blake Cochran was not only the most significant producer in the West End, but he also played an integral role in the creation of a distinctly twentieth century style of British musical theatre, eclipsing the reputation of rivals including André Charlot[28]. Often called 'The Ziegfeld of Britain', Cochran was born in Sussex in 1872 and began his career in the theatre working as an actor before turning to theatrical production and management. He gained experience as a producer by managing both the Oxford Music Hall and the Royal Albert Hall[29]. Cochran is primarily remembered for producing musical theatre revues, although in reality, he had a hand in almost every type of entertainment in Britain, producing musicals, ballets and operas and, infamously, the Wembley Rodeo in 1924[30].

Cochran's revues, including those by Noël Coward, epitomized the height of style for London theatre. He was the ideal advocate for someone like Weill because of his penchant for producing innovative works created by foreign artists. With Cochran's anticipated support, Weill and Vambery hoped that the production would be a hit, and initially thought that luminary lyricist A. P. Herbert would be asked to do the libretto translation. In a letter dated 2 April

---

[24]. Fox 2000.
[25]. Symonette – Kowalke 1996, p. 87.
[26]. Drew 1986, p. 220.
[27]. Symonette – Kowalke 1996, p. 75.
[28]. Harding 1988, p. 51.
[29]. *Ibidem*, p. 70.
[30]. *Ibidem*, p. 105.

1934 to Lenya in Louveciennes (a suburb of Paris where the couple lived during their time in France), the composer wrote: «I hope that A. P. Herbert will do the translation. He's very enthusiastic. We probably will get the Palace Theatre, the best one in London (Cochran!)»[31]. Indeed, if Cochran had followed through with his promise of sponsorship, it likely would have been successful, as Cochran possessed many important social connections. However, Cochran seemed to be more interested in what he saw as a definite success with Porter than an uncertain outcome with Weill, as the composer complained to Lenya on 24 January 1935: «Instead of my operetta, Cochran is doing *Liebelei* by Oscar Strauss and the new operetta (*Anything Goes*) by Cole Porter, which is a huge success in New York»[32]. Lenya agreed with Weill, stating «This Cochran seems to be an old half-wit, who doesn't want to take any risks»[33]. Despite Lenya's comments, Weill was eager to work with Cochran, who had experienced two bankruptcies was known for his success[34]. Unfortunately for Weill, this collaboration with Cochran never materialized.

The failure of *A Kingdom for a Cow* was a personal blow to Weill because all signs pointed to success: the relative critical success of *Anna-Anna*, the potential backing of Cochran, and the prestige of the Savoy itself. Still, the creative team made some serious miscalculations. Although the choice of the Savoy Theatre for *A Kingdom for a Cow* was likely due to the critical success of Weill's transported production of *Anna-Anna*, it raised immediate associations of place with style. Like most theatres in the West End, the Savoy was known as the site of the D'Oyly Carte light opera company, primarily known for staging Gilbert and Sullivan's works beginning in 1874. By presenting *A Kingdom for a Cow* at the Savoy, Weill was subject to a comparison with the operettas of Gilbert and Sullivan. One critic expressed particularly high hopes, stating «this new adventure on the part of Europe's most gay, daring master of light music should bring back to the Savoy something of the old Gilbertian spirit, with a dash of Walt Disney and at the same time some pungent satire on dictatorial "ambitions" […]»[35]. Similarly, the *Daily Express* called *A Kingdom for a Cow*: «A comic opera of Gilbert and Sullivan structure […] Satire is on the armaments racket — a subject which, in view of one things and another, is best treated lightly on a Peter-Panesque stage such as London's today»[36]. However, other reviewers were not so kind. The very theatre, with its associations with the light operas of Gilbert and Sullivan, proved to be Weill's downfall[37]. «It is like vinegar mixed with sugar», *Horse and Hound* magazine

---

[31]. SYMONETTE – KOWALKE 1996, p. 179.
[32]. *Ibidem*, p. 148.
[33]. *Ibidem*, p. 36.
[34]. COCHRAN 1937 and *THE PERFORMER* 1931.
[35]. *MORNING POST* 1935 and *DAILY EXPRESS* 1935.
[36]. *DAILY EXPRESS* 1935.
[37]. *NEWS OF THE WORLD* 1935.

complained, «but at least the Savoy management have "ventured forth a lance"; at least they have refused to be chained and gagged by musical comedy conventions [...]»[38].

CRITICAL RECEPTION

In several ways, *A Kingdom for a Cow* was a stereotypical operetta, with lush musical orchestrations, large ensembles, and foreign setting such as the French scene in Act III, scene 1 «Les Nuits de Paris». Like many theatrical productions, sheet music of songs in the production was published and marketed by Chappell, specifically 'As Long as I Love', 'Two Hearts', and a separate album of piano selections, all of which could be purchased in the lobby of the Savoy. Musically, the work contained several elements that were typical of British musical theatre, especially operetta, include the large-scale chorus numbers, dances, and balance between the large ensemble and smaller duets and solos, all set in a stylized foreign setting. However, Weill's musical language was combined with biting, politicized satire of the works' arms-race plot. Despite the difference in the various styles, Weill tried to create a balance between the typically British aspects of the production and those from his earlier dramatic and musical roots; it was Weill's test of the artistic waters as he attempted to write a musical work that conformed to the expectations for British operetta this period.

Weill's artistic experimentation met with mixed success as critics grappled with expectations. A few critics praised this musical style, as one noted: «Herr Kurt Weill's wistful melodies fitted with pleasant words that never decline into music, and ably orchestrated trios [...]»[39]. Several struggled to identify the mixture of styles, including a critic for the *Daily Mail*, who noted: «[he] has the reputation of a leader in the *avant garde* of Continental composers, but in this score he has reverted to the classic tradition of Offenbach [...] he has written a score of "sweet" music. Even the stage hands, busy at their work during rehearsals, can be heard whistling these new numbers»[40]. One critic warned that the musical style was not distinctive enough to earn Weill the same notoriety that he had enjoyed for his German works, stating «It is simple and attractive stuff enough [...] but [...] he will have to do something considerably better than this if he is to achieve the same sort of reputation in this country»[41]. Although in some ways the work aligned with British musical theatre in the period, in other ways it represented an entirely divergent style altogether, muddling the expectations for audiences and critics who attempted to parse the exotic theme.

---

[38]. *HORSE AND HOUND* 1935.
[39]. *THE TATLER* 1935.
[40]. HOBSON 1935.
[41]. *GLASGOW BULLETIN* 1935.

The theatre program highlights the exotic theme, and establishes a dichotomy between idealized old world, and the new, and this continues with the arms race, which is also thrust upon this 'native' land with no thought to how they are able to respond to this insertion of technologically-founded progress. The written prologue — an unusual feature for this era in which most shows began with a glamorous chorus — states:

> There long ago there lived a simple race
> Laughing and loving in that little Heaven;
> Hunting and fishing — happy for a space
> Till fourteen-ninety-seven
> Upon a morn in May
> There came a shop from Portugal
> And anchored in the bay.
> They landed on the Eastern cape
> And shot the native men,
> They seized their women, burnt their crops and started there and then
> A new and better Government
> Upon that summer morn.
> And that is how the little state of Santa Maria was born.

The poem and a map of the imaginary setting printed in the program established the mood for the idealized tropical world and its reckonings with Western Imperialism, despite the prologue's strangeness in the context of the genre.

In addition to the critical reception, the BBC added another later of complication to the perception of Weill and his work. It controlled every radio broadcast and much of the entertainment industry as a result. Leading up to the Second World War, contemporary German musicians and composers were increasingly marginalized. Although the war did not bring an outright ban on German music, the BBC did restrict copyright payments to living German composers, discouraging the performance of their work[42]. As Robert MacKay points out, the BBC formulated a list of «alien composers» who were to be ignored: «Sheltering behind the technical explanation that the enemy should not benefit, even retrospectively, from royalties for the performance of compositions whose copyright he controlled, the BBC operated a form of cultural censorship that constituted a departure from its established artistic criteria and which was never publicly announced»[43]. The political backlash against music by German composers had been evident for several years, and was directed by the BBC, who saw themselves as the cultural establishment during and after the war, publicly endorsing certain works and composers, while often enacting a form of censorship.

---

[42]. MACKAY 2000.
[43]. *Ibidem.*

The level of critical debate indicates that while on the surface, Weill's London failure stemmed from aesthetic and musical concerns, other factors were at play. Hans Keller, himself an Austrian-born émigré who worked as a critic and in several senior roles within the BBC, hinted at the longstanding opinions of Weill even 30 years later when he wrote about the BBC broadcast of *The Threepenny Opera*. He deemed it «the weightiest possible lowbrow opera for highbrows and the most full-blooded highbrow musical for lowbrows [...] Weill grimly ironizes, amongst other things, our own conception of decadence [...]»[44]. Decadent is a problematic term that seemed to only be used to describe German-Jewish composers in this period and that appears to have served as coding for the press[45].

During the 1933-1935 seasons in which Weill's works were staged in London, musical comedies like Cole Porter's *Nymph Errant* and *Anything Goes* were referred to as such, partly because they involved lighter music, popular forms and clear, non-satiric comedy (as distinct from Music Hall with vaudevillian-esque or slapstick comedy). Thus, the use of 'opera' in critical reviews is not inappropriate, but rather establishes a specific set of genre expectations, audience makeup, theatrical space and conventions. Related to this, there are multiple accounts of Weill's time in Britain in the press, and several titles used for his work (*Ha'penny, Tuppeny Opera, Beggar's Opera, Dreigroshenoper*), and he is addressed as Herr Kurt Weill and Mr. Weill. Further complicating theatrical expectations is the use of censorship which exacerbated natural British skittishness in terms of political representation onstage.

Some critics, and likely members of the public, felt that the political aspects of *A Kingdom for a Cow* were still far too contentious and reeked of leftist leanings. As an anonymous reviewer for *The Stage* argued: «[it] is one of those anti-capitalist, anti-government, anti-everything else kind of plays which might have flattered a self-satisfied audience in Moscow several years ago»[46]. This critic dismisses Weill's work as being part of a long-past political movement that was both undesirable and fleeting. The response to the political aspects of Weill indicated the British desire to stay out of German political entanglements. As Noël Coward's satirical song 'Don't Let's Be Beastly to the Germans' points out, the British press couched their disdain for politics in polite, disinterested terms until they were forced to act. As these issues came to light, the press was more and more unable to separate Weill the German/Jewish émigré from the German modernist turned operetta composer[47].

Weill dismissed the accusations of political agenda, arguing that this work was the continuation of his earlier German compositions and the pervasive style of his youth. In his response, Weill tried to shift the focus to optimistic views on his work; where there was no

---

[44]. KELLER 1956.
[45]. DUCHEN 1999.
[46]. *THE STAGE* 1933.
[47]. *EAST ANGLIAN DAILY TIMES* 1935.

room for innovation in the current political climate of Germany, Weill purported to see a land of opportunity in London, however insincere. He stated, «this is my first experience of the London stage, and it is a great adventure for me»[48]. However, Weill's artistic arguments were not enough to quell harsh critical opinions. The harshest rejection of the work came from *The Sphere*, a publication known for its biting critiques:

> I am now wondering whether that was the sole reason why Herr Weill's presence in Germany is now considered to be undesirable, or whether the quality of his music may not have something to do with it. Much of it, which I suspect to be the real Weill, is steely, heartless stuff. It is deftly scored, but there is a sneer behind it [...] And however much we detest (or admire) militaristic dictators, their adventures or misadventures do not amuse us as comic-operatic theater [...][49].

The work's commercial failure pointed to the divide between high and low culture, and was, as one critic believed, more a fault of audiences than the composer:

> [...] this delightful entertainment would run for months in Paris — in London once more about to prove the assertion of the Continental wag that the main difference between the English and the French is that the Frenchman is witty — the Englishman merely humorous? Judging from the emptiness of the large and comfortable Pit (all seats bookable), the answer to the latter will be YES.

This critic further stated: «it is a joyous and tuneful satire on armament firms, and the way by which their astute representative get business. Pacifists should revel in it; shareholders in armaments should find it genuinely funny [...] However the trouble may be that it's too full of brains»[50]. This idea of satire with an intellectual bent was in opposition to London theatre in which political satire was strictly controlled by the Office of the Lord Chamberlain, which controlled theatrical censorship from 1737-1968, and which outlawed any use of direct political references in theatre[51].

The *Saturday Review* dated July 6, 1935 stated: «Kurt Weill's music did little or nothing to relieve the monotony. It was a hotch-potch of various style, from classical to Gershwinesque and it landed absolutely nowhere»[52]. An anonymous critic in *The Telegraph* noted that the greatest issue with the production's plot was its focus on the arms race. Drawing a comparison to the style of Gilbert and Sullivan, critic stated: «The problem is too serious to be ridiculed

---

[48]. DAILY MAIL 1935.
[49]. THE SPHERE 1935.
[50]. THE REFEREE 1935.
[51]. SHELLARD 2004.
[52]. WILLIAMS 1935B.

out of existence, and it needed a more serious treatment than this Gilbertian fun fair, if it was to make the audience think». The review continues:

> The music comes out of a familiar stockpot, which the composer keeps boiling assiduously without the uncomfortable deterrent of self-criticism. To change the metaphor, it has a recognisable and tolerably respectable pedigree, from Offenbach and Johann Strauss, through the café-concert and the modern revue. Mr. Weill has most of the tricks of the trade in his pocket and exploits them for all they are worth[53].

The review also calls the musical style a «hotch-potch» and a «mixed grill», indicating that although Weill's works combined many elements of London theatre in the period, he was still decidedly too foreign for London tastes and that the musical style wavered between traditional operetta and popular musical styles.

In response, Weill argued that his work was a continuation of past operatic traditions utilizing modern idioms and not a commercial sellout — a criticism that would continue to plague him. He argued against the implication that he was exploiting other idioms, crying: «Well, you will hear very little jazz in this score. The jazz is implicit, so to speak, but not external [...] compared with the operetta this is, of course, what you would call "serious music"»[54]. He was subsequently disheartened by the work's failure. He confided to Lenya: «This London flop was heavy blow for me. But just don't get soft, baby!»[55]. After anticipating such an easy success, Weill was crushed by the flop of *Kingdom* in London, and lamented to Lenya in a letter from 17 July 1935: «I've had a lot of time to think about myself. I would be so happy to be able to do something big again, something right — without having to think about those dull-witted audiences of Europe's big cities. Maybe it'll be possible to build up something in America so that I can write my kind of operas again»[56]. Regardless, the critical reception was a serious blow to Weill, contributing to a bitter end for his London period.

The response to Weill in London reflects not only his own status as a German émigré, but also that of other artists during this period. Had Weill not been subjected to such dismal critical evaluations, it is possible that he would have stayed on in London, perhaps composing more works for the London stage. The effects of prejudice against Weill remained for decades, and this influence of his identity on the reception of his works in Britain was only acknowledged at the end of the twentieth century. The Weill centenary, celebrated with a series of concert performances, marked a turning point in which critics openly acknowledged what one critic

---

[53]. THE TELEGRAPH 1935.
[54]. WILLIAMS 1935B.
[55]. SYMONETTE – KOWALKE 1996.
[56]. *Ibidem*.

called «the harsh effects that his turbulent times brought to bear on music»[57]. The shift in the rhetoric suggested that although Weill was subjected to scrutiny because of identity, 50 years later his work had assumed its rightful place in terms of British theatre. The very difference that marked Weill as an outsider in the 1930s and 40s was reinterpreted in the late twentieth century as being a mark of individualistic and artistic integrity in the face of opposition. By contextualizing Weill's London exile as a product of political change, scholars and critics are able to understand the broader implications of his musical evolution.

Bibliography

Cochran 1937
Cochran, Charles B. 'Charles B. Cochran discusses his plans and describes... Hollywood as I See It', in: *Continental Daily Mail*, 24 August 1937.

Daily Express 1935
Anonymous. 'A Kingdom for a Cow', in: *Daily Express*, 24 June 1935.

Drew 1986
Drew, David. 'Reflections on the Last Years: *Der Kuhhandel* as a Key Work', in: *A New Orpheus: Essays on Kurt Weill*, edited by Kim H. Kowalke, New Heaven (CT), Yale University Press, 1986.

Duchen 1999
Duchen, Jessica. 'Degenerate Composer Number One', in: *The Guardian*, Friday 1 October 1999.

East Anglian Daily Times 1935
Anonymous. 'London Plays and Players. Season's Cleverest Musical Play', in: *East Anglian Daily Times*, 8 July 1935.

Einstein n.d.
Einstein, Alfred. Undated article located in B.B.C. written archives, Series 30, Box 22, Folder 7 B.B.C. publications.

Everett 2008
Everett, William A. 'American and British Operetta in the 1920s: Romance, Nostalgia and Adventure', in: *The Cambridge Companion to the Musical*, edited by William A. Everett and Paul R. Laird, Cambridge, Cambridge University Press, ²2008 (Cambridge Companions to Music), pp. 72-88.

Fox 2000
Fox, Jo. *Filming Women in the Third Reich: Heavy Hands and Light Touches' Approaches to the Study of Cinematic Culture in the Third Reich*, Oxford, Berg, 2000.

---

[57]. Duchen 1999.

Kurt Weill's London Works

Glasgow Bulletin 1935
Anonymous. 'A Kingdom for a Cow', in: *Glasgow Bulletin*, 29 June 1935.

Harding 1988
Harding, James. *Cochran*, Bloomsbury, Methuen, 1988.

Hinton 2012
Hinton, Stephen. *Weill's Musical Theatre: Stages of Reform*, Berkeley-Los Angeles, University of California Press, 2012.

Hirsch 2002
Hirsch, Foster. *Kurt Weill on Stage: From Berlin to Broadway*, New York, Alfred A. Knopf, 2002.

Hobson 1935
Hobson, Harold. 'Kurt Weill', in: *Observer*, 30 June 1935.

Horse and Hound 1935
Anonymous. 'A Kingdom for a Cow', in: *Horse and Hound*, 6 July 1935.

Hughes 1935
Hughes, Spike. 'Close Up 13 Gaybrow', in: *Daily Herald*, 29 June 1935.

Keller 1956
Keller, Hans. 'Review of *The Threepenny Opera*', in: *Music Review*, XVII (May 1956), p. 153.

MacKay 2000
MacKay, Robert. 'Being Beastly to the Germans: Music, Censorship and the B.B.C. in World War II', in: *Historical Journal of Film, Radio and Television*, XX/4 (2000), pp. 513-514.

Marriot 1965
Marriot, R. B. '«Happy End» – Weill Cabaret and Brecht Stockyards', in: *The Stage*, Thursday 18 March 1965.

Martin 1981
Martin, Gerald. *American Operetta: From H.M.S. Pinafore to Sweeney Todd*, Oxford-New York, Oxford University Press, 1981.

Morning Post 1935
Anonymous. 'Review of *A Kingdom for a* Cow', in: *Morning Post*, 8 June 1935.

News of the World 1935
Anonymous. 'There is a Chorus up to Grand Opera Standard', in: *News of the World*, London, 30 June 1935.

OVERY 2009
OVERY, Richard. *The Twilight Years. The Paradox of Britain during the Wars*, New York, Penguin Books, 2009.

PURSER 1955
PURSER, Philip. 'The Greatest Musical Service since Mr. Gilbert Met Mr. Sullivan', in: *The Daily Times*, 25 May 1955.

SHEFFIELD DAILY TELEGRAPH 1930
ANONYMOUS. 'The Wireless Programs: *Beggar's Opera*', in: *Sheffield Daily Telegraph*, 5 May 1930.

SHELLARD 2004
SHELLARD, Dominic. *The Lord Chamberlain Regrets: A History of British Theatre Censorship*, London, The British Library, 2004.

SYMONETTE – KOWALKE 1996
Speak Low (When You Speak Love): The Letters of Kurt Weill and Lotte Lenya, edited and translated by Lys Symonette and Kim H. Kowalke, Berkeley-Los Angeles, University of California Press, 1996.

THE DAILY INDEPENDENT 1933A
ANONYMOUS. '«All-American Variety Bill: German Version of English Music Classic» by Our Own Correspondent', in: *The Daily Independent*, 8 February 1933.

THE DAILY INDEPENDENT 1933B
ANONYMOUS. 'Threepenny Suite', in: *The Daily Independent*, 10 March 1933.

THE DAILY MAIL 1935
ANONYMOUS. 'Week of Parties', in: *The Daily Mail*, 24 June 1935.

THE ERA 1930
ANONYMOUS. 'The Beggar's Opera (In French)', in: *The Era*, 22 October 1930.

THE ERA 1931
ANONYMOUS. 'Metamorphosis: Tuppenny, Ha'penny Opera', in: *The Era*, 7 January 1931.

THE JEWISH CHRONICLE 1935
ANONYMOUS. Untitled, in: *The Jewish Chronicle*, 22 February 1935, p. 46.

THE PERFORMER 1931
ANONYMOUS. 'American Vaudeville', in: *Performer*, 11 February 1931.

THE REFEREE 1935
ANONYMOUS. 'A Kingdom for a Cow', in: *The Referee*, 23 June 1935.

Kurt Weill's London Works

The Scotsman 1930
Anonymous. 'Radio Programs: *Der Lindberghflug*', in: *The Scotsman*, 7 May 1930.

The Scotsman 1932
Anonymous. 'Wireless Programmes and Foreign Stations: *Die Bürgschaft*', in: *The Scotsman*, 8 March 1932.

The Scotsman 1933
Anonymous. 'Wireless Programmes and Foreign Stations: *Der Jasager*', in: *The Scotsman*, 29 December 1933.

The Sphere 1935
Anonymous. 'Review of *A Kingdom for a Cow*', in: *The Sphere*, 6 July 1935.

The Stage 1933
Anonymous. 'American Stage: *Der Jasager*', in: *The Stage*, 18 May 1933.

The Star 1935
Anonymous. 'Kurt Weill', in: *The Star*, 25 June 1935.

The Tatler 1933
Anonymous. 'Kingdom for a Cow', in: *The Tatler*, no. 1673 (19 July 1933).

The Tatler 1935
Anonymous. 'Kingdom for a Cow', in: *The Tatler*, no. 1777 (17 July 1935).

The Telegraph 1935
Anonymous. 'A Kingdom for a Cow', in: *The Telegraph*, 29 June 1935.

The Western Morning News 1933
Anonymous. 'More Ballet at the Savoy', in: *The Western Morning News and Daily Gazette*, Tuesday 4 July 1933.

Western Daily Press 1934
Anonymous. 'The Women's Club', in: *Western Daily Press and Bristol Mirror*, 20 January 1934.

Williams 1935a
Williams, Stephen. 'Review of *A Kingdom for a Cow*', in: *Evening Standard*, 27 June 1935.

Williams 1935b
Id. 'Review of *A Kingdom for a Cow*', in: *Saturday Review*, 6 July 1935.

Wright 2012
Wright, Adrian. *West End Broadway: The Golden Age of the American Musical in London*, Woodbridge, Boydell, 2012.

Kurt Weill's 'Song of the Free' (1942): A «United Nations Anthem»?[*]

Tim Carter
(University of North Carolina, Chapel Hill)

On 30 May 1942, Kurt Weill presented Gertrude Lawrence as a token of his «undying affection» the manuscript of his 'Song of the Free', a setting of verse by Archibald MacLeish[1]. Its original title on the first page of the music was 'The Free Men', but by the time Weill wrote the cover sheet with the dedication to Lawrence, it had changed, also with a parenthetical addition: 'The Song of the Free (The United Nations Anthem)'. Weill's gift was to acknowledge Lawrence's role as the star of his latest Broadway success, *Lady in the Dark*: 30 May was the last night of its long run in New York from 23 January 1941. But his parenthesis reflected a particular set of circumstances that were not to last. To be sure, a 'Declaration by United Nations' had been signed on 1-2 January 1942 by twenty-six governments representing the Allied Powers, headed by the 'big four' — the United States, United Kingdom, U.S.S.R., and China — and including the key members of the British Commonwealth, countries in Central America (including Cuba, the Dominican Republic, and Haiti, but not yet Mexico), India, and eight European governments-in-exile. Their sharing an 'anthem' was never in the cards, however, and even if it were, it was hardly likely to be written by a German-Jewish refugee residing in the United States.

---

[*]. This essay builds on the fine discussion of 'Song of the Free' in Graber 2021, pp. 149-150. I am grateful to Dave Stein, archivist of the Weill-Lenya Research Center (henceforth WLRC) for providing me with copies of materials held in the Papers of Kurt Weill and Lotte Lenya, MSS 30, Irving S. Gilmore Music Library, Yale University (henceforth WLA) and elsewhere. All my transcriptions have been silently edited to correct obvious typographical errors and to standardize punctuation, etc. I also thank Annegret Fauser, Naomi Graber, Elmar Juchem, and Kim Kowalke for their comments on my draft.

[1]. The manuscript (now in the Library of Congress, Washington, DC) is written on 'NBC Chicago' manuscript paper (although the cover sheet is Weill's more normal 'Chappell no. 2' paper), and the song is in G major, but with a penciled annotation, «in F», i.e., the key of the published version. There are other minor variants in the music.

Tim Carter

Weill's 'Song of the Free' often gets grouped among a series of so-called propaganda songs that he produced in the first half of 1942, sometimes extended to 'wartime songs' by virtue of the three settings of poetry by Walt Whitman that he wrote in this same period, and the arrangements of American patriotic songs made for actor Helen Hayes (as reciter). Those labels are not entirely helpful, however, given that these various works were created with different purposes in mind. His 'Song of the Free' is a free-standing case in point: my aim is to ask what brought it about, how it was used, and why Weill somehow felt justified in calling it a 'United Nations Anthem' at least in late May 1942. The answers lie not just in the song and the contexts of its creation, but also in a complex set of circumstances driving Weill's activities in this period that, in turn, reveal the personal and professional relationships that could determine the success, or not, of his career in his adopted country.

First Contact

The story begins in late summer 1941, and with Archibald MacLeish, a poet, dramatist, and all-round intellectual who had been appointed Librarian of Congress in 1939 — a position he held until 1944 — and who would soon become the unpaid Director of the wartime Office of Facts and Figures (OFF). He was also a close friend of President Roosevelt and therefore a powerful Washington insider.

MacLeish provided some of the background to the poem he variously titled 'The Free Men's Song' and 'The Free Men (A Song for Drums)' in a letter to the composer Irving Berlin written on 2 December 1941, describing a plan he had hatched with the famed film director, John Ford, recently commissioned in the U.S. Navy[2]:

> [...] Some months ago, when John Ford first came to Washington, he and I were discussing the possibility of doing a picture on the defense effort — on the effort of the American people in their own defense. In the course of this discussion, Ford asked me if I would try to put down in words something that might serve as the theme of the picture. I did, and the result was a poem — or rather words for a song — which seemed to me to say what I thought should be said.
>
> As time went on, the original plan for the picture was snowed under by events over which none of us had very much control. The song, however, remained, and Jack [Ford] now wants to use the song as the theme and scenario of a defense picture, a briefer picture, which would attempt to realize the meaning of freedom over the generations of American life.

---

[2]. Library of Congress, Washington, DC, Archibald MacLeish Papers (henceforth AMP), Box 3 Folder 20 (which also has Berlin's reply of 9 December cited below). AMP, box 34, folder 27, has three carbon copies of the text of 'The Free Men's Song' and the top copy of 'The Free Men (A Song for Drums)', all without a date. The last is closest to the version set by Weill.

Kurt Weill's 'Song of the Free' (1942)

Various documents allow us to pin things down more precisely. Ford had been assigned to work in the Office of the Coordinator of Information (OCI), headed by Colonial William J. Donovan. At a gathering at Donovan's house one evening in early September, the movie idea was raised, and MacLeish mentioned his poem. He then sent it to Ford on 5 September, saying that he had been «casting around recently for a composer» but was willing to wait to see how their current plan played out[3].

According to his later biographer, MacLeish wrote 'The Free Men's Song' as one of two «choruses» in August 1941[4]. The other one is not named, but it may have been MacLeish's 'The Western Sky: Words for a Song to Roy Harris', which was published in the inaugural edition of *The Free World*, the monthly magazine of the International Free World Association, in October 1941. Harris had already set it to music as 'Freedom's Land', which he then registered for copyright on 1 November[5]. Eleanor Roosevelt also noted her receipt of Harris's «very delightful song» in her syndicated 'My Day' column of 27 November 1941, quoting its final appeal to liberty[6].

MacLeish did not give any details of the poem of current concern when writing to Irving Berlin on 2 December, but clearly it was 'The Free Men's Song', and he went on to make a predictable request:

> [...] You can see what this brings us to. To use the words in this way, they should be set to music which can really speak to the American people and of all the writers of such music, the master is surely Irving Berlin. My question, therefore, is this: Would you be willing to consider writing music for these words for such a purpose?

Berlin politely declined on 9 December on the grounds that he was «not good at setting music to a lyric» given that he preferred to write both the words and the music of any song. He suggested that MacLeish should approach Jerome Kern, Sigmund Romberg, or Richard Rodgers instead. This put MacLeish and Ford in a quandary. Ford favored Romberg, but in the meantime, MacLeish had had a conversation with Burgess Meredith and Melvyn Douglas, both of whom brought Kurt Weill to his attention. MacLeish was enthusiastic, telling Ford on 22 December that «I admire Weil's [*sic*] music enormously». Ford agreed on the 29th («I think

---

[3]. AMP, Box 8 Folder 18, which also contains MacLeish's subsequent correspondence with Ford.

[4]. DONALDSON 1992, p. 287 (no source given).

[5]. Library of Congress Copyright Office, *Catalog of Copyright Entries: Part III, Musical Compositions*, new series, vol. XXXVI, no. 2 (1941), p. 1826 (E pub. 98860). Harris dropped MacLeish's fifth and final stanza. The song was completed by 23 September, when MacLeish pitched it (with music «which seems to me to be simply superb») to Howard Dietz, producer of the *Treasury Hour*, a prominent radio program; AMP, Box 6 Folder 19.

[6]. See <https://www2.gwu.edu/~erpapers/myday/displaydoc.cfm?_y=1941&_f=md056046>, accessed April 2023.

we've got something there. Hope we get at it as soon as possible»). On 30 December, MacLeish confirmed the choice of Weill to set his poem, leaving Meredith to take the next steps.

Burgess Meredith was a close friend of Weill's. Both he and Melvyn Douglas were prominent movie actors, and they had been talking with MacLeish about creating a pool of writers «and other talented people» to be available to the OFF for the production of government movies and other propaganda, although this never came to fruition[7]. On 8 January 1942, Meredith cabled MacLeish that Weill had already read the poem, and that Ford wanted to meet with Weill and MacLeish «to discuss [the] nature of [the] production»[8]. MacLeish sent a telegram to Weill on 19 January asking him to come to Washington, DC, «tomorrow for dinner and a chat in the evening»[9]. Weill did so, and then wrote on 24 January to thank MacLeish and his wife «for a lovely evening in your house»:

> [...] I am very excited about your beautiful poem and John Ford's film project, and I am very happy that you called me in on this project. I hope I will have finished the song in a few weeks, and then I would like to see you again and decide what we are going to do next.

He wrote to his wife, Lotte Lenya, on 28 January that he had «started working on the MacLeish song», and he then kept her updated on his progress with it[10].

MacLeish sent Weill «the new form of 'The Free Men' song with one or two changes» on 31 January, and on 17 February, Weill was able to tell him that

> [...] the song is finished, and I think it is a good song. I wanted it to be dignified and exciting at the same time — an anthem and a battle cry — that's what the words suggested to me. So I wrote a melody of great simplicity, based on a strong sustained drum r[h]ythm and building into a great climax at the end.

MacLeish responded on 25 February expressing delight that the song was done, and excitement at the prospect of hearing it. Weill had written to Lenya also on 17 February that he had already played it to Max Dreyfus at Chappell the day before («who said that it is a great song and might become very important»); he managed to get a plug for it into the *New York Times* on

---

[7]. MacLeish outlined the proposal made by Meredith and Douglas in a letter to Eleanor Roosevelt (addressed to her in the Office of Civilian Defense), 17 January 1942; AMP, Box 19 Folder 13.

[8]. AMP, Box 15 Folder 38.

[9]. AMP, Box 23 Folder 14, which also contains MacLeish's subsequent correspondence with Weill save where noted.

[10]. Weill to Lenya, 15 February 1942; SYMONETTE – KOWALKE 1996, no. 221. All subsequent letters between Weill and Lenya cited in this essay can be found here by date; I have slightly edited them for the sake of consistency. Lenya was currently on tour with Helen Hayes in a production of Maxwell Anderson's *Candle in the Wind*; she and Weill wrote almost daily.

Kurt Weill's 'Song of the Free' (1942)

22 February («a patriotic air, not a show number»); on 25 February he told Lenya that «they are all crazy about the MacLeish song»; and the next day he wrote to his friend, the dancer and choreographer Ruth Page, that it «turned out exceedingly well»[11]. By 19 March, however, Weill was grumbling to Lenya that MacLeish was not responding to his letters, with the result that «this beautiful song is lying around in my drawer — with all the others». There was a reason for that, although Weill was not aware of it.

Kurt Weill, 'Enemy Alien'

It is not at all surprising that Weill should have been preoccupied with the war effort in early 1942: many U.S. composers and performers were seeking how best to meet the challenge of Serge Koussevitzky's proclamation that «We, as musicians, are soldiers, too»[12]. But there were other issues at stake for him as well. He had arrived in New York in September 1935 just to work with Max Reinhardt on the massive opera-oratorio, *The Eternal Road* (1937), but it soon became clear that the political circumstances in Europe meant that he could never return. It is well known — and for some a source of criticism — that he made every effort to adapt, enthusiastically proclaiming himself an 'American' in spirit even before he gained U.S. citizenship on 27 August 1943[13].

However, the declaration of war in Europe on 3 September 1939 had put him and other immigrants from countries now in the Axis in a difficult position, and after the official entry of the United States into World War II in December 1941, all German, Italian, and Japanese nationals were explicitly designated as 'enemy aliens' subject to stringent limitations and controls. Weill tried to mitigate the damage by rousing fellow Germans in New York to the Allied cause (none too successfully); he registered for the draft on 14 February 1942 (as he was required to do); and he took part in Civilian Defense operations — he and his friend and neighbor, the playwright Maxwell Anderson, spent four hours every other week on a hilltop near their homes, keeping watch for enemy aircraft over the Hudson Valley[14]. But he remained viewed as a foreigner, with the added burden of the anti-Semitism prevalent in some New York circles.

Weill and Lenya may have been strapped financially when they first arrived in the United States. But they were now in a very secure position thanks to the weekly royalties and film

---

[11]. *New York Times* (henceforth *NYT*), 22 February 1942, p. X1 (in a brief report on the *Fun To Be Free* revue). Weill to Page, 26 February 1942, copy in WLRC, from New York Public Library for the Performing Arts, Jerome Robbins Dance Division, Ruth Page Collection, folder 42C25, which is also the source of other letters between Weill and Page cited here.

[12]. Fauser 2013, p. 15.

[13]. Kowalke 2000, p. 111.

[14]. Schebera 1993, pp. 268-270.

rights from the highly successful *Lady in the Dark*[15]. The first share of those rights enabled Weill and Lenya to purchase (on 28 May 1941) Brook House on South Mountain Road on the northern edge of New City, NY (in Rockland County, near the New Jersey border on the west side of the Hudson). Their neighbors included a who's who of the New York theatre world, including Maxwell Anderson, Ben Hecht, Burgess Meredith, and the actor Helen Hayes with her husband, the producer Charles MacArthur.

For the most part, it was a congenial artistic community, enlivened by regular dinner parties and other social gatherings. It also reinforced the support networks that helped foster Weill's career. For example, he collaborated with Maxwell Anderson on two works for the stage, *Knickerbocker Holiday* (1938) and *Lost in the Stars* (1949), plus the unfinished *Ulysses Africanus* and *Huckleberry Finn*. They also joined forces for the radio-cantata, *The Ballad of Magna Carta* (1940), and 'Your Navy' for the OFF's *This Is War!* radio series (on which more below), broadcast on 28 February 1942. The narrator of *The Ballad of Magna Carta* was Burgess Meredith, who had taken the role of Crooked Finger Jack in the 1933 Broadway production of *The Threepenny Opera*, and with whom Weill had promised to work since at least 1937, when they formed the idea of a new 'Ballad Theatre' company (that never came to fruition)[16]. We have seen how Meredith nudged MacLeish to consider Weill for his 'The Free Men' song in December 1941; he probably helped him gain the commission to write the music for the wartime propaganda film, *Salute to France* (1944), in which he starred; and he was a great champion of the composer until his own death in 1997. Another figure involved in *The Ballad of Magna Carta*, the producer Norman Corwin working for the Columbia Broadcasting Service (CBS), also had an impact on Weill's subsequent career: they had various projects cooking in the second half of 1941, and Corwin was the producer of the *This Is War!* series to which Weill and Anderson contributed in February 1942[17].

Weill had his enemies, however, and some could be very dangerous. On 13 April 1942 he wrote to Lenya that another friend (and former student), the conductor Maurice Abravanel, had told him about a recent dinner party when the composer Virgil Thomson badmouthed Weill at great length for having «behaved very badly to him in a personal matter». Three days later (on the 16th), Weill told Lenya about even fiercer criticism coming

---

[15]. According to the itemized spreadsheet (covering 1941 to 1950) prepared later by Weill's accountant, Milton Coleman (now in WLRC), their combined income in 1941 was $37,520.59, then $27,4654.56 in 1942 and $62,759.73 in 1943, not counting Weill's share of the extraordinary amount paid by Paramount Pictures for the rights to his latest musical, which brought him $30,000 in 1942 and $12,750 in 1943. These are rather large sums for the period.

[16]. CARTER 2011, p. 320.

[17]. For the 1941 plans, see Weill to Lenya, 17 September 1941. Corwin wrote to Weill about *This Is War!* on 8 January 1942, saying that he would be happy to have music by him in one of its programs; see LANGGUTH 1994, p. 63.

from another quarter, based on a conversation with Gilbert Gabriel (a journalist and another of Weill's friends):

> [...] He told me that one day he was working with John Steinbeck in the [Robert] Sherwood office and a man came in and talked about the propaganda broadcasts to France, Germany etc., which are under the direction of John Houseman. The man said: «What we need most is a great song». Steinbeck said: «Why don't you talk to Kurt Weill[?]». The man said: «I mentioned him the other day and Houseman answered: I don't want this name mentioned any more!». It seems those pansies will never forget that I turned them down with Mahagonny[18]!

This was probably the «personal matter» that had prompted Thomson's wrath as well: he and Houseman were close friends and collaborators[19]. But so far as Weill was concerned, the problem was the failed attempt to stage what Thomson thought would be his *Aufstieg und Fall der Stadt Mahagonny* at the so-called Festival of the Friends and Enemies of Modern Music in Hartford, CT, in February 1936[20]. This festival was Thomson's fiefdom, and with Houseman initially slated to direct Weill's opera, they both must have thought that they were doing him the favor of a U.S. premiere, boosting his reputation just a few months after his arrival. However, it turned into a fiasco caused by miscommunication, misinterpretation, and a certain amount of stubbornness on Weill's part, leading to the whole venture being dropped at very short notice. Weill may have thought he had dodged a bullet, but by any reckoning, he made a serious mistake.

Thomson's power now lay in the fact that he was a regular critic for the *New York Herald-Tribune*: he had written a scathing review of *Lady in the Dark*, accusing it of piling banality upon banality[21]. Weill was able to dismiss that as mere professional jealousy. Houseman was more troublesome, however. He was firmly embedded in the avant-garde of the New York theatrical world, not least by way of his work with the Federal Theatre Project and as co-founder (with Orson Welles) of the Mercury Theatre. More to the present point, by the time

---

[18]. Robert Sherwood was a playwright and a founding member of the Playwrights' Producing Company, but he now worked as Director of the Foreign Information Service Branch of the OCI, based in the Rockefeller Center in New York City.

[19]. THOMSON 2016, pp. 424-425.

[20]. One side of the story belonging to A. Everett Austin, jr., director of the Wadsworth Atheneum, is given in GADDIS 2000, pp. 290-297. The full opera was never in the cards given that Weill only had with him the 'Paris' version of the *Mahagonny Songspiel* (i.e., with added numbers from the opera); see SCHUBERT 2016, p. 26. It is not clear how long Houseman's intention to direct it lasted. By 15 January, when Weill wrote a long letter (copy in WLRC) to Austin trying to set the record straight, he said that the production was to be directed by Edwin Denby (another of Thomson's friends).

[21]. McCLUNG 2007, p. 109.

of that derisory comment on Weill in spring 1942, he was in charge of the radio arm of the U.S. Foreign Information Service (under Robert Sherwood), a position which then mutated into his becoming head of the overseas radio division of the Office of War Information (and hence, the first director of Voice of America). He was someone of influence not to be crossed.

ITCHY FINGERS

By early 1942, Weill was getting restless. He must have been glad to see the cast of *Lady in the Dark* perform on the official opening night of the Stage Door Canteen (2 March 1942) in the Forty-fourth Street Theatre, an important institution sponsored by the American Theatre Wing where volunteers entertained off-duty military personnel[22]. But as the first anniversary of Weill's show came and went, he was looking for additional ways to draw attention to his music. The performance of his 1935 song 'Complainte de la Seine' in a theremin recital by Lucie Bigelow Rosen at the Town Hall in midtown Manhattan on 18 January 1942 would not have counted for much in that regard, despite its being advertised as a «U.S. premiere»[23]. He was also getting anxious to start work on a new Broadway show. He briefly revisited the idea of adapting Ludwig Fulda's 1911 comedy *Der Seeräuber* for the Lunts as *The Pirate* (a notion that dated back to 1939), but that project collapsed due to a fundamental disagreement with the Playwrights' Producing Company over the nature and amount of the music they wanted to include[24]. Meanwhile, he was also in discussion with director and producer Cheryl Crawford, to whom Weill was close from the days of the Group Theatre and his first U.S. musical play, *Johnny Johnson* (1936). Their new plan concerned an adaptation of the 1885 novella, *The Tinted Venus*, by Thomas Anstey Guthrie (publishing as F. Anstey). However, there were rights issues needing to be sorted out, putting everything on hold (*One Touch of Venus* eventually opened on 7 October 1943).

Another project hit the rocks as well: the revue *Fun To Be Free*, initially planned for a two-week run on Broadway beginning on 27 January (although that date was repeatedly postponed). This was based on successful 1941 benefit of the same name and sponsored by the 'Fight for Freedom' Board with Broadway and Hollywood luminaries offering their services

---

[22]. Theatre critic Brooks Atkinson noted the opening performance at the Canteen, paying special attention to 'The Saga of Jenny', «which will probably turn out to be the theme song of the United States forces»; *NYT*, 3 March 1942, p. 26.

[23]. *New York Herald-Tribune*, 19 January 1942, p. 8.

[24]. Weill had an uneasy relationship with the Playwrights' Producing Company, Its founders included Maxwell Anderson, S. N. Behrman, Elmer Rice, and Robert Sherwood (now head of the Foreign Information Service). The PPC had taken Weill on as a music consultant following its production of *Knickerbocker Holiday*. His tribulations over *The Pirate* (to be adapted by Behrman) — and the musical research he did for it — merit a separate study.

for the benefit of the war effort. The original was a one-night extravaganza staged in Madison Square Garden on 5 October 1941 before an audience of 17,000, produced by Ben Hecht and Charles MacArthur. That event had included motivational speeches, a pageant of American luminaries (with music by Weill), and a series of star-studded spots, memorably including Bill 'Bojangles' Robinson tap-dancing on Hitler's coffin to Irving Berlin's 'When That Man Is Dead and Gone'[25]. A version of the show then went on tour. Now, however, the plan was for a more conventional revue of sketches and variety acts put together by an organizing committee comprised of Oscar Hammerstein 2ᵈ, George Kaufman, Robert Alton, and Hassard Short (who had staged the musical sequences of *Lady in the Dark*): Hammerstein was placed in charge of the music. Despite a promising start, however, plans soon fell apart because of a lack of funds and «internal friction» within the cast (prompted in part, it seems, by Groucho Marx)[26]. On 26 February 1942, Weill told Ruth Page that he was writing two songs for the revue, one with Howard Dietz, 'Schickelgruber' — «sung by Hitler's mother (staged like Whistler's mother)» — and the other by Hammerstein, 'The Good Earth'[27]. On 16 April, he wrote to Lenya that he had just met with Hammerstein when they «finished» their song, «which is definitely a hit», with the plan now to sell it to the movies (but it does not seem that they did). 'Schickelgruber' was left hanging until it later found a place in the *Lunchtime Follies*.

Weill may have been hoping for more from Hammerstein, who was also at a loose end following Jerome Kern's move to Hollywood plus a recent flop (*Sunny River* with Sigmund Romberg). They had two lunches together on 6 and 10 March, and Weill tried to get him interested in *The Pirate*, another project that never came to fruition. Although Hammerstein soon went in a very different direction with Richard Rodgers, he was currently looking to write «the great War Song»[28]. Weill had similar ambitions with his three settings of poetry by Walt Whitman (a fourth was added in 1947), one of which ('Beat, Beat Drums!') was included in his arrangements of American patriotic songs for male chorus, orchestra, and Helen Hayes

---

[25]. The report of *Fun To Be Free* in *NYT*, 6 October 1941, p. 1, gives a good idea of its contents. Part of the Hecht-Weill pageant ('What Is America?') was repeated by the R. H. Macy Choral Society at Carnegie Hall on 8 June 1942, conducted by Simon Rady (who had conducted *Fun To Be Free* in October 1941); *New York Herald-Tribune*, 8 June 1942, p. 6. That program also included George Kleinsinger's cantata, *I Hear America Singing* (1941; with settings of poetry by Walt Whitman).

[26]. The fate of the new *Fun To Be Free* revue can be traced through newspaper articles reporting on its ups and downs. For the rehearsals and eventual intended opening, see the *New York Herald-Tribune*, 5 March 1942, p. 16. Groucho Marx is mentioned in *NYT*, 12 March 1942, p. 25. *NYT*, 26 March 1942, p. 26, reports on «internal friction» and also the return of money raised by the 'Fight for Freedom' committee when the revue was dropped.

[27]. On 2 May 1942, Weill told Ira Gershwin that he wrote «some songs» with Hammerstein; WLRC, series 40 (copy from the Library of Congress). However, we know only of 'The Good Earth' and 'Buddy on the Nightshift' (the latter later associated with the *Lunchtime Follies*).

[28]. CARTER 2020, p. 11.

as reciter, which she recorded in late March 1942[29]. As was so often the case with Weill's projects, however, it was difficult to get things off the ground. For example, he was deeply disappointed when plans fell apart for him and Anderson to work on a War Department film with Frank Capra (now a major in the Army Signal Corps) and Anatole Litvak (whom Weill had known in Germany). This would presumably have been a documentary in Capra and Litvak's *Why We Fight* series (the first of which, *Prelude to War*, was on the verge of being released). They had held a successful conference in Washington, DC, on or around 18 May. Weill was excited, so he wrote to Lenya on 20 May: «Of course I would love to get into this kind of work because it would be my best contribution to the war effort»[30]. He also thought that when his citizenship came through, he might apply for a commission in Capra's department. Weill told MacLeish on 8 July that the project was still in play. However, Anderson withdrew with the excuse that he wanted time to finish another play (*The Eve of St. Mark*, which opened in October).

All these on-off ventures were somewhat typical of Weill's career (and that of many others); so, too, was the need to juggle as many balls in the air as possible. But he certainly hoped for something more concrete from his MacLeish song, also within a branch of the U.S. wartime administration that was not tainted by prejudices from the likes of Houseman.

The Office of Facts and Figures

When MacLeish, Ford, and Donovan spent that evening together in early September 1941, part of their discussion presumably included the plans afoot to establish an Office of Facts and Figures (OFF) to deal with what was becoming an increasing problem for the U.S. government: the coordination and control of the gathering and dissemination of information related to the war effort. It was established by executive order on 24 October 1941, and MacLeish somewhat reluctantly agreed to be its director, although his position as Librarian of Congress made him a logical choice[31]. He treated the OFF's original brief more broadly, however, to create a large administrative structure that included a Bureau of Operations directed by William B. Lewis, formerly a vice-president of CBS. This had a number of divisions concerning public outreach, including one for Radio (headed by Douglas Meservey, from the National Broadcasting

---

[29]. Hayes was also wondering about recording 'How Can You Tell an American' from *Knickerbocker Holiday*, although she said that some of the words would need changing; see Lenya to Weill, 7 and 9 March 1942.

[30]. Weill also wrote to Lenya on 26 May that Litvak had told him that Capra was «very impressed» by him.

[31]. Created by Executive Order 8922; <https://www.presidency.ucsb.edu/documents/executive-order-8922-establishing-the-office-facts-and-figures>, accessed April 2023. The OFF operated under the auspices of the Office for Emergency Management, part of the Executive Branch and thus outside the direct control of Congress.

Company [NBC]) and another for Motion Pictures (Leo Rosten)[32]. Indeed, the whole OFF ballooned into something far greater than had been anticipated when it was established, as did its total operating budget. But in effect, MacLeish turned it into the main wartime propaganda arm of the U.S. government, at least for a time.

As the OFF inserted itself into the alphabet soup of government organizations and started to gain increased funding, competing agencies engaged in a series of turf wars to preserve their own budgets and their status. Even just within the Executive Branch, MacLeish had to contend with the rival interests of the Office of the Coordination of Information (OCI), which had been established in July 1941 with Donovan at its head, and with the longer-standing Office of Government Reports (OGR) under the direction of Lowell Mellett. Other bodies attached to the military and to the U.S. Congress added to the bureaucratic complexities. The direct entry of the United States into World War II in December 1941 also turned everything on its head. MacLeish himself soon realized that the OFF was not fit for purpose, and on 20 February 1942 he wrote a long memorandum suggesting that it be liquidated and replaced by a better organized Office of War Information with a clearer set of instructions as to its function[33]. That came to pass a few months later: the OWI was established on 13 June (with broadcaster Elmer Davis, a prominent CBS news reporter, at its head), the same day that the OCI mutated into the Office of Strategic Services (OSS). Although MacLeish continued to serve in the OWI for a short period, he had effectively, and perhaps deliberately, written himself out of a job.

When Weill wrote about his newly completed song to MacLeish on 17 February, he raised some issues that clearly were crucial for him:

> [...] I hope I will soon have an opportunity to show it to you. In the meanwhile I would like to bring up the question: what is the next thing we can do with the song? I could show it to some important singers like Paul Robeson, Lawrence Tibbett, Richard Crooks or — maybe — Kate Smith. I also thought of making an arrangement for Chorus and Orchester [sic] for one of the big radio programs. Or do you think we should wait for John Ford[34]?

MacLeish responded on the 25th:

> [...] As regards your question, I don't think we should wait for John Ford. The prospect is too uncertain and there is too great a question that he will be able to work

---

[32]. For Lewis, see HORTEN 2002, p. 123. Horten is incorrect that he was «head of the Radio Bureau» of the OFF given that he was higher up the chain; for the structure of the Bureau of Operations, see the *Official Register of the United States, 1942*, compiled (as of 1 May 1942) by the United States Civil Service Commission (Washington, DC, U.S. Government Printing Office, 1942), p. 21.

[33]. All these shenanigans are clear in the typed historical account of the OFF in AMP, Box 52 Folder 7.

[34]. *The Kate Smith Hour*, featuring the well-known singer and radio star, ran on CBS from 1936 to 1945.

> on the movie he has in mind when he gets back. Therefore, if I were you I would show it to some of the singers you mention — preferably to a man. But wouldn't it be well for you and me to go over it and talk about it a little before anything is done?

This is the first of two «lovely letters» from MacLeish that Weill forwarded to Lenya on 9 March: the other, written on 3 March, praised Weill's «simply superb» music for the 'Your Navy' program broadcast on 28 February[35]. But so far as his song was concerned, this may not have been what Weill wanted to hear. In fact, MacLeish was being not just cautious, but also economical with the truth. In mid-December 1941, President Roosevelt assigned to Lowell Mellett, director of the OGR, all responsibility for government movies within the Executive Branch (the War Department was another matter under the control of Congress). This was probably the result of yet another turf war, but it put an instant halt to any movie-making initiatives within the OFF with John Ford or anyone else, at least until some accommodation could be reached between it and the OGR. MacLeish told Weill that the Ford project was «too uncertain», but in fact it was dead in the water, at least so far as any OFF involvement was concerned.

MacLeish was very distressed about the Mellett assignment and feared losing still more. On 20 December 1941, he wrote to President Roosevelt asking for confirmation that the OFF would «continue to act as an intermediary between the government and the radio companies and to coordinate government requests for radio time, as well as to handle such programs such [sic] as those Steve [Early] has asked us to handle»[36]. He cited in support the OFF's involvement in the nationwide broadcast on 15 December of *We Hold These Truths*, a star-studded program written by Norman Corwin (with music by Bernard Herrmann) to celebrate the sesquicentennial of the U.S. Bill of Rights. This was the brainchild of William B. Lewis, the former radio executive now in charge of the OFF's Bureau of Information, who used the OFF's power to commandeer all the major networks to air the hour-long program simultaneously. MacLeish, in turn, had persuaded President Roosevelt himself to provide concluding remarks. It was a significant coup.

If MacLeish lost control over the movies, he kept it over radio, so the president decreed on 16 January 1942; indeed, the OFF's work in that regard became its most important function. The thirteen programs in the *This Is War!* series, under Corwin's aegis, were broadcast on all networks on Saturday evenings, 7:00-7:30, from 14 February to 9 May 1942. Lewis had other such grandiose initiatives in mind, as well, one of which eventually provided a solution to MacLeish's current dilemma over what to do with Weill's song.

---

[35]. Weill also told Lenya on 9 March that MacLeish had said to Maxwell Anderson that «Weill's score was the best radio music we have ever heard». On the same day, Weill wrote to Ruth Page that MacLeish had called it «a model score for all future programs».

[36]. AMP, Box 19 Folder 14. Stephen Early was the White House Press Secretary from 1933 to 1945.

Kurt Weill's 'Song of the Free' (1942)

Moving ahead

Weill responded to MacLeish's two letters of 25 February and 3 March on the 7th, agreeing that they should meet to go over their song together. He also noted that «I showed the song to some friends and it makes a great impression everywhere». But his complaint to Lenya that MacLeish had gone silent, made on 19 March, crossed with a letter from him sent on the 17th, proposing a meeting in Washington. Weill's schedule was busy, however — he was in Chicago at the end of March working on the Helen Hayes recordings — so he only made the trip down on 9 April. He described the outcome to Lenya on the 12th:

> My visit in Washington was extremely successful. When I had played the song MacLeish sprang up and said: «That's what we've been waiting for all the time». He was in extasy [sic] and so was his wife. He is going to do everything to get a big start for the song, probably he will write himself one of the 'This Is War' programs around the song.

MacLeish also raved over the Hayes recordings that Weill had brought with him, calling the music «miraculous» and leaving Weill very pleased with himself: «all this is very important and very promising», he wrote, not least because MacLeish «is Roosevelt's closest friend, and a wonderful man»[37]. He returned to the meeting in another letter to Lenya the next day:

> [...] This enthousiasm [sic] of MacLeish for me is most important. His wife said to me: «You don't know what it means to my husband to have at last found a composer who can do with poetry what you are doing».

Now that he had MacLeish's approval, Weill set in motion the publication of the song with Chappell. MacLeish was unable to accept any royalties as a government employee, so he decided to donate his to the Red Cross, and Weill followed suit. He wrote to MacLeish on 24 April saying that Chappell had finished the proofs, which would be sent that day, although there was still some discussion about the title: one floating around was 'The Thing We Mean', but Chappell thought that sounded «a little like a 'popular' song» and wanted «a very strong and unsophisticated title», instead[38]. 'Song of the Free Men' (or 'Song of the Freemen' — Weill gave both options) was the favorite. MacLeish agreed in principle on 30 April, and on 4 May he approved keeping the title «as it was»: 'Song of the Free Men'. Weill originally called it 'The Free Men' on his inked autograph manuscript, but he added 'Song of' at the beginning and

---

[37]. There is a copy of MacLeish's telegram of 7 April in WLRC (from WLA, Box 48 Folder 36).
[38]. 'The Thing We Mean' refers to the eighth line of the second stanza of the song: «If they touch the thing we mean».

deleted 'Men', producing what became the final version: 'Song of the Free'. The sheet music was registered as such for copyright on 14 May, although an initial definite article sometimes got inserted into the title, as Weill did on the cover sheet for that same manuscript presented to Gertrude Lawrence[39].

One can see why MacLeish liked the song. His text is in a Walt Whitman mold, with three regular eight-line stanzas. Weill's setting has an oddly dissonant march-like piano opening, but the first stanza («We were born free men [...]») has a stirring enough melody, repeated for the second («There are some that kiss the rod [...]»)[40]. Clearly, he viewed this as being in a triumphal vein given that his music for the last four lines of those stanzas is exactly the same as the end of 'March to Zion' in *The Eternal Road*: Weill was not averse to re-using old works that no longer had any currency. However, the accompaniment is harmonically quirky and has too many minor-key tinges to strike an unambiguous note. Moreover, having the third stanza («We have heard the cowards speak [...]») set differently enters the realm of art song, as does the five-measure piano postlude[41]. Despite Weill's claim to MacLeish on 17 February that he had written «an anthem and a battle cry», the song is scarcely anthemic, and if it were to be used for anything other than a concert performance, some changes would have to be made. We shall see what they were.

As Weill noted to Lenya on 12 April (quoted above), MacLeish's plan was to use the 'Song of the Free' in one of the *This Is War!* programs, and he now mobilized his colleagues in the OFF to that end[42]. William B. Lewis wrote to Weill on 16 April, noting that «Archie has told me about the swell music you have written for his song which I understand you are thinking of calling, 'The Thing I Mean'». He also asked for a photostat copy in case they could find a place for it in *This Is War!* On the 20th, Weill corrected him on the title («we called it 'Song of the Freemen' lately») and said that Chappell was now mailing Lewis a proof:

---

[39]. Library of Congress Copyright Office, *Catalog of Copyright Entries. Part III: Musical Compositions*, new series, XXXVII/1 (1942), p. 1050 (E pub. 104890).

[40]. FAUSER 2014, pp. 254-255, notes the brief allusion of the piano introduction to the 'Battle Hymn of the Republic' ('Mine Eyes Have Seen the Glory'). One wonders whether Sigmund Romberg's 'Stout-hearted Men' in his *The New Moon* (1928) was also an unwanted intertext. A second movie version of Romberg's operetta had been released by MGM on 19 July 1940, starring Nelson Eddy and Jeanette MacDonald.

[41]. For similar issues in the second of the Whitman songs, 'Oh Captain! My Captain!', see KOWALKE 2000, p. 121. The reading of 'Song of the Free' in HAMM 2009, p. 68, as having a «double-release structure (ABABCB´)» somewhat misses the poetic point.

[42]. This forced a shift in filing protocols. Most of the correspondence between MacLeish and others cited thus far were kept in MacLeish's 'personal' files (hence their location in AMP), but now (with some exceptions), they entered the official record. Save where noted, the documents cited from here on come from the Office of War Information files in the National Archives and Records Administration (College Park, MD), Record Group 208 (henceforth NARA, RG 208), collected in WLRC, Series 30 Box 23 Folder 8.

Kurt Weill's 'Song of the Free' (1942)

> [...] Everybody seems to agree that this can become a very important song and that we should find a very important spot for its first performance on the air. Archie had the splendid idea to make it a kind of theme song for one of the 'This Is War' programs, possibly for the one about the young boys in this country, and he even thought he might write himself this program — but I doubt if he'll have the time for it. If something in this line would work out I would suggest that we get Kate Smith to sing it for 'This Is War'. And, of course, anything I can help, you know you can always count on me[43].

Lewis acknowledged receipt of the song on 24 April and said that he had forwarded it to the producers of *This Is War!* (Norman Corwin and H. L. McClinton) with a recommendation that it be used to close the program on 2 May (dedicated 'To the Young')[44]. On 30 April, however, MacLeish wrote to Weill making no promises, given that the OFF's relationship to the program was «merely advisory and fairly distant at that», and on 1 May, Weill himself informed MacLeish that Corwin had said that the script for the 2 May program had changed, leaving no place for the song. Johnny Green composed and conducted the minimal music for that broadcast instead. In the meantime, Weill showed the song to the producers of the CBS series, *They Live Forever*, but they did not think it right for their purpose. Weill told MacLeish about all this in a letter of 9 May, also informing him that Chappell was now printing «The Song of the Free», a title with which everyone «seems satisfied». But he had also identified another possible idea for it:

> [...] Max Anderson had been asked to write a pageant for 'United Nations Day' on June 14, and we tried to work out an idea of writing a pageant around our song. Then he was told to do it very simply, without music. But it occurred to me that here might be an opportunity for a great 'send-off' for our song. The idea would be to get the song performed on one (or several) of the official radio programs and public meetings on June 14. At the same time we would get a number of singers to do it on their own programs on or around June 14, and I would get a good French translation to be broadcast in France on the same day. It would certainly be the perfect 'United Nations Song'.

United Nations Flag Day, 14 June 1942

Weill was ahead of the news. He wrote that letter to MacLeish on the same day that President Roosevelt issued his declaration that 14 June, treated as 'Flag Day' in the United

---

[43]. For Weill's use of the term «theme song» to mean something that can become thematic across an entire work, see GRABER 2021, p. 240.

[44]. Lewis to Weill, 24 April 1942; copy in WLRC (from WLA, Box 50 Folder 69).

States, would instead be named «United Nations Flag Day» with appropriate celebrations across the country[45]. This was an OFF initiative: MacLeish had suggested to the president on 28 February that he might proclaim 15 May as a «United People's Day», «made the occasion of a country-wide observance which would give point and meaning to the basic idea underlying the whole concept of the United Nations»[46]. By 2 April, the idea had emerged of combining it with the annual Flag Day commemoration, although there was some resistance to overcome from the Daughters of the American Revolution and the United States Flag Association, who did not wish to politicize their yearly event.

Anderson did indeed write a pageant, which was included in a concert by the National Symphony Orchestra at the Watergate Steps (on the waterfront side of the Lincoln Memorial) in Washington, DC, on the evening of Sunday 14 June, with Eleanor Roosevelt in attendance[47]. But when Anthony Hyde, in the OFF's office of Campaign Coordination, responded (at MacLeish's request) to Weill's letter of 9 May, he came up with a different idea: the OFF was in touch with theatres planning to feature the United Nations in their shows during the week of 14 June, and he hoped that 'Song of the Free' would somehow figure in them.

Weill also took matters into his own hands. He approached Jack Partington at the Roxy Theatre and Gus Eysell at Radio City Music Hall, and worked with Chappell to line up singers, choral groups, and radio programs to adopt the song[48]. He went into more detail in a letter to Hyde of 26 May. The Roxy Theatre, Weill reported, was highly enthusiastic — it was «the song they have been waiting for» — and would put it into their new stage show. Radio City Music Hall was also keen, but they had already fixed their own new show, so his song could only be used later in the summer (we do not know if it was). In addition, Weill told Hyde that he had been working with Chappell to identify some seventy-five singers and conductors to do the piece on the air, and that the head of the song department at Chappell was now contacting the sponsors of radio programs, hoping for the same cooperation from the OFF as he had gained from the War Department for 'The Bombardier Song' by Richard Rodgers and Lorenz Hart. Moreover, Chappell was preparing a four-part choral arrangement of 'Song of the Free', and

---

[45]. 'Flag Day' commemorated the adoption of the U.S. flag on 14 June 1777. President Roosevelt's proclamation was made on 9 May and reported by the newspapers on the 10th. The 1942 event also marked the signing of the 'Declaration by United Nations' by two additions to the alliance: Mexico and the Philippines (the latter now fully occupied by the Japanese following the Battle of Corregidor on 5-6 May).

[46]. AMP, Box 19 Folder 13. This was part of MacLeish's strategy for the OFF to build its initiatives on the four principal themes that President Roosevelt had established in his State of the Union address to Congress on 6 January 1942. Subsequent developments of the United Nations idea can be seen in the various minutes of OFF meetings now in AMP, Box 52 Folder 8.

[47]. See <https://www2.gwu.edu/~erpapers/myday/displaydoc.cfm?_y=1942&_f=md056214>, accessed April 2023.

[48]. So Weill communicated by telegram to David Bernstein of the OFF.

would do one for high schools and colleges if there were thought to be sufficient interest[49]. Weill continued:

> [...] Bob Trout, CBS reporter in London, talked from London on Saturday about the urgent demand for a 'United Nations Anthem'. I feel, and I am sure Mr. MacLeish agrees with me, that this is exactly what our song should be, and I want to do everything in my power to give the song some kind of international distribution. We are sending copies to Chappell in London (who happen to be the largest music publishing firm in England). I'll also give a copy to Norman Corwin before he leaves for England, and I have asked my friend Darius Milhaud, the great French composer who lives in California, to make a French translation.

The very large Roxy Theatre was popular for offering double bills of movies and variety shows, the latter emceed by the theatre's 'singing host', Bob Hannon. Weill's account of the proposed show to Hyde on 26 May — «They are planning a production of the song, using flags of all United Nations» — squares with the final result first seen on 4 June, as described in the *New York Herald-Tribune* the next day[50]:

> [...] 'The Song of the Free', a patriotic song by Archibald MacLeish, director of the Office of Facts and Figures, is introduced to the public in the Roxy Theater stage show. While Bob Hannon, singing host of the theater, sings the lyrics, the Roxyettes, dressed in brilliant red, white and blue costumes, perform a marching routine to the music, which was written by Kurt Weil [*sic*]. The finale of the spectacle is signalized by a grouping of the flags of the United Nations against an enormous American flag.

Weill reported on the outcome to MacLeish on 9 June[51]:

> [...] as you probably know, our song is a very big success as the Finale of the stage show at the Roxy. I went to see it yesterday and I must say it has a very stirring effect on the audience although the singer is far from first-rate and the production

---

[49]. Weill says that «We are preparing an arrangement for four-part mixed chorus which could be used on June 14», but the «we» here is Chappell: the arrangement was done by William Stickles (Chappell's in-house arranger); see FARNETH 2000, p. 211.

[50]. *New York Herald-Tribune*, 5 June 1942, p. 13. The show accompanied the premiere of *Ten Gentlemen from West Point* (Twentieth Century-Fox), a historical drama about the eponymous military academy in the early nineteenth century. *Variety*, 3 June 1942, p. 3, gave a briefer report of the song's intended use in the Roxy as well as in a 'New York at War' parade on 13 June, and in the radio broadcast (discussed below) of 14 June. The routine was still in the Roxy show in the week following the 4 July celebrations; see *Variety*, 15 July 1942, p. 47 («This whole number could be revived from time to time in the interests of patriotism»).

[51]. Copy in WLRC (from a carbon copy in WLA, Box 47 Folder 11). For the reluctance against 'patriotic songs' (for fear of jingoism) in the early years of the war, see HORTEN 2002, pp. 41-54.

is typical 'Roxy'. To me it was a very interesting test for the song because I feel a song of this type should be able to endure any kind of treatment — and it seems that the 'Song of the Free' can stand on its feet. I hope we will have a good singer for the performance on the air next Sunday which I consider the first 'authentic' performance. The publisher tells me that the first reaction from singers and conductors is quite favorable. But we have to overcome a certain reluctance against 'patriotic songs' on the part of the radio sponsors and the recording firms. If we can break this 'bottleneck' we hope to get very good results.

MacLeish responded on 12 June: «I am delighted to know the song is going well — I hope it goes well on Sunday. If it does, it will be your music that makes it so»[52].

Toward the Century of the Common Man

That «performance on the air» to which Weill referred in his latest letter to MacLeish — «on Sunday» as MacLeish replied — had been in discussion since early March, with an idea on the lines of the broadcast of *We Hold These Truths* on 15 December 1941. During his visit to Washington on or around 18 May 1942 to discuss the War Department film with Capra and Litvak, Weill took the time to visit MacLeish's office where they agreed that 'Song of the Free' would «be used on 'United Nations Day', June 14, in several mass meetings and on the radio»[53]. Weill asked Hyde about it in his long letter of 26 May, again suggesting Kate Smith as a possible singer of 'Song of the Free', plus Nelson Eddy, Marion Anderson, and Paul Robeson[54]. However, matters seem to have been unclear within the OFF, which is not untypical of large-scale organizations where right and left hands were not always in direct coordination in fast-changing circumstances. On 28 May, David Bernstein in the OFF cabled Weill that the radio plans for 14 June were «still indefinite», although on the 29th, Hyde wrote that «It now looks as if we are going to have an hour show on four networks» which would use MacLeish and Weill's song. On 2 June, Douglas Meservey, head of the radio division at the OFF, sent the music to Frank Black, general music director of NBC (his previous colleague):

> If you think it as [*sic*] lousy, I know you'll say so. We like the song over and above its technical qualities because of the United Nations concept which, as you know, we are trying to push.

---

[52]. Copy in WLRC (from WLA, Box 48 Folder 46).
[53]. Weill to Lenya, 20 May 1942.
[54]. Weill also tried to recruit Robeson for the Whitman songs and 'Song of the Free' in a letter to the singer's wife, Eslanda (Essie), on 11 June 1942; see Kowalke 2000, p. 128, n. 19.

Kurt Weill's 'Song of the Free' (1942)

The next day (3 June), however, Meservey's bureau chief, William B. Lewis, went one step further by sending a «first draft» of a script for the «United Nations program» to Nat Wolff in Hollywood, who was head liaison there for the OFF's Radio Division[55]. Lewis also included the sheet music of 'Song of the Free', which was «needed in the show». This script was written by George Faulkner (who later gained some reputation as a writer for radio), but Lewis notes that revisions to it were being made by Stephen Vincent Benét, a distinguished poet, novelist, librettist, and sometime author of radio dramas (he also wrote for the *This Is War!* series). Faulkner himself sent a letter to Wolff (and to the intended director of the broadcast, Cal Kuhl) with notes on the program, saying that MacLeish had approved the script with some changes, that NBC still needed to do so, and that Benét was doing some rewriting. He also included some casting suggestions, including Nelson Eddy, Lawrence Tibbett, and Paul Robeson as the baritone for Weill's song. The choice now for a male singer was probably inevitable given the subject matter, although we have seen that it had always been MacLeish's preference anyway.

Faulkner's script was titled *Toward the Century of the Common Man*, «a dramatic sermon for the Sabbath Flag Day». This picked up on Vice-President Henry Wallace's speech made for a dinner of the Free World Association in New York on 8 May 1942[56]:

> [...] Some have spoken of the American Century. I say that the century on which we are entering, the century which will come out of this war, can be and must be the century of the common man.

That speech was somewhat controversial both at home and abroad, not just because of its patent internationalism, but also given that any plans for world peace seemed premature in the spring of 1942 save to those who really did believe that the war would be a short-term affair. The «common man» theme was by no means new: it was a frequent trope in the 1930s[57]. But it was now taken up with some enthusiasm in the press and reworked in other speeches by government officials.

This time, Lewis did not manage to get all the radio networks onboard. The OFF program was broadcast from Hollywood on the NBC-'Red' network on Sunday 14 June at 5:00 p.m. EST (station WEAF in New York), although it was designed to dovetail with a ten-minute address to the nation by President Roosevelt across all networks at 5:50. One surviving script of *Toward the Century of the Common Man*, labeled «First Revision», is very close to what

---

[55]. For Wolff and the OFF, see *Variety*, 6 May 1942, p. 37. He then became head of the West Coast Radio Bureau of the OWI.

[56]. <https://www.americanrhetoric.com/speeches/henrywallacefreeworldassoc.htm>, accessed April 2023.

[57]. Conn 2009, p. 114.

was aired, save for minor edits and some small additions[58]. A portion of the text published in Benét's posthumous collection of radio scripts also included an expanded version of the final speech of the Principal Voice (the narrator) — which was used in the broadcast — plus a «prayer» (written «at the request of the Librarian of Congress, Archibald MacLeish») that was incorporated into the president's address[59].

The program began with the Pledge of Allegiance, followed by Beethoven's 'victory' notes from the Fifth Symphony, before the Principal Voice invoked the Four Freedoms (as articulated in President Roosevelt's famous 1941 State of the Union address), dismissed those voices objecting to the present war, and used the sound of a mother singing a lullaby to soothe her fretful child to claim high stakes for the present fight. He quoted Jefferson as the voice of «reason», juxtaposed with the sounds of the «beast» (a Hitler rant): «But the United Nations will prevail. Listen to harmony and unity» (a *maestoso* repeat of the lullaby). The program then moved into what the script called a 'March of Time'-style narrative (a reference to the famous newsreel series) covering events in the 1930s as a direct result of the failure of the League of Nations: the Japanese invasion of Manchuria (1931) and Mussolini's of Ethiopia (1935) — with a voice representing Haile Selassie warning against the threat to world freedom — plus Hitler's rise to power, Franco's march on Madrid, Neville Chamberlain's refusal to intervene, Nazi atrocities against the Jews, and the bombing of Pearl Harbor. All this was accompanied by a tolling bell that also allowed the Principal Voice to quote John Donne's sonnet, 'No Man Is an Island'.

From there, the pace shifted to a series of vignettes focusing on 'common man' representatives of the principal Allied powers, each matched by music in a corresponding national style (see TABLE 1): Russia, Great Britain and the Commonwealth, and China, ending with France and the resistance movements in other occupied countries. There was a clear attempt to negotiate tricky diplomatic circumstances here; the Russian spokeswoman argued that despite their differences, Russia and United States can be friends united by a common enemy, while the Chinese spokeswoman said that she «forgives» the West for selling materials to the Japanese that could be used for war. But at the end of each vignette, the Principal Voice formally saluted the flag of each nation represented.

---

[58]. NARA, RG 208, Entry 93 Box 612 Folder «Celebration 'United Nations Flag Day' — June 14, 1942». I have consulted the copy in WLRC. A different (seemingly earlier) version of the script in NARA, RG 208 (not further identified), is discussed in BENNETT 2012, pp. 116-117. I am grateful to Andy Lanset, director of the New York Public Radio (WNYC) Archives, for providing me with a recording of the actual program.

[59]. BENÉT 1945, pp. 203-210. A typescript of this addition was appended to the copy of the 'First Revision' script in NARA, RG 208. The 'Prayer' was also published elsewhere, and Eleanor Roosevelt included an extract in her 'My Day' column of 16 June 1942; see <https://www2.gwu.edu/~erpapers/myday/displaydoc.cfm?_y=1942&_f=md056213>, accessed April 2023.

Kurt Weill's 'Song of the Free' (1942)

Table 1: Music Cues in *Toward the Century of the Common Man*
(excluding standard sound effects) as identified in the so-called First Revision of the script. Variants in the final broadcast are noted in square brackets.

Beethoven's 'V' notes [in broadcast: Fifth Symphony, mm. 1-4; continues as underscoring]

«Repeat Beethoven notes, and segue into theme march of broadcast, 'Song of the Free', *forte* and fade. It is not sung at this point. It is used as a transition theme several times, to be sung at the end of broadcast». [In broadcast: 'Song of the Free' was sung by the baritone, with the first stanza fading into underscoring.]

Lullaby («should be well known, and a simple, immediately recognizable melody» [in fact, Brahms])

«Menace» theme [omitted from broadcast]

«Cathedral-organ like iteration of lullaby theme for full orchestra»

«Discord» theme […] *segue* to

«'Dirge' theme, with tolling bell»

«Menace» theme — «Dirge» theme

«Original March theme» (= 'Song of the Free' [omitted from broadcast])

«Red Army Song: 'Border to Border' sung by male chorus» (the Cossack song from Dzerzhinsky's opera *Quiet Flows the Don* [sung in English in broadcast])

'Border to Border' sung by baritone and chorus, in English if possible: «Treat as a set, musical number»

March theme (= 'Song of the Free')

«British theme: 'Waltzing Matilda' with bagpipes» [plus chorus in broadcast]

'Waltzing Matilda' with bagpipes and baritone [plus chorus in broadcast]: «It is a 'number', not just a transition»

March theme (= 'Song of the Free')

«Marching song of China ('Chi Li') sung by chorus long enough to establish»

«Conclusion of 'Chi Li' song, with single voice predominant» [a chorus in the broadcast, sung in English]
March theme (= 'Song of the Free')
The 'Marseillaise' sung by a woman's voice [a male voice in the broadcast]
«March chosen to represent occupied countries. It is sung by male chorus» [new march in broadcast]
March theme (= 'Song of the Free' [omitted from broadcast])
[In broadcast: Beethoven 'V' notes *segue* directly into]
«'Song of the Free', sung by baritone and chorus» [just baritone in broadcast]

This led to a grand peroration. The Principal Voice was asked to identify himself, and the response was that he has been known by many names across the ages, all of whom have fought for Liberty: inevitably, Americans figure prominently. This led to a resounding summons, to quote from Benét's ending and its continuation in the 'First Revision':

> [...] It is I who command men and win battles. I have called them forth in the past, I am calling them forth today. I call the brave to the battle-line, I call the sane to the council — I call the free millions of earth to the century ahead — the century of the common man, established by you, the people. *For this world cannot endure, half slave and half free*[60]!
> My name is FREEDOM and my command today is...
> CHORUS (*unison*): Unite[61]!
> PRINCIPAL VOICE: Unite in brotherhood — for a people's victory!
> CHORUS: Unite!
> PRINCIPAL VOICE: Unite in brotherhood — for a people's peace!

The announcer then cued the presidential address, concluding with a chorus singing *The Star-Spangled Banner*.

According to the opening credits of the broadcast, the actors included Charles Boyer, Joseph Calleia, Ronald Coleman, Ray Collins, Melville Cooper, Peter Lorre, Thomas Mitchell, Alia Nazimova, and Maria Ouspenskaya (all Hollywood notables), with music by Robert Armbruster (also the conductor) and Weill. The singer was operatic baritone Donald Dickson,

---

[60]. The reference is to Abraham Lincoln's 'House Divided Speech' (1858), to which Vice-President Wallace also referred in his address on 8 May 1942.

[61]. The text published by Benét ends here, but the broadcast continued with the ending in the 'First Revision'.

known for his radio broadcasts (including in NBC's *The Chase and Sanborn Hour* in 1939). Armbruster was head of the NBC Hollywood Orchestra as well as a composer and arranger: he probably provided all the music, including the rather flamboyant orchestration of 'Song of the Free' (shorn of its introduction and conclusion) which makes it sound not at all like one might expect for Weill. The other musical choices were predictable enough, including Brahms's 'Lullaby' and characteristic songs for the Russians and Chinese, although 'Waltzing Matilda' with bagpipes may have seemed a quirky choice for the British, even with their Commonwealth extension. 'Song of the Free', however, clearly had pride of place, used at the beginning and end, and serving to link the various episodes, even though some of those links were cut in the actual broadcast. The intention in the script was to have it used initially just in instrumental form, with the full song delivered by a baritone and chorus at the end. One suspects that Weill was involved in that decision, given that he did the same thing of saving the full song to the end in *The Eternal Road* (the 'March to Zion' borrowed for 'Song of the Free'), *Johnny Johnson* ('Johnny's Song'), and *Lady in the Dark* ('My Ship'). However, Armbruster seems to have nixed the idea given that in the broadcast, the first appearance of the song was with the voice. Timing seems to have been an issue as well, for the final presentation of the song included just the first and third stanzas, with a rather awkward break between the two.

On 18 June 1942, William B. Lewis sent a telegram to James C. Petrillo, head of the American Federation of Musicians, requesting permission to release recordings of *Toward the Century of the Common Man* for broadcast on local radio stations without further fees, which was granted[62]. The program also remained in the news. Shortly after the broadcast, Phineas J. Biron, whose gossip column 'Strictly Confidential' was widely syndicated across the Anglo-Jewish press, noted (all the ellipses are in the original)[63]:

> [...] Have you heard 'The Song of the Free' launched on United Nations Day?... If you liked the tune, you'll be glad to know that the composer is a man who can really appreciate the freedom of our country... He's Kurt Weill, who came here only a few years ago as a refugee from Hitlerism... And to show his gratitude, he's donating all royalties from this song to the Red Cross.

MacLeish thought that the song in its new context was «simply marvelous [...] It is really, really good», so he wrote to Weill on 16 June, although he wanted to hear it done first by a male voice and then by a full chorus[64]. Weill was less happy, however, as he replied on the 21st:

---

[62]. NARA, RG 208, General Records of William B. Lewis, July 1941 to April 1943, Box 603.

[63]. Cited from *The American Israelite* (Cincinnati, OH), 18 June 1942, p. 1. Phineas J. Biron was the anagrammatic pseudonym of journalist and writer Joseph Brainin; he tended to keep track of Weill in his columns.

[64]. This letter and subsequent exchanges between MacLeish and Weill returned to MacLeish's 'personal' files in AMP, Box 23 Folder 14.

[...] Personally, I was a little disappointed because they changed the song, cut out one verse, messed up the words and did other things that only Hollywood arrangers would do. I agree with you that the song should be done by a male voice first and then repeated by a full chorus, and I have worked out an arrangement and orchestration on that line. Let's hope that somebody will use it soon[65].

The Aftermath

The review of the Roxy Theatre show in *Variety* noted of 'Song of the Free' that «It's a fairly rousing tune, but a trifle complicated for mass popularity», which is entirely true[66]. Weill may not have been too concerned over the fact that the United States Flag Association approved 'Wave That Flag, America' by Phelps Adams and Howard Acton as the 'Flag Week' song[67]. But a greater threat came from another quarter. 'Song of the Free' was copyrighted on 14 May, and less than two weeks later (on the 25th), so was 'The Hymn of the United Nations' by the prominent leftist Harold Rome, published by the Am-Rus Music Corporation[68]. Weill had already accused Rome (and George Kaufman) of having «taken and used all my ideas» for the *Fun To Be Free* revue (so he wrote to Lenya on 31 January 1942), and it is hard not to suspect something similar going on here. Rome did not write anything new, however: he took Dmitri Shostakovich's well-known 'Song of the Counterplan' (written for the eponymous Russian propaganda movie of 1932), which had also been adopted by the French Popular Front as 'Allons au devant de la vie', with words by Jeanne Perret (1935)[69].

By chance, what Weill called his «anthem» went head-to-head with Rome's «hymn» on Sunday 5 July 1942. 'Song of the Free' was included as the final number in the CBS radio program, 'The Pause that Refreshes on the Air' (sponsored by Coca-Cola), broadcast at 4:30-5:00 p.m. (EST), sung by tenor Frank Parker with Andre Kostelanetz's Orchestra, orchestrated by David Terry[70]. Rome's 'Hymn of the United Nations' was premiered that very same day

---

[65]. It is not clear how the words were «messed up» save by cutting the middle stanza: Dickson sang the text as printed. No arrangement/orchestration by Weill of 'Song of the Free' survives, however, to the best of my knowledge.

[66]. *Variety*, 10 June 1942, p. 23.

[67]. *Billboard*, LIV/23 (6 June 1942), p. 23. The song was published by Broadway Music.

[68]. For Rome's song, see Library of Congress Copyright Office, *Catalog of Copyright Entries. Part III: Musical Compositions*, XXXVII/1 (1942), p. 1070 (E pub. 104826).

[69]. Riley 2004. Another leftist version was Nancy Head's 'Salute to Life' for the British Worker's Music Association (1941). But Rome's new words certainly owe something to the French text.

[70]. North 2011, p. 325. Weill informed MacLeish of the broadcast on 21 June; MacLeish responded on 14 July that he had missed it, «but my secretary heard it and thought it was grand». The program aired in New York on WABC (the CBS station) and affiliates elsewhere (e.g., Washington, DC, and Chicago). Weill sent Kostelanetz

by the baritone Igor Gorin at a concert by the National Symphony Orchestra in Washington, DC, conducted by Charles O'Connell, who did the orchestration. Here it was announced as «Dmitri Shostakovich's new 'Song of the United Nations'» and received to great acclaim[71]. Leopold Stokowski then did a transcription of it as the 'United Nations March'. In turn, Rome's song, with lyrics for the verses (but not the refrain) revised by Yip Harburg, provided the grand finale of the MGM blockbuster movie, *Thousands Cheer* (released on 13 September 1943), as 'United Nations on the March', sung by Kathryn Grayson with an orchestra conducted by José Iturbi and a massed choir standing before the flags of the United Nations and 'V' signs, with segments sung in Russian, Mandarin, and Spanish[72]. Shostakovich was now the favorite foreign modernist composer by virtue of the performances of his 'Leningrad' Symphony in the summer of 1942. Weill made a pointed reference to that symphony in his 'Russian War Relief' song («this latest Shostakovich melody»), written for him and Lenya to perform at a local Rockland County revue on 20 August 1942[73]. But he was not going to be able to compete with Shostakovich on any larger musical platform.

The United Nations Flag Day celebrations on 14 June marked the last hurrah of the OFF given its official replacement the day before by the OWI. MacLeish stepped out of the limelight and his correspondence with Weill gradually fizzled out. Weill's last letter to him in the sequence was written on 8 July, telling him that he thought the Kostelanetz broadcast was «the best performance we've had so far», that the Roxy show was still running, that «We had already a nice number of radio performances», and that Chappell was sending out the choral arrangements. But with Robert Sherwood now as Director of the Overseas Branch of the OWI, and John Houseman as Chief of its Radio Program Bureau, Weill was bound to be shunted to the margins of such official circles. 'Song of the Free' was performed in a German translation by Walter Mehring in the first broadcast of the OWI-supported radio series *We Fight Back: The German-American Loyalty Hour* on 27 September 1942 on WHOM, an AM station operated by the New Jersey Broadcasting Company mostly focused on foreign-language programming[74]. Now that Rome had stolen Weill's thunder, however, the song was destined to lapse into

---

a telegram on 6 July congratulating him on the performance («It was everything a composer could dream of»); see <https://www.loc.gov/item/muskostelanetz.1004989/>, accessed April 2023. The orchestration is in Library of Congress, Washington, DC, Andre Kostelanetz Collection, Box 376 Folder 2.

[71]. '«United Nations Song» Cheered in Capital: Listeners Rise as Gorin Sings New Shostakovich March', in: *NYT*, 6 July 1942, p. 18. Gorin also recorded the song (with O'Connell conducting the Victor Symphony Orchestra) on Victor Red Seal, 11-8250.

[72]. BOMBOLA 2017, pp. 239-250, traces the iterations of this final scene from «a military air» (5 March 1942) through «a song for America at war» (27 April; with Stokowski conducting) to «the United Nations Victory song composed by the gifted modern Russian composer, Dmitri Shostakovich» (29 August).

[73]. FARNETH 2000, p. 215.

[74]. HORTEN 2002, pp. 77-78.

obscurity. Typically undaunted, Weill shifted his wartime contributions in a different, probably more familiar direction, with his energetic and time-consuming contributions to the American Theatre Wing's *Lunchtime Follies* from June 1942 forward[75]. Not until 1944 was he able to regain a toehold in official propaganda efforts, with his score for *Salute to France* and another 'wartime song', 'Wie lange noch?' (to lyrics by Mehring)[76].

'Song of the Free' represents a clear statement of Weill's fervent commitment to the war effort. But it also provides a useful case study of the circumstances that would make, or sometimes break, his career in the United States. He needed constantly to work hard at it, seizing or creating chances with no guarantee of success. But he was heavily reliant on networks that could fail him, on personal relationships that could make it hard to distinguish real friends from fair-weather ones or the enemies working behind his back, and on pure luck. Like many foreigners, he could misread situations and their nuances, making missteps with long-term consequences. He sometimes also had grandiose ideas beyond any capacity to reach fruition. 'Song of the Free' was never going to become a «United Nations Anthem». But one cannot blame Weill for trying.

Bibliography

Benét 1945
Benét, Stephen Vincent. *'We Stand United' and Other Radio Scripts*, New York-Toronto, Farrar and Rinehart, 1945.

Bennett 2012
Bennett, M. Todd. *One World, Big Screen: Hollywood, the Allies, and World War II*, Chapel Hill, University of North Carolina Press, 2012.

Bombola 2017
Bombola, Gina. «*Can't Help Singing*»: *The 'Modern' Opera Diva in Hollywood Film, 1930-1950*, unpublished Ph.D. Diss., Chapel Hill (NC), University of North Carolina, 2017.

Carter 2011
Carter, Tim. 'Celebrating the Nation: Kurt Weill, Paul Green, and the Federal Theatre Project (1937)', in: *Journal of the Society for American Music*, v/3 (2011), pp. 297-334.

Carter 2020
Id. «*Oklahoma!*»: *The Making of an American Musical*, Revised and Expanded Edition, Oxford-New York, Oxford University Press, 2020.

---

[75]. For Weill, the *Lunchtime Follies*, and his subsequent interactions with the OWI, see Fauser 2013, pp. 58-64.
[76]. Stein 2019.

CONN 2009
CONN, Peter. *The American 1930s: A Literary History*, Cambridge-New York, Cambridge University Press, 2009.

DONALDSON 1992
DONALDSON, Scott. *Archibald MacLeish: An American Life*, Boston (MA), Houghton Mifflin, 1992.

FARNETH 2000
FARNETH, David (with Elmar Juchem and Dave Stein). *Kurt Weill: A Life in Pictures and Documents*, Woodstock (NY), The Overlook Press, 2000.

FAUSER 2013
FAUSER, Annegret. *Sounds of War: Music in the United States during World War II*, Oxford-New York, Oxford University Press, 2013.

FAUSER 2014
EAD. 'Music for the Allies: Representations of Nationhood during World War II', in: *Crosscurrents: American and European Music in Interaction, 1900-2000*, edited by Felix Meyer *et al.*, Woodbridge, Boydell, 2014, pp. 247-258.

GADDIS 2000
GADDIS, Eugene R. *Magician of the Modern: Chick Austin and the Transformation of the Arts in America*, New York, Alfred Knopf, 2000.

GRABER 2021
GRABER, Naomi. *Kurt Weill's America*, Oxford-New York, Oxford University Press, 2021.

HAMM 2009
Popular Adaptations of Weill's Music for Stage and Screen, 1927-1950, edited by Charles Hamm, New York, Kurt Weill Foundation for Music / European American Music Corporation, 2009 (The Kurt Weill Edition, IV/2).

HORTEN 2002
HORTEN, Gerd. *Radio Goes to War: The Cultural Politics of Propaganda during World War II*, Berkeley-Los Angeles, University of California Press, 2002.

KOWALKE 2000
KOWALKE, Kim H. '«I'm an American!»: Whitman, Weill, and Cultural Identity', in: *Walt Whitman and Modern Music: War, Desire, and the Trials of Nationhood*, edited by Lawrence Kramer, New York-London, Garland, 2000, pp. 109-131.

LANGGUTH 1994
Norman Corwin's Letters, edited by A. J. Langguth, New York, Barricade Books, 1994.

McClung 2007
McClung, Bruce D. *'Lady in the Dark': Biography of a Musical*, Oxford-New York, Oxford University Press, 2007.

North 2011
North, James H. *Andre Kostelanetz on Records and on the Air: A Discography and Radio Log*, Lanham (MD), The Scarecrow Press, 2011.

Riley 2004
Riley, John. 'From the Factory to the Flat: Thirty Years of the «Song of the Counterplan»', in: *Soviet Music and Society under Lenin and Stalin: The Baton and Sickle*, edited by Neil Edmunds, Abingdon-New York, RoutledgeCurzon, 2004, pp. 67-80.

Schebera 1993
Schebera, Jürgen. 'Der «alien American» Kurt Weill und seine Aktivitäten für den *War Effort* der USA 1940-1945', in: *A Stranger Here Myself: Kurt Weill-Studien*, edited by Kim H. Kowalke and Horst Edler, Hildesheim, Georg Olms, 1993, pp. 267-283.

Schubert 2016
Kurt Weill: 'Mahagonny: Ein Songspiel', edited by Giselher Schubert, New York, Kurt Weill Foundation for Music / European American Music Corporation, 2016 (The Kurt Weill Edition, I/3).

Stein 2019
Stein, Danielle. '*Wie lange noch?*: Kurt Weill and the Allied Propaganda Effort', paper presented at the Forty-fifth Annual Conference of the Society for American Music, New Orleans, 20-24 March 2019.

Symonette – Kowalke 1996
Speak Low (When You Speak Love): The Letters of Kurt Weill and Lotte Lenya, edited and translated by Lys Symonette and Kim H. Kowalke, Berkeley-Los Angeles, University of California Press, 1996.

Thomson 2016
Thomson, Virgil. *The State of Music and Other Writings*, New York, Library of America, 2016.

Reconfigurations

How Many Weills?
Rethinking a Musician's Identity*

Nils Grosch
(Universität Salzburg)

«Who am I anyway?»

Who am I anyway, a God or some kind of genius? asks the persona of a song composed in 1943 by Kurt Weill and Ogden Nash, questioning his own identity after having been rejected as a lover by a woman. 'Who am I?' is one of those cut and unsung songs that fill the drawers of theatre composers like Weill[1].

I do not — as music hermeneutics sometimes used to do — tend to directly link the contents of songs to the inner constitution of a composer — or, in reverse, interpret the meaning of the song by reference to a composer's mental state (which would mean to ignore both the constructed persona of the song and the fact that the composer did not author the lyrics). Yet I find this song an interesting starting point to rethink Weill's identity. This is, firstly, because it leads to the idea of a double identity, which is itself a key trope in the reception of Weill and his oeuvre. And secondly because its musical style stands in sharp contrast to its song persona. The song was initially conceived for the God Vulcan, then for self-proclaimed genius and art dealer Whitelaw Savory, and was ultimately cut completely from the score of the show *One Touch of Venus* (1943). The lyric tone of the melody, molded for a smart womanizer with a velvet operatic baritone voice, stands in striking contrast to the breathless, boogie-woogie accompaniment that nodded to the then fashionable style in popular music and dance — anything but what you might expect from either a Roman God or a 1940s modern art dealer, themselves both originators of the unique, the original, and the creatively self-contained.

In the following, I will blatantly re-employ three lines from the song 'Who am I?' in order to shape my reflections into three sections with three hypotheses. In the first section,

---

[*]. With cordial thanks to Ruard Absaroka, who thoroughly helped with editing this chapter.
[1]. Published in WEILL 2002A.

I develop the hypothesis that Weill actively tried to control the impression that he made on others — be it letter addressees or audiences — and thus controlled his public identity, starting from the idea that identity is not something static but dynamic, and not natural but a result of communication, construction, and performance. In the second, I take the perspective of cultural mobility to challenge the paradigm of the holistic, integral, and organic oeuvre — a paradigm that is the starting point for both those in favor of the 'two Weills thesis' as well as for those who espouse the notion of a unified oeuvre. In the third section, I offer a reading of Weill's self-representation as mobile.

The question «Who am I?» might also be the starting point for a theatre character to introduce him or herself, a classical character song. In Weill and Brecht's theatre, character songs contain direct statements such as

Anna I, in *Die sieben Todsünden**

My twin sister and I come from Lou'siana	Meine Schwester und ich stammen aus Louisiana
Where the big Mississippi River ripples in the moonlight...	wo die Wasser des Mississippi unterm Monde fließen...
And we're really feeling homesick	Dorthin wollen wir zurückkehren,
We can't wait to get back there.	lieber heute als morgen.

*. BRECHT, 1982.

or

Charles Lindbergh, in *Der Lindberghflug**

My grandfather was Swedish. I am an American.   Mein Großvater war Schwede. Ich bin Amerikaner.

*. BRECHT 1978.

or

Jenny, in *Aufstieg und Fall der Stadt Mahagonny**

I come from Havana	Ich bin aus Havanna,
But my mother was white and well-born.	meine Mutter war eine Weiße.

*. BRECHT 1977.

In each of those cases, origin is central for the introduction of the persona, and fulfills a specific function in the processes of addressing and of impression management (in the music psychology sense): Anna introduces herself and her sister as a traveling couple, strongly identifying with a homeland to which they wish to return. Charles Lindbergh's relation to two continents can be read as directly related to his transatlantic flight. And Jenny the sex worker establishes that, despite her origin from a multi-racial nation, she has a higher market value because of her white mother (at least in the racial economies of Berlin in 1931). Whereas Anna and Lindbergh address the information to the audience, Jenny's statement is first and foremost for Jakob Schmidt, with the express purpose of raising the price for her services.

How Many Weills? Rethinking a Musician's Identity

So let us see how Weill introduced himself, and if origin has any bearing in how he did this. In his 1922 letter introducing himself to the music director of the Donaueschinger Kammermusik, which turned out to be a landmark event for contemporary music in the early 1920s, Weill outlines his identity as follows: «Ich stamme aus Freiburg i.Br., bin 22 Jahre alt und gehöre zur Meisterklasse von Ferruccio Busoni»[2].

Of course, in those years Weill was a member of Busoni's master class at the Berlin Academy of Arts. But the other details are not accurate: not only was he not yet 22 (his 22nd birthday was more than a week after this letter), nor was he born or raised in Freiburg. Of course, we could read this false ascription as a hint of his life-long difficult relationship to the town of his birth, Dessau. The fact is that before moving to Dessau, his family had lived in Kippenheim and Ettlingen (where also his eldest brother was born), over 40 kilometers to the north of the city of Freiburg. But this is also not an adequate explanation. Remarkably, in an interview from 1941, he traced his family back to 1329, Freiburg[3]. But why did this young musician use a genealogical rather than a biographical attribution of his origin for introducing himself in such an important letter addressed to a gatekeeper of one of the most influential institutions for contemporary music? I presume that in mentioning the city of Freiburg, he intended to hint at a shared cultural identity and origin under the Grand Duchy of Baden, to which the principality of Donaueschingen belonged, as did the city of Freiburg until the end of World War I. In actual fact, the Weimar Republic had abrogated nobility in all German territories, and so the Grand Duchy of Baden and the Principality of Donaueschingen had ceased to exist. But former nobles continued, nevertheless, to use the emblems of nobility, as did Max Egon of Donaueschingen, with the help of the Donaueschingen Festival, to which the young Weill was commending himself in this letter. Of course, the festival was nothing but a staging of noble cultural patronage[4]. And this fact framed a whole system of music sponsorship that aspiring young composers of the interwar years strove to access. Weill, who already as a young man was a staunch democrat who despised nobility, and later confessed that he despised the «snobbery» of the festival[5], nevertheless feigned his allegiance to the former house of Baden.

As we learn from the sociologist Ervin Goffman[6], the representation of self in face-to-face or interpersonal communication has a lot to do with identity management, in which the communicator's persona reflects the position of the person they are addressing. Assuming that «the issues dealt with by stage craft and stage management are sometimes trivial but they are quite general», Goffman concluded in 1959 that «they seem to occur everywhere in social life». Thus, he explains that

---

[2]. «I come from Freiburg i.Br., I am 22 years old and I belong to Ferruccio Busoni's master class». WEILL 1922.
[3]. *BIOGRAPHY OF KURT WEILL* 1945.
[4]. GROSCH 2021.
[5]. WEILL 2002B, p. 53.
[6]. GOFFMAN 1959, p. 26.

> [...] when an individual appears before others he will have many motives for trying to control the impression they receive of the situation. This report is concerned with some of the common techniques that persons employ to sustain such impressions and with some of the common contingencies associated with the employment of these techniques[7].

Here, we see Weill as a young musician standing in front of the gateway to an institution that could prove key for his career, endeavoring to raise the value of his person in the eyes of his addressee, just as Jenny did, by constructing a certain origin and controlling the impression he gives of himself.

This is also important for the reading of Weill's statements regarding national belonging. When he gave an interview for the series 'I'm an American' in 1941, he declared: «I never felt as much at home in my native land as I have from the first moment in the United States»[8]. This may sound to us very much like a wholehearted commitment to American identity, especially when he adds that he «never felt more enthusiastic about any idea than I feel about the American way of life»[9]. Nevertheless, we have to keep in mind that this interview was clearly intended to convey exactly this impression. It was conducted by the U.S. Department of the Interior in collaboration with the National Broadcasting Company, and was one of a series of interviews with recently nationalized immigrants. As the title 'I'm an American!' illustrates, the very aim of the series was to promote the success of the United States by showing that foreign nationals enthusiastically adopted its way of life. Consequently, in his statement in this interview, he strove not only to reinforce his commitment to American values, but also to convey a longer continuity to his identification with America, an identification he claims to have experienced before his immigration.

> Berlin in the years after the First World War was, in spirit, the most American city in Europe. We liked everything we knew about this country. [...] One of my most successful operas, *The Rise and Fall of the City Mahagonny*, was about an American city. We even wrote two songs in English for this opera. Strangely enough, when I arrived in this country, I found that our description of this country was quite accurate in many ways[10].

Of course, this gives the impression of a downright visionary and affirmative Americanism, if we presume that most of the audience for this interview had no idea what *Mahagonny* is about. In fact, *Mahagonny* depicts a city marked by brutal capitalism and corruption — a background

---

[7]. *Ibidem*.
[8]. WEILL 1941.
[9]. *Ibidem*.
[10]. *Ibidem*.

that, given that this «description of this country was quite accurate in many ways» suggests anything but enthusiasm about the American way of life, or about the supposed «decency and humanity in the world» which he associated with the U.S. in a letter to his friends and neighbors Mab and Maxwell Anderson on 22 June 1947[11]. Thus, by mentioning *Mahagonny*, Weill gives his statement an underlying second meaning, which only those who knew that work were able to decode.

In another interview of the same year, Weill returned to the affirmative formula that he had used in the interview quoted above, but now leaves out the continuity narrative of his already pre-War Americanness:

> It's strange, our family goes back to 1329 to Freiburg and I lived in different parts of Germany till I was thirty-five. Yet I never felt the one-ness with my native country that I do with the United States; the moment I landed here I felt as though I'd come home[12].

When Peter Gay used this quote, in his introductory chapter for *Driven into Paradise*, he clarified, with a wink: «The statement sounds like one a press agent would dream up. But», he adds «I believe he made it himself, and that he meant it»[13].

Why this uncritical trust in finally having found Weill's 'real' identity?

The problem is in the concept of identity itself. In cultural disciplines, identity has been read as an aspiration, a premeditation, that can never become a presumption that can be reified (as Jürgen Straub stated convincingly)[14].

In Stuart Hall's words, cultural identity «is always constructed through memory, fantasy, narrative, and myth. Cultural identities are the unstable points of identification or structure, which are made, within the discourses of history and culture. Not an essence, but a positioning»[15]. This premise challenges the existence of identities and also their often-implied durability and stability — in the sense of being true to oneself — as being anything beyond mere discursive aspiration. Instead, such a perspective emphasizes the constructedness of identities as well as the socio-psychological and discursive mechanisms of impression management and of the construction, negotiation, and performance of this identity.

In the case of Weill, who always experimented with genres and was thus not easily pigeonholed by critics, the choice of genres, styles, and collaborations depended upon the anticipated impact that a specific project would have on his own public image. For instance, as I

---

[11]. Quoted in Kowalke 1993, p. 56.
[12]. *Biography of Kurt Weill* 1945.
[13]. Gay 1999, p. 31.
[14]. Straub 2011, p. 279.
[15]. Hall 1990, p. 226.

have pointed out in my chapter on opera as strategy of self-representation and gentrification — partly drawing on Kim Kowalke's observations on 'Weill and the Quest for American Opera' — the designation of *Street Scene* (1947) or of *West Side Story* (1957) as either a musical or an opera was less based on the structure of these works but on a discursive localization of their respective composers against the backdrop of shifting status of the genres in the 1940s and 1950s respectively. Such positioning positioned Weill (and later, Leonard Bernstein) as an American national composer of operas[16].

***

When Weill was approached in 1929 by the dramatist Stefan Grossmann about a potential collaboration on an experimental popular musical for Berlin, one that would include a small number of Lieder (to be composed by Weill), he discussed the offer with his publisher, the Universal Edition A.G. His main concern was the potential impact of such a collaboration on his public image as a composer:

> What appeals to me about this is the following: I can show myself here from a completely different perspective with a minimum of loss of time (I can do the few Lieder in about a week); there are no songs, no "hits", no American milieu, it is completely outside the production circle of my last theatrical works. I would consider this to be of crucial importance prior to *Mahagonny*, otherwise I would soon be accused of a certain one-sidedness[17].

Here we again see Weill's overarching preoccupation with the public reception of his artistic persona as an Americanized composer, and his wariness of being pigeonholed based on his so-called 'Songstil'. For this very reason, he tried to distance himself from his 'Americanized' style in composition and subject matter:

> The vast majority of *Mahagonny* is already completely detached from the song style and already shows this new style, which in regard of seriousness, of "greatness" and expressiveness surpasses everything I have done so far. Almost everything that has been added to the Baden-Baden version is written in a completely pure, thoroughly responsible style, which I firmly assume will last longer than most of what is produced today. *Happy End* has also been completely misunderstood in this regard. Pieces like the *Großer Heilsarmeemarsch* and the *Matrosensong* go far beyond the song character, and the whole music is formally, instrumentally and melodically such a clear continuation beyond *Die Dreigroschenoper* that only helpless ignoramuses

---

[16]. GROSCH 2016.
[17]. WEILL 2002B, pp. 191ff.

How Many Weills? Rethinking a Musician's Identity

like the German critics could overlook it. This is a major development that has not stood still for a moment and which, as you can correctly see, has now made a new advance in the new *Mahagonny* scene and in the *Lindberghflug*[18].

In 1932, when pondering about a collaboration with Erik Charell, Weill was still focused on the uninterrupted subsequent development of his own oeuvre: «The subject matter, that he [Charell] suggested is located so far from everything I have done hitherto, thus I would have to delicately interrupt the consequent development of my works»[19].

On the one hand, we can interpret these arguments as the composer's struggle to construct a self-contained oeuvre, which in itself shows an organic aesthetic identity, not only regarding musical style, but also genre. But we must add two important observations: First, this oeuvre is not conceived as a static unit, but as a line. *Linie*, in German, is the metaphor that returns over and over again in the letters to his publisher to describe the development in his works of the late 1920s and the early 30s. For Weill, the 'line' is, in contrast to a self-contained concept of 'oeuvre', a dynamic development, fluid regarding both style and genre. Second, it is always molded and changed in reflection of, and in interaction with, the demands not only of the audience but also of social and political change that, in Weill's eyes, make certain decisions necessary.

«Is there anyone in the house who would care for an extra identity?»

For musicologists grappling with questions about Weil's identity, there have been few notions as influential as David Drew's assertion that Weill had «done away with his old creative self in order to make way for a new one»[20]. Of course, the so-called 'two Weills thesis', so frequently discussed that I don't need to explain it here[21], reflects a fundamental point in exile discourse, especially regarding émigré artists' biographies, raising the question of whether emigration left its traces in the creative output of an artist, and if one can thus detect a fragmented oeuvre, marked by mobility.

The wish for a homogeneous or integral oeuvre is conditioned by the tendency, to be found in most biographic narratives, to depict personalities as consistent or integrated. Stephen Hinton elaborated that aspect convincingly:

> Biography, as a genre, tends to be implicated in establishing, confirming or reducing the reputation of a figure, deemed historically or culturally significant.

---

[18]. *Ibidem*, pp. 194ff.
[19]. *Ibidem*, p. 392.
[20]. Drew 1980.
[21]. See Hinton 1993, Kowalke 1995, Levitz 1996.

> Composer biographies are no exception, often presented as hagiographies, as tales of artistic integrity on the highest level. [...] Biographers are bound to make critical judgements based on certain expectations: on aesthetic criteria as well as on conceptions of personal identity and individuality[22].

In her study of biographies of musicians, Melanie Unseld has pointed out that «the connection between biography and work was seen as 'natural' in the early nineteenth century, and thus biographic and music-analytical or music aesthetic writing could not be separated»[23]. In biographies of émigré artists such as Weill, this implies certain consequences for the evaluation of art works derived from the person's character. It also, vice versa, creates space for a distrust of a person's integrity, occasioned by observations of aesthetic re-orientations in his or her creations or artistic development.

Nineteenth century biographic narratives also include another axiom that is still present the treatment of historic personae today: the heroic approach in biographical writing, that, as Unseld has shown, is still molded by nationalist discourse[24]. This is the reason why origin is so important in the reception and institutionalization of music — it binds composers' names to spaces. In his 2010 book on mobility, human geographer Peter Adey alerts us to the fact that «Music is marketed through place, while places are marketed through music»[25]. In his introduction to cultural mobility, literature scholar Stephen Greenblatt exposed a fundamental problem in the unspoken assumption of cultural disciplines, that they

> [...] have taken for granted the stability of cultures, or at least have assumed that in their original or natural state, before they are disrupted or contaminated, cultures are properly rooted in the rich soil of blood and land and that they are virtually motionless. Particular cultures are routinely celebrated for their depth, authenticity, and wholeness, while others are criticized for shallowness, disorientation, and incoherence. A sense of 'at-homeness' is often claimed to be the necessary condition for a robust cultural identity[26].

The idea of culture being bound to places, in other words, the concept that the right place for a person, as for a work of art, is where he/she/it comes from, belongs to the field of fixity, in cultural politics as well as in cultural scholarship. But the perception of fixity, as Adey points out, is an illusion, for the normal condition in human history is that of mobility. Fixity is what

---

[22]. HINTON 2003, p. 212.
[23]. UNSELD 2014, 13ff.
[24]. *Ibidem*, pp. 23ff.
[25]. ADEY 2010, p. 196.
[26]. GREENBLATT 2010, p. 3.

How Many Weills? Rethinking a Musician's Identity

Ulrich Beck has called a «Zombie category»: «alive-death categories, that float around in our heads and focus our view to realities, that are more and more about to disappear»[27].

This is clearly the basis on which critics of Weill, like David Drew or Theodor W. Adorno, have argued, and it reveals an important aspect of the critics' problem with Weill's later works. From their perspective, the inner concept of the authentic Weill is bound to his German homeland: here he established the real nucleus of whatever can be seen in his authentic personal style. Nevertheless, this conception of authenticity (one which relies on the inner nature of individuals and which considers their art to be independent of interpersonal construction) is itself a zombie category. With such a starting point, the evaluation of Weill's post-1935 creations depends entirely upon the question of whether we can find elements of continuity from his pre-1935 period. If we are lucky in finding them, we can proclaim Weill to have stayed true to himself, we can invert Drew's assessment, whilst accepting and reaffirming the problematic paradigm on which it is based.

«The Time has come to face realities»

«Habit is like a fluffy blanket», the philosopher Vilém Flusser wrote in his book *The Freedom of the Migrant*, «a blanket that covers over reality as it exists»[28]. «Discovery begins as soon as the blanket is pulled away. Everything is then seen as unusual» he continues[29]. Thus, Flusser explains his hypothesis of the creativity of exile: «In exile, everything is perceived to be undergoing change, and the expellee perceives absolutely everything as a challenge to himself to be changed»[30]. The debate about host countries' influences on émigré composers already was vigorous in the 1940s and 50s. When asked about the influences of the experience of exile on artistic production, composer Ernst Krenek brought the core issue to the fore when he remarked in 1950: «We shall never know what they [the exiled composers] would have written if they had not come to America»[31]. The very notion of an artistic development fragmented by emigration reveals the unstated ideal behind it: an aesthetic development free of interruption, indeed, in case of doubt, free from environmental influences, if not an ideally static, essentialized aesthetic identity. Anyway, the communicative artistic interaction with the environment for the purpose of self-positioning and orientation in the (cultural, national, aesthetic, social) setting (e.g. in a host society), also and especially with the help of artistic means, is dynamic and mobile from

---

[27]. Beck – Willms 2000, p. 16.
[28]. Flusser 2003, pp. 81ff.
[29]. *Ibidem*, p. 82.
[30]. *Ibidem*, p. 83.
[31]. Quoted in Goldberg 1950.

scratch. And for composers like Weill and Krenek, who complained that other, mostly older colleagues had lost contact with their environment, it was a positive component of artistic activity already in the 1920s.

After his emigration, Weill himself initially struggled to construct an image of himself and his creativity that was based more on mobility than on local belonging or citizenship[32]. The word exile usually embraces the concept of at-home-ness and belonging to the place of origin, as I have explained elsewhere[33], but rarely occurs in Weill's self-reflection. In 1934, when Weill lived in France, the Danish journalist Ole Winding conducted an interview with Weill, subsequently published under the headline 'Kurt Weill in Exile'. In his self-representation, Weill, tongue-in-cheek, subverted this concept of exile by constructing a narrative that explained his emigration to France as a consequence of a «change of air» that he had felt necessary already before the Nazi threat. «So, before Hitler and the Nazis thought of re-inventing me, I myself had that idea. I travelled abroad without the slightest bitterness, and, of course, hoping to return in course of time; but anyway with the certainty of being allowed to love my fatherland at least as much as [the] contemporary German patriots do». When asked by the interviewer if this would almost imply that exile was kind of a service, Weill reportedly answered with an undefinable smile, responding: «Why shouldn't we view it that way?»[34]. Although we may doubt the reliability of the biographical anecdote, I would like to emphasize the double entendre of this quote and underline the legitimate insistence upon the agency of a migrant, even in a situation of threat and flight.

This is also true for when he resisted being called a German composer, as he did in 1947 in a column in *Life* magazine upon the occasion of the premiere of *Street Scene*. Vigorously, he responded:

> Although I was born in Germany, I do not consider myself a 'German composer'. The Nazis obviously did not consider me as such either and I left their country (an arrangement which suited both me and my rulers admirably) in 1933[35].

Here he again repeats the alleged agreement between the Nazis and himself, in a rhetorical figure we similarly find in other émigré musicians' self-representations to the American public. The musicologist Alfred Einstein in 1950 described his forced emigration as a decisive liberation that ultimately led him, at the end of his life, to the position that had been denied him long

---

[32]. After 1941 he tended to campaign for a more «local belonging». We can observe that shift if we compare his portrayals of himself in the program for *Lady in the Dark* to the one in *One Touch of Venus*; see GRABER 2021, pp. 174, 193.

[33]. GROSCH 2019.

[34]. WEILL 2000, p. 459.

[35]. WEILL 1947A; see also WEILL 2000, pp. 186ff.

before the Nazis came to power in his homeland. And he repeated his cynicism in an interview in *Time* magazine:

> When he found his German colleagues had become nonentities in brown uniforms, he decided he "couldn't stand it any longer". [...] Now Einstein looks on his years as a music critic as a "nightmare" when he had time to be "only a bricklayer in musicology". By chasing him out of his rut and back to work as a master mason in music scholarship, Adolf Hitler, he says, became 'my greatest benefactor'[36].

Such rhetoric emphasizes that the development of his academic potential had been decisively hindered by the prevailing anti-Semitism long before 1933, but that, on the other hand, it was only the life-threatening situation of the Holocaust that resulted in emigration. Being «chased out of his rut», as Einstein put it, can be understood as the flip side of the coin to what Vilem Flusser understood as the «creativity of exile». This is Flusser's hypothesis:

> The expellee has been torn out of his accustomed surroundings or has torn himself out of them. In our accustomed surroundings we notice only change, not what remains constant. [...] But in exile everything is unusual. Before defending my hypothesis, I wish to draw attention to the fact that it advances a positive valuation of expulsion. In a situation in which we have become used to pitying expellees, such a positive valuation is itself unusual and should therefore, according to the hypothesis, be informative per se. [...] This statement in no way justifies the expellers but actually demonstrates their vulgarity. Expellees were disturbing factors and were removed to make the surroundings even more ordinary than before. However, the statement does pose the question of whether the expellers might not really have done a service to the expellees, although neither of them intended this outcome[37].

Thus, the narratives, laid out by Einstein, Flusser, or Weill depicting their own expulsion as a service done for them, can be understood as a claim to underline émigrés' agency (and interpretational sovereignty of their identity). In Flusser's words, this «represents a dialectical transformation in the relationship between the expellee and the expeller. Before that discovery, the expeller is the active pole; the expellee the passive. Afterward, the expeller becomes the victim and the expellee, the perpetrator»[38].

In the multiple self-representations Weill gave in articles and interviews, we always find him telling a story of continuation and agency, even through expulsion and exile. Even his reference to the Americanist fashions, topics, and styles in his Berlin works, mentioned earlier,

---

[36]. Quoted in ANON. 1950.
[37]. FLUSSER 2003, pp. 81ff.
[38]. *Ibidem*, p. 85.

can be read as a narrative more about the mobility of his own thinking and aesthetic goals, than, as it may seem on first sight, about his claims to «Americanness». The same is even true in his 1947 statement:

> Ever since I made up my mind, at the age of 19, that my special field of activity would be the theatre, I have tried continuously to solve, in my own way, the form-problems of the musical theatre, and through the years I have approached these problems from all different angles[39].

Hinton reads this as a statement that Weill «wants us to acknowledge the plurality of his oeuvre, to appreciate how theatre always makes the same kinds of demands, yet ones that can be met in various ways»[40]. I would add that Weill also reminds as that music and theatre are mobile forms of art. They cannot be appreciated for their fixed and static identity, but on the contrary, for their suitability, indeed their willingness to be taken along, modified, and re-negotiated.

Bibliography

Adey 2010
Adey, Peter. *Mobility*, Abingdon-New York, Routledge, 2010.

Anon. 1950
Anon. 'Music: a Store of Knowledge', in: *Time*, 24 April 1950, <content.time.com/time/subscriber/article/0,33009,812281,00.html>, accessed April 2023.

Beck – Willms 2000
Beck, Ulrich – Willms, Johannes. *Freiheit oder Kapitalismus: Gesellschaft neu denken*, Frankfurt, Suhrkamp, 2000.

Biography of Kurt Weill 1945
Biography of Kurt Weill, Three-page unpublished typescript, dated April 20, 1945, held in the Yale Music Library, Weill-Lenya Papers, box 74, folder 4, p. 2. Transcript <https://www.kwf.org/pages/wt-biography-breof-kurt-weill.html>, accessed April 2023.

Brecht 1977
Brecht, Bertolt. *Rise and Fall of the City of Mahagonny*, translated by Michael Feingold, in: Id. *Collected Plays. Volume 2*, edited by Ralph Manheim and John Willett, New York, Vintage Books, 1977.

---

[39]. Weill 1947b.
[40]. Hinton 2003, p. 214.

Brecht 1978
Id. *Der Lindberghflug*, translated by Lys Symonette, Weill-Lenya Research Center, Ser.20/L6/1978/Eng.

Brecht 1982
Id. *The Seven Deadly Sins*, translated by Michael Feingold, Weill-Lenya Research Center, Ser.20/S2/1982/Eng.

Drew 1980
Drew, David. 'Weill, Kurt', in: *The New Grove Dictionary of Music and Musicians*, edited by Stanley Sadie, London, MacMillan, ⁶1980, vol. xx, pp. 300-310.

Flusser 2003
Flusser, Vilém. *The Freedom of the Migrant. Objections to Nationalism*, Urbana-Chicago, University of Illinois Press, 2003.

Gay 1999
Gay, Peter. '«We miss our Jews»: The Musical Migration from Nazi Germany', in: *Driven into Paradise: The Musical Migration from Nazi Germany to the United States*, edited by Reinhold Brinkmann and Christoph Wolff, Berkeley (CA), University of California Press, 1999, pp. 21-30.

Goffman 1959
Goffman, Erving. *The Presentation of Self in Everyday Life*, New York, Anchor Books, 1959.

Goldberg 1950
Goldberg, Albert. 'The Transplanted Composer', in: *Los Angeles Times*, 21 Mai 1950, n.p., <http://www.zeisl.com/essays-and-articles/the-reception-of-austrian-composers-in-los-angeles.htm>, accessed April 2023.

Graber 2021
Graber, Noami. *Kurt Weill's America*, Oxford-New York, Oxford University Press, 2021.

Greenblatt 2010
Greenblatt, Stephen. *Cultural Mobility: A Manifesto*, with Ines G. Županov, Reinhard Meyer-Kalkus, Heike Paul, Pál Nyíri, and Friederike Pannewick, Cambridge-New York, Cambridge University Press, 2010.

Grosch 2016
Grosch, Nils. 'Oper als Strategie der kompositorischen Selbstinszenierung und Wertbegriff: *Street Scene* (1946) und *West Side Story* (1957)', in: *In Search for the «Great American Opera»: Tendenzen des amerikanischen Musiktheaters*, edited by Frédéric Döhl and Gregor Herzfeld, Münster, Waxmann, 2016, pp. 101-112.

Grosch 2019
Id. 'Exil und kulturelle Mobilität: Ernst Krenek und Kurt Weill', in: *Zeitgenossenschaft: Ernst Krenek und Kurt Weill im Netzwerk der Moderne*, edited by Matthias Henke, Schliengen, Argus, 2019, pp. 175-182.

Grosch 2021
Id. 'Die Donaueschinger Kammermusik 1921-1926 und die Medienkultur der Weimarer Republik', in: *Laboratorium der Neuen Musik: Die Donaueschinger Kammermusiktage 1921-1926*, edited by Simon Obert and Matthias Schmidt, Basel, Schwabe, 2021 (Resonanzen, 4), pp. 137-151.

Hall 1990
Hall, Stuart. 'Cultural Identity and Diaspora', in: *Identity: Community, Culture, Difference*, edited by Jonathan Rutherford, London, Lawrence & Wishart, 1990, pp. 222-237.

Hinton 1993
Hinton, Stephen. 'Fragwürdiges in der deutschen Rezeption', in: *A Stranger here Myself: Kurt-Weill-Studien*, edited by Kim H. Kowalke and Horst Edler, Hildesheim, Olms, 1993, pp. 23-33.

Hinton 2003
Id. 'Kurt Weill: Life, Work, and Posterity', in: *Amerikanismus - Americanism - Weill: die Suche nach kultureller Identität in der Moderne*, edited by Hermann Danuser and Hermann Gottschewski, Schliengen, Argus, 2003, pp. 209-220.

Kowalke 1993
Kowalke, Kim H. 'Formerly German: Kurt Weill in America', in: *A Stranger here Myself: Kurt-Weill-Studien, op. cit.*, pp. 35-57.

Kowalke 1995
Id. 'Kurt Weill, Modernism, and Popular Culture: Öffentlichkeit als Stil', in: *Modernism/modernity*, II/1 (1995), pp. 27-69.

Levitz 1996
Levitz, Tamara. '«Junge Klassizität» zwischen Fortschritt und Reaktion Ferruccio Busoni, Philipp Jarnach und die deutsche Weill-Rezeption', in: *Kurt-Weill-Studien*, edited by Nils Grosch, Joachim Lucchesi, and Jürgen Schebera, Stuttgart, Metzler & Poeschel, 1996, pp. 9-37.

Straub 2011
Straub, Jürgen. 'Identität', in: *Handbuch der Kulturwissenschaften. 1*, edited by Friedrich Jaeger and Burkhard Liebsch, Stuttgart, Metzler, pp. 277-303.

Unseld 2014
Unseld, Melanie. *Biographie und Musikgeschichte: Wandlungen biographischer Konzepte in Musikkultur und Musikhistoriographie*, Cologne-Vienna, Böhlau, 2014 (Biographik. Theorie, Kritik, Praxis, 3).

Weill 1922
Weill, Kurt. *Letter to Heinrich Burkard*, 22 February 1922, Donaueschingen Music Archives, quoted with kind permission.

How Many Weills? Rethinking a Musician's Identity

Weill 1941
Id. *I'm an American*, Radio program broadcast March 9, 1941 on NBC Blue Network. Transcribed from audiocassette held by the Weill-Lenya Research Center, Ser.122/3. <https://www.kwf.org/pages/wt-im-an-american.html>, accessed April 2023.

Weill 1947a
Id. 'Gentle Beef', in: *Life*, xxii/11 (17 March 1947), p. 17, <https://www.kwf.org/kurt-weill/recommended/gentle-beef/>, accessed April 2023.

Weill 1947b
Id. [Liner Notes for the Original Cast Recording of *Street Scene*], *Street Scene*, Columbia Masterworks set M-MM-683, 1947, <https://www.kwf.org/kurt-weill/recommended/liner-notes-for-the-original-cast-recording-of-street-scene/>, accessed April 2023.

Weill 2000
Id. *Musik und musikalisches Theater. Gesammelte Schriften*, Mainz, Schott, 2000.

Weill 2002a
Id. *Unsung Weill: 22 Songs; Cut from Broadway Shows and Hollywood Films*, edited by Elmar Juchem, European American Music Corporation, 2002.

Weill 2002b
Id. *Briefwechsel mit der Universal Edition Wien*, edited by Nils Grosch, Stuttgart, Metzler, 2002.

Changes in Kurt Weill's Music: Cross-Cultural Reception between Jazz and Avant-garde

Leo Izzo
(Università degli Studi di Udine)

This article examines how jazz musicians, especially those in the U.S. between 1940 and 1965, drew on Kurt Weill's music, with a coda devoted to his Italian interpreters. Before taking into account musical recordings and historical facts, it is crucial to focus on two sets of issues. The first is a lexical one and concerns what is meant by the term 'jazz'. 'Jazz' is a very fluid category that refers to different phenomena depending on the historical period, place, and cultural context. Throughout the article, the term 'jazz' will encompass its broadest meaning, which may include also musical practices that lie at the boundaries of the concept of 'jazz music', such as the European light music bands that played jazz repertoire in the 1920s and the academically trained composers who included stylistic references to jazz in their scores in the 1950s.

The second issue concerns the cultural and geographical contexts of the reception of Weill's music. The story of how jazz musicians have reinterpreted Weill's works begins, understandably, with his productions for Broadway and takes place predominantly in the U.S. music scene. However, the reception of Weill's works in Western Europe took a different course. This paper will pay particular attention to the Italian case. When the fascist regime ended in Italy, a group of left wing intellectuals (including theatre directors, playwrights, literary critics, and composers) considered Bertolt Brecht's theatre as a political and aesthetic reference point. In the early 1950s, some of them worked together to popularize Weill's and Brecht's works, achieving remarkable results. This interest in Weimar's theatrical productions also resulted in some new jazz arrangements of Weill's songs, recorded by Italian musicians.

Jazz Performances of Kurt Weill's Broadway Songs

Although the first jazz-influenced recording of Weill's songs appeared in Germany as early as 1929 (which will be discussed later), the long-lasting interest of jazz performers in Weill's music started after his first work in American mainstream commercial theatre, *Lady in the Dark*, in 1941. The first jazz rendition of one of his songs is also one of the most interesting cases: in 1941, swing singer Mildred Bailey recorded Weill's 'The Saga of Jenny', with contributions from the harmony choir The Delta Rhythm Boys (Decca, 1941). In *Lady in the Dark*, Weill and Ira Gershwin conceived the musical sequences as the dreams or reveries of the protagonist Liza who recounts them during her psychoanalytic therapy. Liza, the editor-in-chief of a fashion magazine, suffers from constant indecision in her professional and personal life. In 'The Saga of Jenny', she tells the story of an imaginary female character who is capable, unlike her, of making up her mind. As Naomi Graber explains in her *Kurt Weill's America*,

> As Liza descends into the depths of her psyche, her music becomes progressively more "primitive" and "exotic". She starts in the idealized "white" world of operetta, passes through "brown" in the second dream, and finally finds herself in "black" musical context, each time coming closer and closer to her submerged sexuality. [...] Liza finally unleashes herself in 'The Saga of Jenny', a blues-inspired number that Lawrence turned into a bump-and-grind performance, which Hart remembered as almost a "strip tease"[1].

The exotic connotation, sexual innuendo, and sense of risk that characterize 'The Saga of Jenny' are reminiscent of the Broadway blues specialty number, where female stars get a chance to be sexy, usually with a strophic ballad about a 'bad girl'. Although not using the traditional 12-bar blues form, Weill draws on many typical blues stylistic features, as Graber remarks: swung rhythms and blue notes (e.g., the oscillation between perfect fifths and sharp fourths/flat fifths). More likely, for this song Weill drew on blues-oriented jazz music from the 1920s, such as the style that was in vogue at the Cotton Club in Harlem and which became famous with the bands of Duke Ellington and Cab Calloway[2]. The music accompanying Cotton Club's exotic shows featured mostly minor-key, dark-sounding tunes and, usually, a trumpet or trombone solo with guttural and growl sounds. In particular, the melody and chords of the chorus of 'The Saga of Jenny' have several elements in common with 'Minnie the Moocher', Cab Calloway's 1931 hit. Both are in a minor key, with a succession of chords insistently echoing the tonic (C minor in 'The Saga of Jenny', E minor in 'Minnie the Moocher'), in both songs the vocal line accentuates the bluesy effect of the flat fifth, and the lead vocals alternate with a chorus. As Nate Sloan explains, «Calloway reused the harmonic structure and instrumental introduction of Louis Armstrong's recording of 'St. James Infirmary' and based the lyrics on 'Willie the Weeper', a vaudeville tune about a drug-addled chimney sweeper that had been recorded by Frankie "Half-Pint" Jaxon in 1927»[3].

---

[1]. GRABER 2021, pp. 181-182.
[2]. See WOIDECK 2017.
[3]. SLOAN 2019, p. 381.

Changes in Kurt Weill's Music

The similarities between the songs of Weill, Calloway, and 'Half-Pint' Jaxon are striking. All of them begin with a narrator in the act of telling a story. For his lyrics, Calloway quoted the opening of 'Willie the Weeper' directly, substituting the name of the protagonist: «Folks here's a story 'bout Minnie the Moocher», while the lyrics by Ira Gershwin in 'The Saga of Jenny' begin with «There once was a girl named Jenny». All songs feature a girl with uninhibited sexuality. In 'Willie the Weeper', there is only a brief mention, «He told the gal who's dancing to make it kind of jerky», while in 'Minnie the Moocher' the female dancer becomes the main character of the story: «She was a red-hot hoochie-coocher»[4]. Finally, in all three songs, the telling of a dream is an important feature: 'Willie the Weeper' is, basically, a dream narrative, and, in Calloway's song, Minnie's drug-related misadventures are interrupted to describe a dream: «She had a dream about the King of Sweden / He gave her things that she was needin'». Calloway also performed this song in the Betty Boop cartoon *Minnie the Moocher* (1932)[5]. The cave scene, featuring both Calloway and Betty Boop, is characterized by exoticism, danger, otherness, and sexual disinhibition that white concertgoers experienced firsthand in Harlem Cotton Club during the 1920s and 1930s. Teenage Betty Boop, straying from her safe family environment, enters a dark cave and encounters Calloway (depicted as a ghostly walrus) and other frightening characters in a hallucinatory nightmare.

Despite the similarities between these songs, no direct source confirms that Weill drew on 'Minnie the Moocher' to write his piece. More likely, in his search for widespread stylistic features in the African American musical tradition, Weill drew on the jazz style best suited to the character of Liza/Jenny. The similarity between the two pieces is particularly evident in the closing bars of each chorus of Weill's song, such as on the words «Little Jenny was an orphan on Christmas Day», and at the end of each stanza of 'Minnie the Moocher' («But Minnie had a heart as big as a whale»). Here, the chords and vocal lines of the two songs almost overlap, featuring a descent from the fifth to the first degree that touches the fourth and minor third.

The strong resemblance between 'The Saga of Jenny' and 'Minnie the Moocher' probably did not go unnoticed in 1941, and Mildred Bailey, in her interpretation of Weill's song, seems to underscore this connection. Mildred Bailey's performance is deeply rooted in Bessie Smith's classic blues. Taking inspiration from Smith's vocal style, Bailey sings at a slower tempo and in a lower register than the original piece, and floats behind and ahead of the beat. Her performance departs from Weill's melody both with new rhythmic articulations and with blues-inflected

---

[4]. In Harlem slang, called 'jive' (to which Calloway devoted a dictionary), the term 'hoochie coochie' refers to a sexually provocative dance.

[5]. Kristin McGee discusses the role of Betty Boop cartoons in the debate about the 'modern women' during the 1920s and the 1930s in her *Some Like It Hot: Jazz Women in Film and Television*. In particular, she analyzes the sexualized representation of the woman in the cartoon *I'll Be Glad When You're Dead You Rascal You* (Dave Fleischer, Paramount, 1932). See MCGEE 2009, pp. 22-26.

pitches and grace notes, such as the descending third added at the end of the first two-bar phrase, on the words «when she was three». In addition to her blues-rooted singing style, which is closer to Calloway than to the musical-theatre singing tradition, the band's arrangement at several moments seems to reference Calloway's song. In particular, at the closing of several choruses, the piano and the background vocals hint at a momentary doubling of tempo, with an effect similar to the Cab Calloway recording.

After Bailey's recording paved the way for a long association between Weill's music and the jazz world, musicians started to record instrumental arrangements of his songs. Artie Shaw recorded an orchestral version of 'September Song' with an arrangement by Ray Conniff (Victor, 1945) from the Weill-Anderson musical *Knickerbocker Holiday* (1938). Weill wrote 'September Song' at the request of actor Walter Huston, who wanted the powerful and aged governor of Nieuw Amsterdam (the villain of the play) to have a wistful romantic moment with the young heroine. Weill drew on one of his own previous songs ('Juan's Lied' from the operetta *Der Kuhhandel*, written in German in 1934 and first performed in an English adaptation as *A Kingdom for a Cow* in London in 1935) and adapted the melody to the characteristics of Huston's character and voice, with a slow pace and limited range. In this song of restrained emotion, harmonies play a crucial role, creating delicate passages of tension that do not compromise the elegance of the whole. This song had already been recorded by Tony Martin (1939) and Bing Crosby (1943, both for Decca) and was among the few Weill's songs included in the film *Knickerbocker Holiday* (1944). Shaw could then produce an instrumental arrangement, one of the earliest examples of a jazz score for orchestra based on one of Weill's songs, confident that audiences would recognize the melody even without the lyrics: this, too, was a step toward Weill's full integration into U.S. popular culture.

Ray Conniff's recording of 'September Song' was especially innovative, with a very balanced score, respectful of the original song and full of innovative details. In keeping with the usual practice of swing orchestras, his arrangement retains only the choruses and ignores the verse. The introduction and first chorus are the most interesting parts, based on a tonic bass pedal for twenty-four bars. Above this foundation, trombones, trumpets, and saxes build a rhythmically complex and poignantly dissonant ostinato. Overall, the atmosphere is ethereal and dreamy until the arrival of the bridge, at which point Barney Kessel's electric guitar responds contrapuntally to the melody. In the next chorus, Shaw has a 16-bar improvised solo, leading to the final chorus, in which the initial ostinato returns. In 1948 Conniff returned to the same piece, writing a successful new arrangement for Harry James's orchestra, and further developing the complexity of the opening ostinato and dissonant clusters of muted trumpets.

Thanks to these recordings, among many other ones, 'September Song' became the Weill's 'calling card' to enter the inner circle of musical theatre creators. The dissemination of his music outside the New York community of musical theatre-goers reinforced the legitimacy of Weill's contribution to America's cultural heritage. The symbolic event that marks this transition is the inclusion of 'September Song' (sung by Helen Forrest) in one of the V-Discs that the US Army sent to boost soldiers' morale among American troops in Europe (Army V-Disc 613, 1946). Within a short time, 'September Song' became a firmly established song in the standard jazz repertoire, with an impressive number of recordings by great singers, such as Frank Sinatra (Columbia, 1946) and Sarah Vaughan (with Teddy Wilson, Musicraft, 1947), and jazz musicians such as Sidney Bechet (Circle, 1946), Errol Garner (Savoy, 1949), Dave Brubeck (Fantasy, 1950), and Red Norvo (in trio with Charles Mingus and Tal Farlow, Discovery, 1951). 'September Song' also received some attention in Europe, as evidenced by the recording by the Italian pop singer Teddy Reno, accompanied by Lelio Luttazzi and his orchestra (GDC, 1950).

From then on, several of Weill's songs, in particular his slow, moody ballads such as 'Speak Low' and, since the late fifties, 'My Ship', were chosen by jazz musicians and singers. Weill's American works were becoming part of the American musical heritage, on par with the songs of George Gershwin, Cole Porter, and Irving Berlin. Nevertheless, by the end of the 1940s, most American audiences still ignored Weill's European scores, such as *Die Dreigroschenoper* (1928).

George Avakian, between Pop Hits and avant-garde Jazz

After Kurt Weill's sudden death in 1950 and the sensational success of the off-Broadway production of *The Threepenny Opera* with Marc Blitzstein's English translation in 1954, the way America looked at Weill's music changed dramatically. As Kim Kowalke summarized:

> Blitzstein's version of *The Threepenny Opera* guaranteed for Weill what his Broadway works had not: a posthumous impact on the course of American musical theater and the impetus to resurrect some other works composed before his arrival in the United States. *Die Dreigroschenoper* had preceded Weill across the Atlantic, but it took twenty years longer than its composer to adapt successfully to the new cultural setting[6].

The off-Broadway production featured Weill's widow, the singer Lotte Lenya. She appeared in the first European staging of *Die Dreigroschenoper* in the 1920s and had been singing 'Die Moritat von Mackie Messer' in German for years. Her turn in *The Threepenny Opera* won a Tony award, a rarity for an off-Broadway performance. Within a short time, the popularity of *The Threepenny Opera* led listeners to rediscover Weill's European works, beginning with the album *Lotte Lenya sings Kurt Weill* (Philips-Columbia, 1955). Another consequence of the *Threepenny Opera* popularity was the transformation of 'Die Moritat von Mackie Messer' into a jazz-pop hit. In Germany in 1929, on the wave of the German success of *Die Dreigroschenoper*, band

---

[6]. Kowalke 1990, p. 79.

leader Hans Schindler had the intuition to turn the melody of 'Moritat' into a jazz-style song, a 'slow-fox' (Parlophon, 1929). In the version by Schindler and his Haller Jazz Revue Orchestra, 'Moritat' undergoes a gradual transformation. It begins as a street tune accompanied by a barrel organ, similar to the original version. It then mutates into a jazz tune: the central chorus for the reed section in three-part harmony recalls the arrangements of Fletcher Henderson. A repeated figure of two notes (an eighth note followed by a sixteenth note) creates a 3 + 3 + 2 rhythm over the duple-metered bass and adds an effect similar to the 'secondary rag' pattern, typical of ragtime, a common feature of European jazz bands at the time.

In the United States, these kinds of recordings were utterly unknown. In the early 1950s, amid Cold War and McCarthyism, American pop stars and the Marxist-leaning German theatre of the Weimar Republic belonged to two seemingly irreconcilable cultural worlds.

The person who could bridge this gap was a young record producer named George Avakian, then director of both the Popular Album and International Departments of Columbia Records. Avakian played a crucial role in the development of jazz in the 1950s. He recorded and released vast amounts of music by numerous jazz artists such as Duke Ellington, Miles Davis, Dave Brubeck, Erroll Garner, Tony Bennett, Benny Goodman, and Buck Clayton. Occasionally he produced recordings of contemporary composers, such as *The 25-Year Retrospective Concert of the Music of John Cage* (Not On Label, 1959). Avakian soon realized that 'Die Moritat von Mackie Messer', in Blitzstein's new translation, had the potential to catch the public's imagination. The story of how Avakian involved Louis Armstrong in the recording of 'Mack the Knife' has been told several times[7].

The two met in 1940, when Avakian was in his early twenties, working for Columbia Records. Avakian, at that time, was making the first series of jazz records reissues. With great persistence, he searched the archives for old, forgotten jazz 78 rpm records from the twenties and reissued them for the Hot Jazz Classics Series. He also curated and corrected Charles Delaunay's *Discography*, and paved the way for the emergence of a historical perspective on jazz music. In the mid-1950s, Avakian produced some of Armstrong's most famous albums, such as *Louis Armstrong Plays W.C. Handy* (1954) and *Satch Plays Fats* (1955).

At the same time, however, Avakian shared with his wife Anahid Ajemian, a distinguished violinist devoted to contemporary music, a strong interest in avant-garde music. According to *Billboard* on 29 October 1955, Avakian listened to European Weill's music for the first time through his wife.

> An unorthodox chain of events will result this week in two unusual single record issues by Columbia. Both will feature 'Mack the Knife', the opening song from Kurt Weill's *Three Penny Opera*, and the artists are jazz stars Louis Armstrong

---

[7]. See Pollack 2012 and Riccardi 2012.

and Turk Murphy, in vocal and instrumental versions respectively. It all began last winter when Anahid Ajemian, the classical violinist, gave the first American performance of the late Weill's Violin Concerto, which she subsequently recorded for MGM. Miss Ajemian's husband, George Avakian, became interested in Weill's music as a result and was particularly taken with the *Three Penny Opera* which, in an English adaptation by Marc Blitzstein, has been holding forth at a local off-Broadway theater and which also had been recorded by MGM. For months Avakian, who is head of Columbia's jazz and pop album departments, tried to interest various of his jazz artists in the 'Ballad of Mack the Knife', and finally he succeeded with Murphy[8].

Avakian was initially interested in the melody of 'Mack the Knife' and not in Brecht-Blitzstein's lyrics. He then commissioned trombonist and jazz revivalist Turk Murphy to record an instrumental version of the piece. 'The Ballad of Mack the Knife' tells of heinous murders and violence in which the perpetrator goes unpunished. The lyrics have a cynical tone, and Avakian knew that it would have been difficult to propose such a song to radio stations. A few months earlier, for the recording of the cast album (MGM, 1955), Blitzstein had been forced to soften the rawness of the original lyrics, removing the more brutal stanzas in which Brecht describes the killing of Sloppy Sadie and the rape of Little Susie. However, even with some stanzas censored, verses like «When the shark bites with his teeth, dear / Scarlet billows start to spread» were still much cruder than most jazz and pop song lyrics. According to Avakian's testimony, as reported by Ricky Riccardi, Armstrong accepted the producer's proposal without any hesitation, replying: «Hey, I'll record that. I knew cats like that in New Orleans. They'd stick a knife in you as fast as say hello»[9].

Armstrong's reference to the New Orleans social environment reveals a hidden affinity between two seemingly distant musical traditions. In Brecht and Weill's conception, the opening 'Moritat' was to introduce the character of Macheath in the style of a folk ballad accompanied by a street organ. As Una McIlvenna explains in her research paper on *Singing complaintes criminelles across Europe*, songs recounting heinous crimes from recent or past chronicles were widespread in the nineteenth century. They were distributed by street singers through «chapbook format, usually in eight-page pamphlets, with a prose account of the crimes followed by a song»[10]. Something similar also existed in the U.S. folk tradition of murder ballads from both black and white traditions, popular in both the early blues and early country recordings, in which the deeds of outlaws and their brutal crimes were told[11]. Armstrong himself, in his autobiography

---

[8]. *Billboard* 1955.
[9]. Riccardi 2012, p. 113.
[10]. McIlvenna 2021.
[11]. In 1938, at Alan Lomax's request (for *The Library of Congress Recordings* series) Jelly Roll Morton performed some murder ballads, such as 'The Robert Charles Song' and 'Aaron Harris'. Other typical songs in this repertoire are 'Crow Jane', which narrates the murder of a prostitute, recorded by blues guitarist Julius Daniels

Satchmo: My Life in New Orleans, recounts the many «bad guys» he met when he was a boy[12]. Lotte Lenya attended the recording session, and Armstrong added a playful dedication to Weill's widow in the song, including her name in the concluding list of Mackie's victims[13]. The recording was released under the title *A Theme from the Threepenny Opera*, mentioning 'Mack the Knife' in brackets (Columbia, 1956). Still, despite Armstrong's enthusiastic participation, Avakian planned to record an instrumental version as well to circumvent any probable future censorship actions by radio stations. Avakian's efforts in promoting Weill's work did not stop with Armstrong's hit. He also produced some recordings of Weill's music by Lenya for Columbia (*Kurt Weill's The Seven Deadly Sins*, 1957 and *Lotte Lenya Sings Berlin Theatre Songs by Kurt Weill*, 1958).

The unexpected success of this song became even greater when Bobby Darin, who had recently made some rock'n'roll records, recorded 'Mack the Knife', accompanied by a swing-style big band (ATCO, 1959). Darin's recording held on to the top spot on the Hot 100 for nine weeks in 1959 and earned the singer a Grammy for Record of the Year. Richard Wess wrote a simple yet effective jazz-style arrangement for this recording. He conceived the whole instrumental background as a long *crescendo*: in the first stanza, the rhythm section plays 'in two', emphasizing the first and third beats with a 'boom-chick' feel and lends it an old-fashioned flavor. In the second stanza, the brass adds short *staccato* interjections in response to the vocal line. From the third stanza on, the double bass plays a more modern walking line, and the arrangement introduces the first of several truck-driver modulations. At the end of the performance, the orchestra reaches a climax on Darin's sustained high note.

The popularity of this song, which was ranked number three on *Billboard*'s All-Time Top 100 Singles chart, probably lies in the social transformations that took place in America during those years. Kowalke summarizes these changes by writing about the reasons for the fortunes of *The Threepenny Opera* in 1954:

> It is a simplistic but irrefutable fact that the off-Broadway production also "came at the right time". The reopening of the show in 1955 coincided with the date of James Dean's car crash; that year Brando won an Academy Award for *On*

---

for the Victor in 1927, and 'Crazy Blues', recorded by Bessie Smith for the Okeh in 1920. The latter track, where an abandoned woman plans to kill a police officer, is one of the first blues recordings ever released. On the role of violence in the lyrics of the blues tradition, see GUSSOW 2014 and HERSCH 2009.

[12]. See ARMSTRONG 1986.

[13]. During the recording session, at Avakian suggestion, Armstrong and Lenya worked up a duet on the spot. The jazz rendition of the melody at the 'Suky Tawdry' stanza needed a particular syncopation: a rhythmic tool far from Lenya's usual vocabulary. The studio reels recorded some minutes or their rehearsal, where Armstrong is showing her how to add a jazz rhythm to the song. The previously unissued track is contained in a 11-CD Deluxe Box Set titled *Lenya*, a complete retrospective of Lenya's musical and spoken-word recordings (Bear Family Records BCD 16019 KL).

the Waterfront; the rebellious beat generation could identify with certain anti-Establishment aspects of *The Threepenny Opera* as well. McCarthyism was finally precipitating an inevitable cultural backlash, even in middleclass America[14].

The formidable performances by Armstrong and Darin also came at the right time. Recorded a few years apart, however, these two interpretations tell slightly different stories to different generations. By 1955, Armstrong was an acknowledged global star. Nevertheless, he still represented the golden age of New Orleans jazz, a glorious and vanished era nostalgically fueling the jazz revival. Armstrong's entire recording of 'Mack the Knife' looks toward the past, playing in two, with a 'boom-chick' feel. Before the band starts playing, Armstrong announces: «Dig, man, there goes 'Mack the Knife'». He seems to prepare the listeners, explaining that the music about to begin comes from the distant past. On the other hand, Darin, who was then 22 years old, addressed the new generation, which in the late 1950s rejected the establishment and parental authority, singing the disengaged and provocative songs of rock'n'roll music. The commercial radio network The Mutual Broadcasting System had banned his previous hit, 'Splish Splash' (along with 'Hard Headed Woman' by Elvis Presley), because it was considered «distorted, monotonous, noisy music and/or suggestive or borderline salacious lyrics»[15]. Darin performed Weill's song in a vocal style that was both relaxed and energetic. Moreover, he insightfully replaced Blitzstein's frequent use of 'dear' with a more sexually charged 'babe'.

The success of 'Mack the Knife', therefore, is also related to a profound change in American society. By the mid-1950s, the portrayal of teenagers was changing rapidly: news reports of youth gang riots were the basis for other musical theatre masterpieces of the period, such as *West Side Story* (1957). Films such as *Jailhouse Rock* (1957), starring Elvis Presley at the beginning of his film career, conveyed the model of rebellious youth. All these factors contributed to the popularity of Darin's 'Mack the Knife'. By narrating Macheath's crimes in a confident manner, Darin offered a light-hearted but cynical view of teenage life in the rougher neighborhoods of the contemporary metropolis. At the same time, he constructed his image by adopting a relaxed, comfortable, and cool attitude. As Joel Dinerstein explains in *The Origins of Cool in Postwar America*, in the early 1950s the word 'cool' crossed over through Beat writers, such as Clellon Holmes and William Burroughs, attuned to the new hipster and jazz slang, and then spread into the popular culture:

> To be cool was inherently anti-authoritarian and opposed to legal norms —
> in other words, in quiet rebellion against "the heat" or the cops. At the individual

---

[14]. KOWALKE 1990, p. 114.
[15]. MARTIN – SEGRAVE 1988, p. 25. In the banned lyrics, Darin narrated about getting out of a bathtub wearing only a towel and joining a party.

level, cool was a quest for existential stillness, relaxation, and self-control. A cool person projects a calm center through economy of motion and has an implied intensity. [...] The cool person does not explain the content of his or her rebellion. This is a salient difference between being hip and being cool[16].

With hits by Armstrong and Darin, 'Mack the Knife' became part of the standard repertoire of jazz musicians and pop singers, with countless recordings. Sonny Rollins included 'Moritat' on his 1956 career-changing album, *Saxophone Colossus*, and Wayne Shorter recorded the song in 1959 on his debut *Introducing Wayne Shorter*.

One of the most famous jazz versions of 'Mack the Knife' was the live recording of Ella Fitzgerald's performance in Berlin in 1960, collected on the Grammy-winning album *Ella in Berlin* (Verve, 1960). Introducing the song, Ella Fitzgerald warns the audience: «We hope we remember all the words». Then, as announced, having reached the fourth stanza, she replaces Blitzstein's lines with new improvised words, maintaining the meter and rhyme. In doing so, she engages the audience in a game of metatextuality and intertextuality: «Oh, what's the next chorus? To this song, now / This is the one, now. I don't know». The informal mood of Armstrong's 1955 recording now comes alive in Ella's performance. Just as Armstrong had included Lotte Lenya's name in the song's lyrics, Ella, while singing the melody, pays homage to the performances of those who preceded her: «Oh Bobby Darin, and Louis Armstrong / They made a record, oh but they did / And now Ella, Ella, and her fellas / We're making a wreck, what a wreck of 'Mack the Knife'». Ella closes the performance with a final *coup de théâtre* during her subsequent scat-style improvisation, where she imitates Armstrong's vocal style and drawling pronunciation of the word 'dear' in the lower range.

Several factors contributed to the success of *Ella in Berlin*, including changes in the record industry during the 1950s and the audible sense of connection between Fitzgerald and the audience during her concert. In 1956, Norman Granz, the producer who invented the famous series of concerts Jazz at the Philharmonic, gave a twist to Fitzgerald's career by having her sign for the newborn label Verve Records. As he explained, «I was interested in how I could enhance Ella's position, to make her a singer with more than just a cult following amongst jazz fans»[17].

In some respects, *Ella in Berlin* differs from previous live recordings of jazz performances: even though maintaining a clear jazz identity, its conception is closer to the typical live album of a popular music performer, such as Ray Charles's *In Person* (Atlantic 1960, recorded in 1959). In his brief liner notes, Granz avoided the word 'jazz', instead stating that this album substantiates his «belief that people who love good popular music are the same everywhere». Indeed, the entire *Ella in Berlin* album celebrates Fitzgerald's strong connection with the audience and

---

[16]. DINERSTEIN 2018, p. 231.
[17]. Quoted in HERSHORN 2011, p. 217.

places more emphasis on her than on the band. This is exemplified by her performance of 'Mack the Knife': it features a memorable and well-known melody and the song title is highlighted on the album cover. The recording emphasizes the audience's response throughout the entire performance, such as the applause at the beginning of Fitzgerald's performance, the moment after the public recognizes the song, and when she imitates Armstrong's voice.

In 1960, when the album was released, jazz was going through «a decisive cultural moment in establishing an autonomous art-form», and many musical landmarks were «recorded in every style of jazz (from mainstream to avant-garde)»[18]. By then, the average jazz listeners could by then appreciate how musicians handled imperfections during the unexpected turns of an improvised performance. In this perspective, 'Mack the Knife' track is particularly noteworthy because Fitzgerald's creative process is so transparent. As the track progresses, we witness how she expertly navigates unexpected challenges, which allows listeners a glimpse into her decision-making process. During the performance of this song, she skillfully weaves a network of relationships with the band members (a quartet led by pianist Paul Smith, featuring guitarist Jim Hall), the audience/listeners and their expectations, the singers who have previously performed this song, the composer, and virtually, the Berliners who attended the first staging of *Die Dreigroschenoper*. During her performance there are slight hesitations, such as the rhythmic indecision between the lines «You won't recognize it / it's a surprise hit», but she manages these moments with ease and naturalness. In doing so, she creates an informal atmosphere, shortens the distance between herself and the audience, and puts the listener in a comfortable position.

As Philip Auslander suggests in *Jazz Improvisation as a Social Arrangement*, during a jazz performance «real suspense or surprise [...] results from the collaboration between performers and audience, each of whom plays multiple roles within mutually recognized social frames»[19]. In his view, «listening to recorded jazz requires the assumption of an information state that makes it possible to hear the recording as an improvisation taking place in the present moment of listening, not as a document that refers us to an original (past) action»[20]. In this light, Fitzgerald's version of 'Mack the Knife', as described by David Ake, stands as «the clearest example of the aesthetic of imperfections in action»[21].

Meanwhile, as Armstrong's 'Mack the Knife' was being taken up and transformed by numerous other performers, George Avakian became interested in another trend: to bridge the gap between 'art' music and modern jazz. His plans met with interest from a group of jazz composers committed to combining jazz with concert music. For them, Weill's music,

---

[18]. BRUBECK 2003, p. 177.
[19]. AUSLANDER 2013, p. 66.
[20]. *Ibidem*, p. 67.
[21]. AKE 2010, p. 46. Here Ake is referring to the relevant study of jazz by Ted Gioia, titled *The Imperfect Art*. As Gioia wrote, «If jazz music is to be accepted and studied with any degree of sophistication, we must develop an aesthetic that can cope both with that music's flaws as well as its virtues». GIOIA 1988, p. 56.

and particularly his European and modernist works, became a model of possible coexistence of different musical genres. In 1957, Avakian and Ajemian co-produced a four-concert series at Town Hall titled *Music for Moderns* with a radically innovative goal. A short article in *Billboard* explained Ajemian's intentions:

> The series, which will be annual project, will attempt to present varied types of modern music, including jazz, on the same programs in an effort to broaden tastes, demonstrate cross-developments, etc. According to Miss Ajemian: «Similar and contrasting uses of the same basic materials will be explored, thus attempting to bridge the traditional but artificial barrier between the so-called 'serious' and light interpretations»[22].

The opening night, on 28 April 1957, was titled *From Twelve Tone to Ellingtonia*. In the first half of the concert, Ajemian performed Kurt Weill's *Concerto for Violin and Wind Orchestra*, Op. 12, with Dimitri Mitropoulos conducting. In the second half, the Duke Ellington Orchestra gave the world premiere of one of Ellington and Billy Strayhorn's masterpieces: the suite *Such Sweet Thunder*, based on the work of William Shakespeare[23]. Avakian and Ajemian's choices were in line with the idea of 'third stream music', as defined by composer Gunther Schuller: a new musical genre located about halfway between jazz and classical music. In May of that year, Avakian succeeded in one of his most ambitious recording projects. He planned to put Miles Davis at the center of a large orchestral jazz setting, with a series of arrangements by a first-rate arranger and an ensemble sound close to a classical orchestra. The title of the album was already set: *Miles Ahead* (Columbia, 1957). Initially, Avakian had thought of Gunther Schuller as the arranger for the record. Finally, the choice fell to Gil Evans, who had already collaborated with Davis on *Birth of the Cool* (Columbia, 1957)[24].

The album tracklist features a selection of pieces composed by leading jazz musicians such as Johnny Carisi, Ahmad Jamal, Dave Brubeck, James Louis 'J. J.' Johnson, plus two original scores by Evans himself. In this selection, there is only one piece from Broadway musical theatre: Weill's 'My Ship'. Unlike 'September Song', 'Speak Low', or 'Mack the Knife', 'My Ship' had not been much performed by jazz musicians previously, except for Sarah Vaughan's recent recording for the album *Great Songs from Hit Shows* (Mercury, 1957). Gil Evans' arrangement of 'My Ship' is a masterpiece of balance between innovation (complex harmonies, chromatic tensions

---

[22]. BILLBOARD 1957.

[23]. In 2016 the New York Public Library for the Performing Arts organized an exhibition titled *Music for Moderns: The Partnership of George Avakian and Anahid Ajemian*. The information here comes from the website of the New York Public Library for the Performing Arts, see SNYDER 2016. The website also shows a group photograph that includes George Avakian, Duke Ellington, Lotte Lenya, and Anahid Ajemian at Town Hall after the opening concert of *Music for Moderns*, dated 28 April 1957.

[24]. See STEIN CREASE 2003, pp. 190-191.

and unusual distribution of the parts) and expressiveness[25]. Evans achieved a unique orchestral sound, developing Weill's idea of an 'Andante Misterioso'. Evans took the original introduction and expanded it with chromatic passages in counterpoint to the lead voice, achieving an effect of tonal ambiguity. With its slow opening tempo and complex harmonies, Evans' arrangement reflects the song's function in *Lady in the Dark*: a dark, removed memory in the unconscious.

Miles Ahead marked the beginning of a new phase in the reception of Weill's music among jazz musicians. Like Schuller and Evans, other jazz composers became interested in exploring the complexity of Weill's music. These jazz composers had specific characteristics in common: they had attended (at least in part) formal studies in composition; they were interested in contemporary classical music and experimentation; they promoted, through records and concerts, an idea of jazz as an intellectual, artistic product and not just as entertainment; and they gave composition and improvisation equal importance.

The first album to mark this new interest in Weill's music was recorded by a little-known band from Australia, named The Australian Jazz Quintet, which worked in the United States in the second half of the 1950s. This recording, issued in 1958 under the programmatic title *Modern Jazz Performance of Kurt Weill's Three Penny Opera* (Bethlehem Records, 1958), is almost a concept album based on a selection of the songs from the play. The order of the tracks closely mirrors their appearance in *The Threepenny Opera*, except for 'Polly's Song' and 'Jealousy Duet', postponed on the disc. The title tracks are the following: on side A: 'Mack the Knife', 'Army Song', 'Love Song', 'Barbara's Song'; on side B: 'Tango Ballad', 'Solomon's Song', 'Polly's Song', 'Jealousy Duet', 'Finale'. The quintet included Dick Healey (alto saxophone, flute), Erroll Buddle (clarinet, tenor, and baritone saxophone), Bryce Rohde (piano), Jack Brokensha (vibraphone), Jack Lander (bass), and Jerry Segal (drums).

The main point for interest here, however, lies in the collaboration of composer and vibraphonist Teddy Charles, who supervised the recording for Bethlehem Records, wrote all the arrangements, and performed on two tracks ('Mack the Knife' and 'Solomon's Song'). Teddy Charles was an important innovator in jazz music in the 1950s, although his contributions are still little-known, and so deserves an extended introduction. As Noal Cohen writes in an insightful biographical article: «While his music has sometimes been portrayed as a precursor of both free jazz and the so-called 'third stream', it was his intent neither to jettison the conventional framework of jazz nor to create a fusion with classical music»[26]. Charles briefly attended the Juilliard School of Music in New York, then continued his studies privately with composer and pianist Hall Overton[27].

---

[25]. See REEVES 2002.

[26]. COHEN 2000.

[27]. Overton is best known for being Thelonious Monk's arranger for several big band concerts including *The Thelonious Monk Orchestra at Town Hall* (Riverside, 1959). However, his most important scores are close to

In 1958, when Charles collaborated with the Australian Jazz Quintet, he was at the height of his artistic creativity. Two years earlier, he had participated in the recordings of Mingus's Jazz Composers Workshop, which included major musicians and composers interested in experimentation, such as George Russell, Gil Evans, and Teo Macero. Some of them took part as composers/arrangers on Charles's next record: *The Teddy Charles Tentet* (Atlantic Records, 1956). It is also worth mentioning that in 1957 Teddy Charles took part in a little-known experiment. He partecipated in a workshop for improvisers conducted by Edgard Varése and based on the musical interpretation of a graphic score[28].

Hall Overton described Charles's compositional thought in the liner notes for the album *New Directions 4* (Prestige, 1954). Overton summarizes the features of Charles's music into four essential points: «1. longer forms than the usual 32-bar song form; 2. a much more varied type of harmony (polytonality, 4th chords); 3. spontaneous counterpoint, whenever performers feel an extra melodic line fits; 4. fluctuating tonal centers»[29]. It is, therefore, not surprising that Teddy Charles, as a composer, was interested in Weill's European works. Interviewed in the liner notes of *Modern Jazz Performance of Kurt Weill's Three Penny Opera*, Charles himself described the way he approached Weill's music, and mentioned the off-Broadway show, which was still in the running during the interview:

> I've tried to realize Weill's intentions in creating a work with an ironic twist. Some of the pieces have just been re-orchestrated while others I've translated fully into the modern idiom — chords and all. I felt that Weill's music was so strong that I purposely didn't go to see the show; in that way I could concentrate on and really feel only the music. Incidentally, I've occasionally used some modern jazz clichés just as Weill used some of the obvious ones of his day[30].

Charles' arrangements on this recording are very respectful of the original music. Although he only had a small ensemble at his disposal, Charles tried to keep some elements of Weill's arrangements, such as the counterpoint to the primary melody in songs like 'Army Song', 'Barbara Song' and 'Tango Ballad'. The latter two are the most interesting tracks on the album because Charles takes advantage of the many changes in mood and tempo in Weill's music and succeeds in writing a modern jazz score. These pieces feature frequent and challenging changes of tempo and rhythm (from slow ballad to medium swing to latin rhythm). They also include sudden stops and complex forms. These elements are comparable to what Charles Mingus was experimenting with his bands.

---

avant-garde and contemporary classical music. His loft in New York was attended by jazz musicians, artists, and composers, and Steve Reich was among his students.

[28]. For more detailed information on this exciting experiment, see COHEN 2018.
[29]. OVERTON 1954.
[30]. MURANYI 1958.

Changes in Kurt Weill's Music

Avakian's final contribution to this story of jazz arrangements of Weill's music is the album *Mack the Knife and other Berlin Theatre Songs* (RCA Victor, 1965), which features a variable sextet that included Eric Dolphy (alto saxophone and bass clarinet), Thad Jones (cornet), and John Lewis (piano). Although Michael Zwerin's arrangements are not particularly innovative, the record includes one track of great expressive power, 'Alabama Song', thanks mainly to the improvisation of Eric Dolphy on the bass clarinet. This recording took place at a particular time in the history of African-American people and the Civil Rights Movement. On 15 September 1963, four African American girls were killed in a Baptist church in Birmingham, Alabama, when Ku Klux Klan members bombed the building with dynamite. The same year, John Coltrane recorded an original composition titled 'Alabama' later published on Coltrane's album *Live at Birdland* (Impulse, 1964). Coltrane's introspective melody, played with a mournful saxophone voice, was his elegy to the four victims. Dolphy's solo in 'Alabama Song' and Coltrane's 'Alabama' are two completely different pieces. They have nothing in common except for their titles. However, it is possible that Dolphy, who had played 'Alabama' as a member of Coltrane's quintet shortly before, tried to express through improvisation the sense of anger in reaction to that racist violence.

In 'Alabama Song', Dolphy develops his solo against the constant background of the melody, repeated in unison by trumpet and trombone with an almost irritating monotony. Dolphy's improvisation on bass clarinet, according to the style he was experimenting with at the time, is atonal. He reaches the extreme points of the instrument's range, makes guttural growls reminiscent of human cries, and plays very fast and dissonant lines. On one hand, Weill's simple theme is motionless, impassive, and almost ironic in the context of a modern jazz recording. Nevertheless, on the other hand, Eric Dolphy's clarinet seems to fight against this melody in an awkward, expressionistic manner. Combining these irreconcilable yet concurrent elements has an estranged and intense effect that intensifies features already present in Brecht-Weill's original piece. In his playing against the melody, Dolphy seems to consider Brecht's advice to the actors in his *Threepenny Opera Notes*. In Brecht's idea, the actors should «not follow [the music] blindly», because «there is a kind of speaking against-the-music which can have strong effects»[31]. There is no evidence to suggest that Dolphy intended his solo as a political statement against racial discrimination and the recent tragic events in Alabama. Nevertheless, the contrast between his clarinet and the melody can be read as a way to add a distancing effect to the whole, and to invite the listener to reflect on the inner motivations of the performer in such a musical context.

---

[31]. BRECHT 1964, p. 45.

Leo Izzo

Brecht-Weill Reception in Italy, between Jazz and Avant-garde Music

The main reason Italy played a significant role in the reception of Weill's music is due to the cultural awakening in the postwar period and a group of leftist intellectuals eager to renew Italian culture. In this climate of new opportunities, the gradual rediscovery of Brecht's work and, to a lesser extent, Weill's music, played a significant role. The highlight of Weill's reception in those years was the performance of *L'opera da tre soldi* (*Die Dreigroschenoper*) at the Piccolo Teatro in Milan in 1956, directed by Giorgio Strehler: one of the most influential events in the history of postwar Italian theatre. Brecht attended rehearsals and the premiere and expressed his admiration for Strehler's direction[32]. For the younger generation of Italian intellectuals, Brecht and Weill were role models due to their expressive means and their ethical and political motivations. Among the many intellectuals who attended the premiere of *L'opera da tre soldi* in Milan, there was the music scholar and critic Roberto Leydi. His many interests encompassed artistic production under the Weimar Republic, music of oral tradition, political singing, and jazz music. Today, Leydi is widely recognized as one of the founders of Italian ethnomusicology[33]. In 1950, when Kurt Weill died, Leydi wrote a long and insightful reflection on the composer's life and music[34]. In that article, Leydi regretted that American periodicals did not mention Weill's German masterpieces:

> With the death of Kurt Weill, we have lost not only one of the greatest musicians of our century — certainly the most distinguished representative of German revolutionary music of that other postwar period — but, above all, a man who, through his work and his own existence, laid down several fundamental principles to our consciousness as modern men. That is why Kurt Weill continues to be beloved and considered great, even though he devoted the years of his American life to crafting banal songs and operettas. Because Kurt Weill was a flag, a guide to that cultural movement that deluded itself that he could renew old Europe in the aftermath of the other war[35].

Although he initially neglected Weill's American achievements (a position that he reconsidered in later years), in the still myopic view of Italian 1950s press, Leydi declared his profound admiration for his European works. During the 1950s, Leydi undertook direct efforts to popularize Weill's work to Italian audiences, producing radio and television broadcasts. During the performance of *L'opera da tre soldi* at the Piccolo Teatro, the orchestra conductor was the composer Bruno Maderna, co-founder with Luciano Berio of the Studio di Fonologia in

---

[32]. See Guazzotti 1961 and Hinton 1990.
[33]. See Ferraro 2015.
[34]. Leydi 1950.
[35]. *Ibidem*, p. 233. Translated from Italian by the author.

Milan (Italy's first electronic music center) and a point of reference for the younger generation of avant-garde musicians.

Leydi and Maderna's shared interest in Kurt Weill's music led to a collaboration in 1963, for the recording of the two LPs *Kurt Weill 1900-1933* and *Kurt Weill 1933-1950* (Ricordi, 1963)[36]. Maderna had at his disposal an orchestra with variable personnel, gathering some of the best Italian jazz musicians, such as Gianni Basso (tenor saxophone), Oscar Valdambrini (trumpet), and Gil Cuppini (drums). Also playing with them were great performers of contemporary music, such as flautist Severino Gazzelloni, to whom Dolphy dedicated the flute piece 'Gazzelloni', on the album *Out to Lunch!* (Blue Note Records, 1964), recorded a few days after 'Alabama Song'.

Since there was no monograph in Italian dedicated to Kurt Weill, Leydi seized the opportunity to write a comprehensive portrait of the composer. Leydi organized the tracks on the two albums in an almost chronological sequence, and included two booklets with exceptionally long liner notes and illustrations, similar to musicological essays. Most of the lyrics were translated to make the meaning clearer to an Italian audience. The vocalist for these albums was the young actress Laura Betti. During those years, Betti was touring in Italian theatres with *Giro a vuoto*, a provocative and unconventional recital of songs in which she played the character of an ironic and uninhibited woman. Many of her songs described couple relations in a way that subverted the hypocrisy of bourgeois morality. Several distinguished poets and writers, such as Pier Paolo Pasolini and Alberto Moravia, contributed to her recitals, writing the lyrics of many of her songs. The track list of the two albums dedicated to Weill's music is the following. Spelling and language of the track titles are quoted as they appear in the record cover. Songs sung in the original language are marked with an asterisk.

Kurt Weill 1900-1933
from *Die Dreigroschenoper* (1928): 'Barbara song', 'Ballata della schiavitù sessuale', 'Tango Ballade', 'Jenny dei pirati', 'Moritat', 'Salomon song', 'Ballata dell'agiatezza';
from *Happy End* (1929): 'Surabaya Johnny';
from *Das Berliner Requiem* (1929): 'La ragazza annegata';
from *Mahagonny* (1927-1930): 'Moon of Alabama'*, 'Wie man sich bettet'.

Kurt Weill 1933-1950
from *Maria Galante* (1934): 'Le grand lustucru'*, 'J'attends un navire'*;
from *Der Silbersee* (1934): 'Lied der Fennimore';
from *Die sieben Todsünden* (1933) 'I sette peccati capitali' [pieces from the ballet];
from *One Touch of Venus* (1943): 'Speak low'*, 'That's him'*;
from *Knickerbocker Holiday* (1938): 'How can you tell an American'*, 'September song'*;
from *Street Scene* (1947): 'Lonely house'*.

---

[36]. See Izzo 2022.

Laura Betti had previously sung Weill's music during a performance of *Die Sieben Todsünden* in Rome in 1961 alongside the famous Italian ballet dancer Carla Fracci. In addition, she included several of Weill's songs in her repertoire, and in the recital *Giro a vuoto n. 3 - Omaggio a Kurt Weill*. Maderna had also previously written instrumental arrangements of three pieces by Weill ('Tango-Ballade', 'Ballade von der sexuellen Hörigkeit', 'Die Moritat von Mackie Messer') for a radio broadcast titled *Arcidiapason* (1960). In these arrangements for orchestra, Weill's music is the starting point for imaginative stylistic variations by Maderna. Maderna often adds passages of simulated improvisation for a small jazz band in these arrangements for the radio. Some instruments move away from the melody and chords of Weill's piece and dialogue with each other with contrapuntal phrasing reminiscent of Jimmy Giuffre's chamber jazz[37].

However, on the recording with Laura Betti, many Maderna's arrangements closely adhere to the original compositions. In only a few pieces does Maderna explore more adventurous writing: these are the songs that had already become firmly established in the jazz repertoire, such as 'Moritat', 'September Song', and 'Speak Low'. For 'Speak Low', Maderna wrote a highly original score, based on the timbral treatment of the orchestra at the opening of the piece. From the silence emerges the faint sound of the flute, joined in pianissimo by other wind instruments, with a canon-like effect. The progressive overlapping of the parts generates a delicate polyrhythm, and the beat remains vague and unstable even after the entrance of the voice. After Betti sings the theme, Maderna introduces a section of seemingly improvised, but entirely written, contrapuntal jazz, with continuous tonality shifts. The piece ends mirroring the opening: the orchestra's sound gradually fades out, as if commenting on the last lines: «The curtain descends, everything ends too soon». The combination of these features makes this score a creative rewriting of 'Speak Low' rather than an arrangement, in which the original piece is rethought and morphed into a 'new' Weill/Maderna composition.

Although Maderna was not a jazz musician, on a few occasions he experimented ways to include jazz-style passages in his compositions. Some of his scores for radio-plays and films features passages in dodecaphonic jazz, somewhat anticipating the experiments Gunther Schuller made ten years later in the album *Jazz Abstraction* (Atlantic, 1960).

Maderna's contribution to the jazz reception of Weill's music may be seen as the Italian counterpart to the aforementioned George Avakian project, which aimed to promote Weill's music by involving modern jazz composers close to Schuller's 'third stream'. From a broader perspective, studying how jazz musicians of various stripes drew on the music of Kurt Weill leads to an investigation of how these figures reinterpreted the music of neighboring genres,

---

[37]. These tapes have never been published and are held in the archives of the Ex-Studio di Fonologia in Milan, now at the Museum of Musical Instruments in Milan. For more detailed information and discussion on the role of jazz in Bruno Maderna's music, see Izzo 2007.

such as the Broadway musical and twentieth-century classical music. From its origins, jazz has shown great versatility and openness to other musical traditions. Jelly Roll Morton was one of the first musicians to define the concept of 'jazz', during the *Library of Congress Recordings* by Alan Lomax in 1938[38]. The New Orleans pianist and composer claimed, with an attitude that was both braggart and thoughtful, that he had devised a way to transform every musical piece, including the 'Miserere' from Giuseppe Verdi's *Il trovatore*, into a swung performance; he called this transformation «my creation [...] jazz music. In fact, I changed every style to mine» (Jelly Roll Morton, *The Complete Library of Congress Recordings*, Rounder Records, 2005, Disc 3). From early twentieth-century New Orleans (the period Morton was referring to) to the global music scene of the 1960s, jazz music has passed through many phases. As a result, the boundaries between jazz and 'other' kinds of music have become increasingly blurred. Nevertheless, the general principle theorized by Morton remains valid, and jazz — or at least part of it — may still be considered as the art of changing other kinds of music. The story of how jazz performers have interpreted Weill's music is long and varied. Along with changes in society, the recording industry, and culture, Weill's own music has also been transformed through countless performances. At each stage of this journey, Weill's music has been reimagined and transformed, and, through these new appropriations, it continues to live on, resonating in an ever-changing world.

Bibliography

Ake 2010
Ake, David. *Jazz Matters: Sound, Place, and Time since Bebop*, Berkeley (CA), University of California Press, 2010.

Armstrong 1986
Armstrong, Louis. *Satchmo, My Life in New Orleans*, New York, Da Capo Press, 1986.

Auslander 2013
Auslander, Philip. 'Jazz Improvisation as a Social Arrangement', in: *Taking It to the Bridge: Music as Performance*, edited by Nicholas Cook and Richard Pettengill, Ann Arbor, University of Michigan Press, 2013, pp. 52-69.

Billboard 1955
'Unorthodox Events Lead to 2 Disk', in: *Billboard*, 29 October 1955, p. 15.

Billboard 1957
'New Concert Series «Music For Moderns»', in: *Billboard*, 13 April 1957, p. 45.

---

[38]. See Izzo 2002.

BRECHT 1964
BRECHT, Bertolt. 'The Literarization of the Theatre: Notes on *Threepenny Opera*', in: ID. *Brecht on Theatre: The Development of an Aesthetic*, edited and translated by John Willett, New York, Hill and Wang, 1964, pp. 43-47.

BRUBECK 2003
BRUBECK, Darius. '1959: The Benning of Beyond', in: *Jazz Changes*, edited by Mervyn Cooke and David Horn, Cambridge, Cambridge University Press, 2003, pp. 177-201.

COHEN 2000
COHEN, Noal. 'New Directions Revisited – The Rich and Unique Legacy of Teddy Charles', 2018, <https://attictoys.com/new-directions-revisited/>, accessed April 2023. [Originally published in: *Coda Magazine*, no. 29 (July/August 2000), pp. 22-29.]

COHEN 2018
COHEN, Brigid. 'Enigmas of the Third Space: Mingus and Varèse at Greenwich House, 1957', in: *Journal of the American Musicological Society*, LXXI/1 (2018), pp. 155-211.

DINERSTEIN 2018
DINERSTEIN, Joel. *The Origins of «cool» in Postwar America*, Chicago, University of Chicago Press, 2018.

FERRARO 2015
FERRARO, Domenico. *Roberto Leydi e il «Sentite buona gente»*, Rome, Squilibri, 2015.

GIOIA 1988
GIOIA, Ted. *The Imperfect Art*, Oxford-New York, Oxford University Press, 1988.

GRABER 2021
GRABER, Naomi. *Kurt Weill's America*, Oxford-New York, Oxford University Press, 2021.

GUAZZOTTI 1961
«L'opera da tre soldi» di Bertolt Brecht e Kurt Weill: uno spettacolo del Piccolo teatro di Milano, regia di Giorgio Strehler, edited by Giorgio Guazzotti, Bologna, Cappelli, 1961.

GUSSOW 2014
GUSSOW, Adam. *Seems like Murder Here: Southern Violence and the Blues Tradition*, Chicago, University of Chicago Press, 2014.

HERSHORN 2011
HERSHORN, Tad. *Norman Granz: The Man Who Used Jazz for Justice*, Berkeley (CA), University of California Press, 2011.

HERSCH 2009
HERSCH, Charles. *Subversive Sounds: Race and the Birth of Jazz in New Orleans*, Chicago, University of Chicago Press, 2009.

HINTON 1990
HINTON, Stephen. 'The Premiere and after', in: *Kurt Weill: «The Threepenny Opera»*, edited by Stephen Hinton, Cambridge, Cambridge University Press, 1990 (Cambridge Opera Handbooks), pp. 50-77.

IZZO 2002
IZZO, Leo. 'La conservazione dell'identità culturale creola nella musica di Jelly Roll Morton', in: *Il Saggiatore musicale*, X/2 (2003), pp. 287-315.

IZZO 2007
ID. *Il ruolo del jazz nelle musiche composte da Bruno Maderna per la radio e per il cinema*, Ph.D. Diss., Bologna, Università di Bologna, 2007, <http://amsdottorato.unibo.it/228/1/Leo_Izzo_Tesi_dottorale.pdf>, accessed April 2023.

IZZO 2022
ID. 'Bruno Maderna and His Arrangements', in: *Utopia, Innovation, Tradition: Bruno Maderna's Cosmos*, edited by Angela Ida De Benedictis, Basel, Paul Sacher Stiftung; Woodbridge, Boydell, 2022, pp. 245-276.

KOWALKE 1990
KOWALKE, Kim H. '*The Threepenny Opera* in America', in: *Kurt Weill: «The Threepenny Opera»*, op. cit., pp. 78-119.

LEYDI 1950
LEYDI, Roberto. 'La musica «da tre soldi» ricorda lo scomparso Weill', in: *Cinema*, III/37 (April 30 1950), pp. 233-234.

MARTIN – SEGRAVE 1988
MARTIN, Linda – SEGRAVE, Kerry. *Anti-rock: The Opposition to Rock 'n' Roll*, New York, Da Capo Press, 1988.

MCGEE 2009
MCGEE, Kristin A. *Some Liked It Hot: Jazz Women in Film and Television, 1928-1959*, Middletown (CT), Wesleyan University Press, 2009.

MCILVENNA 2021
MCILVENNA, Una. 'Singing Complaintes Criminelles across Europe', in: *Criminocorpus*, no. 17 (2021), <http://journals.openedition.org/criminocorpus/8608>, accessed April 2023.

MURANYI 1958
MURANYI, Joe. Liner notes in: *A Modern Jazz Performance of Kurt Weill's Three Penny Opera*, The Australian Jazz Quintet, Bethlehem Records BCP-6030 LP, 1958.

OVERTON 1954
OVERTON, Hall. Liner notes in: *New Directions 4*, Teddy Charles Quintet, Prestige PRLP 169, 1954.

POLLACK 2012
POLLACK, Howard. *Marc Blitzstein: His Life, His Work, His World*, Oxford-New York, Oxford University Press, 2012.

REEVES 2002
REEVES, Scott D. 'Gil Evans: The Art of Musical Transformation', in: *Annual Review of Jazz Studies*, xii (2002), pp. 1-40.

RICCARDI 2012
RICCARDI, Ricky. *What a Wonderful World: The Magic of Louis Armstrong's Later Years*, New York, Vintage, 2012.

SLOAN 2019
SLOAN, Nate. 'Constructing Cab Calloway: Publicity, Race, and Performance in 1930s Harlem Jazz', in: *Journal of Musicology*, xxxvi/3 (2019), pp. 370-400.

SNYDER 2016
SNYDER, Matt. 'Music for Moderns at Town Hall, 1957, August 19, 2016', in: *The New York Public Library for the Performing Arts*, 2016, <https://www.nypl.org/blog/2016/08/19/anahid-ajemian-avakian>, accessed April 2023.

STEIN CREASE 2003
STEIN CREASE, Stephanie. *Gil Evans – Out of the Cool: His Life and Music*, Chicago, A Cappella, 2003.

WOIDECK 2017
WOIDECK, Carl. 'Authentic Synthetic Hybrid: Ellington's Concepts of Africa and Its Music', in: *Duke Ellington Studies*, edited by John Howland, Cambridge, Cambridge University Press, 2017 (Cambridge Composers Studies), pp. 224-264.

Die Dreigroschenoper in Japan:
The 'Threepenny Fever' in Its Early Days

Misako Ohta
(Kobe University)

Introduction: Memories of
Die Dreigroschenoper in Japan[1]

From its premiere in 1928, *Die Dreigroschenoper* (*Sanmon Opera* in Japanese) was popular for a number of reasons, including its freshness of expression and mix of opera and theatre, Brecht's sharp social commentary, and Weill's music, which blended popular dance and song styles with the language of classical music. The number of new productions reached 50 in the premiere season alone, and 130 by 1933[2]. Although it was banned under the Third Reich as 'degenerate art', the piece continued to have a powerful influence in the postwar period, and to this day it is revived around the world. In 2018, 90 years after its premiere in Berlin, four different new productions of the play were staged in Japan: in Kanagawa, Miyazaki, Osaka, and Tokyo[3].

---

[1]. This study is based in part on oral presentations at the IMS International Musicological Society Conference in Tokyo (March 2017) and the Peking University, Fudan University, and Kobe University Three Schools Humanities Symposium (November 2018). The author would like to thank Professor Emeritus Shuhei Hosokawa of the International Research Center for Japanese Studies, Professor Carol J. Oja of the Department of Music at Harvard University, and Section Chief Chiaki Shinohara of Kobe University Human Library for their advice and support.

[2]. Hinton 1990, p. 50.

[3]. Japanese productions of *Die Dreigroschenoper* are flourishing, partly due to the expiration of Weill's and Brecht's copyright in Japan. Here are some examples from 2018: 23 January-4 February, KAAT Kanagawa Arts Theatre, directed by Kenichi Tani; 22-24 June, Medikit Arts Center (Miyazaki Prefecture), directed by Tomoyuki Nagayama; 27 June, Orquesta Libre plays *Die Dreigroschenoper*, Ibaraki City Civic Center; 18-28

According to the German scholar of English literature Aleida Assmann, art functions within society as «active cultural memory»[4], and we can reuse that memory to imagine and situate historical meaning of those works of art within the contemporary world. As the location and time period of a stage production changes, new interpretations emerge, reflecting the unique cultural conditions of the region. For example, when *Die Dreigroschenoper* premiered in Austria in 1929, it was called a 'new type of operetta' that reinvigorated a genre that was beginning to lose relevance, and critics attributed its novel form to the tradition of Johann Nestroy (1801-1862), a nineteenth-century Viennese popular dramatist whose works were full of social satire. The 1933 premiere in the U.S. was a box-office failure due to translation problems, but the second American production in 1954 was a major hit with a long run, and the play established the viability of 'Off-Broadway' productions, that is, those that ran in small theatres outside of established Broadway houses[5].

In this essay, I focus on the reception of *Die Dreigroschenoper* in Japan, especially in its early years, and clarify the characteristics of its reception. The Japanese premiere of *Die Dreigroschenoper* was in 1932, only three and a half years after the Berlin premiere, and one year earlier than the premiere in the United States, where Weill and Brecht eventually settled. I will explore why this work premiered so early in Japan, and why it has continued to have such an impact on Japanese audiences. I will also examine what kind of memories the work evoked in Japanese society, and what kind of transformations it has undergone depending on the media through which the work has been transmitted. As primary historical sources, I referred to Japanese newspapers, magazines, professional journals, and performance programs from the time of the first performance.

This essay consists of three parts. In the first part, I focus on the encounter between Japan and *Die Dreigroschenoper*, and how the work was introduced to Japan, based on various documents from the period. In the second part, I examine the reception of the work and its relationship to Japanese musical culture and social history of the interwar period, focusing on the questions posed through the stage recordings of *Die Dreigroschenoper* and the various 'reviews' of the time. Finally, the conclusion summarizes the characteristics of the early reception of *Die Dreigroschenoper* in Japan, which came through films, sound recordings, and stage performances.

October, Tokyo Art Festival Open-Air Theatre, *Die Dreigroschenoper* directed by Giorgio Barberio Corsetti, Ikebukuro Nishiguchi Park. In 2019 other venues at universities staged the piece with casts drawn from the younger generation. (8-10 February 2019 directed by Takashi Masuyama, Kyoto University Yoshida Dormitory Cafeteria; 20-21 December 2019 Kobe Gakuin University, etc.)

[4]. Assmann 2008, pp. 100-101.
[5]. Ohta 2014, pp. 85-87.

Die Dreigroschenoper in Japan

The 'Threepenny Fever' of 1932

Behind the enthusiastic reception of *Die Dreigroschenoper* in Japan, there was a major change that took place in the urban areas in the 1920s, in which aspects of the cultural situation in Berlin and Tokyo became synchronized[6]. In the process of reconstruction after the Great Kanto Earthquake of 1923, new movie theatres, theatres, and other entertainment venues were built in Tokyo, and the city saw a surprising growth in popular entertainment. It was also during the reconstruction period that the culture was transformed and the salaried employee — who became the new consumers of entertainment — appeared on the scene. The revue, which became an icon of the roaring twenties, was a «new genre that symbolized the luxury, opulence, variety, and machinism of Tokyo as well as Europe, and the bubbles of all social phenomena appeared and flowed, distorted and jazzed up by the revue as icon of that time»[7]. Around the 1930s, the «proletarian revue» took the world by storm, including subtypes such as the «current affairs report revue» which combined comedy, satire, enlightened propaganda, and chant slogans. The special form of revue was also performed at leftist theatres, such as in *Living Newspaper*, a revue from 1931.

Even in Germany during the interwar period, *Zeitopern*, such as *Neues vom Tage* (1929) by Paul Hindemith in collaboration with librettist Marcellus Schiffer (1892-1932), were performed. The art cabarets that became popular from the turn of the century to the 1920s in Germany were also popular in Japan, as were groups of workers' agitprop performers such as the 'Red Revue' and the 'Red Cabaret'.

In addition, the rapid development of the media was also evident in Tokyo, and media collaboration was born. The launch of national newspapers, the rush to launch weekly magazines, and the establishment of foreign-affiliated record companies such as Nippon Columbia and Victor Company of Japan all contributed to a Western-style culture of consumption and enjoyment in Tokyo:

> The proletarian culture, supported by Marxism, grew in power against the established bourgeois culture, and the two cultures rebelled against each other, eroded each other, and finally, a barracks-like leveling progressed and settled on a lower level. The sense of order that existed before the earthquake, of left and right, high and low, collapsed, and the population became endlessly populist[8].

Thus, in the late 1920s and 1930s, Tokyo's cultural climate was predisposed to welcome *Die Dreigroschonoper* as a fresh form of expression that opposed the established bourgeois

---

[6]. Ito 1983, pp. 176-204.
[7]. *Ibidem*, p. 185.
[8]. *Ibidem*, p. 201.

culture of opera. After its premiere in Berlin on 31 August 1928 and the German release of the film *Die 3 Groschen-Oper* by Georg Wilhelm Pabst (1885-1967) in 1931, the work was the subject of heated discussion in major Japanese newspapers such as the *Asahi* and *Yomiuri Shimbun*. The discussion also spread to specialized magazines and was covered by music journals such as *Ongaku Sekai* (Music World), which was first published in 1929[9].

Even before the film was released in Europe in 1931, on 18 February 1930 the *Asahi Shimbun* reported that conductor Otto Klemperer (1885-1973) had given a successful concert of *Die Dreigroschenoper* in Russia, which had enthralled the young people there. Klemperer was already prominent in Japanese music circles. The article quotes Weill, not Brecht:

> You are mistaken if you think I am an artist. I used to be, but people make too much grandiose music. With my *Threepenny Opera*, I wanted to make people's music. We are always fighting against the complicated Wagner. What we're trying to present is life and its depravity. We don't aim for more than that. Wagner wrote for the rich, and *Threepenny Opera* was written for someone else. For the latter, there are only the rich and those without bread[10].

The original source of this interview is unknown, but Weill here refers to Richard Wagner, who in the nineteenth century composed operas based on Nordic and Germanic mythology, using the comparison to distinguish between conventional opera and *Die Dreigroschenoper*. He declares here that the audience is not the wealthy, but rather the «breadless» poor and the lower classes. Weill's statement was misunderstood in Japan, likely because his «epic» is a mode of narration and not merely an audience response. However, Weill's statement was repeatedly quoted in several Japanese newspapers and magazines at the time[11]. Indeed, Weill had stated that he aspired to create a music drama that was not about heroes and myths, but rather a collaboration with contemporary writers that «mirrored» the people of the city and dealt with real social issues[12]. In this article, published in a Japanese newspaper, class struggles were emphasized.

Cross-Border Critics and Artistic Jazz Pieces

Interestingly, *Die Dreigroschenoper* attracted the attention of prominent critics and musicians of the 1930s in Japan, as it did in its home country of Germany. After the Taisho

---

[9]. GOTO 2001, p. 7.
[10]. *ASAHI SHIMBUN* 1930.
[11]. This translation of Weill's remarks was also quoted in the *POLYDOR MONTHLY BULLETIN* 1932, p. 20 and in the text of KAMITSUKASA 1932A-B-C.
[12]. WEILL 1928, p. 66.

Democracy, critical assessment of Western art music had come to play a greater role as a source of instruction in Western culture[13].

First, in March 1931, the music magazine *Ongaku Sekai* published two articles by Shu Ninomiya, a composer born in Kobe and living in Berlin, introducing *Die Dreigroschenoper* from the perspective of music and theatre, delivered as a report from abroad. Although Ninomiya was a composer and researcher of proletarian music, he himself had never seen *Die Dreigroschenoper* on stage. The article was based on the film and the recording, and it introduced the synopsis of the film in advance of its release in Japan in February 1932. The article is interesting from a comparative cultural perspective. Ninomiya wrote that «This play is not monotonous for a Western play, but has changes, just like the Japanese Kabuki play Shiranamimono»[14]. The article also describes the novelty of the work, arguing that it «broke with people's conceptions of conventional opera and music in which beggars, thugs, and whores play an active role instead of the court and aristocracy». Regarding the music, after listing Weill's published works, including his instrumental music, Ninomiya quotes Alfred Baresel (1893-1984), a jazz critic active in Germany in the 1920s. According to Ninomiya's article, Baresel described Weill as «an accomplished composer on the cutting edge of jazz» and «a progressive who could use jazz with assured artistic skill». Weill himself was aware of this perspective, and Ninomiya introduced Weill's assertion from his 'Notiz zum Jazz',

> Today we are undoubtedly at the end of the epoch in which one could speak of an influence of jazz on art music. The most essential elements of jazz have been absorbed by art music, they form integral parts of the musical structure in those composers who cannot do without them, but they no longer appear as jazz, as dance music, but in a superior form[15].

In the second article of the series, Ninomiya also introduced the scores of 'Die Moritat von Mackie Messer' and 'Zuhälterballade' from *Die Dreigroschenoper* and explained in detail how the music is divided into rhythm, melody, harmony, timbre (instrumentation), and structure of the piece. It is described as «semi-mundane but artistic», employing a jazz vocabulary but sounding lively through the various techniques of art music[16]. Ninomiya also described the musical life of Berlin in the context of this work, in which he observed a division between a conservative audience and a youth culture:

> The majority of the elderly are gray-haired old ladies whose dreams of the 19th century have yet to subside, followed by their daughters, and very few young

---

[13]. GOTO 2001, pp. 11-24.
[14]. A Kabuki play featuring a bandit. A story about a thief. NINOMIYA 1931A, p. 130.
[15]. *Ibidem*, p. 132. WEILL 1929, p. 82 (translated into English by the author).
[16]. NINOMIYA 1931A, p. 131.

people. The young people and adults here only catch a glimpse of music concerts, but are happy to listen to new music in cafes, cinemas, or radio stations. Most of it was jazz music[17].

Ninomiya stated that the work was written not for those elderly ladies, but for the «general populace», the «citizens living in the big city». In other words, the work had a significant impact on the young, urban audiences.

It is important to note that, from the time of the work's debut in Berlin, the music press in Japan had already taken notice of the hybrid nature of the music, with its more complex devices than works of popular entertainment[18]. The image of Weill as a 'people's' composer who eschewed traditional art music and advocated 'anti-Wagnerism' after the performance of his *Die Dreigroschenoper* in Europe[19] was already established in Japan before the work itself arrived[20]. For example, the novelist Shoken Kamitsukasa, in his article series 'A Cry from Art Denial', which appeared in the *Yomiuri* for three consecutive days beginning on 5 April 1932, took up the subject of *Die Dreigroschenoper*, and Weill's remarks were quoted in it. In the first installment, Kamitsukasa praised the «cry from art denial» that came impulsively from the mouth of the artist himself, and praised 'Mackie Messer's Crime Story', which he had heard on a gramophone. On the second day, he commented that he was «deeply impressed» by the music of *Die Dreigroschenoper* because it was «jazzified modern music» of European origin, rather than pure jazz, which his boss had rejected because he «felt the stench of America». On the third day, he explained the cause and effect of Weill's «cry of art denial», that he chose the proletarian path by depicting the lives of the people, unwilling to indulge in the «grandeur and complexity of the old bourgeois art»[21]. The work also had repercussions in the Japanese literary world; novelist Rintaro Takeda saw Pabst's film and the stage production, and in June 1932 he published *Nihon Sanmon Opera* (Japan's *Die Dreigroschenoper*), set in an downtown Asakusa apartment, in which he vividly depicted the lives of ordinary people from various walks of life,

---

[17]. NINOMIYA 1931B, p. 70.

[18]. The challenges of class society and artistic genres also extended to radio and music education theatre.

[19]. It is also related to the 'Two Weill Issues', which discussed the reception and creation of the composer's works before and after his exile. For details, see OHTA 2014. As for his position on Wagner, the content of his pre-university education and his correspondence with his brothers suggest that Wagner's technique of indicative motive had a significant influence on Weill's own conception of the words and sounds of music drama. See also WEILL 2000B.

[20]. Even after *Die Dreigroschenoper*, interest in the works of Brecht and Weill remained high, and in the 1930s the two musical education plays *Der Lindberghflug* and *Der Jasager*, were introduced. The latter was performed at the Tokyo Music School by Klaus Pringsheim, who was a professor there. HAYASAKI 1994, pp. 46-55.

[21]. KAMITSUKASA 1932A, KAMITSUKASA 1932B, KAMITSUKASA 1932C.

including a love affair between a café waitress and her lover, an earnest cook who was a beauty queen, and the agony and madness of middle management over a movie theatre strike[22].

At the time, foreign specialist journals were the source of information on Western music in Japan, and they were surprisingly quick to follow the discussions in German and Austrian journals of the interwar period, with topics such as 'neoclassicism' and 'Return to Mozart'[23] introducing neo-classical currents.

In July 1931, the Japanese magazine *Gekkan Gakufu* (Monthly Sheet Music) introduced Weill along with Darius Milhaud, Igor Stravinsky, Alois Haber, Georges Auric, and others in an article entitled 'Rag-music as Pure Music', and noted that Weill's *Kleine Dreigroschenmusik* (1929) performed at the 91st concert of the New Symphony Orchestra, the predecessor of the NHK Symphony Orchestra, was «a complete jazz work for wind instruments»[24]. The piece itself attracted a great deal of attention from Japanese musicians not only in Japan and but abroad. For instance composer and conductor Kosaku Yamada (1866-1965) saw the Russian premiere of *Die Dreigroschenoper*, directed by Alexander Tailov at the Kamelny Theatre in Moscow during a two-month trip[25] across the Soviet Union in the early summer of 1931. He commented that «compared to Tailov's production that he saw in Moscow, the sound film is superior in its musical direction, although the tempo is a little looser»[26]. Yamada pointed out the novelty of Weill's music, noting that Weill's use of simple, vernacular musical material had a major impact on existing genres:

> The appearance of *Threepenny Opera*, with its simplicity of structure and appropriate use of vernacular music throughout, can be rightly seen as providing a new challenge to the world of opera and operetta, which had become stagnant and moribund due to its verbosity. In this sense, we admire the composer Weill for breaking out of his orthodox musical training and using simple vernacular music that is appropriate for the material he has created[27].

One of the most important Japanese champions of *Die Dreigroschenoper* was Kamesuke Shioiri (1900-1938), who was one of the first critics to appreciate the work, was the leading

---

[22]. In 1932, Rintaro Takeda published 'Nihon Sanmon Opera (Japan's *Die Dreigroschenoper*)' in the June issue of *Chūō Kōron*. According to literary critic Masaaki Kawanishi, Takeda, who was «suffering from the difficulty of finding new material for writing since he had left proletarian literature», was inspired by the film and stage versions that «won applause for satirizing the idea that the bourgeois were worse than robbers» and «aiming at socialism while satirizing capitalism». TAKEDA 2000, p. 265. Also, OTANI 1982, pp. 158-160.

[23]. KOIZUMI 1932.
[24]. ITO 1931, p. 22.
[25]. GOTO 2014, p. 365.
[26]. YAMADA 2001, p. 239.
[27]. *Ibidem*, p. 238.

critic of his time[28]. Shioiri was born in Tokyo in 1900, the same year as Weill. After working as a reporter for the *Yomiuri Shimbun*, he moved to the literary department of the New Symphony Orchestra. He worked in the editorial department of the New Symphony Orchestra's journal *Philharmony*, and later edited the new music magazine *Ongaku Sekai*, which launched in 1929. The magazine was not only devoted to classical music, but also to symphonic jazz music by Irving Berlin, George Gershwin, and others. It also covered minstrelsy. Shioiri was well versed in jazz having published a book entitled *Jazz Ongaku* (Jazz Music) in 1930[29]. He regarded jazz and jazz songs as representative of the modern age, and his critical activities were not limited to classical music. He not only introduced *Die Dreigroschenoper*, but also translated the original lyrics into Japanese. His translation was recorded in Nagoya in April 1932, followed by a revue version in March of the same year and a stage version at Hibiya Public Hall on 14 June[30]. Thus, *Die Dreigroschenoper* was sung in Japanese and heard on record. Shioiri's Japanese translations of both 'Tango-Ballade' and 'Die Moritat von Mackie Messer' were not literal translations of the original poems, but rather euphemistic translations, designed to be sung in Japanese[31]. In 1935, he produced and directed a stage version of Brecht and Weill's radio cantata *Der Lindberghflug* (1931) at the Military Hall in the center of Tokyo. Motoo Otaguro's review of *Der Lindberghflug* appeared in the *Asahi Shimbun* on 30 May 1935[32]. The review noted the restrictive method of musical expression in a «cantata», viewing it as «too flat», and also acknowledged the difficulties of adapting a radio drama for the stage.

Media Development and the Japanese «Die Dreigroschenoper»

The reception and success of *Die Dreigroschenoper* in Japan was multilayered, involving magazines, newspapers, films, and records. The year 1932 truly marked a 'Threepenny Fever', in Japan, with the release of a records in German in January, the Pabst film in February, and the Japanese premiere of a stage production at the end of March. To coincide with the release of the film, Nippon Polydor released *Die kleine Dreigroschenmusik* ('The Little Threepenny Opera Suite')[33], a recording by a brass band conducted by Otto Klemperer and featuring members of the Berlin State Opera Orchestra, which created quite a stir. The cover of the January 1932

---

[28]. Goto 2001, p. 7.
[29]. Shioiri 1930.
[30]. Ongaku Shincho 1932, pp. 92-93.
[31]. Released by Asahi Records April 1932.
[32]. Otaguro 1935.
[33]. Polydor 30082-30083 double disc set. *Kleine Dreigroschenmusik* is a suite of eight pieces by Weill for brass ensemble, first performed at the Berlin State Opera on 7 February 1929, by the Berlin State Opera Orchestra conducted by Otto Klemperer: '2. Die Moritat von Mackie Messer', '4. Die Ballade vom angenehmen Leben', '6. Tango-Ballade', '7. Kanonen-Song'.

Ill. 1: *Polydor Monthly Bulletin*, January 1932.

issue of *Polydor Geppo* (Polydor Monthly Bulletin) featured an illustration by Weill and Brecht (Ill. 1) with the words «Two Threepenny Opera Artists Who Became a Culture» and «New Music: Listen! Music of the People» above and below the images. The article on the composer and his works was mostly quoted from Ninomiya's article in *Ongaku Sekai*, along with quotes from Weill's interview that accompanied the Klemperer recording, titled 'Threepenny Opera is the People's Music'. The article also touted the success of the Moscow concert[34]. The professional magazine *Record* also introduced a new album in the 'Jazz Records' category in January, noting the appeal of crossover performances: «One can only marvel at how beautiful jazz can be when played by such professional musicians, as when it is played by an orchestra specializing in dance»[35]. The new Klemperer score is a good example. Klemperer's new album was also introduced as «the sharp end of jazz» in the *Yomiuri Shimbun*'s Masterpiece Disc Brief Review[36].

---

[34]. Polydor Monthly Bulletin 1932, p. 20.
[35]. *Ibidem*, p. 20.
[36]. 'Meiban Sunpyo' (Brief Review) 1932.

In the January 1932 issue of *Sound Record* magazine, the vocal scores of two songs from the film, 'Lied von der Unzulänglichkeit menschlichen Strebens' and 'Tango-Ballade' were published in Shiori's translations as «Shiho Kamei»[37]. In the February 1932 issue of *Sound Record*, *Die Dreigroschenoper* was introduced with a focus on the Pabst film, and the three discs (78rpm) of opera with solo voices, 'Barbara Song' (5287), 'Moritat' (5346), 'Moritat, and Kanonen Song' (5358), released by Nippon Parlophone, advertisements of the albums were also included in the issue, and two suites from Nippon Polydor, 'Crimes of Mackie Messer, Songs of Life' (30082), 'Tango Ballad and Kanonen Song' (30083), for a total of five discs.

After the release of Klemperer's *Die kleine Dreigroschenmusik* in Japan, Japanese performers also began to play the piece. On 14 February 1932, the Tokyo Radio Orchestra under Hidemaro Konoe broadcast it on Radio 1 at 8:30 pm. The commentary was provided by Shioiri[38]. In 1932, the New Symphony Orchestra, conducted by Hidemaro Konoe (1898-1973), released a record on the Nippon Polydor label[39]. The recordings were released just after the film appeared in Japan on 25 February. Later, in April 1932, the Nagoya-based Tsuru label released two Japanese songs from *Die Dreigroschenoper*, 'Moritat' and 'Tango-Ballade', both accompanied by the Asahi Orchestra, as part of 'Jazz Songs'[40]. The song was sung by Susumu Kuroda (1904-1956), a tenor singer from the Tokyo Music School. In the first half of twentieth century, he often sang theme songs for movies and became an indispensable popular singer for 'Koga melodies' created by composer Masao Koga such as 'Jinsei Gekijo (Life Theatre)' and 'Tonkobushi'. Yoichi Uchida also released 'Lied von der Unzulänglichkeit menschlichen Strebens' on the Taiyo label. The light Dixieland jazz-style accompaniment by the Taiyo Orchestra shows the high-performance ability of the Japanese jazz musicians of the time[41].

March 1932 issue of *Eiga Hyoron* (Film Critique) featured Pabst's film as its cover and ran a special feature on it (ILL. 2). The issue featured two articles on *Die Dreigroschenoper*: the film music expert Hiroshi Nakane wrote an essay on 'The Sound Value of the *The Threepenny Opera*', and Shioiri wrote an essay on 'The Music of the *The Threepenny Opera*'.

---

[37]. RECORD 1932, p. 130.
[38]. ASAHI SHIMBUN 1932B.
[39]. Japan Polydor 1140. 4 pieces: '1. Overture', '8. Finale', '3. Alternative song', '5. Polly's song'. The finale is only the chorale part. As an early recording of the New Symphony Orchestra, it is regarded as a challenge to the 'contemporary music' of the time. Combined with Klemperer's selections, all of the Suite for the *Threepenny Opera* could be heard at that time. NOZAWA 2004, pp. 20-21.
[40]. MORI 2012.
[41]. The soundtrack has been reissued and is included in *Jazz in The Great Tokyo - 1925-1940* (supervised by Masato Mori), Gramoclub, 2014.

Ill. 2: *Eiga Hyoron*, March 1932 issue, special issue on 'The Threepenny Opera'.

Nakane praised the appropriate ratio of playing and singing in the film, but criticized it for its slow pacing[42]. Comparing the stage and film versions, Shioiri pointed out that the success of the film's philosophy lay in the «realistic use of jazz music» that matched the nihilism and realism of Brecht's script. In addition, he said that Weill wrote this music based on the essence of the earlier jazz of the early 1920s, unlike contemporary American jazz, which was characterized by an increasingly enormous orchestra and was gradually moving toward the romanticism of the mid-nineteenth century. Shioiri wrote of Weill's score:

> He uses bold new harmonies, simplifying the orchestral technique as much as possible. For example, quartal harmony, polytonality, and seventh chords can be found throughout. However, once the music plays, this new harmonic technique

---

[42]. NAKANE 1932, p. 65.

does not seem at all difficult to the listener. Instead, it evokes a sense of vitality and color. The melody is simple and beautiful. Weill has also created a new style of declamation. This new style of chanting is appropriate for this realistic opera. It is the best way to express the lyrics and the character of the person singing them. The melody he uses would be completely meaningless without the lyrics[43].

The method of declamation pointed out by Shioiri makes the words easier to hear and understand. Shioiri, who also translated the lyrics, must have been keenly aware that the relationship between words and music is one of the most appealing things about the music in *Die Dreigroschenoper*. Unlike in the earlier examples of «destroying the whole of the opera by unreflectively including the music from the opera»[44], the way the music is used in the film is different. The film was praised for its ingenuity in adapting the music to the film medium:

[…] Pabst, while making films dependent on opera, could make full use of music within the dramaturgy of his sharp realism. A director who does not understand music well might have killed the music if he tried to imitate Pabst, but the effect of the music, moving freely as it does here, is never less than in the original work, and the fact that this music, composed for the stage, never has an unnatural presence in the film is a great thing. […] This *Threepenny Opera* is a film that has given me, as a music critic, a lot to think about. At the same time, it will also provide great lessons to those in the film industry[45]

THE TOKYO ACTING TROUPE'S 'BEGGARS' THEATRE' AND HIBIYA'S *DIE DREIGROSCHENOPER*

The stage version of *Die Dreigroschenoper*, which became popular through records and movies, was finally performed at the New Kabuki-za Theatre in Tokyo from 26 to 30 March 1932. The person who proposed and led the production was Koreya Senda (1904-1994), brother of the famed Japanese dancer Michiro Ito. Senda was one of the pioneers of Shingeki, a new 'realist' style of theatre, in contrast to traditional Japanese theatre such as Kabuki and Noh.

Remarkably, Senda saw the actual performance of *Die Dreigroschenoper* in Berlin in 1928[46]. He left Tokyo's Tsukiji Little Theatre[47] in the 1920s and became committed to

---

[43]. SHIOIRI 1932, pp. 66-67.
[44]. *Ibidem*, p. 68.
[45]. *Ibidem*, p. 68.
[46]. SENDA 1976, p. 34.
[47]. Tsukiji Little Theatre is the first theatre founded in 1924 especially for Shingeki (literally, the new play) in Tokyo. They translated Western plays from mainly Germany and Russia.

proletarian theatre, staying in Berlin from April 1927 to November 1931, where he established extensive personal contacts and was himself active in German agitprop theatre[48]. Among the many plays he saw during his stay there, he particularly enjoyed *Die Dreigroschenoper*, and like Kosaku Yamada, he also saw the Tairoff production of the work at the Kamerny Theatre in Moscow. Other Brecht performances he saw included *Man is a Man* and a trial performance of *Die Massnahme* by Hanns Eisler in December 1930[49].

After returning from Berlin in 1931, Senda felt that just as in

> [...] Germany, where there were calls for a broad united front to oppose the rapid rise of Nazi forces, the same issues were emerging in Japan, where the danger of fascism looms [...] it is more necessary than ever to reach out to the peasants, middle class, intellectuals, etc., as well as to win a large number of working-class people. In Japan, too, the danger of fascism is coming, and it is more necessary than ever to reach out to the peasants, the middle class, the intelligentsia, etc.[50]

In response to this realization, he launched a new theatre company, Tokyo Acting Troupe, with a new concept. The first performance of *The Beggar's Play* at the end of April 1932 was an adaptation of *Die Dreigroschenoper*. *The Beggar's Play* was the first Brecht work to be performed in Japan. Although Brecht himself revised the opera several times, *The Beggar's Play* is based on the 1928 version[51]. It was the first of many such productions. The Tokyo Acting Troupe was unique in that it «introduced a kind of producer system centered on freelance actors and aimed to be a mixed theatre troupe, bringing together members of the former Tsukiji Little Theatre and those involved in the then-popular revue and light theatre»[52]. In short, since *Die Dreigroschenoper* called for performers with mixed genre backgrounds, the casting matched Senda's vision of the Tokyo Acting Troupe. In a newspaper review of the Troupe, Tomoyoshi Murayama first refers to the mixed cast as an «adventure» in relation to the audience of the time:

> [...] First, the group itself is an adventure. The target audience is the petty bourgeoisie and the intelligentsia. However, since the downfall of the old Tsukiji Little Theatre,

---

[48]. In the background of the performance of *Die Dreigroschenoper*, the connection to Japanese Agit-prop theatre can be seen through Senda. HAGIWARA 2009, pp. 53-73. On the other hand, the diversity of theatre in the early 1930s, from proletarian theatre to revues, is also suggestive in considering the connection between popular culture and *Threepenny Opera*. NAKANO 2007B, pp. 331-344.

[49]. SENDA 1975, pp. 133-252.

[50]. *Ibidem*, p. 235.

[51]. There are different editions, such as the 1928, 1932, and 1948 editions, in terms of beginning, end, song placement, and lyrics; BRECHT 2004 and the Kurt Weill edition (WEILL 2000A) also include notes in response to the changes.

[52]. NAKANO 2007A, p. 189 and *ASAHI SHIMBUN* 1932A.

real-world analysis of the theatrical needs of this group has been largely neglected, even though it is becoming more and more important. This group is made up of freelancers who are anti-capitalist and anti-fascist in their political tendencies, German in their theatrical style, large-scale performers in terms of the form of the show, and miscellaneous freelancers with a small cadre in terms of the organization of the theatre company.

The practical results of this adventure will depend on if the progressive approach can be taken to the decadent and fashionable Japanese bourgeoisie, and how rigorously the group will examine each achievement and make it their own[53].

Senda himself called the cast of *The Beggar's Play* an «unprecedentedly lively lineup»[54]. The cast included Senda himself as Mekichi (Macheath); Hisashi Sumikawa, a baritone, from the Tsukiji Little Theatre as the street singer (ballad singer); Sadao Maruyama as Heichamu (Jonathan Peachum); Akiko Tamura as Otora (Mrs. Peachum); Chikako Hosokawa as Orie (Polly Peacham); Toyoko Takahashi as Osen (Jenny Diver); Kenichi Enomoto from the Casino Folies, a theatre in Asakusa as Reverend Kimbal; Teiichi Futamura as the thief Yokota (a member of Macheath's gang); and from the kabuki world, Nakamura Genemon, who played Tiger Brown. The production was directed by Hijikata Yoshi, one of the founders of the Shingeki movement. The stage set was designed by Senda's brother Yoshiro Ito, the costumes were by Nuiko Kawashima, and the musical direction, arrangement, and lyrics were written by Saburo Moroi, a composer who went on to study in Berlin. Moroi worked with Gen Ichikawa and Shinjiiro Katayama, who were in charge of music for the Proletarian Theatre League (Plot), and the TES Orchestra.

German press about the Senda production also reveals how Senda adapted the work for Japanese audiences. The Japanese 'Threepenny Fever' of 1932 was also reported in Germany in the *Berliner illustrierte Zeitung*, which noted that three different productions of *Die Dreigroschenoper* had already been staged in Tokyo. The third was a nonsense revue *Die Dreigroschenoper* performed at the Moulin Rouge Shinjukuza, which opened at the end of the previous year, using Pabst's film as the basis for the production[55]. The article featured

---

[53]. Murayama 1932.

[54]. Senda 1975, p. 235. The names of 37 actors are listed in *Shinko Gikyoku*. Shinko Gikyoku 1932, pp. 22-23. Some actors played more than one role, such as Tomoko Ito, who played the three roles of an old woman, Hanako the town woman, and Heichamashi's (Peacham's) wife (on the first day).

[55]. Berliner illustrierte Zeitung 1932, p. 995. Weill-Lenya Research Center. Regarding information on Japanese productions, there is a statement that Walter Benjamin reported on this information: Hinton 1990, p. 50. The performance at the Moulin Rouge Shinjukuza, which opened at the end of 1931, was called the nonsense revue *Die Dreigroschenoper*, and was held from 10 to 13 March. The title of the performance was «From the film The Threepenny Opera by Brecht», indicating that Pabst's film was the original. The text was translated by Kamesuke Shioiri and adapted and directed by Keiichi Shimizu. Nakano 2011, pp. 95-96.

photographs of the Tokyo Theatre Group, and reported the production to be a mixture of Japanese and Western styles, with a knack for timelessness in both the costumes and the overall performance. In the stage costumes, Orie (Polly) wore a Western-style dress, while Osen (Jenny) wore a kimono (Ills. 3 and 4). Osen also played the shamisen on stage like a Geisha girl to accompany 'Okazaki Ondo', a folksong that was added (discussed further below).

Ill. 3: Koreya Senda as Mekichi/Macheath, Chikako Hosokawa as Orie/Polly and Keinichi Enomoto as Reverend Kimbal. Courtesy of The Tsubouchi Memorial Theatre Museum, Waseda University, F54-03682 *The Beggar's Play*.

Ill. 4: At the Bordello Toyoko Takahashi as Osen/Jenny on the right side. Courtesy of The Tsubouchi Memorial Theatre Museum, Waseda University, F54-03681 *The Beggar's Play*.

On the evening of 14 June 1932, another performance of Shiori's adaptation of *Die Dreigroschenoper* took place at the Hibiya Public Hall, directed by Yobun Kaneko, a proletarian playwright. It was arranged by Masao Shinohara, a graduate of the Tokyo Music School who as active in the Asakusa Opera, who also conducted the Corona Orchestra at the performance. Macheath was played by tenor Yuzuru Kuroda, a graduate of Asakusa Opera; Peacham was played by Musei Tokugawa, an actor as well as a Benshi (narrator of silent films); Mrs. Peacham by soprano Akiko Sato; Polly Peacham by soprano Takane Nanbu; and Jenny by Kikuyo Amano, a graduate of Asakusa Opera who also sang popular music by Nipponophone. The role of Brown was cast with baritone Keisuke Shimoyagawa[56].

Compared to the Tokyo Acting Troupe's *Beggar's Play*, Keneko's cast included many classically trained vocalists, and the lineup was particularly focused on the music. Kumazawa Mataroku, a Russian literature scholar who published regularly in *Gekkan Gakufu*, quoted someone who had already seen the show five times in England as saying that the Japanese productions of *Die Dreigroschenoper* were «less musical and more theatrical than the original, which is more like an operetta»[57]. He criticized Kaneko's production in harsh terms for the technical challenge in the music, saying that first of all, it was necessary to clarify why this piece should be performed[58].

«The Beggar's Play» – The First Performance of «The Threepenny Opera»

There is prior research on the stage premiere of Tokyo Acting Troupe's *The Beggar's Play* by Masaaki Nakano, who reprinted the script[59]. A characteristic feature of this performance, as found in the script, is that the original work was adapted to suit the tastes, comprehensibility, and social conditions of Japanese audiences. According to a commentary by the Tokyo Acting Troupe, *Die Dreigroschenoper* is Brecht's «free adaptation» of John Gay's *The Beggar's Opera* and Weill's «modern artistic jazz and orchestra that created a melodramatic free form in the most entrenched theatre since naturalism»[60], and following this, Tokyo's *The Beggar's Play* was also positioned as a freely adapted *Die Dreigroschenoper* by the Tokyo Acting Troupe. Nakano wrote:

> […] This work was not, of course, written as an opera in this sense, but as a play in which the traditional drama, which had not yet escaped its naturalistic and ideological character, was given a pure theatrical interest in form, and in content,

---

56. Ongaku Shincho 1932, pp. 92-93.
57. Kumazawa 1932, pp. 92.
58. *Ibidem*, pp. 92-93.
59. Nakano 2007a.
60. Shinko Gikyoku 1932, p. 21.

> a form of drama that was perfectly suited to the times and the public. This is where
> Brecht's outstanding dramatic value should be recognized[61].

Nakano goes on to point out that since Pabst's film was highly acclaimed in Japan, «the Tokyo Acting Troupe's aim was to create a popular theatre aimed at the urban middle class by staging Die Dreigroschenoper as a musical drama rather than a Brecht-style morality play»[62]. The concept was led by Senda, who had seen the first performance in Berlin[63]. But in the Japanese version, which he and Hijikata created together, the setting was changed to Tokyo in the first year of the Meiji era. In the beginning of the first act, Macheath/Mekichi listens to the 'Moritat', sung by a street singer, at «a place near the Tsukiji riverbank where the Honganji temple worshippers gather». In Brecht's version, Macheath is pardoned by Her Majesty's envoy in a lively 'recitative' and promised a knighthood and a lifetime pension, while the whole cast sings a chorale of celebration, followed by indictment of the audience and a call to action at the end. In contrast, in the Japanese version of *The Beggar's Play*, the Queen's coronation ceremony is replaced by 'Daihoe' (Great Buddhist Memorial Service), and Mekichi is told by a messenger on horseback that he has been pardoned and «appointed commissioner of the colony». On the stage almost 20 songs were played, but Nakano also observes: «A few songs were reduced from the original and Japanese-style doubles were increased»[64].

The songs in *Die Dreigroschenoper* are characterized by the fact that they are not integrated into the plot of the story[65], so it is not unusual for them to be replaced by other numbers. *The Beggar's Play* added Japanese traditional folk songs, such as Hauta 'Naramaru Kuzushi' in Act I and 'Okazaki Ondo' in Act II, in which Okazaki Ondo is sung by Osen as Jenny: «Sleep with You or shall we take 5000 koku?» (ILL. 5).

These songs are clearly dissimilar to the musical concept of Weill's *Die Dreigroschenoper*, which musically focuses on western dance rhythms like the minuet, tango or march. However, given the nature of these two changes, a song's replacement can also be interpreted as analogous to a 'ballad opera', which was composed of existing folk songs and operatic arias, essentially continuing the tradition of Gay and Pepush's ballad opera *The Beggar's Opera* of 1728 (ILL. 6).

Another important difference is the treatment of the finale. In the original version of *Die Dreigroschenoper*, the finale in each act follows the form of an opera or operetta. Traditionally, the finale is usually deeply connected to the dramatic catharsis, such as the happy or tragic ending

---

[61]. *Ibidem*, p. 21.
[62]. NAKANO 2007a, p. 190.
[63]. SENDA 1976, p. 37.
[64]. NAKANO 2007a, p. 191. In connection with the TES Orchestra, which was in charge of music, the TES Ensemble was organized immediately after the performance of *The Beggar's Play*. An analysis of the members of the ensemble indicated that it had a strong orientation toward jazz.
[65]. BRECHT 1985, p. 58.

Ill. 5: Toyoko Takahashi as Osen/Jenny with Shamisen. Courtesy of The Tsubouchi Memorial Theatre Museum, Waseda University, F54-03691 *The Beggar's Play*.

Ill. 6: TES (Tokyo Engeki Shudan / Tokyo Acting Troupe) Orchester. Courtesy of The Tsubouchi Memorial Theatre Museum, Waseda University, F54-03691 *The Beggar's Play*.

of the drama. In this respect, the finale of *Die Dreigroschenoper* produces the «estrangement effect» (*Verfremdungseffekt*), as it issues a call for action rather than discharging tension. In *The Beggar's Play*, the original finale was not placed at the end of each act, but was freely arranged, sung at the beginning of the opening act or the second act. Only the third finale is sung at the end of the act.

The decisive difference between *The Beggar's Play* and *Die Dreigroschenoper* is that the former does not engage with 'opera' or the European tradition of 'Christianity'. 'Opera' played a decisive role in the for Brecht's 'estrangment effect' and for the dramaturgy of Weill's 'gestic' music. This was also shown in the fact that the title of the Japanese version was changed to *The Beggar's Play* without the word 'opera' in it. The meaning of Kurt Weill's musical gestures, which were supported not only by contemporary jazz and dance music but also by Baroque music styles, was an element that was difficult to convey to Japanese audiences. In the *Asahi Shimbun*, Tomoyoshi Murayama praised the individuality of the actors, but criticized the «painful breakdown of conventional opera in both content and form» which did not work «for Japanese audiences who still have no operatic tradition», noting that it was important to improve the actors' singing skills to respond to opera and jazz[66].

THE BEGGAR'S PLAY – CULTURAL MEMORY AS A MUSICAL THEATRE FOR COMMON PEOPLE IN JAPAN

The change of characters' names to Japanese and the positioning of characters by their costumes were a form of Japanese-Western fusion, but they also reflected the process of modernization of Japanese society. As *Shinko Gikyoku* wrote, Macheath/Mekichi, is «a man of a refined taste pretending to be a gentleman from the high-culture» and is «Westernized in every way»[67]. In contrast, Osen/Jenny, in her kimono, symbolizes the old world, with sex as a commodity.

For Senda, who had seen the premiere in Berlin in person, these changes were necessary for *Die Dreigroschenoper* to be performed on the Japanese stage. What was important was that these changes were made for a performance for a general Japanese audience. In fact, according to actor Hisaya Morishige's memoirs, at the time «this theme song 'Mackie Messer no Uta' (Mack the Knife) sung also in Japanese by street vendors was truly impressive», and through film, record, and stage, «the song (sung in the play) was sung with love among new students»[68]. In the early years, Weill's music attracted even more attention than Brecht's libretto. Perhaps

---

[66]. MURAYAMA 1932.
[67]. *SHINKO GIKYOKU* 1932, p. 24.
[68]. MORISHIGE 1977, p. 28.

this was due, in part, to the fact that film and recordings played a greater role in the reception of *Die Dreigroschenoper* than the stage in Japan. Songs of *Die Dreigroschenoper* have been passed down from generation to generation.

The basic idea of localizing Western works and presenting them in a form familiar to the 'Japanese public' was also a characteristic of Asakusa Opera. It later became the source of the 'memory' of Japanese performances of *Die Dreigroschenoper* and was carried over into postwar productions[69]. However, even at the time of the first 'Threepenny Fever' in 1932, the oppression of proletarian theatre people in particular grew more severe every day, including the May 15 Incident, the torture and death of novelist Takiji Kobayashi, and the repeated imprisonment of Koreya Senda. Japan was soon plunged into total war[70]. It was not until the 1950s, after the end of the war and the occupation, that *Die Dreigroschenoper* was again performed on the stages that housed various genres of theatre[71]. From the 1950's the cultural memory of *Die Dreigroschenoper* as a theatre for common people in Japan was strongly brought back to Japanese audience, also with Kurt Weill's beloved songs from the era of the Japanese Threepenny Fever.

Bibliograhiy

Asahi Shimbun 1930
'Obelisk – *The Threepenny Opera*', in: *Asahi Shimbun*, 18 February 1930.

Asahi Shimbun 1932a
'Koreya Senda, the Man in Question, Launches New Theater Company, Stopping the Ideological Trend toward a Single Ideological Direction, the quirky Variety Theatre', in: *Asahi Shimbun*, 28 January 1932.

---

[69]. In 1988, *Die Dreigroschenoper* by the Black Tent, an *avant-garde* troupe, was based on a libretto by Kiyokazu Yamamoto and directed by Makoto Sato. It was set in Tokyo in the first year of the Meiji era (1868-1912).

[70]. The last time a newspaper advertisement for a translation of Brecht's novel *Die Dreigroschenoper* (translated by Hideo Kikumori, Nikko Shoin) appeared on 27 March 1941 (*Asahi Shimbun*), and in June, 'Recent Translation (Germany)' commented, «The fact that Bertolt Brecht's Die Dreigroschenoper was translated at this time is only ironic because it is a mockery of the anti-Nazi Jewish proletarian writers' attack on London, a stronghold of the moneyed class». The advertisement for the film was for a screening at the Shin-eiza Theatre in October 1941. In Germany, *Die Dreigroschenoper* was labeled a decadent art form and could not be performed after 1933. In Japan *Die Dreigroschenoper* was still being screened and translated and published in the 1940s.

[71]. During the occupation period, Weill's American-era work, the folk opera *Down in the Valley*, was planned (but never realized) by the Ernie Pyle Theatre and performed at a record concert at the CIE Library, but there is no record of a performance of *Die Dreigroschenoper*. During the occupation period, the *Yomiuri Shimbun* 1950 reported, on 11 January, that Kenichi Enomoto, who played Reverend Kimbal in the 1932 *The Beggar's Play* was planning a comic opera and had *Die Dreigroschenoper* as a candidate. Also see Ohta – Oja 2021, p. 70 and p. 80 (note 88).

ASAHI SHIMBUN 1932B
'A Small Suite of *The Threepenny Opera* Conducted by Hidemaro Konoe', in: *Asahi Shimbun*, 14 February 1932.

ASSMANN 2008
ASSMANN, Aleida. 'Canon and Archive', in: *Cultural Memory Studies – An International and Interdisciplinary Handbook*, edited by Astrid Erll and Ansgar Nünning, Berlin-New York, Walter de Gruyter, 2008, pp. 97-107.

BERLINER ILLUSTRIERTE ZEITUNG 1932
Berliner illustrierte Zeitung, no. 30 (1932), p. 995.

BRECHT 1985
BRECHT, Bertolt. 'Über das Singen der Songs', in: *Brechts Dreigroschenoper*, edited by Werner Hecht, Frankfurt, Suhrkamp, 1985.

BRECHT 2004
ID. *Die Dreigroschenoper – Text und Kommentar*, edited by Joachim Lucchesi, Frankfurt am Main, Shurkamp, 2004 (Basisbibliothek, 48).

GOTO 2001
GOTO, Nobuko *et al. Music Criticism Magazine in the Early Showa Period: Budding of Music Criticism, Index of Articles*, Tokyo, Yamada Kosaku Kenkyujo Publishing, 2001.

GOTO 2014
ID. *Creating, Not Producing – Kosaku Yamada*, Kyoto, Minerva Shoten, 2014.

HAGIWARA 2009
HAGIWARA, Ken. 'On the Theatre of the Agit-prop-Tai (Mezamashitai) – Deinstitutionalized Theatre, Its Transformation during the Fifteen Years War', in: *Theatre Studies Review*, 2009, pp. 53-73.

HAYASAKI 1994
HAYASAKI, Erina. *Berlin-Tokyo Story*, Tokyo, Ongaku no Tomo Sha, 1994.

HINTON 1990
HINTON, Stephen. 'The Premiere and after', in: *Kurt Weill «The Threepenny Opera»*, edited by Stephen Hinton, Cambridge, Cambridge University Press, 1990 (Cambridge Opera Handbooks), pp. 50-77.

ITO 1931
ITO, Noboru. 'Rag Music as Pure Music', in: *Gekkan Gakufu*, July 1931, pp. 18-22.

ITO 1983
ITO, Toshiharu. 'Nihon no 1920s: Tokyo o Chushin tosuru Toshi Taishu Bunka no Tenkai' (The 1920s in Japan: The Development of Urban Popular Culture Centering on Tokyo), in: *Toshi Taishubunka no Seiritsu* (Formation of urban popular culture), Tokyo, Yuhikaku Sensho, 1983, pp. 176-204.

KAMITSUKASA 1932A
KAMITSUKASA, Shoken. 'The Cry of Art Denial (1)', in: *Yomiuri Shimbun*, 5 April 1932.

KAMITSUKASA 1932B
ID. 'The Cry of Art Denial (2)', in: *Yomiuri Shimbun*, 6 April 1932.

KAMITSUKASA 1932C
ID. 'The Cry of Art Denial (3)', in: *Yomiuri Shimbun*, 7 April 1932.

KOIZUMI 1932
KOIZUMI, Ko. 'Return to Mozart', in: *Ongaku Sekai*, February 1932, pp. 29-31.

KUMAZAWA 1932
KUMAZAWA, Mataroku. 'I Saw the *Threepenny Opera*', in: *Gekkan Gakufu*, XXI/7 (1932), pp. 92-95.

MORI 2012
MORI, Masato. 'Brief History of Tsuru Records', in: *Jazz in the Central City – Great Nagoya's Tsuru-Asahi Jazz Song Collection 1929-1938*, Gramoclub, 2012.

MORISHIGE 1977
MORISHIGE, Hisaya. 'Memories of *The Beggar's Play* in Its Japanese Premiere (1932)', in: *Teigeki The Threepenny Opera Pamphlet*, 1977, p. 28.

MURAYAMA 1932
MURAYAMA, Tomoyoshi. 'Watching *Beggar's Play* – Tokyo Theater Group's Flagship Show', in: *Asahi Shimbun*, 29 March 1932, morning edition.

NAKANE 1932
NAKANE, Hiroshi. 'The Value of Music in the *Threepenny Opera*', in: *Eiga Hyoron*, March 1932, pp. 63-66.

NAKANO 2007A
NAKANO, Masaaki. 'Bertolt Brecht's Original Play, Freely Adapted by Tokyo Acting Troupe's Literary Department, *The Beggar's Opera* (*The Threepenny Opera*) in Three Acts and Three Scenes (1)', in: *Theatre Research and Theatre Museum Bulletin*, XXXI (2007), pp. 189-222.

NAKANO 2007B
ID. 'From Shinko Geijutsuha to Revue Theater: Kagerouza, Magazine Kindai Seikatsu to Casino Folie, Moulin Rouge', in: *Bulletin of the Center for Theatre Research*, Tokyo, Waseda University VIII, 2007, pp. 331-344.

NAKANO 2011
ID. *Moulin Rouge Shinjukuza: A Short History of Light Theater in the Showa Period*, Tokyo, Shinwasha, 2011.

николиуа 1931a
Ninomiya, Shu. 'On *Dreigroschenoper (The Beggar's Opera)*', in: *Ongaku Sekai*, iii/10 (1931), pp. 126-132.

Ninomiya 1931b
Id. 'On *Dreigroschenoper (The Beggar's Opera)*', in: *Ongaku Sekai*, iii/12 (1931), pp. 64-73.

Nozawa 2004
Nozawa, Christopher N. 'Musicians and Their Backgrounds', CD1, Domestic Recordings of Japanese Musicians, in: *Rohm Music Foundation SP Record Reissue CD Collection*, 2004, pp. 20-21.

Ohta 2014
Ohta, Misako. 'Kurt Weill: A Sociocultural History of Musical Theatre', in: *Bungaku (Literature)*, Tokyo, Iwanami Shoten, 2014, pp. 84-98.

Ohta – Oja 2021
Ohta, Misako – Oja, J. Carol. 'US Consert Music and Cultural Reorientation', in: *Sounding Together – Collaborative Perspectives on U.S. Music in the 21st Century*, edited by Charles Hiroshi Garrett and Carol J. Oja, Ann Arbor, University of Michigan Press, 2021, pp. 51-81.

Ongaku Shincho 1932
'*The Threepenny Opera* Performance', in: *Ongaku Shincho* (Music New Wave), July 1932, pp. 92-93.

Otaguro 1935
Otaguro, Motoo. 'The Flight of Lindbergh', in: *Asahi Shimbun*, 30 May 1935.

Otani 1982
Otani, Koichi. *Critique of Takeda Rintaro*, Sendagaya-Shibuya-Tokyo, Kawade Shobo Shinsya, 1982.

Polydor Monthly Bulletin 1932
'Music of Kurt Weill's *Threepenny Opera*', in: *Polydor Monthly Bulletin*, January 1932, pp. 17-20.

Record 1932
'Talkie; Music in the *The Threepenny Opera*', in: *Record*, January 1932, pp. 130-135.

Senda 1975
Senda, Koreya. *Another Shingeki History*, Tokyo, Chikuma Shobo, 1975.

Senda 1976
Id. *Theatre in the 20th Century: Brecht and I*, Tokyo, Yomiuri Shimbun, 1976.

Shinko Gikyoku 1932
'Bertolt Brecht's original *Threepenny Opera*, freely Adapted by the Literary Department of the Tokyo Acting Troupe, *Beggar's Play*: Overture and Twelve Scenes in Three Acts', in: *Shinko Gikyoku* (New Play), May 1932, pp. 21-25.

SHIOIRI 1930
SHIOIRI, Kamesuke. *Jazz Music*, Tokyo, Keibunkan, 1930.

SHIOIRI 1932
ID. 'The Music of *Threepenny Opera*', in: *Eiga Hyoron*, March 1932, pp. 66-69.

TAKEDA 2000
TAKEDA, Rintaro. *Nihon Sanmon Opera (Japan's Threepenny Opera)*, commentary by Masaaki Kawanishi, Tokyo, Kodansha, 2000.

WEILL 1928
WEILL, Kurt. 'Zeitoper', in: *Melos*, VII/3 (1928), pp. 106-108 [also in: *Kurt Weill Musik und Musikalisches Theater: Gesammelte Schriften*, edited by Stephen Hinton, Jürgen Schebera and Elmar Juchem, Mainz, Schott Musik International, 2000, pp. 64-67].

WEILL 1929
ID. 'Notiz zum Jazz', in: *Anbruch*, March 1929, p. 138 [also in: *Kurt Weill Musik und Musikalisches Theater: Gesammelte Schriften*, op. cit., pp. 82-83].

WEILL 2000A
ID. *Die Dreigroschenoper*, edited by Stephen Hinton and Edward Harsch, New York, Kurt Weill Foundation for Music / European American Music Corporation, 2000 (The Kurt Weill Edition, I/5).

WEILL 2000B
ID. *Briefe an die Familie (1914-1950)*, edited by Lys Symonette and Elmar Juchem, Stuttgart, J. B. Metzler, 2000.

YAMADA 2001
YAMADA, Kosaku. '*The Threepenny Opera* no Mondai', (23 February 1932, *Tokyo Nichinichi Shimbun*), in: *Yamada Kosaku Zenshu 2*, Tokyo, Iwanami Shoten, 2001, pp. 238-239.

YOMIURI SHIMBUN 1950
'Enoken, Inspired by the Public's Opinion of Him, Is Planning an Operetta, and Is also Keen on a 10,000-Circus Play' in: *Yomiuri Shimbun*, 11 January 1950.

«Hard to Distinguish from Cole Porter»: On the Deeper Truth of an Invective by Adorno

Tobias Fasshauer
(Independent Scholar, Berlin)

In 1956, Theodor W. Adorno, in a dispute with Horst Koegler concerning the critical assessment of Kurt Weill's American works and especially of *Street Scene* (1947), made the following statement:

> That Weill still came up with extremely suggestive song melodies even in emigration, no one will deny. But under the explicit or unspoken pressure of a conformism that uses "he is too artistic" as a death sentence, he was certainly *no* longer able to do everything he was able to do. [...] You only need to play songs from the old version of *Mahagonny* and from the *Threepenny Opera* and immediately afterwards from *Lady in the Dark* and *One Touch of Venus*, and you will hear what Weill had to sacrifice to the slick smoothness of popular music. This is really, except for a few alien moments in *Down in the Valley*, hard to distinguish from Cole Porter, save for the fact that the light idiom caused some difficulties for Kurt Weill and that, to his credit, he never spoke it quite as fluently as the models[1].

---

[1]. «Daß Weill auch in der Emigration noch überaus suggestive Songmelodien eingefallen sind, wird niemand bestreiten. Sicherlich aber konnte er unter dem ausgesprochenen oder nichtausgesprochenen Druck eines Konformismus, der 'he is too artistic' als Todesurteil verwendet, *nicht* mehr alles, was er konnte. [...] Man braucht nur Songs aus der alten Fassung von *Mahagonny* und aus der *Dreigroschenoper* und unmittelbar danach solche als [*sic*] *Lady in the Dark* und *One Touch of Venus* zu spielen, und man wird hören, was alles Weill der geschleckten Glätte der popular music opfern mußte. Das ist wirklich, außer ein paar fremden Momenten auch in *Down in the Valley*, von Cole Porter nur schwer zu unterscheiden, es sei denn dadurch, daß das leichte Idiom Kurt Weill ein wenig schwerfiel und daß er es, zu seiner Ehre, nie ganz so fließend sprach wie die Modelle». Adorno 1984, pp. 800ff., emphasis in original.

In the more recent scholarly discourse on Weill, which shifted the emphasis from the ruptures in his oeuvre to its continuities, this quote came to epitomize everything that was problematic about Adorno's view of the composer. Giselher Schubert wrote:

> None of Adorno's comments on Weill from the time after the Second World War are based on a renewed engagement with Weill's works; and the few judgments on more recent works that he intersperses seem egregious and downright annoying in their bizarre uninformedness [...][2].

In a footnote, Schubert explains: «I mean, above all, the comparison of Weill with Cole Porter [...], with which he believed to disavow Weill completely, but which now documents his narrow-mindedness»[3].

While Schubert did not elaborate on the question of how exactly Adorno's alleged «bizarre uninformedness» about Weill manifested itself, Kim Kowalke was more specific in his criticism of Adorno's comparison. He addressed what in fact was Adorno's main target, the aspect of musical style:

> If Adorno had experienced Weill's American scores as performed in their original Broadway productions, he would not have found the music «hard to distinguish from Cole Porter». Rather he would have encountered (and surely recognized) familiar Weillian elements: melodies, harmonic procedures, formal structures, text-music relationships, tonal language [...][4].

Without question, Adorno drew the comparison between Weill and Porter to devalue the American work of the former. What is striking about Schubert's and Kowalke's comments, however, is their implicit premise that the two composers did not play in the same artistic league. Tacitly, if perhaps subconsciously, Weill is ranked higher than Porter, which is evident from the fact that Kowalke and Schubert seek to defend him against Adorno's attack while Porter does not receive such treatment. One might wonder who would have protested if Adorno, or anybody else, had stated that Porter's songs were hard to distinguish from Weill's.

Kowalke implies that Weill's so-called 'American' style differs substantially from Porter's, and that this difference is due to the presence of certain elements that were typical of Weill in

---

[2]. «Keine seiner [Adornos] Ausführungen zu Weill aus der Zeit nach dem Zweiten Weltkrieg beruhen auf einer erneuten direkten Auseinandersetzung mit den Werken Weills; und die wenigen Urteile über neuere Werke, die er einstreut, wirken in ihrer bizarren Uninformiertheit unsäglich und schlechterdings ärgerlich [...]». SCHUBERT 2000, pp. 35ff.

[3]. «Gemeint ist vor allem der Vergleich Weills mit Cole Porter [...], mit der [sic] er Weill vollends zu desavouieren glaubte, die nun aber seine Borniertheit dokumentiert». *Ibidem*, p. 36.

[4]. KOWALKE 1995, p. 36.

the 1920s. In contrast, this essay aims to demonstrate that, not only are there many similarities in style and creative thinking between Weill and Porter, but the latter also received formative impulses from French modernism of the 1920s, which makes him seem closer to Kurt Weill than might be expected if one has only Porter's Broadway career in mind. In other words, this essay attempts to reveal a deeper truth in Adorno's statement about Weill and Porter. Considering that Adorno is referring to musical style and structure, it does so on the basis of musical analysis. Analyzing popular songs, however, involves problems that result from the fact that such pieces usually lack the quality of a 'work in the emphatic sense', the *Werkcharakter*. Don M. Randel described this challenge with regard to Porter:

> Before studying or performing a work, musicologists like to satisfy themselves that they have established a suitably reliable text of the work [...]. Cole Porter's songs, however, do not lend themselves to such a pursuit, for complete autographs of both words and music are relatively rare, and the character of such autographs and of the first printed editions of this music were clearly shaped by the nature of the intended audiences and performances. For example, a song of this type was often first published in a form and for an audience that required it to be relatively easy to play on the piano. [...] It is thus rather difficult to establish what features of any given song can be thought to be essential to its identity. [...] We will no doubt wish to get as close as we can to what Porter himself had in mind, but Porter himself almost certainly contemplated modifications by others [...]. This greatly complicates anything we might like to produce in the way of voice-leading graphs [...], since apart from the melody itself, register is not in general specified at all as essential to the identity of a song, and there may be considerable variety even in the inversion in which a given harmony is presented. One will thus not be able to speak with much confidence of a pitch in the melody that is given support in the bass[5].

Matthew Shaftel assessed the source value of Porter sheet music editions much more favorably: «[U]nlike composers such as Irving Berlin, Porter had the training and experience to write the piano-vocal scores for his songs in their entirety and we have demonstrated that the printed sheet music resembles these piano-vocal scores almost exactly»[6]. This statement, however, does not invalidate Randel's basic claim that the simplification of the songs for the sheet music market caused uncertainty about their identity.

While Randel's observations apply probably to the vast majority of U.S. popular music before recordings overtook sheet music, Kurt Weill is an exception; for the elaborate scores of his stage works — contrary to Broadway practice, he used to orchestrate them himself — do indeed offer «reliable texts» to a sufficient degree (as is proven by the Kurt Weill Edition). That is why,

---

[5]. RANDEL 2016, pp. 222f.
[6]. SHAFTEL 1999, p. 321.

in line with Kowalke's reference to «Weill's American scores as performed in their original Broadway productions», the stage versions of the songs can be considered authoritative manifestations of their identity. It remains a fact, however, that Weill's songs achieved their greatest impact, apart from recordings, through their dissemination as authorized sheet music, and it is only in this guise that they can be compared with Porter's songs. A comparative analysis of Weill's and Porter's songs must therefore be limited to an examination of what is basically preserved in the simplified sheet music versions: melody and harmonic substance, which can be assumed not to have been significantly altered by an arranger. This limitation does not devalue the analytic approach, for even if melody and harmony do not constitute the whole of Weill's composing style, they are its most formative elements. Orchestration and how the basic harmony translates into specific figures of accompaniment cannot be the object of such analysis.

Porter's European Modernist Experience: *Within the Quota*[7]

In 1917, Cole Porter came to France as a volunteer with a relief organization, and stayed in Paris when World War I was over. He studied with Vincent d'Indy at the Schola cantorum and frequented the soirées of the famous patron Princesse Edmond de Polignac (who was later to commission Weill's Second Symphony). In the summer of 1922, Porter approached Igor Stravinsky about receiving composition lessons, but they did not come to terms, reportedly because of the high fee Stravinsky demanded[8]. In June 1923, Porter took a private intensive course in orchestration with Charles Koechlin, to whom he had been introduced by Darius Milhaud. About the same time, Rolf de Maré, director of the Ballets Suédois, was planning an American tour for the following year and, according to Milhaud, wanted «an authentic American work, but did not know whom to approach. He was afraid of coming across some composer struggling in the wake of Debussy, Ravel, or someone composing music *à la Brahms*, or *à la Reger*»[9]. Thanks to a recommendation from Milhaud, he chose Porter. Collaborating with the painter Gerald Murphy, who provided the scenario and designed the scenery, Porter composed *Within the Quota*, which depicts the adventures of a Swedish immigrant on his arrival at New York. When Porter became pressed for time, Koechlin took over the orchestration of the ballet. It premiered on 25 October 1923 at the Théâtre des Champs-Élysées as part of a program that also featured the première of Milhaud's ballet *La Création du monde*, works by

---

[7]. Information on *Within the Quota*, its genesis and background is compiled from Orledge 1975, Harbec 2015, Morrison 2016, and Van den Brande 2016.
[8]. See Van den Brande 2016, p. 44.
[9]. As cited in Orledge 1975, p. 20.

Erik Satie, and young composers of the École d'Arceuil promoted by Satie. In an interview for the Paris edition of the *New York Herald*, Porter said the following about his work:

> The object is of course to get the quintessence of Americanism out of its newspapers. It is not cubism, but its composition is inspired by cubism. [...] The characters are all out of real life. There is a Jazz Baby who is a composite of Goldie [*recte*: Gilda] Gray and Ann Pennington, a millionaire who is a study of an American woman entering the Ritz, a sweetheart of the world who is of course Mary Pickford. [...] Well, it is nothing but a translation on to the stage of the way America looks to me from over here. I put into the play all the things that come out of America to me, [...] as I get things into perspective and distance. Paris is bound to make a man either more or less American[10].

It should be added that the female characters Porter mentions are joined by a «colored gentleman», a cowboy, a sheriff, and others.

Within the Quota was a highly ironic project: expatriate Americans exploited stereotypes of America for a ballet that was to be performed by a European company before an American audience. Musically, the work represents quintessential Cocteauesque modernism, which combined up-to-date composing methods and sonic materials such as polytonality and polymodality, the whole-tone system, quartal harmony, ostinato technique, and emancipated dissonance, with elements of popular music of American provenience, indiscriminately labeled as 'jazz'[11]. In the Paris *Herald*, Porter explained: «It's easier to write jazz over here than in New York [...]. One reason is because you are too much under the influence of the popular song in America, and jazz is better than that. It has a very large value for the future of music, as is shown by the influence it has on most European composers. Perhaps some of them take it a little too seriously [...]». The interviewer added: «The music of 'Within the Quota' is described as American rhythms worked into ballet form, and is an exhibition of the possibilities of native melodies in an art form by a composer who has already had a hand in the making of popular tunes [...]»[12]. Porter's efforts to distance the piece from American popular song seems remarkable for someone who would soon become one of the leading American songwriters. *Within the Quota* remained his only endeavor as a composer of so-called 'serious' music.

The combination of European modernist and American popular idioms, the latter mainly represented by syncopated dance rhythms and some blues tonality, is well exemplified by movement no. 4 from *Within the Quota*, 'The Colored Gentleman'. It is a sort of distorted ragtime, which employs an arsenal of impressionist harmonic means such as parallel seventh

---

[10]. HERALD 1923, p. 6.

[11]. Statements about the musical structure of *Within the Quota* refer to the transcription for two pianos or piano, four hands, by William Bolcom and Richard Rodney Bennett, Edward B. Marks Music/Hal Leonard, 2017.

[12]. HERALD 1923, p. 6.

chords, chords with added dissonant notes, and the emancipation of dissonance within the diatonic material. A set of harmonic sequences that occur in the middle of the movement gives a sense of Porter's compositional sophistication (see Ex. 1).

Ex. 1: Cole Porter, *Within the Quota*, 4. 'The Colored Gentleman', bars 200-203, pair of chromatic sequences based on a whole tone scale (schematic representation).

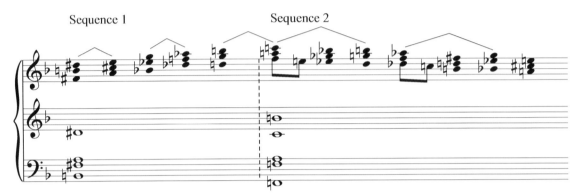

The first sequence consists of pairs of major triads ascending in major thirds, in bar 200: B-A, E♭-D♭, G-F. Second inversion (first chord of a pair) and root position (second chord of a pair) are alternating in this progression, so that the whole tone scale, which determines its construction, does not become evident melodically. This sequence leads immediately into another one, a progression descending in major thirds using the same roots as the first sequence, but in a different order and grouped in threes instead of pairs: F-e♭-G, D♭-b-E♭, A. Here, the first two chords of each group of three appear in root position, but nonetheless their whole tone relation is blurred by a passing semitone in the lowest voice. The whole harmonic complex is underlaid with the progression of a B major seventh chord into an F major triad with the addition of a dissonant Lydian fourth (the chord change takes place when the first sequence reaches F major, which, according to the key signature, is the tonic of the movement).

The assimilation of American popular idioms on the basis of an aesthetic that erased the boundaries between high art and mass culture was a major contribution of French composers, namely Satie and Milhaud, to European non-expressionist art music after World War I, and their model was followed by German composers of the New Objectivity movement, including Kurt Weill — the Americanism of *Mahagonny* is not too far from either Satie's and Cocteau's *Parade* or Porter's *Within the Quota*[13]. Thus it may be said that Porter and Weill shared, to some extent at least, a common aesthetic and technical inspirations. Kowalke rightly points out that Weill's experience as an avant-garde composer in the Weimar Republic is still evident in his work as a popular American composer. Now the question is, does something similar apply

---

[13]. On this influence, see FASSHAUER 2014.

to Cole Porter, whose engagement with art music was much shorter and less intense? A positive answer to this question would not necessarily depend on the evidence of specifically modernist configurations of the musical material. A modernist attitude may also become evident when conventional textbook form and harmony are not taken for granted but are treated as material for creative manipulation, something which Hanns Eisler and Adorno called the independence of resources and composing methods in their book *Composing for the Films* from 1947[14]. However, composers striving for popularity were not as free in their creative choices as those of art music, but had to be careful not to deviate too far from established genre standards regarding form, tonality, meter, and rhythm in order to keep their music accessible. The power of convention seems weakest with regard to harmony, for an appealing melody allows for considerable freedom in the harmonic treatment.

'Night and Day'

One of Porter's most famous songs, 'Night and Day', from the musical *Gay Divorce* (1932), serves as a good starting point for discussing his modernism and artistic originality. Since Matthew Shaftel has analyzed the song in detail (applying Schenkerian theory)[15], it may suffice here to point out some of the features that specifically constitute the modernist attitude mentioned above.

The melody of the refrain (see Ex. 2) starts with the fifth note of the scale, which would normally call for a tonic or dominant chord. Instead, it is harmonized with an unexpectable major seventh chord of the lowered sixth degree in pre-dominant function. Technically, this chord can be described as an instance of vertical montage, i.e. harmonizing a melody against its historically determined implication, which is in fact a typically Weillian technique. Another Weillian technique is the structural integration of the surprise chord through chromatic voice leading. The effect here is stunning: the contrast between the bluesy, dissonant pre-dominant chord from the depths of the minor subdominant region on the one hand and the major seventh chord of the tonic on the other can be heard as a tone painting of the words «night and day», undercut with an ironic asynchronicity between the lyrics and the music, however, as the word

---

[14]. See EISLER 1947, p. 82. (Adorno had resigned from his co-authorship prior to publication in order to avoid being drawn into the political campaign against Eisler.) In the latest German edition, the crucial passage reads: «Trügt jedoch nicht alles, dann hat die Musik heute eine Phase erreicht, in der Material und Verfahrensweise auseinandertreten, und zwar in dem Sinn, daß das Material gegenüber der Verfahrensweise relativ gleichgültig wird». ADORNO – EISLER 2006, p. 74.

[15]. SHAFTEL 1999. It should be mentioned that Schenkerian analysis, which aims to reveal the integral, organic character of a musical work of art, does not help much in explaining the originality of a piece of popular music against the backdrop of conventions.

«day» coincides with the somber, dissonant pre-dominant chord ♭VI⁷. The sweet brightness of the major tonic is given additional emphasis by putting the third in the melody and encircling it chromatically in the triplet on the upbeat to the third bar[16]. As this motivic configuration — the third of the major tonic in the melody embellished with its neighboring semitones — refers back to the nineteenth century parlor style[17], we have a clever montage of blues feeling and romantic sentimentality.

Ex. 2: Cole Porter, 'Night and Day' (New York, Harms Inc., 1932), bars 21-23, reduced to melodic-harmonic outline.

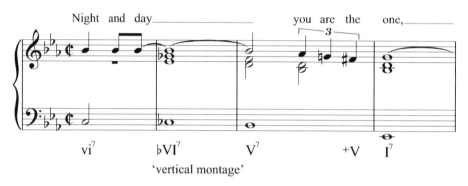

Alec Wilder, in his book *American Popular Song*, tells a revealing anecdote about Porter introducing the song to his publisher: «The story goes that when Porter played this song for Max Dreyfus of Harms Music, he received an unenthusiastic reaction due to the bass notes beneath the melody at its opening. The resultant dissonance convinced Dreyfus that it would prejudice the audience». Wilder, referring to the song's obvious popular success, comments: «If a melody appeals, it would take a cacophonous background to turn an audience off. As I have said before, very few non-musicians hear any harmony, good or bad»[18].

The completion of the refrain's first strain (see Ex. 3) displays a typical feature of Porter's music: a mathematically constructive rather than tonal understanding of chromaticism. Beginning after the pick-up, melody and bass descend chromatically and in parallel sevenths, aiming at a predominant seventh chord on the second degree. However, the harmonic progression is neither an overall consistent parallelism, nor would it make much sense to describe it in terms

---

[16]. A technically and aesthetically comparable effect occurs in the refrain of Porter's 'What is This Thing Called Love' (*Wake Up and Dream*, 1929). In this case, too, a V-I progression is chromatically embellished with the leading tone to the major tonic's third. These chords are preceded by I⁷♭ (a blues chord) and °ii⁷ (or respectively, the minor subdominant iv⁺⁶) above a pedal point of the tonic.

[17]. This configuration occurs e.g. in Fryderyk Chopin's waltzes Op. 34 Nos. 1 and 3, Op. 69 No. 1, Johann Strauss Jr's waltzes *G'schichten aus dem Wienerwald* Op. 325 and *Frühlingsstimmen* Op. 410, and John Philip Sousa's *The Stars and Stripes Forever*.

[18]. WILDER 1975, p. 230.

of functional harmony. The second sonority is a half-diminished seventh chord on the raised fourth degree, suggesting either a double dominant or a predominant second degree within a g minor cadence that fails to materialize. The third and fourth are minor seventh chords. The substantial harmony of the fourth full bar is not so easy to determine. It may be the third inversion of the diminished seventh chord on the raised fourth degree. This chord is not related to the following predominant in any other way than by linear voice leading. The notorious term from Weill analysis, «semitonal instability»[19], comes to mind.

Ex. 3: Cole Porter, 'Night and Day', bars 29-33, reduced to harmonic outline.

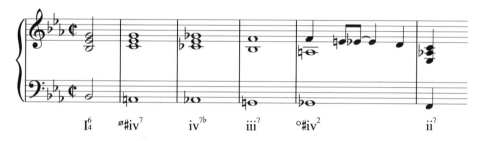

'In the Still of the Night'

A Porter song that does indeed make it hard to distinguish its composer from Kurt Weill is 'In the Still of the Night' from 1937, which starts with a harmonic-melodic pattern that had been a hallmark of Weill's songs since 1929: the alternation of the major tonic and its parallel minor, the latter in the form of a minor triad with an added sixth in the melody, which is identical to the first inversion of a half-diminished seventh chord on the sixth degree. This pattern can be found e.g. at the beginning of the second strain of Weill's 'Zu Potsdam unter den Eichen' (*Das Berliner Requiem*, 1929) and at the beginning of the refrain of his 'Surabaya Johnny' (*Happy End*, 1929, Ex. 4a). Ex. 4b presents the fourth occurrence of the pattern in Porter's song, in the cadential phrase of the first strain. Here, the harmony finally moves to the third degree via its dominant VII, just as it does in the second four-bar phrase of the refrain of 'Surabaya Johnny'. To be sure, 'minorizing' a major tonic, even without making it a subdominant in a cadence modulating to the key of v, is an old rhetorical device; in the context of a foxtrot song and with the added sixth, however, it has a decidedly Weillian flavor. It must be admitted,

---

[19]. Introduced in WATERHOUSE 1964, p. 897: «A cursory glance at Weill's scores will reveal that one of the most persistent characteristics of his harmony is what could be called 'semitonal instability', whereby one chord or harmonic complex dissolves into the next through the chromatic shift of a semitone by one or more of its notes. The result is a continual hovering between major and minor keys, and a constant threat to tonality itself [...]».

though, that the apparent 'Weillism' of 'In the Still of the Night' may be purely coincidental, since there is no solid evidence that Porter was familiar with Weill's Berlin song style in the 1930s. A well-known American Weill song that features the I-i^{+6} pattern, 'September Song' from *Knickerbocker Holiday* (based on 'Juans Lied' from the earlier operetta *Der Kuhhandel*), was not published until 1938.

Ex. 4a: Kurt Weill, 'Surabaya Johnny' (Vienna, Universal Edition, 1929), bars 27-33, reduced to melodic-harmonic outline.

Ex. 4b: Cole Porter, 'In the Still of the Night' (New York, Chappell & Co., Inc., 1937), bars 26-33, reduced to melodic-harmonic outline and transposed up a minor third to facilitate comparison with 'Surabaya Johnny'.

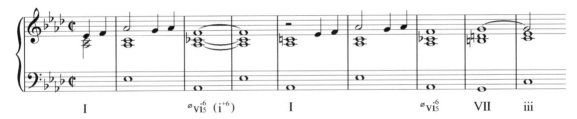

'Begin the Beguine'

While 'In the Still of the Night' sounds very close to Weill, there is at least one Weill song that may not have been written the way it was had it not been for a model from Porter's pen. This song is 'Speak Low' (from *One Touch of Venus*, 1943), which bears some similarity to Porter's 'Begin the Beguine' (from *Jubilee*, 1935).

The characteristics of the beguine, a subgenre of the rhumba that was popularized not least by Porter's composition, account for a gestic analogy between the two songs. Both contrast the dactylic, pavane-like pattern of the basic rhythm with a broad sweeping melody whose quarter note triplets make it hover, so to speak. Both are unusually long songs, albeit organized in different forms, and neither has a verse.

In both songs we find compositional peculiarities that constitute an artistic originality beyond mere craftsmanship. In 'Begin the Beguine' this is, in the first place, the continuous variation of a motivic pattern of four bars while avoiding symmetry by placing the triplets on different beats. However, the most interesting detail in regard to a relationship to Weill's music is a modulating descending chain of fifths in the bridge, which takes the form of a sequence that combines the Weillian idiosyncrasy of minorizing the tonic with conventional ii-v-i cadential progressions (Ex. 5).

Ex. 5: Cole Porter, 'Begin the Beguine' (New York, Harms Inc., 1935), bars 36-44, reduced to harmonic outline.

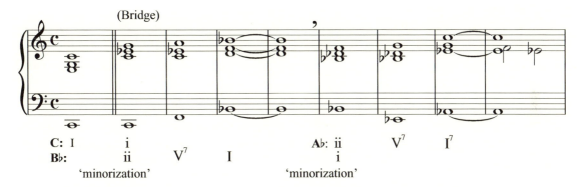

Because 'Begin the Beguine' is such a long and for that matter relatively un-catchy song, Wilder, who otherwise held Porter in high esteem, did not like it very much. He did, ironically, like 'Speak low', in spite of his general dismissal of Kurt Weill:

> I happen not to be a Kurt Weill fan. I don't swoon at the mention of *The Threepenny Opera*, as I'm told I should; I don't weep at the downbeat of 'September Song' [...]. Part of my irritation in listening to his music stems from my feeling that there was no personal involvement on his part.
> However, 'Speak Low' [...] is a very good song and one in which I feel that Weill was, indeed, involved[20].

(Note how Wilder, with his theory about Weill's lacking «involvement», an emotional distance from what he wrote, comes close to Adorno's claim that the composer was not at home in the Broadway style.) Admittedly, Weill's *cliché*-avoiding composing methods in 'Speak Low' appear more sophisticated than Porter's in 'Begin the Beguine'. The syntax of Weill's song undermines periodic symmetry and its harmony is unconventional throughout[21].

---

20. WILDER 1975, p. 511.
21. See the analytical reflections on 'Speak Low' in FASSHAUER 2007, pp. 178-180, 192-194.

Tobias Fasshauer

'Love for Sale'

With the Porter songs mentioned above, the list of his compositions that demonstrate inventiveness beyond textbook harmony is far from complete. Another remarkable case is 'Love for Sale' (*The New Yorkers*, 1930), whose «licentious harmony and counterpoint» has been discussed in detail by Michael Buchler. In the verse Buchler identifies the following «licentious» elements[22]:

- irregular phrase length (two ten-bar phrases);
- harmonic progression by whole tones while melody and bass move in parallel sixths, so that «any sense of tonal function or directionality» is opposed, «creating a musical fog»[23];
- dichotomy between major and minor tonic (see the Weillian I-i^{+6} pattern described above);
- «surprisingly direct progressions» (from A major to A♭ major to F major: VII-♭VII-V). Such harmonic surprises may recall Weill's technique of 'horizontal montage'; see e.g. the employment of the double minor subdominant (♭vii^{+6}) in the refrain of the 'Zuhälterballade' from *Die Dreigroschenoper*.

The refrain of 'Love for Sale' begins with a harmonically ambiguous complex, the double alternation of IV and i, a Dorian combination (in B♭) that may alternatively be perceived as I-v in the Mixolydian key of the subdominant (E♭). Buchler refers to this harmonic pendulum of eight bars, which appears three times in the course of the refrain, as a «Chopinesque play of tonality that obscures the roles of tonic and subdominant»[24]. Again, it is the «dichotomy between major and minor tonic», i.e. the minor third in a major context, that accounts for the special flavor of the passage.

Conclusion

Porter, like Weill, and like any popular composer who did not content him- or herself with merely serving a market, faced the dialectical challenge of reconciling the standardization of a basic musical language with individual artistic originality in the service of meaningful communication with the audience. In fact, the repertoire of American Broadway song between 1920 and 1950 can be seen in its entirety as a response to this challenge, as shown by the studies of Alec Wilder and Allen Forte[25], who based their analyses of this music on criteria otherwise

---

[22]. BUCHLER 2016, pp. 210-212.
[23]. *Ibidem*, p. 210.
[24]. *Ibidem*, p. 215.
[25]. WILDER 1975 and FORTE 1995.

applied to art music. In 1937 Weill himself credited American popular music with higher sophistication than that of other, i.e. European, countries[26], implying that his own efforts to develop a both artistic and popular style in Europe was an individual project with no support from a corresponding general trend in popular music. Systematic comparison of Weill's songs with those of Jerome Kern, Richard Rodgers, George Gershwin, and others would probably reveal similarly striking analogies as those pointed out in Porter. Such a comparison would be consistent with the approach taken here, since Adorno himself uses Porter's name as just a proxy for Broadway. Nevertheless, Porter's experience in the Parisian *avant-garde* of the 1920s makes him a most interesting case study. Extending the analysis to the relationship between music and lyrics, which is beyond the scope of this article, might perhaps support the assumption that there is a special affinity between Weill and Porter. One of Weill's most important American lyricists, Ira Gershwin, shared with Porter a predilection for sophisticated puns, which in turn may have made Weill approach Porter's musical style more closely. Note e.g. the gestic analogy between two songs from *The Firebrand of Florence* (1945), 'A Rhyme for Angela' and 'Sing Me not a Ballad', and Porter's 'I Get a Kick out of You' (*Anything Goes*, 1934): The refrain of each song begins with a pronounced ascending scale in the melody, spanning a four-bar phrase. The subgenre of the 'list song' in particular seemed to awaken a Porteresque spirit in Weill, see also 'The Nina, the Pinta, the Santa Maria' from the film *Where Do We Go from Here* (1945).

Of course, in Adorno's view, creating art within the confines of a standardized genre was an impossible task. However, if we set aside Adorno's condemnation of popular music and the culture industry and take an unbiased look at the matter, we may conclude that the claim that Weill and Porter are hard to distinguish from each other is in fact a compliment to both.

Bibliography

ADORNO 1984
ADORNO, Theodor Wiesengrund. 'Vortrupp und Avantgarde: Eine Replik', (1956), in: ID. *Gesammelte Schriften. 18*, Frankfurt, Suhrkamp, 1984, pp. 800-804.

ADORNO – EISLER 2006
ID. – EISLER, Hanns. *Komposition für den Film*, edited by Johannes Carl Gall, Frankfurt, Suhrkamp, 2006.

---

[26]. WEILL 2000, pp. 159ff.: «Es scheint, daß der musikalische Geschmack des großen Publikums hier [in the United States] besser ist als in vielen anderen Ländern, weil sich die populäre Musik auf einem höheren Niveau befindet und weil die Jazzmusik [...] das musikalische Empfinden mehr kultiviert hat als die flache, unzeitgemäße populäre Musik anderer Länder».

BUCHLER 2016
BUCHLER, Michael. 'Licentious Harmony and Counterpoint in Porter's "Love for Sale"', in: *A Cole Porter Companion*, edited by Don M. Randel, Matthew Shaftel and Susan Forscher Weiss, Urbana, Chicago-Springfield, University of Illinois Press, 2016, pp. 207-221.

EISLER 1947
EISLER, Hanns. *Composing for the Films*, Oxford-New York, Oxford University Press, 1947.

FASSHAUER 2007
FASSHAUER, Tobias. *Ein Aparter im Unaparten. Untersuchungen zum Songstil von Kurt Weill*, Saarbrücken, Pfau, 2007.

FASSHAUER 2014
ID. 'Amerikanismus bei Weill: A French Connection?', in: *Kurt Weill und Frankreich*, edited by Andreas Eichhorn, Münster, Waxmann, 2014 (Veröffentlichungen der Kurt-Weill-Gesellschaft Dessau, 9), pp. 39-62.

FORTE 1995.
FORTE, Allen. *The American Popular Ballad of the Golden Era, 1924-1950*, Princeton, Princeton University Press, 1995.

HARBEC 2015
HARBEC, Jacinthe. '*Within the Quota* de Cole Porter et Charles Koechlin: la francisation du jazz américain', in: *Les Cahiers de la Société québécoise de recherche en musique*, XVI/1-2 (2015), pp. 39-50.

HERALD 1923
'American Ballet Will Give Paris All the Latest Broadway Whims', in: *The New York Herald: European Edition*, Paris, 25 October 1923, p. 6.

KOWALKE 1995
KOWALKE, Kim H. 'Kurt Weill, Modernism, and Popular Culture: Öffentlichkeit als Stil', in: *Modernism/modernity*, II/1 (1995), pp. 27-69.

MORRISON 2016
MORRISON, Simon. 'Landed: Cole Porter's Ballet', in: *A Cole Porter Companion*, op. cit., pp. 57-69.

ORLEDGE 1975
ORLEDGE, Robert. 'Cole Porter's Ballet *Within the Quota*', in: *The Yale University Library Gazette*, L/1 (July 1975), pp. 19-29.

RANDEL 2016
RANDEL, Don M. 'About Cole Porter's Songs', in: *A Cole Porter Companion*, op. cit., pp. 222-241.

Schubert 2000
Schubert, Giselher. 'Surrealismus bei Weill? Zu einer Weill-Deutung Adornos', in: *Kurt Weill: Auf dem Weg zum 'Weg der Verheißung'*, edited by Helmut Loos and Guy Stern, Freiburg im Breisgau, Rombach, 2000 (Litterae, 75), pp. 23-36.

Shaftel 1999
Shaftel, Matthew. 'From Inspiration to Archive: Cole Porter's 'Night and Day'', in: *Journal of Music Theory*, XLIII/2 (Autumn 1999), pp. 315-347.

Van den Brande 2016
Van den Brande, Wilfried. 'Cole Porter, European', in: *A Cole Porter Companion*, *op. cit.*, pp. 34-56.

Waterhouse 1964
Waterhouse, John C. G. 'Weill's Debt to Busoni', in: *The Musical Times*, CV/1462 (December 1964), pp. 897-899.

Weill 2000
Weill, Kurt. 'Oper in Amerika', in: Id. *Musik und musikalisches Theater. Gesammelte Schriften*, edited by Stephen Hinton and Jürgen Schebera, with Elmar Juchem, Mainz, Schott, 2000, pp. 155-161.

Wilder 1975
Wilder, Alec. *American Popular Song: The Great Innovators, 1900-1950*, Oxford-New York, Oxford University Press, 1975.

Street Scenes

Rebecca Schmid
(Humboldt Universität, Berlin)

In 1947, following a performance of *Street Scene*, Leonard Bernstein was heard backstage by Weill's assistant and piano coach, Lys Symonette, muttering: «This isn't worth *drei Groschen!*»[1]. Three decades later, in 1977, following a matinee performance of the same work at New York City Opera, Bernstein commented to the performance's conductor John Mauceri over dinner, «I am not convinced»[2]. Mauceri recalled: «That was one of the most telling lines [...] he was not convinced in the musical language that Kurt Weill had adopted when he came to New York City [...] that he was using the traditions, rules [...] of Broadway and American pop song — which indeed he [Weill] had been studying — as a way of writing his opera, and that in some ways it was synthetic [...]». These comments present a paradox: As the following intertextual analysis will reveal, Bernstein derived essential impulses from *Street Scene* in his most famous stage work, *West Side Story* (1957).

Andreas Jaensch credits Bernstein for landing upon his «own new style in that he combined the arias, duets and ensemble technique of traditional opera with the form schema of popular song»[3] in *West Side Story*. And yet, while the work is more often considered a culmination of the integrated musical[4], Nils Grosch argues that *West Side Story* embodies a Brechtian separation of the elements («Trennung der Elemente») characteristic of Brechtian

---

[1]. Kowalke 1996, p. 12. The remark echoes that of Alban Berg, who in 1928 admitted that «the likes of us cannot make up our minds in favor of a *Threepenny Opera* or a *Ten-Thousand-Dollar Symphony*». Hinton 2012, p. 472.

[2]. Interview with the author of 30 January 2020.

[3]. Jaensch 2003, p. 167.

[4]. See, for example, Martin Charmin's liner notes to the Original Broadway Cast Recording (Sony Music. 01-060724-10), p. 10.

theatre rather than American Broadway shows[5]. Elizabeth Wells has similarly placed *West Side Story* in a tradition of «intentionally antiorganicist works» that have their lineage in *Die Dreigroschenoper*[6] (1928). Bernstein of course knew *Dreigroschenoper* intimately. In June of 1952, two years after Weill's death, he had premiered Marc Blitzstein's English adaptation, *The Threepenny Opera*, in a concert performance, conducting from and putting his own markings into Weill's original holograph full score[7].

The kinship between *Street Scene* and *West Side Story* is clear on the level of setting and plot. Both scores explore thwarted love stories amid social tensions in mid-twentieth-century New York City. The similarity in wording that introduces the works in their scores cannot be a coincidence. In Weill's «American Opera» (which was billed as a «Dramatic Musical») «the action takes place on a sidewalk in New York City», with Act I set on an evening in June and Act II the following day. In Bernstein's score, «the action takes place on the West Side of New York City during the last days of summer»[8]. The stories both feature romance between New Yorkers of different ethnicities who must cope with heartbreak. Weill's male protagonist, Sam, is a Jewish-American hopelessly in love with Rose, a young woman of Irish-Catholic heritage who also dreams of running away with Sam. The tragedy that takes the foreground is the troubled relationship between Rose's parents: Mrs. Maurrant is murdered by her husband for having an affair. *West Side Story*, meanwhile, tells of a romance amid warring Puerto Rican and Caucasian-American gangs (the Sharks and the Jets) but was originally conceived as *East Side Story*, «a modern version of Romeo and Juliet» in which Juliet would be of Jewish origin and Romeo an Italian-American from Greenwich Village[9].

Bernstein wished to tell what he called «a tragic story in musical-comedy terms, using only musical-comedy techniques, never falling into the "operatic trap"». «Can it succeed?» he asked rhetorically in January of 1949. «It hasn't yet in our country. I'm excited. If it can work — it's the first». On the one hand, *West Side Story* did dodge the «operatic trap» through the

---

[5]. See GROSCH 2017, p. 296.

[6]. The connection to Weill is mentioned in a footnote, as she argues «it is not the organicism of *West Side Story* that places it among the important musicals of the era, but those aspects of it that diverge from a homogeneous, organic, and singular artwork». WELLS 2011, p. 59 and p. 93.

[7]. See WEILL 1996.

[8]. Nigel Simeone also notes that «the portrayal of humanity in Weill's show (and the Elmer Rice play on which it is closely based) includes poverty, abuse and murder, as *West Side Story* was to do, and the action of both takes place in the city within a time-span of 24 hours». SIMEONE 2009, p. 75. Weill chose unity of time, place and action «to avoid the conventional musical comedy technique and to work it out as a kind of popular Broadway opera», as he wrote to Rouben Mamoulian, his first choice of director (Mamoulian turned down the offer in favor of more lucrative projects in Hollywood but would go on to direct Weill's *Lost in the Stars*). See HIRSCH 2000, p. 259 and KOWALKE 2003, p. 291.

[9]. BERNSTEIN 1982, p. 144 and BURTON 2017, p. 274.

narrative role of dance[10]. On the other hand, the form is deceitful, its operatic DNA at times disappearing beneath the work's slick surface[11].

Opera Reform

Weill did not consider opera an obsolete art form but one in need of renewal or reform for the contemporary time and place. «My entire life has been devoted to the theatre», he said in 1946, «and I have dedicated it to combining the theatre of our time with a higher form of music [...]». In the same interview, he expressed hopes that *Street Scene* would «open new vistas for American composers»[12]. *Street Scene* tells a «tragic story in musical-comedy terms» but leaves the fissures between opera and American musical theatre bare, an «unresolved tension» which Stephen Hinton calls a form of dramaturgical counterpoint[13]. While *West Side Story* manages to smooth over and to some extent neutralize (in Josef Straus's sense) operatic content, it still thrives on this formal tension between tragic content and entertainment[14].

Bernstein achieved a structural unity unprecedented in his output for the stage[15]. He cited the 'Maria' motive (a rising tritone from D to G-sharp that resolves to A) as the «kernel» of the entire score[16] or «sort of a leitmotif»[17]. That the score creates organic unity through the use of motives, both melodic and rhythmic, has invited comparisons with the scores of Beethoven

---

[10]. Burton 2017, p. 264.

[11]. In a similar observation, the critic Kenneth Tynan called the score «as smooth and savage as a cobra; it sounds as if Puccini and Stravinsky had gone on a roller-coaster ride into the precincts of modern jazz». Cited in Simeone 2009, p. 129.

[12]. Weill 1946.

[13]. Hinton 2012, pp. 371-387.

[14]. «Aus der Spannung zwischen tragischem Inhalt auf der einen und der durch das theatralische Unterhaltungsgenre geprägten Form auf der anderen Seite erwächst das Experimentelle und Neuartige der Show, die Etabliertes nicht verwirft, sondern in neue Zusammenhänge stellt, ihm neuartige Funktionen zuweist, es in andere Erzählstrukturen einbaut». Grosch 2017, p. 297. The concept of «neutralization» comes from Josef Straus, who identified a process by which «musical elements are stripped of their customary function, particularly of their progressional impulse. Forward progress is blocked». Straus 1990, p. 17.

[15]. See, for example, Smith 2011, p. 168.

[16]. «[...] the three notes of Maria pervade the whole piece — inverted, done backward. I didn't do this on purpose. It seemed to come out in "Cool and as the gang whistle". The same three notes». Simeone 2009, p. 81. Via an interview of Bernstein with Mel Gussow.

[17]. See Jaensch 2003, p. 95. Grosch calls the compositional technique a «hidden critique» of the genre of the musical. Grosch 2017, p. 312.

and Wagner, to whom Bernstein directly alludes. Wells has further identified intertextual references to Berlioz, Stravinsky, Chopin, Gershwin and Diamond[18].

The most famous allusion, however, is to Blitzstein's *Regina* (1949), a work which Bernstein actively championed, pushing for performances at La Scala in 1955[19]. The words «And suddenly that name» in 'Maria' directly quote the introduction to the dinner party scene in the first act of *Regina*, a passage which is also in E-flat major[20]. Bernstein had written a preview piece for the *New York Times* upon *Regina*'s premiere, proclaiming an operatic tradition had emerged from a «natural musical theatre — one which is unique in the world, and wholly an outgrowth of our culture»[21] (Exs. 1a and 1b).

Ex. 1a: *West Side Story*, No. 5 'Maria'.

[18]. WELLS 2011, Chapter 3. Also see SHAWN 2014, pp. 150-151; BLOCK 1997, pp. 261-266; and SIMEONE 2009, p. 83 and p. 102.

[19]. SIMEONE 2013, pp. 330-332.

[20]. Shawn writes that «the continuation of the melody after the initial three-note cell comes so close to the orchestral introduction to the dinner party scene in Blitzstein's *Regina*, completed in 1948, that one can assume it is directly influenced by it». SHAWN 2014, p. 144. Also see BLOCK 1997, pp. 251-252.

[21]. BERNSTEIN 1949.

Ex. 1b: Regina, Act I: No. 1&2. Introduction and Birdie.

By placing a fragment of Blitzstein's melody in the foreground, Bernstein pays homage to Blitzstein and establishes *West Side Story* as another American tragedy by an American composer. That Bernstein neither acknowledged Weill's influence on what he calls «the Broadway equivalent of what was once known as opera» nor quoted any of *Street Scene*'s melodies may stem from his theory of a «wholly» American tradition to which Weill only partly belonged. The few statements he made about Weill evince ambivalence, conflict, and competition. In Bernstein's 1976 Norton Lectures at Harvard University, Stravinsky emerges as the foremost model of neo-classicism and bi-tonality (a key feature of both the *West Side Story* and *Street Scene* scores, discussed below), while Weill is mentioned only once as an example of a German composer who couldn't help but be seduced by American vernacular.

In her study of *West Side Story*, Wells wonders if Bernstein was «simply trying to absolve himself of any unintended plagiarism by allying himself» with canonic composers such as Stravinsky[22]. «By creating a kind of evolutionary narrative of musical style», she writes of the Norton Lectures, «Bernstein ultimately places himself within a tradition that extends at least back to Berlioz [...] without appearing to be so presumptuous as to baldly state this»[23]. Indeed, Bernstein was inclined to align himself either with European canonic composers or those born in the United States. In a 1948 talk on national television, he created a narrative in which Weill becomes a secondary figure in serious Broadway music theatre, reversing a logical chronology and omitting the precedent of *Die Dreigroschenoper*: «One serious composer, Marc Blitzstein, had even invaded Broadway with his odd, original opera,

---

[22]. WELLS 2011, p. 60.
[23]. *Ibidem*, p. 90.

The Cradle Will Rock. Then Kurt Weill had brought his whole German training to Broadway in works such as *Lady in the Dark* »[24].

Rather than acknowledge the formative role of the German-born Weill on American tradition, Bernstein expressed confidence that a movement in musical theatre « borrowing this from opera, that from revue, the other from operetta, something else from vaudeville » had led to a new, indigenous form: « opera but *in our own way* »[25]. An intertextual analysis of *West Side Story* and *Street Scene* shows, however, that there are structural, harmonic and motivic parallels, above all in the numbers of Tony and Maria.

Analysis

The instrumental introductions to *Street Scene* and *West Side Story* each weave together a highly chromatic harmonic language with distinctly American jazzy or bluesy material. If the role of the tritone in setting the mood in Bernstein's 'Prologue' and establishing harmonic tensions that will permeate the entire work has been given consideration attention in studies of *West Side Story*[26], the same interval takes on a prominent role in the 'Introduction' and 'Opening Ensemble' to *Street Scene*. A double set of tritones in the first bar foreshadows the impending tragedy, right on the streets of New York (Ex. 2a). Clashes of semi-tone intervals go on to conjure the unstable, frenetic urban setting, with a falling appoggiatura figure in the violins (B-sharp and C-sharp, in measure 11) that is passed on to the second clarinet and oboe.

Bernstein's music opens with C major and A major chords[27] that are offset by semi-tone clashes in the electric guitar. By the eighth measure, an A-flat in the bass creates a tritone with D-natural while the semi-tones persist (Ex. 2b). Upon the entrance of a solo vibraphone, marked « with a jazz feel », the melody descends from A to D-sharp. When a Shark trips a Jet, the drama escalates with an upward sliding tritone in the electric guitar, from B-flat to

---

[24]. BERNSTEIN 1959, pp. 152-179.

[25]. *Ibidem*.

[26]. Swain writes that «[...] by beginning with the tritone so brazenly, Bernstein's careful motivic development is pre-empted [...] the Prologue establishes not only the significant melodic and rhythmic elements for the play, but also significant harmonic procedures and pitches, C, A and F-sharp, which will unify the musical numbers in a way that no other Broadway composer has attempted». SWAIN 1990, p. 217 and p. 370. Simeone states that the tritone was « a crucial unifying feature of the musical language of *West Side Story* » and « came to represent irresolvable conflict » (SIMEONE 2009, p. 80). Block notes that only the characters who represent the triumph of love over hate, Tony and Maria, « can unambiguously and convincingly resolve the tritone tension embodied in the gang's signature motive » (BLOCK 1997, p. 269). Also see BURTON 2017, GOTTLIEB 1994, SHAWN 2014; and SMITH 2011.

[27]. Wells traces this « double-tonic complex » back to Wagner's *Tristan* prelude. WELLS 2011, pp. 73-75.

Ex. 2a: *Street Scene*, No. 1 Introduction and Opening Ensemble.

E-natural, doubled by the bassoon and flute. In contrast to Weill, who exploits continuous chromatic movement, Bernstein guides the listener through the Prologue in almost leitmotivic fashion through recurring tritone and semitone intervals, and the overlaying thereof, which persists into the 'Jet Song'.

Ex. 2b: *West Side Story*, No. 1 Prologue.

In both *Street Scene* and *West Side Story*, the dissonance of tritones and semitones in the opening bars subtly alert the listener that the sweltering summer in New York harbors existential danger. While Bernstein has been credited by Joseph Swain and Helen Smith for creating a musical structure that allowed for tragedy on the Broadway stage, Weill had already explored a similar formula[28]. If he received crucial impulse from Gershwin's *Porgy and Bess*, Weill distinguishes himself by not blending but rather juxtaposing musical idioms[29]. The irony of his earlier works more often than not cedes to an earnest endeavour, that of creating an American tragedy for the Broadway stage. And as Hinton has explored, Weill's pursuit becomes a meta-dramatic thread in the score[30].

Also in both works, the male protagonist is assigned the most prominent solo number (Sam's 'Lonely House' in *Street Scene* and Tony's 'Maria' in *West Side Story*), in a style that neatly bridges opera and American theatre style. Sam, in particular, with his musical idiom

---

[28]. Swain calls tragedy «the most elusive dramatic expression for the Broadway tradition». SWAIN 1990, pp. 205 and 218. Also see SMITH 2011, p. 145. Elise K. Kirk differentiates between the two works through a negative comparison: «Weill appears to shift between operatic and pop techniques rather than assimilate them as Gershwin does so successfully». KIRK 2001, pp. 262-263. Again, there is this tension between tragedy and entertainment.

[29]. *Porgy and Bess* emboldened Weill to write serious musical plays for the American stage after attending a rehearsal in October of 1935, one month after he arrived in the U.S. He went on to advise Cheryl Crawford for a posthumous 1942 revival that replaced most of the recitative with spoken dialogue and would later cite the prominence of dialogue underscored by orchestra as an important feature of *Street Scene* that improved upon Gershwin's stage work. WEILL 1946. Elise K. Kirk differentiates between the two works through a negative comparison: «Weill appears to shift between operatic and pop techniques rather than assimilate them as Gershwin does so successfully». KIRK 2001, pp. 262-263.

[30]. HINTON 2012, pp. 379-381.

evoking late Romanticism, emerges as a possible personification of the composer: alienated from his surroundings, lonely and excluded from the tradition of which he is rightfully a part[31].

Weill considered 'Lonely House' the theme song of the opera[32]. In a stage work in which alienation from the urban environment is a constant undercurrent, Sam gives the clearest expression to a sense of isolation («Funny you can be so lonely with all these folks around»). Over a bluesy ostinato bass in the strings and uneasy semitones in the clarinet, the celeste and harp alternate with a wistful violin figure. Sam enters in a restrained, recitative-like style before breaking out into a sweeping melody («Lonely house, lonely me!»). Hinton has drawn attention to the climax of the Arioso, when Sam declares that the night «is not romantic» in a cadenza-like style marked «free»[33]. As his melody rises up to A-flat, the wistful figure from the opening measures re-emerges in the woodwinds, the worlds of opera and musical theatre chafing against each other self-consciously. Perhaps like Weill himself, Sam tries, but cannot distance himself from the world of late nineteenth-century opera.

TABLE 1

West Side Story	*Street Scene*
No. 5 'Maria' *Moderato con anima* Hybrid of popular song and operatic aria (Jaensch)	**No. 10 Arioso 'Lonely House'** *Moderato assai* «At once song and aria, a soulful blues that crosses over into the sound world of late-nineteenth century opera» (Hinton)
Central key of E-flat major (key of romance)	Central key of E-flat major (one of the opera's «most romantic moments», Hinton)
Protagonist (Tony) standing alone onstage (Robbins complains to Sondheim: a «static song with no one else in the scene»)	Protagonist (Sam) standing alone onstage
Opens with recitative (B major), *slowly and freely*; rises to A-flat on final utterance of 'Maria'	Opens with recitative (E-flat major with flourishes of bluesy augmented second); climaxes in a cadenza-like passage marked *free*, rising to A-flat
ends on an E-flat major chord	ends on an E-flat major chord

---

[31]. Kowalke notes the «palpable autobiographical resonance» of «Sam, the shy Jewish intellectual» for both Rice and Weill. Quoting Adorno's *Philosophie der Musik*, he also draws a parallel between Sam's loneliness and the «expressionist» who «reveals loneliness as universal». KOWALKE 1995, p. 11.

[32]. Weill wrote to Langston Hughes that the song is about the building («the house») where Sam feels trapped, «the house being a prison for the spirit etc. It could almost become a theme song for the show. It should be passionate and very moving, but as personal as we can make it, that means: not abstract!». Cited in HIRSCH 2000, p. 269.

[33]. Hinton calls the number «at once song and aria, a soulful blues that crosses over into the sound world of late-nineteenth century opera». He also notes the irony that this is one of the opera's «most romantic moments» as Sam pities himself. HINTON 2012, pp. 383-384.

In a setting which rubbed the choreographer Jerome Robbins the wrong way[34], 'Maria' features the protagonist Tony standing alone onstage. He is more extroverted than Weill's protagonist, however[35]. Consolation lies only in possessing Maria, and he wants the whole world to know how he feels. While Sam's Arioso is labeled «Moderato assai», Bernstein turns up the heat with «Moderato con anima». Tony is not afraid to wear his heart on his sleeve: he repeats the name «Maria» over twenty times. Triplet figures, first ascending, then descending, underscore the urgency of his emotion.

Despite an effusiveness that places the number in the tradition of American musical theatre, it maintains a proximity to operatic convention[36]. After a recitative-like passage in B major marked «slowly and freely»[37], the main aria enters in E-flat major, with an ostinato, rhumba-style bass that persists for all but the last seven bars of the number. Unlike in Sam's solo number, there is no dark irony or a sense of alienation that might link him to the late Romantic aspects of *Street Scene*. His melody, in place of bluesy ambivalence, follows a predominantly whole-tone scheme, although the alternation between A-natural and A-flat starting in measure nine creates a tension between major and minor modes. And while the orchestra in 'Lonely House' contradicts Sam toward the end of the Arioso with a wistful violin figure and bluesy semitones, here the orchestra can only be swept up in Tony's world, echoing the second two notes of the original 'Maria' motive (A-natural to B-flat) before ending on an E-flat chord with added sixth, recalling the final measure of 'Lonely House' but in a spirit of pure optimism (Exs. 3a and 3b. The no. 18 Duet of Rose and Sam also ends on an E-flat chord with an added sixth).

Weill's *Street Scene*, meanwhile, deploys intertextual allusions for specific dramaturgical effects. Kowalke has demonstrated that references to Puccini create a subtext for understanding the romance of Sam and Rose: like Pinkerton and Cio-Cio-San in Puccini's *Madama Butterfly*, the two characters occupy potentially incompatible worlds. The duet 'Remember that I care' specifically alludes to the moment after the title character fills the house with flowers in anticipation of Pinkerton's arrival from America, thereby informing the listener that the attraction of Sam and Rose is hopeless[38]. On another level of commentary, Rose's musical

---

[34]. Sondheim recalls that Robbins had a negative reaction to a «static song with no one else in the scene» (SONDHEIM 2010, p. 29).

[35]. In a slight contrast, Grosch notes an evolution within the number from an introverted atmosphere into an erotically charged *Habanera*. GROSCH 2017, pp. 308-309.

[36]. «Auch wenn die Nummer sich formal stark an den Popular Song anlehnt, fallen doch auch arienhafte Züge auf: so vor allem der extreme Umfang der Melodiestimme und die über dem Orchesterpart stehende "Kadenz"». JAENSCH 2003, p. 81 and p. 83.

[37]. This recalls the cadenza marked «free» in 'Lonely House'. Simeone calls it «one of the very few moments of recitative-like music in the show». SIMEONE 2009, p. 98.

[38]. «The cultural chasm between first-generation Russian-Jewish and Irish-Catholic immigrants living within the same apartment building seems even more forbidding than that separating Puccini's couple: the

Ex. 3a: *Street Scene*, No. 10 Arioso 'Lonely House'.

Ex. 3b: *West Side Story*, No. 5 'Maria'.

idiom — particularly in the solo number 'What good would the moon be' — is less operatic than that of Sam despite pentatonic figures evoking *Butterfly* in the opening measures[39].

Sam's idiom in «Remember that I care» is meanwhile distinguished by sobbing two-note figures in the accompaniment, rising triplets in the vocal line and Wagner-infused chromatic harmonies[40]. Toward the end of the opera, in a desperate plea to keep Rose from fleeing, the orchestra introduces a full-blown *Tristan* allusion (Ex. 4). The association of Rose with *Madama Butterfly* and Sam with the Wagnerian tale of star-crossed (detailed further below) lovers makes clear the characters' respective stances: While she has a hunch that their backgrounds will stand in the way of their dreams (and is warned to that effect by Sam's sister, Shirley, in Act II), he believes that they should consummate their affection for one another, even if it means losing touch with reality and alienating their families.

Ex. 4: *Street Scene*, No. 22 Finale 'Don't forget the lilac bush'.

allusion tells us that Sam and Rose's relationship is doomed, before it has a chance to blossom». KOWALKE 1995, pp. 17-18.

[39]. In the original production, the role of Rose was the only to be cast with a soprano who did not have an operatic background, while the tenor playing Sam had sung in *Il barbiere di Siviglia* at the Metropolitan Opera. HIRSCH 2000, p. 262.

[40]. Kowalke writes that Sam's entrance «wrenches the musical idiom out of melodrama and onto a highly charted operatic plane, accompanied by full orchestra and characterized by the greatest density of chromaticism, dissonance, and asymmetries in Act 1». KOWALKE 1995, p. 16.

Street Scenes

That the lovers in both *Street Scene* and *West Side Story* are ultimately destined to go separate ways is further revealed in the tonal scheme of their duets. In 'Remember that I care', Rose's flowery, pentatonic-colored C major idiom interrupts Sam after he has reflected on the pain of human existence in the key of E-flat major. When they dream of fleeing their New York tenement in No. 18 Duet and Scene 'We'll go away together', Rose's music gravitates toward the minor mode, even when her words are optimistic, while that of Sam repeatedly pulls the music toward A-flat (the home key) or E-flat major (the key of romance).

Table 2

No. 6 Balcony Scene	No. 18 Duet and Scene
Orchestra quotes 'Maria' melody in a-flat minor	Orchestral opening/Rose singing in a-flat minor
modulates to B-flat major	modulates to B-flat major for Sam
Maria pulls music toward C major with chromatically descending bass line from D to B-natural («In my eyes, in my words...»)	Rose pulls music toward c minor with chromatically descending bass line from D to B-flat («we'll leave behind our yesterdays»)
Tony responds in c minor («And there's nothing for me but Maria»)	Sam reflects in c minor («Life is a sky-tall mountain / Where clouds play hide and seek»)
Modulates to E-flat major their kiss	Sung refrain 'When we go away' lands in E-flat major with added sixth
Modulates to B-flat major for 'Tonight'; home key wins out with final cadence in A-flat major	After Rose has pulled orchestra to c-minor, Sam sings in B-flat major in double-tonic complex over A-flat major; final chord overlays key of romance (E-flat major) with key of dreams (C-major) and the high F of Sam's exaltation
Segues to spoken dialogue over orchestra accompaniment	Segues to spoken dialogue over orchestra accompaniment

Also in this number, only Sam is capable of sustaining idealist feelings. After Rose opens the number in a-flat minor, the accompaniment modulates to B-flat major for Sam's entrance about two people who «grow wings and say [...] Come away, love, come away!». His melody rises up to an F that is sustained for over three measures, at which point the chirping woodwind figures symbolizing birds «who spread their wings and fly» are passed to the strings for the first time.

It is he who introduces the refrain «with warm and tender expression» in the home key. Rose joins optimistically, but a chromatically descending bass line from D to B-flat pulls the music away from Sam's goal (Ex. 5a), leaving him no choice but to reflect philosophically in c-minor, the parallel minor of the key of romance. Following an ardent cadenza that again lands on a sustained F, underscored by a chromatic figure in the trumpet, he finds his way back to the home key. Rose again brings the music back to c-minor when they join for one line ('We'll go away together'), but this does not prevent Sam from breaking out into sweeping lyricism with a cadenza-like passage that climaxes in E-flat major and ushers in an orchestral statement of the full refrain. Rose, however, is unable to join, breaking out into dialogue over the orchestra as the clarinet quotes Sam's words «We'll build a house to shelter us beneath a happier sky».

When she does sing again, the music has modulated back to c minor. Sam manages to end the number with a refrain in the key of romance that begins with a rising sixth from E-flat to C major ('When we go'). The orchestra ends the number on a jazzy, brassy E-flat chord with added second and sixth, but the strings will join and continue to gently sing the refrain in A-flat major as Sam and Rose continue in spoken dialogue. After Rose's aggressive suitor Easter enters, however, tritones underlie the orchestra's melody (A and E-flat, then F-sharp and C). And when Rose introduces the two men, the first violins stop singing «We'll go away together», instead ceding to a mourning solo violin that foreshadows her crucial words «Loving and belonging / they're not the same» in her final exchange with Sam ('Don't forget the Lilac Bush').

The following segment, the finale, begins with Sam exclaiming Rose's name on C and then F-sharp as the chirping bird figures from the No. 18 duet return briefly in the woodwinds. He addresses her in a chromatic recitative line that foreshadows an impending allusion to Wagner's *Tristan*, landing hopefully on A-flat while an A-natural in the double-bass, harp and bassoon offsets his ardor. Rose's music proceeds to sink chromatically into f minor. When she does succumb to Sam's upward sweeping lyricism («I never dreamed/it would be this way»), lingering on F for a full measure, a b minor chord with an added sixth in the bass ushers in climbing *Butterfly* chords.

Sam's desperation is indicated by a highly chromatic idiom, his insistence on the home key again offset by A-natural in the bass when he declares, «I'll go where you go». His full avowal of love takes place in Rose's forlorn key of f minor, with the trumpet figure of «We'll go away together» returning to underscore his loneliness and alienation. Rose can only join briefly in his sobbing idiom («Oh if it could be!»), landing on an e-flat minor chord with an added second and sixth. A C creates a tritone with G-flat (in the cello, second violin and trombones) before ushering in foreboding, chromatic chords across the orchestra.

A new courageous idiom enters for Rose with percussive chords that alternate between C major (the key of dreams, as noted in TABLE 2) undercut by B-natural and F-sharp and e minor overlaid with D-flat major. Tellingly, her first utterance of «alone» is set to a harmonic accompaniment including the tritone of C and F-sharp. When she sings the word a second time, the music races back to Sam's desperate idiom: «No!» he exclaims on the high F that once represented the exaltation of love. «Not alone!». On the second syllable of the word «together», another *Tristan* allusion emerges, rising chromatically from G to C and then continuing to rise upward until the orchestra stammers the first two notes of Sam's E-flat major refrain «We'll go away together» from the No. 18 duet (Ex. 5a).

Ex. 5a: *Street Scene*, No. 18 Duet and Scene 'We'll go away together'.

Sam, however, can no longer join in his own song. As the full melody emerges in the solo violin, he admonishes Rose in counterpoint, «There's no hope for us unless we love each other». Rose admits that love is all she wants in the world but seems to know that a romance with Sam would be doomed. «Loving and belonging», she sings. «They're not the same». The word «belonging» features an F-sharp that offsets the double-tonic chord of C major and the parallel a minor. With the full backing of orchestra, she then adopts the Grand Opera idiom of her parents and reminds Sam of love's dangers («Look at my father, / my poor mother, / If she had belonged to herself [...]»[41]). After Sam responds briefly in his chromatic idiom, she breaks out into dialogue over the orchestra's nostalgic reminiscences of the C major refrain from «Remember that I care».

When Rose returns to song, she reminds Sam that hope is still on the horizon for both of them («don't forget the lilac bush») while the orchestra's pentatonic, arpeggiated *Butterfly* chords indicate the harsh reality. Sam again cannot join the refrain when Rose sings, «Remember that I care», her final F landing in the parallel minor of the home key, an f minor chord with an added sixth in the bass. After she packs her suitcase, she turns back and kisses Sam briefly while the bass clarinet quotes, transposed down a third, his line about «staying here, / in this slum never seeing you». A tritone of C and G-flat in the bass indicates the gravity of the situation. The full orchestra will sing Sam's lines after he breaks away and runs into the house, ending on a half-diminished chord that juxtaposes the same tritone, C and F-sharp.

Maria and Tony also join for three duets in *West Side Story*. They do not occupy separate musical worlds to the same extent as Rose and Sam, although dance rhythms indicate their

---

[41]. Edward D. Latham considers the music of Sam and Rose to represent «the best example of the stylistic synthesis Weill sought to achieve in *Street Scene*», while Mr. and Mrs. Maurrant reside in the idiom of «pure grand opera». LATHAM 2008, p. 148.

respective cultural backgrounds. Like Rose, Maria also is prone to push the music away from the home key or break out into dialogue. In the 'Balcony Scene', she is the first to sing, yet a chromatically descending bass line in the cellos from D to B-natural brings instability to what would otherwise be an effusively optimistic expression of love on the line, «In my eyes, in my words, in everything I do» (Ex. 5b). The moment alludes to the Duet and Scene 'We'll go away together' when Rose sings «we'll leave behind our yesterdays» over a chromatically descending bass line from D to B-flat, pulling the music away from Sam's goal (see Ex. 5a). Here, A-flat major is also the home key, and it is Tony who keeps pushing the music in this direction.

Ex. 5b: *West Side Story*, No. 6 'Balcony Scene'.

He first sings in c minor but will bring the music into E-flat major, the key of romance, in which Tony had swooned over Maria's name. At this point, in the film score, they kiss (Ex. 6). Tonal stability does not last long, however. The music modulates to c minor, tonic chords overlaid with d minor so that the music can move back to Maria's initial key of B-flat major for the refrain, 'Tonight'. At this point, the accompaniment shifts between a tonic chord with an added second and g minor with added sixth. The foxtrot rhythm may indicate Tony's power over her (by contrast, as Helen Smith has observed, the rumba in 'Maria' indicates that he is consumed by her world[42]).

---

[42]. See SMITH 2011, pp. 153-160, for more insight into the implications of the rhythms in *West Side Story*.

Ex. 6: *West Side Story*, No. 6 'Balcony Scene'.

They sing in unison in the bright key of A major until a composite chord of the tonic and the parallel f-sharp minor brings the music back to the home key. But the stability is short-lived: Tony sings one verse of the refrain, and the music turns to a-flat minor. While the orchestra continues to sing the 'Tonight' refrain, in A-flat major, Maria is reduced to spoken dialogue: «I cannot stay. Go quickly». Like Rose, she cannot indefinitely join in her lover's optimism.

When Maria and Tony do sing again together, A-flat major is offset by composites joining it with B-flat and D-flat major until the home key eventually wins out. The text indicates, however, that only in their dreams can they be together («Sleep well and when you dream, / dream of me / tonight»). Just as in *Street Scene*, the music and text foreshadow the tragic resolution. The number ends with two intra-textual references, in which the bassoon sings «There's a place for us» and provides then the answer, «Somewhere», together with oboe and clarinet: the place where Tony and Maria can be together is not on earth.

They continue to dream unto the end, however. In the quintet 'Tonight', the aggressive, double-tonic chords indicating the stand-off of the Sharks and Jets cede, if only briefly, to

A-major and C-major (the double-tonic complex, as Wells has noted, of the *Tristan* prelude[43]) for Maria and Tony. The duet 'One Hand, One Heart', originally conceived as a love duet for *Candide*[44] (1956), modulates from D major to C major (the key of dreams, as in *Street Scene*) for their mock wedding but reaches E-flat major when Tony declares «till death do us part». Tony and Maria mostly sing in unison, beginning in G-flat major and ending in the home key of A-flat major. The refrain features a chorale-like figure in the accompaniment recalling the mock-Lutheran passages in *Die sieben Todsünden* (1933) or the final chorale of *Die Dreigroschenoper*, but is free of irony, taking on an earnest, prayerful tone.

Conclusion

The intertextual relations between *Street Scene* and *West Side Story* reveal that Weill's formal experimentation on Broadway tilled the soil for what would become Bernstein's most popular stage work. The score exploits double-tonalities that are unconventional for the American musical; allows the orchestra to have the last word; and includes subtle intertextual allusions to canonic composers such as Wagner. Yet Bernstein achieved a streamlining of syntax that makes the music accessible to a wide audience. *Street Scene*, meanwhile, had set a precedent by bringing realist tragedy from the streets of New York onto the Broadway stage. The juxtaposition of harsh, one might say modernist dissonance with breezy, popular vernacular is a key part of its formal identity. Within his pursuit to establish a viable tradition of Broadway Opera, Weill also dared to self-consciously maintain continuity with European tradition through the dramaturgically strategic placement of intertextual allusions. Building upon on this unique blend of elements, Bernstein reached the «moment in history» he had predicted in which a «new form» would emerge[45].

Credits
Leonard Bernstein, *West Side Story*.
Copyright ©1956, 1957, 1958, 1959 by Amberson Holdings LLC and Stephen Sondheim. Copyright renewed. Leonard Bernstein Music Publishing Company LLC. Provided courtesy of Boosey & Hawkes Bote und Bock Berlin.
Kurt Weill, *Street Scene*.
An American Opera (Based on Elmer Rice's Play). Lyrics by Langston Hughes (Chappell Music Company, 1948) Lyrics by Langston Hughes Music by Kurt Weill © 1945 (Renewed) Chappell & Co., Inc. and Tro-Hampshire House Publishing Corp., New York, NY All Rights for the World Outside of the U.S. Administered by Chappell & Co., Inc. All Rights Reserved Used by Permission of Alfred Music.

---

43. Wells 2011, pp. 73-75.
44. Jaensch 2003, p. 86.
45. Bernstein 1959, p. 179.

Bibliography

Bernstein 1949
Bernstein, Leonard. 'Prelude to a Blitzstein Musical Adaptation', in: *The New York Times*, 30 October 1949.

Bernstein 1959
Id. 'American Musical Comedy', in: *The Joy of Music*, London, Weidenfeld & Nicolson, 1959, pp. 152-179.

Bernstein 1982
Id. *Findings*, New York, Simon and Schuster, 1982.

Block 1997
Block, Geoffrey. *Enchanted Evenings: The Broadway Musical from Show Boat to Sondheim*, Oxford-New York, Oxford University Press, 1997.

Burton 2017
Burton, Humphrey. *Leonard Bernstein*, London, Faber & Faber, 2017.

Gottlieb 1964
Gottlieb, Jack. *The Music of Leonard Bernstein: A Study of Melodic Manipulations*, DMA Diss., Urbana-Champaign (IL), University of Illinois, 1964.

Grosch 2017
Grosch, Nils. '*West Side Story*', in: *Leonard Bernstein und seine Zeit*, edited by Andreas Eichhorn, Laaber, Laaber-Verlag, 2017, pp. 296-316.

Hinton 2012
Hinton, Stephen. *Weill's Musical Theater: Stages of Reform*, Berkeley-Los Angeles, University of California Press, 2012.

Hirsch 2000
Hirsch, Foster. *Kurt Weill on Stage. From Berlin to Broadway*, New York, Random House Publishing, 2000.

Jaensch 2003
Jaensch, Andreas. *Leonard Bernsteins Musiktheater. Auf dem Weg zu einer Amerikanischen Oper*, Kassel, Bärenreiter Verlag, 2003.

Kirk 2001
Kirk, Elise K. *Music in American Life*, Urbana-Chicago, University of Illinois, 2001.

Kowalke 1995
Kowalke, Kim H. 'Kurt Weill, Modernism, and Popular Culture: *Öffentlichkeit als Stil*', in: *Modernism/modernity*, II/1 (January 1995), pp. 27-69.

Kowalke 1996
Id. '*The Threepenny Opera*: The Score Adapted', in: Weill 1996, pp. 11-17.

Kowalke 2003
Id. 'Kurt Weill and the Quest for American Opera', in: *Amerkanismus/Americanism/Weill*, edited by Hermann Danuser and Hermann Gottschewski, Schliengen, Edition Argus, 2003, pp. 283-301.

Latham 2008
Latham, Edward D. *Tonality as Drama. Closure and Interruption in Four Twentieth-Century American Operas*, Denton (TX), University of North Texas Press, 2008.

Shawn 2014
Shawn, Allan. *Leonard Bernstein: An American Musician*, New Haven-London, Yale University Press, 2014.

Simeone 2009
Simeone, Nigel. *Leonard Bernstein: West Side Story*, Farnham-Burlington, Ashgate, 2009.

Simeone 2013
Id. *The Leonard Bernstein Letters*, New Haven-London, Yale University Press, 2013.

Smith 2011
Smith, Helen. *There's a Place for Us: The Musical Theatre Works of Leonard Bernstein*, Farnham-Burlington, Ashgate, 2011.

Sondheim 2010
Sondheim, Stephen. *Finishing the Hat. Collected Lyrics (1954-1981) with Attendant Commetns, Principles, Heresies, Grudges, Whines and Anecdotes*, New York, Alfred A. Knopf, 2010.

Straus 1990
Straus, Joseph N. *Remaking the Past: Musical Modernism and the Influence of the Tonal Tradition*, Cambridge (MA)-London, Harvard University Press, 1990.

Swain 1990
Swain, Joseph. *The Broadway Musical: A Critical and Musical Survey*, Oxford-New York, Oxford University Press, 1990.

Weill 1946
Weill, Kurt. 'Broadway Opera: Our Composers' Hope for the Future', as told to Edward J. Smith, in: *Musical Digest*, xxix/4 (December 1946), pp. 16, 42.

Weill 1996
Weill, Kurt. *«Die Dreigroschenoper»: A Facsimile of the Holograph Full Score*, Series i, Vol. 1, edited by Edward Harsh, New York, Kurt Weill Foundation for Music, 1996.

Wells 2011
Wells, Elizabeth A. *«West Side Story»: Cultural Perspectives on an American Musical*, London-Toronto, The Scarecrow Press, 2011.

What Makes Weill Weill?[1]

Kim H. Kowalke
(University of Rochester / The Kurt Weill Foundation for Music)

I came up with the title of this essay when I was invited to present a lecture about Kurt Weill for the Glimmerglass Opera Festival in 2012. I intended it to sound a bit enigmatic when spoken aloud. After Kurt Weill arrived in New York in 1935, he altered his pronunciation of his surname from 'Vile' to 'Wile'. It has not been standardized since, becoming something of a 'you say e̱ither, I say ei̱ther' situation. If one chooses to pronounce it as an Americanized 'Wile', then 'What makes Weill Weill?' presents no more confusion than 'what makes Puccini Puccini?'. But that isn't the case for the German analogue: 'What makes Vile Vile?'. Depending on inflection, that could be an inquiry about some wretched performance practice of the composer's music or a wholesale condemnation of his entire output. And if one wanted to play into the hands of critics dismissive of his American oeuvre, one could ask 'what makes Wile Vile?'. On the other hand, if the German and American pronunciations are reversed into 'What makes Vile Wile?', my title hints at the central issue in Weill studies since his premature death in 1950. Modernist aesthetic agendas and critical constructs have been hard-pressed to cope with the dichotomies and ambiguities of Weill's career and output: European and American, German and Jewish, serious and popular, *Amerikanismus* and Americanism. Weill does not conform to the unitary stylistic and biographical identity conventionally expected of a 'genuine' composer. So 'two Weills' had to be created:

> While some notable artists have simply stopped creating at a certain stage of their careers and a few have put an end to their lives, Weill is perhaps the only one

---

[1]. Earlier versions of this essay were presented as lectures at the Glimmerglass Opera Festival, Cincinnati College Conservatory, Oberlin College, University of Minnesota, and University of Buffalo. I am grateful for colleagues' comments, suggestions, and critiques offered on each of those occasions. Dave Stein, Archivist of the Weill-Lenya Research Center, was particularly helpful in preparing this print version at a time when COVID-19 limited access to some of my sources.

> to have done away with his old creative self in order to make way for a new one [...].
> It means that in Weill we have not one, but two composers. The first and important
> one can and should be evaluated without reference to the second.

In fact, David Drew, the pioneering dean of Weill scholarship and author of the Weill entry in the *New Grove Dictionary of Music and Musicians* in 1980 (quoted above), even entitled its concluding section 'The Two Weills'. In a final flourish he asserted that the composer's failure to conform to modernist expectations of artistic development resulted in his being «one of music's great might-have-beens»[2].

Weill's Last Year

To anchor a brief exploration of 'What makes Weill Weill?' let's begin by time-traveling back to 1949, the last day of March, a Thursday, 8:30 p.m. If you were living on the East Coast or in certain parts of the Midwest, you could have turned on your black-and-white television set and tuned in to the fledgling and by no means yet nationwide NBC network to catch a half-hour weekly variety program called *The Swift Show*[3]. Each week a segment of the program showcased a musical then running on Broadway, with a small ensemble of singing theatre-goers exclaiming that ticket prices started at $1.10 and capped at $8.80. That evening's featured musical was *Love Life* (1949) a *vaudeville* by Alan Jay Lerner and Kurt Weill, which had opened the previous October. But the primitively produced *Swift Show* was not all that 'swift'. It lasted for just that one season, as did Weill's most innovative Broadway musical. Seated at a grand piano in his purported 'studio', a tongue-twisted Weill was obviously uncomfortable in front of the camera. He accompanied Martha Wright and host Lanny Ross plugging 'Here I'll Stay', *Love Life*'s big romantic duet. But the television exposure didn't help ticket sales all that much. Although now recognized as the first non-linear 'concept musical' — the prototype for *Cabaret* (1966), *Chicago* (1975), *Company* (1970), *Assassins* (1990), and even the *Scottsboro Boys* (2010) — *Love Life* closed six weeks later, after 252 performances. Two boycotts had prevented the recording of an original cast album as well as radio stations' broadcasting songs from the show. After its run ended in mid-May, Weill would be without a show on Broadway, but for only a few months.

That summer he and Maxwell Anderson were still hard at work adapting Alan Paton's anti-apartheid novel *Cry, the Beloved Country* as a 'musical tragedy'. They had persuaded the original Porgy, Todd Duncan, to take the lead role and recruited Rouben Mamoulian, the

---

[2]. DREW 1980. Drew apparently borrowed the «unhappy might-have-been» epithet from Gerald Abraham, whose target for the phrase had been Max Reger; see ABRAHAM 1938, p. 230.

[3]. The *Love Life* sequence from the telecast of *The Swift Show* on 31 March 1949 can be viewed at <https://vimeo.com/444251513>, accessed April 2023.

What Makes Weill Weill?

director of *Porgy and Bess* (1935), *Oklahoma!* (1943) and *Carousel* (1945), to stage it. In September, Weill wrote to his parents, who had fled Germany to Palestine in 1935, to reassure them that things were going well, that life was good: «Yesterday I finished composing the music and now I must work flat out to complete as much orchestration as possible before rehearsals begin on 19 September». In the next paragraph he reported, with some satisfaction and surprise, that «after twenty-five years of difficult, tireless work, it almost looks like I am to reap some sort of reward — not in a financial, but in a purely idealistic sense [...]. I've suddenly been promoted to the rank of "classical composer", and people are even beginning to talk about the historical significance of my work»[4].

On 30 October, *Lost in the Stars* debuted at the Music Box Theatre to generally favorable reviews, particularly for Weill's score and the musical's daring treatment of racial injustice in South Africa, and, by extension, in the United States as well. Shortly after the new year, NBC televised its first opera production, Weill's *Down in the Valley* (1948), just three weeks after CBS had beaten it to the punch with its first opera telecast, *Carmen*. By then Anderson and Weill had already started work on a musical adaptation of *Huckleberry Finn*. Workaholic Weill celebrated his fiftieth birthday on 2 March 1950. Two weeks later he suffered a heart attack. At first he rallied. But on 3 April, he took a sudden turn for the worse and died, almost exactly one year after his appearance on the *Swift Show*.

Obituaries of 'The Two Weills'

The morning after Weill's death, the *New York Times* carried a lengthy, unsigned obituary. Its four-part heading read: «KURT WEILL DEAD; COMPOSER, WAS 50 / Wrote Music for *One Touch of Venus*, *Lady in the Dark* and Other Broadway Hits / ALSO TURNED OUT OPERAS/ *Der Protagonist* and *Tsar Has Himself Photographed* His Best-Known Works». Note that Weill is identified not as a 'songwriter' or 'tunesmith', but as a 'Composer'. This was not an unconsidered choice of words. The obituary later quotes the *Times*'s chief drama critic Brooks Atkinson's review of *Lady in the Dark* from 1941: «he is not a song writer but a composer of organic music that can bind the separate elements of a production and turn the underlying motive into song». Note also which of Weill's works qualify for mention. Predictably, the list begins with his two longest running shows on Broadway, *Lady in the Dark* (1941) and *One Touch of Venus* (1943). But then, an unlikely assertion: «*Der Protagonist* and *Tsar Has Himself Photographed* his best-known works». These were two of Weill's first operas, both one-acts with librettos by the famous German expressionist playwright, Georg

---

[4]. Letter in German from Weill to Albert and Emma Weill, 6 September 1949, reprinted in SYMONETTE – JUCHEM 2000, pp. 419-420. All translations from the German included in this essay are the present author's.

Kaiser. Performed separately and as a double bill by a fair number of Germany's opera houses in the late 1920s, they indeed had almost instantly established Weill's standing as the foremost operatic composer of his generation in Germany. But by 1950, both had all but vanished — on both sides of the Atlantic. At the time of his death, they were a far cry from being his «best-known works». *Down in the Valley* would soon lay sole claim to that distinction, with almost six thousand performances in the 1950s[5].

The Threepenny Opera warranted no marquee billing in the *Times* obituary. Although it had been produced in virtually every major European city (and beyond) before the Second World War, it had flopped when it was mounted on Broadway in 1933, lasting only 12 performances. Not until 1954, when Marc Blitzstein's adaptation would be staged off-Broadway in the Theatre de Lys, with Weill's widow, Lotte Lenya, again playing Jenny, did it find success in English-speaking countries. By the end of that decade, *The Threepenny Opera* would displace *Oklahoma!* as the longest running musical in history, and Bobby Darin, Louis Armstrong, Ella Fitzgerald, and Frank Sinatra would propel 'Mack the Knife' to the head of the hit parade. The song sold more than 10 million records. Weill's obituary would have read much differently had he lived to be sixty.

Across the Atlantic, delayed news of Weill's death elicited an obituary in the *Frankfurter Rundschau* about two weeks later than the one printed in the *Times*. Its author was no less a figure than Theodor W. Adorno, the apostle of musical modernism and a principal spokesman for the Frankfurt School of Marxist critical theory. Its headline read: «Kurt Weill – Musiker des epischen Theaters»[6]. 'Musician of the Epic Theatre' has subsequently become a key document in postwar Weill reception, demanding quotation at some length here:

> The image of this composer, who died in America, is scarcely accommodated by the notion of a "composer". His gift, like his influence, resides far less in musical capacities as such (in creations whose substance and structure would stand on their own) than in an extraordinary and original feeling for the function of music in the theater [...]. Working with limited powers of organization, he made a virtue of the necessity of subordinating the artistic to theatrical effect and to some degree even the political [...]. With flair, mobility and a very individual mode of expression, he defined a new role: that of a "music stage director" [*Musikregisseur*].

After noting that Weill had been a pupil of Busoni, Adorno lamented that Weill's «lack of real craftsmanship, from the simplest harmonization to the construction of large forms, was his inheritance from a school that was more aesthetic than strictly technical». The harshest and least informed judgment was reserved for the American Weill: «with a disarmingly shy

---

[5]. See KOWALKE 2003, p. 285.
[6]. *Frankfurter Rundschau*, 15 April 1950. (Reprinted in ADORNO 1984, pp. 544-547.)

and crafty innocence, he became a Broadway composer, with Cole Porter as his model, and talked as if concession to the commercial field were no concession, but only a pure test of his ability, which made everything possible even within standardized boundaries». There is no evidence, however, that Adorno had ever attended a production of any of Weill's American stage works, nor of Weill attending or commenting on any of Porter's stage musicals[7]. It is likely that Adorno heard on the radio songs such as 'Speak Low', the closest Weill approached the Porter of 'Begin the Beguine'. Another possibility is that Adorno, like so many others, mistook the almost unrecognizable Hollywood adaptations of *Lady in the Dark* (1944) and *One Touch of Venus* (1948) for a reasonable facsimile of Weill's original stage scores. Yet with his own supremely crafty confidence, Adorno thereby sowed the seeds of necessity for two Weills in the postwar European reception of his (then almost entirely unknown) American works: «In this endeavor he had to renounce all those elements in his musical language which had once created a Weillian atmosphere. He could no longer do what he knew how to do». 'Wile' could no longer be 'Vile', so to speak.

In contrast, on the Sunday following Weill's death, American composer-critic Virgil Thomson had devoted his column in the *New York Herald Tribune* to an appraisal of Weill's historical significance and had come to conclusions very different from Adorno's:

> Everything [Weill] wrote became in one way or another historic. He was probably the most original single workman in the whole musical theater, internationally considered, during the last quarter century [...]. Whether Weill's American works will carry as far as his German ones I cannot say. They lack the mordant and touching humanity of Brecht's poetry. But the loss to music and to the theater is real. Both will go on, and so will Weill's influence. But his output of new models — and every work was a new model, a new shape, a new solution of dramatic problems — will not continue[8].

These three obituaries vividly demonstrate how limited and parochial were mid-century perspectives on both sides of the Atlantic at the time of Weill's death. A few months later Hans Redlich wrote in London's *Music Survey*:

> It is a well-known fact that most of the representative composers of this age [...] have been driven into exile by indiscriminate forces of political factions which brutally denied them vital contact with their respective national climates. This sorry fate overtook Kurt Weill while still in his early thirties and nothing can express more poignantly the sinister implications of this enforced exodus than the sinister fact

---

[7]. There is no record of contact between Porter and Weill, though Porter did introduce himself to Lenya in April 1938 when she was singing at the Ruban Bleu nightclub in New York.

[8]. THOMSON 1950.

that Weill's mature music, composed by the homeless artist in France, England and ultimately in the United States, has remained a *terra incognita* even to his admirers[9].

In a review of a memorial concert for Weill at Town Hall a year after his death, even Virgil Thomson now suggested that «after Weill came to live in America, he ceased to work as a modernist»[10].

Little had changed a decade later, when, at the height of the Cold War, Weill's first biographer, Hellmut Kotschenreuther, declared that «Whoever accepts Weill's *Johnny Johnson* forgoes the right to accept *Die Dreigroschenoper*, *Aufstieg und Fall der Stadt Mahagonny*, and *Die sieben Todsünden*»[11]. Already the Weill-with-Brecht was being pitted against the Weill-without-Brecht. The construct of the 'two Weills', one German, the other American, had been collapsed and simplified into Weill-With and -Without, despite the fact that Weill and Brecht's collaboration had lasted less than four years and was characterized by fruitful but ultimately irreconcilable aesthetic, political, and personal tensions almost from the outset. Such was the starting point for the long and still incomplete process of trying to put Weill back together, to figure out 'What makes Vile Wile or Wile Vile'.

As the Berlin Wall was being dismantled, the debate around Weill's identity prompted the formidable musicologist Richard Taruskin to declare him to be «perhaps the twentieth century's most problematical major musician»[12]. By then the composer was being viewed from both sides of the Atlantic as a key figure reifying the central issues at hand, and not only in musicological discourse: modernism versus counter- or post-modernism; elitism versus popularism; autonomy versus accessibility; originality versus comprehensibility; atonality/serialism versus tonality; stylistic diversity versus authenticity. In asserting already in 1936 that the «recital hall is obsolete» and that absolute music has reached its historically appointed dead end, Weill anticipated what might now be seen as the central 'problem' of music in the second half of the twentieth century and beyond[13]. Absent a compelling replacement for a modernist 'progress narrative', how can music in a post-Adornian pluralistic, postmodern, and aesthetically entropic world be productively situated?

---

[9]. REDLICH 1950. A variant of Redlich's observation about Weill's fate has been preserved, without identification of source, as a photocopy filed as Ser.80.200 in the Weill-Lenya Research Center: «The tragedy of our contemporary world is nowhere more vividly expressed than in the fact that the compositions of the mature Kurt Weill, written between his 34th and 50th year, have so far remained a closed book even to his most faithful admirers in the Old World. It must have been a keen disappointment to him that the country of his origin cold-shouldered him even after the defeat of Nazidom in 1945».

[10]. THOMSON 1951.

[11]. KOTSCHENREUTHER 1962, p. 92.

[12]. TARUSKIN 1988, p. 3.

[13]. WINETT 1936, p. 10.

What Makes Weill Weill?

Weill's Itinerary

«Where does the stable essence of an "I" reside?» asks Milan Kundera in *Testaments Betrayed*, his remarkable collection of essays on modernism. «Over what period of time can we consider a man identical to himself?» Such Weill-relevant questions arise as Kundera interrogates the modern novel, seeking in particular to understand the differences between Dostoyevsky and Tolstoy. Kundera suggests that the stable identities of Dostoyevsky's characters lie in their personal ideologies, whereas «in Tolstoy, man is the more himself, the more an individual, when he has the strength, the imagination, the intelligence, to transform himself». In *War and Peace* Bezukhov and Bolkonsky surprise — «They make themselves different» — and thereby offer another conception of human identity: «He is an itinerary; a winding road; a journey whose successive phases not only vary but often represent a total negation of the preceding phases»[14]. Kundera immediately refines this metaphor, however: «I've said *road*, a word that could mislead, because the image of a road evokes a destination. Now, what is the destination of these roads that end only randomly, broken off by the happenstance of death?».

In the musical realm Kundera focused not on Weill, but Stravinsky, «whose conscious purposeful eclecticism» he finds «gigantic and unmatched». Stravinsky's life, Kundera notes, «divides into three parts of roughly equal length: Russia, 27 years; France and French-speaking Switzerland, 29 years; America 32 years». Despite corresponding radical shifts in Stravinsky's musical language and style, Kundera argues not for three «distinct personalities» but for a single artistic persona who changes as he attempts to master the past, an agenda central to the modernist project. Elsewhere in his book, in a nuanced unpacking of irony entitled 'Paths in the Fog', Kundera might well have chosen Weill (instead of Janácek) to stand as the musical counterpart to Kafka: «In the kingdom of irony, equality rules; this means that no phase of the itinerary is morally superior to another».

Juxtaposition of two crucial milestones along Weill's transatlantic itinerary may prove illuminating: *Die Dreigroschenoper* (Berlin, 1928) and *Lady in the Dark* (New York, 1941). They might seem incompatible, if not antithetical. Yet they have much in common. They were respectively Weill's first successful forays into commercial theatre in Germany and America. *Die Dreigroschenoper* opted out of the state-subsidized system of theatrical and operatic production to engage a new audience in the Weimar Republic. Its instantaneous and unexpected near-global success came as an embarrassment to *enfant terrible* Brecht, who spent the next several years attempting to rework it, first as a literary version of the play, then as a novel and a screenplay, each reflecting his newly acquired Marxist bent ever more radically. With *Lady in the Dark* Weill left behind his affiliations with such left wing collectives as the Group Theatre to embrace

---

[14]. Kundera 2001, pp. 211-213 and *passim*.

mainstream Broadway, with the most illustrious of collaborators, namely Ira Gershwin (in his first return to Broadway since the death of George) and Moss Hart.

Both were generic hybrids, defying conventions of musico-dramatic structure and exploring alternative relationships between text and music, between what was spoken and sung. *Die Dreigroschenoper* ended up as a 'play with music', but a play inhabited with singing actors and acting singers from highly disparate backgrounds. *Lady in the Dark* broke the mold of Broadway musical comedy even more boldly, utilizing music to structure the 'musical play', with its through-composed dream sequences corresponding to the use of color to differentiate Oz from Kansas in 1939's *Wizard of Oz*. This was no ordinary book musical in the era between *Show Boat* (1927) and *Oklahoma!* (1943). It was a radical experiment, one which could not be repeated, but one that inaugurated the possibility of what would be called thirty years later the 'concept musical'. Each work established Weill as the foremost innovator in the musical theatre in its two respective, diverse cultural contexts. And their success allowed him not only to buy a house in Berlin and Rockland County respectively, but also to give him the stature and resources necessary to advance his ambitious agenda to create new models of musical theatre. As such, they lay equal claim as signposts, if not beacons, along Weill's winding road.

In that light, we might now re-direct Kundera's question away from Stravinsky toward Weill: «where does the stable essence of Weill's identity reside?». Perhaps we might consider critic Harold Clurman's oft-quoted characterization of Weill as a musical Gulliver, able to write music in any country so that it would seem as if he were a native: «if he were forced to live among Hottentots he would in the shortest possible span of time become the leading Hottentot composer»[15]. For Clurman, Weill was «all theater, and all mask», a sort of musical shape-shifter who constantly changed identities by assuming characteristics of his collaborators and adapting to his audiences' expectations[16]. Clurman's corollary, that Weill «sold out» to American commercialism, was largely congruent with the aesthetic views of Eric Bentley, as articulated in *The Playwright as Thinker* (1946), the American dramatic analogue to Adorno's *Philosphie der neuen Musik* (1949). Such appraisals by modernist critics on both sides of the Atlantic beg the foundational question: is there anything essential, or even essentialist, that makes Weill Weill?

---

[15]. CLURMAN 1949. Clurman's invocation of the pejorative and racialist term «Hottentot» may not have been intended to refer specifically to the Khoekhoe, indigenous nomadic pastoralists living in southern Africa before the arrival of European explorers. It probably came to mind because Clurman was reviewing *Lost in the Stars*, set in contemporary South Africa.

[16]. CLURMAN 1974, pp. 128-129.

What Makes Weill Weill?

Making Weill Weill

At the risk of gross over-simplification in an attempt to formulate a necessarily brief and provisional answer, one might first compile a short list of constants, aspects of Weill's aesthetics, musical language, and dramatic strategies that characterize his music for the stage on both continents. If this were not an interdisciplinary forum, one might be tempted to begin with a detailed technical examination of musical vocabulary and syntax that remained recognizable as 'Weill' throughout his oeuvre. Such an inventory might include the treatment of strophic and verse-refrain structures: for example, the parallel form and function in the 16-measure, strophic units of 'Die Moritat vom Mackie Messer' and 'The Saga of Jenny'. One could compile a catalogue of characteristically Weillian harmonic progressions, starting with the resemblance linking the refrain of 'Das schöne Kind' (1917) to the climax of Frank Maurrant's 'Let Things Be Like They Always Was' from *Street Scene* (1947). Or chart the unfolding of large-scale 'double-tonic' structural units with explicit non-triadic cadential resolutions, from the Cello Sonata (1920) to 'My Ship' twenty years later. Or the similarity of fifth-generated harmonies and pentatonic melodies in the fourth song of *Frauentanz* (1923) and 'What Good Would the Moon Be?' from *Street Scene*. Or the ubiquitous semitone vacillations between major and minor within melodic and harmonic structures, from the String Quartet in B minor (1918) through *Lost in the Stars*, Weill's last completed work. Such a recital would rapidly grow tedious for most readers, particularly for those whose ears inform them intuitively that the same composer wrote 'Die stille Stadt' (1919) and 'Lonely House' (1946). Therefore, it may be more persuasive to examine broader and ultimately more decisive imperatives that persisted throughout Weill's career.

First and foremost, already at the age of 19 when he was working as a Kapellmeister in a tiny provincial theatre in Lüdenscheid, Weill decided that his special field of activity as a composer would be the theatre. He confided to his sister Ruth that the musical theatre, «where music can best express the unspeakable, will probably turn out to be my life's work»[17]. Although he wrote with some success in other genres and media, for three decades he would indeed focus on the musical theatre in its widest range, writing about twenty-five dramatic works in three languages for audiences in the opera house, the commercial theatre, the school auditorium, the movie theatre, the radio, and even the transportation pavilion at the 1939-1949 World's Fair in New York. He wrote 'absolute' instrumental music less and less as his stage career progressed, putting into practice his belief that «in our time theater-music is far more important than absolute music»[18]. And, as Stephen Hinton has observed, the array of Weill's theatrical works comprised

---

[17]. Letter from Kurt Weill to Ruth Weill, 28 January 1920, published in SYMONETTE – JUCHEM 2000, p. 257 (letter no. 143).

[18]. WINETT 1936, p. 11.

a succession of experimental generic hybrids, each breaking new ground, each laying claim to the status *sui generis*[19]. In that sense Clurman certainly was right: Weill was increasingly 'all theatre'.

As a teenager Weill also confessed with some embarrassment to his brother Hans: «I need poetry to set my musical imagination in motion, for my imagination is not a bird, but an airplane»[20]. He recognized that he would need words to ignite his inspiration, to propel his musical intellect. His earliest surviving compositions were therefore, predictably, lieder. His first two large-scale orchestral works (1919, 1921) were symphonic poems inspired respectively by *Die Weise von Liebe und Tod des Cornets Christoph Rilke* and Johannes Becher's *Arbeiter, Bauern, Soldaten*. When composing the orchestral *Fantasia, Passacaglia, und Hymnus* in 1922, he deemed it necessary to derive much of its musical material from pre-compositional stylistic studies he sketched by setting poetry of Rilke.

During the quarter century extending from his first published and produced opera *Der Protagonist* (1924-1925) through his sketches for the unfinished Huck Finn project, Weill recruited and cultivated as collaborators some of the finest literary and dramatic talents in each language and location in which he labored. He boasted in 1947 that «one of the first decisions I made was to get the leading dramatists of my time interested in the problems of the musical theater»[21]. Indeed, in Germany his two principal collaborators were arguably the leading playwrights of their respective generations, Georg Kaiser and Bertolt Brecht. In America he successfully recruited Paul Green, Maxwell Anderson, Elmer Rice, Ogden Nash, S.J. Perelman, Moss Hart, Langston Hughes, and Alan Jay Lerner. Despite considerable effort, his attempts to collaborate with the likes of Jean Cocteau, John Steinbeck, Herman Wouk, and Eugene O'Neill did not come to fruition. Like Stephen Sondheim a quarter century later, Weill preferred to work not just as a composer or songwriter, but as a 'collaborative dramatist', side by side with the author(s) drafting librettos, which were usually all but completed before Weill started composing: «I need a subject before I can compose. I've never just taken a libretto and made music to it. It must be a libretto I believe in»[22]. In 1944 Weill confessed to Lenya some frustration in this regard while working on *The Firebrand of Florence* (1945):

> I don't get credit for anything but the music. But I am sure that Verdi or Offenbach or Mozart contributed as much to their libretti as I do without getting credit for it. This is a part of a theater composer's job, to create for himself the vehicle he needs for his music[23].

---

[19]. See HINTON 1993, pp. 23-32.

[20]. Letter to Hans Weill, 27 June 1919. Reprinted in SYMONETTE – JUCHEM 2000, p. 234 (letter no. 127).

[21]. 'Two Dreams Come True', published in 1947 as liner note for the original cast recording of *Street Scene*, CBS OL 4139.

[22]. WINETT 1936, p. 12.

[23]. Letter from Weill to Lenya, 12 August 1944, reprinted in SYMONETTE – KOWALKE 1996, p. 417 (letter no. 344).

What Makes Weill Weill?

This was as true with Kaiser and Brecht as with Anderson or Lerner.

And Weill's relationships to those texts was never uncomplicated. In 1933, for example, in an attempt to persuade the designer Caspar Neher that Brecht's lyrics for the «ballet with singing» *Die sieben Todsünden* (1933) weren't just «literary trash», Weill argued: «Everyone who knows anything about me knows that every text I've set looks entirely different once it's been swept through my music»[24]. He frequently cited the example of the «Zuhälterballade» from *Die Dreigroschenoper*, where «a rather obscene text is sung to a tango that is as elegant and seductive as that found in many an operetta»[25]. Such ironic counterpoint, even dissonance, between text and music became a Weillian signature, producing complex layers of reciprocal commentary. In furnishing Langston Hughes with a blueprint for the Nurses' Lullaby in Act II of *Street Scene*, Weill provides a glimpse into the workshop where its 'Brechtian irony' was still being crafted:

> Whatever we will do with the last scene, I am sure the nursemaids will be in, and they need badly an amusing song. As you remember, it should be a sort of waltz song about the newspaper reports and pictures, using the whole *Daily News* terminology which is typical of fifty million women in America who are more interested in murder stories than anything else [...]. This part could be a regular little waltz chorus, then it would be interrupted by a little ditty in a different rhythm (short lines) where they are scolding the babies in the carriages to be quiet [...]. I know that this kind of lyric which should be gay and funny and bitter at the same time is not easy to write[26].

The subtle, shifting, and sometimes subversive relationships among words, notes, rhythms, and instrumentation remained a crucial Weillian characteristic throughout his career.

Unlike most creators of American musical theatre, Weill seldom worked with any librettist or lyricist more than once, Maxwell Anderson and Ira Gershwin the two exceptions. Such inconstancy was both a curse, in that the composer was always breaking in newcomers to the musical stage, and a blessing, in that by working with different writers he avoided repeating himself, by falling back into formulas in the way perennial collaborators such as Gilbert and Sullivan, Rodgers and Hammerstein, or Lerner and Loewe frequently did. Rather, as Weill put it, «each show has to create its own style, its own texture, its own relationship between text and

---

[24]. Undated letter from Weill to Erika Neher (May 1933). Photocopy in Weill-Lenya Research Center.

[25]. Letter from Kurt Weill to Universal Edition, 10 September 1928, published in GROSCH 2002, p. 135 (letter no. 423).

[26]. Letter from Weill to Langston Hughes, 20 September 1946. Photocopy in the Weill-Lenya Research Center. Hughes thought that Weill continually tried to make *Street Scene* into something more like *Die Dreigroschenoper* than what Elmer Rice would allow.

music»[27]. And because he required that each work have its own *Klangbild* or sonic world, he insisted on doing his own orchestrations throughout his entire career, virtually unique among Broadway composers of his time. He remained fiercely protective of them whenever his music was performed in the theatre, whether a *Schauspielhaus* in Germany or an orchestra pit on Broadway.

Almost all of Weill's stage works dealt with serious contemporary issues of relevance to the audience at hand. But such engagement with issues and audiences in the present came with a price. The topicality of what was called *Zeittheater* in Germany is, of course, double-edged: today's urgent issue (whether disarmament, psychoanalysis, or apartheid) frequently becomes tomorrow's ever more dated memory. The standard repertory of American musical theatre in particular has been resistant to politically or socially-engaged works. Weill thus walked a precarious tightrope, hovering precipitously between popularizing the 'serious' and transforming the 'popular' within substantive discourse.

Weill maintained in private and public that all his works were stepping stones along the path toward an accessible modern musical theatre, an accessibility demanding that he take into account his changing audiences. «A creative artist», he wrote in an essay from 1937 entitled 'The Future of Opera in America', «must know for whom he is creating»[28]. Citing Mozart as a model, Weill seldom wavered from a credo he most clearly articulated in 1949: «I have learned to make my music speak directly to the audience, to find the most immediate, direct way to say what I want so say, and to say it as simply as possible»[29]. In attempting to reform opera, to rescue it from what he called its «splendid isolation» and to reach out to the broader audience for theatre, even to society at large, adapting popular idioms and song forms for serious dramatic purposes became an emblematic strategy. In fact, an astonishing polystylism, an eclectic counterpoint of musical idioms, conventions, and styles in the service of dramatic function, characterizes virtually every one of Weill's two dozen stage works. This may be the most distinctive and stable component of his compositional procedure. As he put it, «the musical score itself becomes its own form of storytelling»[30].

And this musical storytelling went far beyond such 'intratextual' techniques as reminiscences and leitmotives which Weill had inherited from operatic predecessors extending back to *Die Zauberflöte*. Instead, he often employed 'intertextuality' as a type of metadramatic musical commentary on a character or situation. This might involve use of such musical idioms

---

[27]. WEILL 1947.
[28]. WEILL 1937, p. 184.
[29]. Letter from Kurt Weill to G. F. Stegmann, 14 February 1949. Original in Weill-Lenya Papers, Irving Gilmore Music Library, Yale University, Ser.IV.A, Box 47 Folder 14.
[30]. WEILL 1946, p. 16.

as a tango, foxtrot, or chorale to capture what he once called the «Gestus» of a scene[31]. Or he would invoke allusions to or quotations from works familiar to many in the audience: the 'Chorale of the Armed Men' from *Die Zauberflöte* and the 'ewige Kunst' of 'Gebet einer Jungfrau' in *Aufstieg und Fall der Mahagonny* (1931); in *Street Scene*, the fate motive from *Carmen* and the 'Strawberries' sales pitch from *Porgy and Bess*; most poignantly the final vocal utterance in Act II of *Madama Butterfly* for Sam and Rose's 'lilac duet'[32].

Although such examples of the constants throughout Weill's *Lebenswerk* put the lie to Adorno's assertion that in America Weill «could no longer do what he knew how to do», generalizations of any sort are inadequate with respect to either Weill. Unmasking one work reveals little about the stylistic identity of another. Thus, even chronologically contiguous pieces such as *Street Scene, Down in the Valley, Love Life,* and *Lost in the Stars* differ from each other as much as they do from most of the European predecessors in Weill's oeuvre. The same could have been said about *Happy End* (1929), *Der Jasager* (1930), *Die Bürgschaft* (1931), and *Der Silbersee* (1933). Yet Weill was still unmistakably Weill in all of them. Contrary to Adorno's assertion, to the end of his tragically foreshortened career, Weill was doing what he knew how to do, from the Kurfürstendamm to the Great White Way, for a post-World War I audience in Berlin and a very different post-World War II one in New York.

Weill's Own Answer

Four months before he died, Weill himself was asked to consider the question 'What makes Weill Weill?'. His last appearance on radio took place in December 1949. The occasion was 'Opera News on the Air', the intermission feature for a broadcast of the Metropolitan Opera's production of Puccini's *Manon Lescaut*. Host Boris Goldovsky first inquired of Weill (and another guest), «what makes Puccini Puccini?» Weill responded, «I'm convinced we have been looking for it in the wrong place»[33]:

> Of course, we could pursue this matter further into a somewhat technical analysis, but even then I doubt if we would have the answer. The answer lies deep

---

[31]. For Weill's most comprehensive explanation of the metadramatic function of music in fixing the 'Gestus' of a dramatic moment, see Weill 1929. Translated in Kowalke 1979, pp. 491-493.

[32]. For a detailed analysis of Weill's utilization of the metadramatic techniques of intertextuality and intratextuality in *Street Scene*, see Kowalke 1995, pp. 27-69. Sondheim's use of 'pastiche' in many of his stage works is a variation on this type of intertextual borrowing.

[33]. 'Opera News on the Air', moderated by Boris Goldovsky, intermission feature during broadcast of Metropolitan Opera performance of *Manon Lescaut*, 10 December 1949. Transcription of audio recording of the feature is available at <https://www.kwf.org/kurt-weill/recommended/opera-news-on-the-air-1949/>, accessed April 2023.

within the composer himself and only a sort of musical psychoanalysis, I would say, could get to the root of it [...] You will notice that in his various operas Puccini consciously colors his music to fit the time and place of his action. For instance, oriental color in *Butterfly* and *Turandot*. But when he hits one of those dramatic situations which he finds most stimulating to himself, the unconscious takes over. He writes pure unadulterated Italian Puccini.

Goldovsky inquired, «Tell me, Mr. Weill, as a composer yourself, are you conscious of any particular emotional appeal that brings forth the most characteristic in you; that brings out the Weill in Weill, so to say? [laughter from audience]» Weill answered without hesitation:

Well, I'm not conscious of it when I actually write music, but looking back on many of my compositions, I find that I seem to have a very strong reaction in the awareness of the suffering of underprivileged people — of the oppressed, the persecuted. I know, for instance, that in the music I wrote for *Lost in the Stars*, I consciously introduced a certain amount of South African musical atmosphere, and yet, in retrospect, I can see that when the music involved human suffering, it is, for better or worse, pure Weill.

Lenya liked to tell the story about Weill's staking out an identity as a composer already as a student in Berlin:

One day during the masterclass in composition at the Akademie der Künste in Berlin, his teacher Ferruccio Busoni had poked fun at Kurt's youthful aspirations to create a popular, but serious and socially-engaged musical theater: "What, you want to become a Verdi of the poor?" "Would that be so bad?" Weill responded.

Perhaps pursuing that goal went a good way toward making Weill Weill.

Bibliography

ABRAHAM 1938
ABRAHAM, Gerald. *A Hundred Years of Music*, London, Duckworth, 1938.

ADORNO 1984
ADORNO, Theodor Wiesengrund. *Musikalische Schriften v*, Frankfurt, Suhrkamp, 1984 (Gesammelte Schriften, 18).

CLURMAN 1949
CLURMAN, Harold. 'Lost in the Stars of Broadway', in: *The Saturday Review of Literature*, 31 December 1949.

CLURMAN 1974
ID. *All People Are Famous*, New York, Harcourt Brace Jovanovich, 1974.

DREW 1980
DREW, David. 'Weill, Kurt', in: *The New Grove Dictionary of Music and Musicians. 20*, edited by Stanley Sadie, London, MacMillan, 1980.

GROSCH 2002
Kurt Weill: Briefwechsel mit der Universal Edition, edited by Nils Grosch, Stuttgart, Metzler, 2002.

HINTON 1993
HINTON, Stephen. 'Fragwürdiges in der deutschen Rezeption', in: *A Stranger Here Myself: Kurt Weill Studien*, edited by Kim H. Kowalke and Horst Edler, Hildesheim, Georg Olms Verlag, 1993, pp. 23-32.

KOTSCHENREUTHER 1962
KOTSCHENREUTHER, Helmut. *Kurt Weill*, Berlin, Max Hesses Verlag, 1962.

KOWALKE 1979
KOWALKE, Kim H. *Kurt Weill in Europe*, Ann Arbor (MI), UMI Research Press, 1979.

KOWALKE 1995
ID. 'Kurt Weill, Modernism, and Popular Culture: *Öffentlichkeit als Stil*', in: *Modernism/modernity*, II/1 (January 1995), pp. 27-69.

KOWALKE 2003
ID. 'Kurt Weill and the Quest for American Opera', in: *Amerikanismus, Americanism, Weill*, edited by Hermann Danuser and Hermann Gottschewski, Schliengen, Edition Argus, 2003, pp. 283-301.

KUNDERA 2001
KUNDERA, Milan. *Testaments Betrayed: An Essay in Nine Parts*, translated by Linda Asher, New York, Harper-Collins Perennial, 2001.

REDLICH 1950
REDLICH, Hans Ferdinand. 'Obituary', in: *Music Survey*, III/1 (Summer 1950), p. 4.

SYMONETTE – JUCHEM 2000
Kurt Weill: Briefe an die Familie (1914-1950), edited by Lys Symonette and Elmar Juchem, Stuttgart, Metzler, 2000.

SYMONETTE – KOWALKE 1996
Speak Low (When You Speak Love): The Letters of Kurt Weill and Lotte Lenya, edited and translated by Lys Symonette and Kim H. Kowalke, Berkeley-Los Angeles, University of California Press, 1996.

TARUSKIN 1988
TARUSKIN, Richard. Review of David Drew, *Kurt Weill: A Handbook*, in: *Kurt Weill Newsletter*, VI/1 (Spring 1988), p. 3.

THOMSON 1950
THOMSON, Virgil. 'Music in Review: Kurt Weill', in: *New York Herald Tribune*, 9 April 1950.

THOMSON 1951
ID. Review of 'Kurt Weill Concert', in: *New York Herald-Tribune*, 5 February 1951.

WEILL 1929
WEILL, Kurt. 'Über den gestischen Charakter der Musik', in: *Die Musik*, no. 21 (March 1929), pp. 419-423.

WEILL 1937
ID. 'The Future of Opera in America', in: *Modern Music*, XIV/4 (May-June 1937), p. 184.

WEILL 1946
ID. 'Broadway Opera: Our Composers' Hope for the Future', as told to Edward J. Smith, in: *Musical Digest*, XXIX/4 (December 1946), pp. 16, 42.

WEILL 1947
ID. 'Score for a Play', in: *New York Times*, 5 January 1947, Section D, p. 3.

WINETT 1936
WINETT, Ralph. 'Composer of the Hour: An Interview with Kurt Weill', in: *Brooklyn Daily Eagle*, 20 December 1936, pp. 10-12.

Abstracts and Biographies

Stephen Hinton, *Weill's Cinematic Imagination: Reality and Fantasy*

Kurt Weill's formation as a composer for the musical theatre was intimately bound up with his experience of the new media. It was a two-way street: as a composer for the stage he wanted to bring his experience in opera houses and the theatre to bear on music composed expressly for the radio and the cinema. But those media, especially cinema, also affected what he wrote for the theatre. Composing for films is something that he speculated about, producing numerous published and unpublished texts on the topic, and which he also fantasized about with projects of various kinds that either remained unfinished or on some level were finished in such a way that left his artistic imagination unsatisfied. Specific projects discussed here include Georg Wilhelm Pabst's *3 Groschen-Oper* (1931), Fritz Lang's *You and Me* (1938), and Gregory Ratoff's *Where Do We Go from Here*? Drawing on recent writings by Wolfgang Ette and Berthold Hoeckner and their expansion of Walter Benjamin's aesthetics of technological reproducibility, the article discusses how Weill's conception of the cinematic song combines the reflective detachment of epic theatre with the subjective, emotional potential of what Hoeckner calls «music's magic».

Stephen Hinton is the Avalon Foundation Professor in the Humanities at Stanford University. He has published widely on many aspects of modern German music history. His book *Weill's Musical Theater: Stages of Reform* (University of California Press, 2012), the first musicological study of Weill's complete stage works, received the 2013 Kurt Weill Book Prize for outstanding scholarship in music theatre since 1900. Together with the St Lawrence String Quartet, he created *Defining the String Quartet*, the series of edX online courses on the music of Haydn and Beethoven.

***

Francesco Finocchiaro, *Kurt Weill and the Principle of 'Concertante Music'*

In a well-known interview with Lotte Eisner titled 'Musikalische Illustration oder Filmmusik?', Kurt Weill declared his personal program of emancipation of film music from the age-old principle of 'illustration', that is, the subordinate role of the musical component to dramatic action. The accompanying music — he claimed — should not simply illustrate the events that take place onstage, but should have a «purely musical shaping», a formal and structural integrity of its own. After this reflection, he strongly criticized Edmund Meisel's principle of *Lautbarmachung*: this idea of 'acoustic manifestation of reality', which had informed Meisel's score for *Panzerkreuzer Potemkin* (1926), in Weill's view would have never been able to provide «a solution to the problem of film music». On the contrary, according to Weill this long-awaited solution was to be achieved through an «objective, almost concertante film music». In film, just like in drama, music should be an independent component that stands in a dialectical relationship with the staged events, instead of sedulously illustrating them. Through this 'concertante' quality, music can become an essential part of the 'epic attitude' of the artwork. Through the tension that it establishes with the action or the visual sphere — for instance by providing an antiphrastic counterpoint to it, or by interrupting its flow — music unmasks the illusion of realism of the narrative fiction. 'Concertante music'

Abstracts and Biographies

prevents spectators from passively identifying with fiction, instead pushing them to actively search for nuances of meaning that hide behind outer behaviors. The principle of 'concertante music' was widely applied not only in Weill's musical theatre, from the music for *Die Dreigroschenoper* (1928) to the opera buffa *Aufstieg und Fall der Stadt Mahagonny* (1931), but also in many scores for cinema of the early 1930s-Germany by art-music composers and film-music specialists such as Paul Dessau, Hanns Eisler, Walter Gronostay and Weill himself. A thorough analysis of audiovisual montage casts light on a variety of dramaturgic choices, from dramaturgical counterpoint to horizontal collage, all of which share two basic features: the preservation of some degree of formal coherence for the musical component and the tendency to treat music and sound like any other montage material. Overcoming any slavish illustration of the narrated events in favor of a type of music that is able to establish a dialectical tension with the stage events, and constitutes an autonomous text with its own formal coherence and semantic density, is the most important legacy cinema received from Weill's principle of 'concertante music'.

Francesco Finocchiaro (Ph.D.) is a Research Scientist in Musicology at the State University of Milan. His research interests focus on the points of connection between composition, theory, and aesthetics in twentieth-century music. He has dedicated his studies to the Viennese School and released the Italian edition of Arnold Schoenberg's theoretical work *The Musical Idea* (Astrolabio, 2011). He has also published extensively on film music, with a special focus on the relationship between musical Modernism and German cinema (Palgrave Macmillan, 2017). His latest monograph, *Dietro un velo di organza* (Accademia University Press, 2020), deals with the film music criticism during the silent film era.

***

William A. Everett, *Kurt Weill and the American Operetta Tradition: «The Firebrand of Florence» and «Where Do We Go from Here?»*

In two works that appeared in 1945, the Broadway musical *The Firebrand of Florence* and the Hollywood home front propaganda film *Where Do We Go from Here?*, both with lyrics by Ira Gershwin, Weill paid homage to the operetta tradition while subverting some of its most recognizable attributes. This chapter provides a context for how audiences in the United States would have experienced operetta in the 1940s before investigating how Weill repurposed many of the genre's features in the two works. These include character- and couple-defining music, the prominent use of dance, and extended musical sequences. Especially notable in *The Firebrand of Florence* is the prominence given to the tarantella, a central role typically associated with the waltz in Viennese operettas, and an inversion of the musical tropes typically associated with social class. Operetta influences are evident in two sequences from *Where Do We go from Here?* The first is a Teutonic tavern scene that evokes Romberg's *The Student Prince* (1924) while the second is a ten-minute sequence set aboard Christopher Columbus's Santa Maria.

William A. Everett is Curators' Distinguished Professor of Musicology Emeritus at the University of Missouri-Kansas City Conservatory. He has published widely on musical theatre and other topics and is contributing co-editor to *The Cambridge Companion to the Musical* (with Paul R. Laird, 3rd ed., 2017), *The Palgrave Handbook of Musical Theatre Producers* (with Laura MacDonald, 2017), and *Intertextualiy in Music: Dialogic Composition* (with Violetta Kostka and Paulo F. de Castro, Routledge, 2021). He currently edits the series 'Cambridge Elements in Musical Theatre', published by Cambridge University Press.

***

Abstracts and Biographies

Naomi Graber, «*Steel Veins*»: «*Railroads on Parade*» *and the Industrial Folk*

During the Great Depression, audiences in the United States searched for a new foundational myth of the nation, which they found in the world of folklore. While initially exploited by the political left, by the end of the decade, the corporate world began to propagate the idea of an 'industrial folk' (Miller 2004). Melding ideas of nature and the 'everyman', this 'industrial folk' aesthetic created a new vision of the nation's history and culture rooted in free-market capitalism. This aesthetic was prominent at the 1939-1940 World's Fair, especially in Kurt Weill's *Railroads on Parade*. With its score based in folk music (pastiche and quotations), *Railroads on Parade* — like many of the Fair's spectacles — linked the natural and industrial worlds, and painted a picture of harmonious relations between labor and capital in order to align the railroad with the broader populist folkloric ethos of the era. While Edward Hungerford's libretto tells the story of the railroad as a series of genius inventions, with politicians applauding from the sidelines, Weill's arrangements of folksongs and other classic Americana portrays the railroad as integral to both the landscape and the culture of the United States. Through his unique orchestration — including the newly invented novachord — Weill painted the railroad as both old and new. The score includes instrumental versions of several folksongs that circulated within militant labor circles, thereby reclaiming the folkloric history of the railroad for industry.

Naomi Graber (Ph.D.) is an Associate Professor of Musicology at the University of Georgia's Hugh Hodgson School of Music. Her book *Kurt Weill's America* was published by Oxford University Press in 2021, and she has also published articles on Kurt Weill in *Musical Quarterly* and the *Journal for the Society of American Music*. Other publications have appeared in *Studies in Musical Theatre* and *American Music*. In addition, she co-edits and writes for *Trax on the Trail*, a website devoted to tracking music in U.S. electoral politics. She is the recipient of the University of Georgia's Willson Center Fellowship and the Virgil Thomson Fellowship from the Society for American Music.

***

Marida Rizzuti, *Shared Authorship and Compositional Process in 1940s Hollywood:* «*One Touch of Venus*» *by Kurt Weill and Ann Ronell*

Kurt Weill's musical productions for Hollywood originated in the 1930s, and by the 1940s displayed a variety of approaches. It is possible, however, to identify some recurring trends, one of which, his close collaboration with the figure of the musical arranger, was unusual in Holywood practice. It is also worth noting the practice of assigning the role of the arranger to women: in the case of Kurt Weill, the arranger who joined him in his work was Ann Ronell, the 'Tin Pan Alley Girl'. This collaboration generated a variety of procedures in the studio system that were reflected both in the creative processes of music for film and in the function of film music itself. The relationship between Weill and the studios was not idyllic: in the most crucial phase of his career (1940-1948), the composer worked intensively in the Broadway system innovating the musical, and in Hollywood he sought possible avenues of experimentation (dramatic structures, narrative flexibility) through exploiting the characteristics of cinematic language. The mediation of the arranger, Ann Ronell, was crucial in this relationship: she accommodated Kurt Weill's insistence on retaining his own compositional authorship by reinterpreting his work, and thereby also protected the interests of the production company. The film musical *One Touch of Venus* (1948) is an ideal case study for investigating this relationship between composer and arranger as it defined a practice of shared authorship in producing a soundtrack.

Abstracts and Biographies

Marida Rizzuti (Ph.D.) is a Research Fellow and Adjunct Professor at the Department of Humanistic Studies at the University of Turin. She coordinates the study group Galaxy Musical (GalMus) within the Italian Society of Musicology. Her areas of study are Musical and Film Musical, Exile studies, and Film Music History. She is the author of the volumes *I musical di Kurt Weill. Prospettive, generi e tradizioni* (Edizioni Studio 12, 2006), *Kurt Weill e Frederick Loewe. Pigmalione fra la 42° e il Covent Garden* (Edizioni Accademiche Italiane, 2015), *Molly Picon e gli artisti Yiddish born in USA* (Accademia University Press, 2021).

***

Arianne Johnson Quinn, *Musical Language, Censorship, and Theatrical Identity in Kurt Weill's London Works (1930-1935)*

This chapter re-evaluates Weill's place in London musical theatre, reframing his period of musical exile between his German and American periods as a period of creative experimentation and cultural assimilation. His German and American period is well-known by scholars, practitioners, and theatre audiences, however, there is much to learn from Weill's London exile, which served as a crossover between Germany and the United States. London period of exile began in 1933, beginning first in Paris and then London. Rather than dismissing this as a transitionary and insignificant era, this chapter demonstrates that Weill's evolution as a musical theatre composer reflected the cultural significance of theatre in London's West End in the pre-World War II landscape of Britain. It explores Weill's London period within the context reception history for *Anna-Anna* (originally *Die sieben Todsünden*, 1933) and *A Kingdom for a Cow* (1935) and the ways in which these works collided with the opinions of the British cultural establishment. Through an exploration of the reception history of Weill's London works, we learn about the intermingled forces of critical opinion, governmental policy, and their effect on the rapidly changing theatre industry in London's West End.

Arianne Johnson Quinn is the Music Special Collections Librarian, Warren D. Allen Music Library, Florida State University. She holds the Ph.D. in Musicology from Princeton University, and has worked as Digital Archivist and Research Associate for the Noël Coward Archive Trust. She has taught at South Georgia State College and Tallahassee Community College. Her research focuses on the intersections between the American and British musical in London's West End from 1920-1970, particularly the works of Noël Coward, Kurt Weill, Lerner and Loewe, Irving Berlin, Cole Porter and Rodgers and Hammerstein.

***

Tim Carter, *Kurt Weill's 'Song of the Free' (1942): A «United Nations Anthem»?*

In the first half of 1942, Kurt Weill was riding high on the huge success of his *Lady in the Dark* (1941) on Broadway. He also wrote a number of what now tend to be called his «wartime songs»: the reason is obvious enough given his otherwise precarious position in the United States as an 'enemy alien'. One of them, 'Song of the Free', needs separating from the others, however, because it was commissioned by the author of its text, Archibald MacLeish, for very specific reasons. MacLeish was Librarian of Congress and currently Director of the wartime Office of Facts and Figures (OFF, the predecessor of the Office of War Information). He originally approached Irving Berlin to set his poem with the aim of using the song in a government propaganda movie to be directed by John Ford. By the time Weill came on board instead, the OFF had been forced by intra-governmental squabbles to focus its attention on radio broadcasts: his 'Song of the Free' eventually anchored a program aired nationwide on what President Roosevelt had designated as United Nations Flag Day, on 14 June 1942. Tracing the song's development and its use across the media, and then how composer Harold Rome managed to scupper Weill's

Abstracts and Biographies

ambitions by way of his own 'Hymn of the United Nations' (using music by Dmitri Shostakovich), reveals a great deal about the issues that could make or break Weill's career in his adopted country.

TIM CARTER is the author of books on opera and musical theatre ranging from the late sixteenth and early seventeenth centuries through Mozart to Rodgers and Hammerstein. His edition of Paul Green and Kurt Weill's musical play, *Johnny Johnson* (1936), received the Claude V. Palisca Prize from the American Musicological Association for an 'outstanding edition or translation' published in 2012. He recently retired from the University of North Carolina at Chapel Hill, where he was David G. Frey Distinguished Professor of Music.

***

NILS GROSCH, *How Many Weills? Rethinking a Musician's Identity*
Are Kurt Weill's oeuvre and his artistic attitude characterized by a unifying, stable identity, or are they best framed according to various periods and parts? This question appears to be fundamental to the appreciation, reception, and research of the composer and his output. And the responses have turned out to be crucial in the history of the interpretation and performance of Weill's works. My essay analyzes strategies of identity management and image construction, from Weill's own identity policy, through critical reception, to the models provided in the scholarship on Weill. I am interested in the tensions that accrue around a composer who worked in different fields and on different stylistic levels, and whose life was split by persecution and escape. I use Stephen Greenblatt's concept of cultural mobility to challenge understandings of cultural identity, artistic coherence, and spatial belonging.

NILS GROSCH holds the chair in Musicology at the University of Salzburg/Austria where he is also Head of Department for Art history, Musicology and Dance studies. He earned his doctorate at the University of Freiburg i. Br. with a dissertation about *Die Musik der Neuen Sachlichkeit*, and completed his habilitation at the University of Basel with a thesis about *Lied und Medienwechsel im 16. Jahrhundert*. His major research interests are music and media, music and migration, and musical theatre. Nils co-heads research projects in the field of music, migration, and mobility: <musik-und-migration.at> and <musicmigrationmobility.com>.

***

LEO IZZO, *Changes in Kurt Weill's Music: Cross-Cultural Reception between Jazz and Avant-garde*
This article examines how jazz musicians drew on Kurt Weill's music, particularly in U.S. recordings between 1940 and 1965, with an appendix devoted to the Italian context. The story of how jazz musicians interpreted Weill's music goes through many historical changes. Along with changes in society, the recording industry, and culture, Weill's music has also been transformed through countless performances by jazz performers. Consequently, each stage of this narration requires a different perspective of analysis. For example, Mildred Bailey's version of 'The Saga of Jenny' in 1941 drew on exotic jazz music of the twenties, while the popularity of 'Mack the Knife' sung by Louis Armstrong and Bobby Darin reflected American societal changes. In the fifties, Weill's reception among jazz musicians was coordinated by record producer George Avakian, who could involve the best jazz composers of the time. He supervised several recordings with new arrangements of Weill's music, starting with *Miles Ahead*, by Miles Davis and Gil Evans. Some of these still little-known recordings with jazz interpretations of Weill's music should be reconsidered. In 1958 The Australian Jazz Quintet recorded the album *Modern Jazz Performance of Kurt Weill's Three Penny Opera*, with insightful arrangements by Teddy Charles, an innovative jazz composer. In 1963 Italian singer Laura Betti recorded two albums titled *Kurt Weill 1900-1933* and *Kurt Weill 1933-1950*. Bruno

Abstracts and Biographies

Maderna — one of the leading avant-garde composers in Italy — wrote the orchestra arrangements; some of the best Italian jazz musicians took part in the recordings, and Roberto Leydi, a relevant music scholar, wrote two essays for the album liner notes.

Leo Izzo obtained his Ph.D. in musicology in 2007 from the University of Bologna. As a musicologist he studies the relationship between improvisation and composition, both in jazz and contemporary music, through the analysis of the sketches. He wrote several essays on music and cinema, the music of Jelly Roll Morton, Bruno Maderna. He is working now on the facsimile edition of the Edgard Varèse's sketches for *Poème électronique*. He has been a music educator in Italian middle-schools since 2001 and a teacher trainer.

***

Misako Ohta, «*Die Dreigroschenoper*» in Japan: The 'Threepenny Fever' in Its Early Days

The acceptance of *Die Dreigroschenoper* in Japan, which began without much delay after its premiere in 1928, coincided with a breakthrough period in the acceptance of Western music against the backdrop of the rise of urban popular culture after the 1923 earthquake. The works were developed through a variety of media, including record releases, radio, concerts, movies, and stage performances. The various discourses exchanged in these media revealed what the people understood from *Die Dreigroschenoper* at that time. In particular, genre-crossing and broad-minded critics such as Shoiri played a special role in the reception of *Die Dreigroschenoper*, which was developed in multiple media. The recordings, films, the success of the translations and the demand for Japanese jazz songs, plus the active critical activities in newspapers and magazines were all factors that contributed to the triumph of the work. By 1932 three different productions of *Die Dreigroschenoper* had already been staged in Tokyo. The Tokyo Acting Troupe's 'Beggar's Theatre', a group of theatre artists of diverse origins and personalities. The tradition of the localization of Western culture, as seen in the Asakusa Opera, is also important. Moulin Rouge's *Die Dreigroschenoper* is connected to the world of revue. These performances already suggested the various possibilities of the genre-crossing 'Threepenny Opera'. In general, the prewar reception of *Die Dreigroschenoper* also reflected the attitude of those who eagerly learned and absorbed the West during the interwar period in Japan. In the early years, Weill's music attracted even more attention than Brecht's. Perhaps this was due, in part, to the fact that film and recordings played a greater role in the reception of *Die Dreigroschenoper* than the stage. The recordings of Weill's music are sung with Japanese translations of the lyrics. However, it was not until after the war that the full-fledged acceptance, development, and transformation of Weill's works, including Brecht's theories, began.

Misako Ohta is an Associate Professor of the Graduate School of Human Development and Environment, Division of Human Expression, at Kobe University. Born in Tokyo, she studied musicology at Tokyo University of the Arts (BA) and German Literature at Gakushuin University (MA). Her Ph.D. in music history (University of Vienna, 2001) examined artistic intention and its public effects in Kurt Weill's musical theatre from the 1920s into the 1930s. She teaches Western music history within its cultural context and transnational perspective and has been a music critic for the regional edition (Kansai area) of the Yomiuri shinbun since 2003. In 2019, co-authored with Professor Carol J. Oja, Katie Callam and Makiko Kimoto, the article 'Marian Anderson's 1953 Concert Tour of Japan: A Transnational History' was published in English and Japanese, and won the 2021 Irving Lowens Article Award). In March 2022 her critical biography of Kurt Weill in Japanese was published by Iwanami Shoten.

***

Abstracts and Biographies

Tobias Fasshauer, «*Hard to Distinguish from Cole Porter*»: *On the Deeper Truth of an Invective by Adorno*

In his 1956 article 'Vortrupp und Avantgarde', Theodor W. Adorno noted that Kurt Weill was «hard to distinguish from Cole Porter» in regard to his American oeuvre, save for the fact that «the light [Broadway] idiom caused him some difficulties». For later Weill scholars, it was precisely this statement that encapsulates Adorno's ignorant and prejudiced attitude towards the composer's artistic development. However, a comparative analysis of songs by Porter and Weill reveals that a certain similarity in style and compositional procedure cannot be dismissed easily, regardless of whether one shares the value judgement implied in Adorno's verdict or not. Interestingly, a common reference point can be identified quite early in Porter's and Weill's artistic careers, namely the direct or indirect connection to French non-expressionist musical modernism of the 1920s with its synthesis of art and entertainment, inspired by American popular culture. Already in 1923, Porter's Cocteauesque aesthetic background, which he had acquired during his residency in Paris, became apparent in his ballet *Within the Quota*. A few years later, Weill's composing became subject to the general, if largely unacknowledged, influence that especially Darius Milhaud exerted on *Neue Sachlichkeit* music and the *Gebrauchsmusik* movement in Germany. Both Porter and Weill were to re-import musical Americanism, as filtered through European culture, to the United States. This article highlights some striking structural und 'gestic' similarities in their work and examines the strategies by which Porter and Weill, two popular composers who strove for more than mere commercial success, met a fundamental challenge: How can originality, individuality, and artistic ambition come into their own in a highly standardized genre?

Tobias Fasshauer studied in Detmold and Berlin; his subjects were musicology and theatre studies, and he took a diploma in music theory. He took his doctorate in 2005 with a thesis on Kurt Weill's song style. Formerly on the staff of the Hanns Eisler Complete Edition, he is the editor of Eisler's Chamber Symphony and co-editor of his Collected Writings. He has lectured in musicology at Berlin universities and at the Universidad de los Andes in Bogotá, Colombia. From 2017 to 2022 he has been conducting the research project *John Philip Sousa and Musical Americanism in Continental Europe*, funded by the Deutsche Forschungsgemeinschaft, at the University of the Arts, Berlin.

***

Rebecca Schmid, *Street Scenes*

Weill hoped that his Broadway Opera *Street Scene* (1947) would «open new vistas for American composers» (Weill 1946). Less than a decade after his death, Leonard Bernstein reached the cultural mainstream with *West Side Story* (1957). A comparative analysis reveals that Weill's formal experimentation tilled the soil for what Bernstein hoped would be the «one, real moving American opera» (Bernstein 1828). That Bernstein reportedly scoffed at *Street Scene* on more than occasion only corroborates musical evidence of his inability to escape Weill's aesthetic precedent. The numbers of Rose and Sam share not only structural but motivic and harmonic parallels with those of Maria and Tony. My analysis builds upon previous studies of *Street Scene* to illustrate how allusions to Puccini's *Madama Butterfly* and Wagner's *Tristan und Isolde* serve a narrative function. Bernstein, meanwhile, includes cross-references to Beethoven, Wagner and — most importantly, Marc Blitzstein — that distract from *West Side Story*'s kinship to *Street Scene*. Weill's aesthetic legacy in *West Side Story* reveals the extent to which the Broadway Opera and other American-period works reified his mission to renew opera with formal hybrids that spoke as directly to a native sensibility as they rooted themselves in Old World tradition.

Abstracts and Biographies

Rebecca Schmid is an independent scholar with a focus on the twentieth and twenty-first centuries. Her book *Weill, Blitzstein, and Bernstein: A Study of Influence* has been published in 2023 by University of Rochester Press/Boydell & Brewer in the series 'Eastman Studies in Music'. Rebecca's research has been supported by the Austrian-American Fulbright Association, the German Academic Exchange Service and the Kurt Weill Foundation for Music. She has moderated and written program notes for the Cleveland Orchestra, Metropolitan Opera, Salzburg Festival and other organisations. Her writing appears frequently in such publications as the *Financial Times*, *New York Times* and *Opernwelt*.

***

Kim H. Kowalke, *What Makes Weill Weill?*

The title of my essay is intended to be pronounced 'What Makes Vile While', thereby invoking the longstanding critical construct that there were two composers: the German and the American. One can trace the origins of this to the 1940s when Weill's box office success on Broadway disqualified him as a 'real composer' for the likes of T. W. Adorno. In his obituary for Weill, Adorno planted the seeds of necessity for two Weills: in this endeavor he had to renounce all those elements in his musical language which had once created a Weillian atmosphere. He could no longer do what he knew how to do wile could no longer be a vile, so to speak. This paper investigates a half dozen constants in Weill's career and works. It concludes with Weill's own answer to the question, posed to him on 'Opera News on the Air' during intermission of the Metropolitan Opera's broadcast of Puccini's *Manon Lescaut*. After speculating what made Puccini Puccini, the question was turned back toward Weill himself. He responded, «in retrospect, I can see that when the music involved human suffering, it is, for better or worse, pure Weill». His answer is the matching bookend to his teacher Ferruccio Busoni's questioning of Kurt's youthful aspirations to create a popular, but serious and socially-engaged musical theatre: «What, you want to become a Verdi of the poor?» «Would that be so bad?» was Weill's prophetic retort.

Kim H. Kowalke is Professor Emeritus of Musicology at the Eastman School of Music and the Turner Professor Emeritus in Humanities at the University of Rochester. He is the author of many articles and four books on twentieth-century music and theatre, including *Speak Low: The Letters of Kurt Weill and Lotte Lenya* (University of California Press, 1996), which inspired the Broadway musical *LoveMusik*, directed by Hal Prince, and *Lenya Story*, premiered in Vienna in 2017. He is a fivetime time winner of ASCAP's Deems Taylor Award for excellence in writing about music and two Irving Lowens Awards for the best articles on American music. Since Lotte Lenya's death in 1981 Kowalke has served as President of the Kurt Weill Foundation, founding both the Kurt Weill Edition and the Lotte Lenya Singing Competition. He has conducted dozens of musical theatre productions and received the 2020 Erwin Piscator Honorary Award for his contributions to the international musical theatre.

Index of Names

A

Abraham, Gerald 248
Abravanel, Maurice 53, 122
Absaroka, Ruard 147
Acton, Howard 140
Adams, Phelps 140
Adey, Peter 154
Adorno, Theodor Wiesengrund x, 14-16, 26, 29-30, 155, 209-211, 215, 219, 221, 233, 250-251, 259
Ainsworth, Gardner 61
Ajemian, Anahid 168-169, 174
Ake, David 173
Alton, Robert 125
Amano, Kikuyo 200
Anderson, John Murray 43, 45
Anderson, Leslie 95
Anderson, Mab [Gertrude 'Mab' Higger] 151
Anderson, Marion 134
Anderson, Maxwell 120-122, 124, 126, 128, 131-132, 151, 248-249, 256-257
Arkell, Reginald 37
Armbruster, Robert 138-139
Armstrong, Louis 164, 168-173, 250
Asche, Oscar 102
Assmann, Aleida 186
Atkinson, Brooks 124, 249
Auric, Georges 191

Auslander, Philip 173
Austin, Everett 123
Autry, Gene 60
Avakian, George 168-170, 173-174, 177, 180

B

Bailey, Mildred 164-166
Baker, Herbert 40
Balanchine, George 104
Barberio Corsetti, Giorgio 186
Baresel, Alfred 189
Barthes, Roland ix
Basso, Gianni 179
Becher, Johannes 256
Bechet, Sidney 167
Beck, Ulrich 155
Becker, John 74
Beethoven, Ludwig van 136-138
Behrman, Samuel Nathaniel 124
Benét, Stephen Vincent 135-136, 138
Benjamin, Walter ix, 3-5, 13-16, 198
Bennett, Richard Rodney 213
Bennett, Tony 168
Bentley, Eric 254
Berg, Alban 225
Berio, Luciano 178
Berlin, Irving 118-119, 125, 167, 192, 211

Index of Names

Berlioz, Hector 228-229
Bernstein, David 132, 134
Bernstein, Leonard x, 41, 152, 225-232, 234, 242
Betti, Laura 179-180
Bing, Herman 52
Biron, Phineas J. 139
Black, Frank 134
Blitzstein, Marc 67, 167-169, 226, 228-229, 250
Blossom, Henry 40
Bolcom, William 213
Bonanova, Fortunio 53
Boyer, Charles 138
Brahms, Johannes 137, 139
Brainin, Joseph 139
Brecht, Bertolt viii, 6, 9, 13, 15, 29-31, 99, 104, 148, 163, 169, 177-178, 185-186, 188, 190, 192-193, 195, 197, 200-201, 203, 251-253, 256-257
Brentano, Felix 39
Brokensha, Jack 175
Bronstein, Ronald 26
Brookes, Sam 45
Brooks, Van Wyck 60
Brown, Forman 40
Brubeck, Dave 167-168, 174
Buchler, Michael 220
Buddle, Erroll 175
Burroughs, William 171
Busoni, Ferruccio 3, 149, 250

C

Calleia, Joseph 138
Calloway, Cab [Cabell Colloway] 164-166
Capra, Frank [Francesco Rosario Capra] 126, 134
Carisi, Johnny [John E. Carisi] 174
Carlisle, Kitty [Catherine Conn] 42
Carluccio, Giulia xi
Carrol, Charles 58
Carter, Desmond 37, 105
Carter, Tim x, 117
Cellini, Benvenuto 38, 43-44, 46-47
Chamberlain, Neville 136
Charell, Erik [Erich Karl Löwenberg] 153
Charles, Ray [Ray Charles Robinson] 172, 176
Charles, Teddy [Theodore Charles] 175-176

Charlot, André 105
Charmin, Martin 225
Chopin, Fryderyk 216, 228
Clarke, Kevin 45
Clayton, Buck [Wilbur Dorsey Clayton] 168
Clurman, Harold 254
Cochran, Charles Blake 102-103, 105-106
Cocteau, Jean 214, 256
Coe, Richard L. viii
Cohen, Noal 175
Coleman, Milton 122
Coleman, Ronald 138
Collins, Ray 138
Coltrane, John 177
Conniff, Ray [Joseph Raymond Conniff] 166
Cooper, Melville 49-50, 138
Copland, Aaron 60, 84
Corwin, Norman 122, 128, 131, 133
Cowan, Lester 83, 88-89
Coward, Noël 42, 105, 109
Crawford, Cheryl 13, 124, 232
Crocker, Charles 67
Crooks, Richard 127
Crosby, Bing [Harry Lillis Crosby] 166
Cuppini, Gil [Gilberto Cuppini] 179

D

Daniels, Julius 169
Darin, Bobby [Walden Robert Cassotto] x, 170-172, 250
Davis, Elmer 127
Davis, Miles 168, 174
Dean, Basil 103
Dean, James 170
Debussy, Claude 212
Delaunay, Charles 168
De Mille, Agnes 94
Denby, Edwin 123
Dessau, Paul 24, 30
Diamond, David 228
Dickson, Donald 138, 140
Dietrich, Marlene [Marie Magdalene Dietrich] 7
Dietz, Howard 119, 125
Dinerstein, Joel 171

Index of Names

Dolphy, Eric 177, 179
Donne, John 136
Donnelly, Dorothy 40
Donovan, William J. 119, 126-127
Dostoyevsky, Fyodor 253
Douglas, Melvyn 119-120
Drew, David 153, 155, 248
Dreyfus, Max 120, 216
Duncan, Todd 248
Dzerzhinsky, Feliks Edmundovich 137

E

Early, Stephen 128
Ebbs, Fred viii
Eddy, Nelson 130, 134-135
Egon, Max 149
Einstein, Alfred 100-101, 156-157
Eisenstein, Sergei 26
Eisler, Hanns 13, 24, 26, 29-33, 197, 215
Eisner, Lotte 21
Ellington, Duke [Edward Kennedy Ellington] 164, 168, 174
Elo, Mika 14
Enomoto, Kenichi 198-199
Ette, Wolfgang ix, 14-16
Evans, Gil [Ian Ernest Gilmore Green] 174-176
Evans, Wilbur 42
Everett, William A. ix, 37, 102
Eysell, Gus 132

F

Fargo, Wells 63
Farlow, Tal [Talmage Farlow] 167
Farquhar, Marion 39
Fasshauer, Tobias x, 31, 33, 209
Faulkner, George 135
Fauser, Annegret 117
Feld, Hans 24
Finocchiaro, Francesco ix, 21
Fitzgerald, Ella 172-173, 250
Fleischer, Dave 165
Flusser, Vilém 155, 157
Flynn, Errol 50
Ford, Jack 118

Ford, John [John Martin Feeney] 118-120, 126-128
Forrest, Helen 167
Forte, Allen 220
Fosse, Bob [Roberto Louis Fosse] viii
Foster, Stephen 63, 67
Foucault, Michel ix
Fracci, Carla 180
Francell, Jacqueline 105
Franco, Francisco 136
Freud, Sigmund 15
Friml, Rudolf 38, 40, 42, 102
Fulda, Ludwig 124
Futamura, Teiichi 198

G

Gabriel, Gilbert 123
Garner, Erroll 167-168
Gay, John 200
Gay, Peter 151
Gazzelloni, Severino 179
Genemon, Nakamura 198
Gershwin, George [Jacob Gershowitz] 60, 84, 167, 192, 221, 228, 232
Gershwin, Ira [Israel Gershowitz] 11, 37-38, 43-47, 52-54, 82, 125, 164-65, 221, 254, 257
Gilbert, Edward 39
Gilbert, William Schwenck 11, 16, 38, 40-41, 102, 106, 110
Gioia, Ted 173
Giuffre, Jimmy 180
Goffman, Ervin 149
Goldovsky, Boris 259-260
Goll, Iwan 5
Goodman, Benny [Benjamin David Goodman] 168
Gordon, Max 43
Gorin, Igor 141
Graber, Naomi ix, xi, 57, 79, 117, 164
Graham, Charles 67
Granz, Norman 172
Gray, Goldie 213
Gray, William B. 67
Grayson, Kathryn 141
Green, Johnny 131
Green, Paul 256

Index of Names

Greenblatt, Stephen 154
Grofé, Ferde 67
Gronostay, Walter 27-28
Grosch, Nils x, 147, 225, 227, 234
Grossmann, Stefan 152
Guthrie, Thomas Anstey 124

H

Haber, Alois 191
Hall, Jim [James Hall] 173
Hall, Stuart 151
Hammerstein, Oscar 38, 40, 125
Hammond, Laurens 66
Hannon, Bob 133
Hansen, Miriam 13
Harbach, Otto 40
Harburg, Yip [Edgar Yipsel Harburg] 141
Harris, Roy 119
Hart, Lorenz 132
Hart, Moss viii, 254, 256
Haver, June 50, 52
Hayes, Helen 118, 120, 122, 125, 129
Head, Nancy 140
Healey, Dick [Richard James Healey] 175
Hecht, Ben 122, 125
Hellman, Lillian 41
Henderson, Fletcher 168
Herbert, Alan Patrick 105-106
Herbert, Victor 38, 40, 42, 51
Herrmann, Bernard 128
Herzig, Sig 50
Hill, Joe 74
Hindemith, Paul 26, 187
Hinton, Stephen vii-ix, 3, 153, 227, 232-233, 255
Hitler, Adolf 101, 125, 136, 156-157
Hoeckner, Berthold ix, 14-16
Holmes, Clellon 171
Hopkins, Mark 67
Horten, Gerd 127
Hosokawa, Chikako 198-199
Houseman, John 123, 141
Hudson, Paul 51
Hughes, Langston 233, 256-257
Hungerford, Edward 57, 64

Huntington, Collis P. 67
Huston, Walter 166
Hyde, Anthony 132, 134

I

Ichikawa, Gen 198
Ihering, Herbert 31
Illiano, Roberto xi
Indy, Vincent d' 212
Ito, Michiro 196
Ito, Tomoko 198
Iturbi, José 141
Izzo, Leo x, 163

J

Jaensch, Andreas 225
Jamal, Ahmad [Frederick Russell Jones] 174
James, Edward 103-104
James, Harry 166
Janácek, Leoš 253
Janney, Russell 40
Jaxon, Frankie [Frank Devera Jackson] 164-165
Jefferson, Thomas 136
Jones, Sidney 102
Jones, Thad [Thaddeus Joseph Jones] 177
Juchem, Elmar 117
Judah, Theodore B. 67

K

Kafka, Franz 253
Kaiser, Georg viii, 103, 249, 256-257
Kálmán, Emmerich 47
Kalynak, Kathryn 79
Kamitsukasa, Shoken 190
Kander, John viii
Kaneko, Yobun 200
Katayama, Shinjiiro 198
Kaufman, George 125, 140
Kawanishi, Masaaki 191
Kawashima, Nuiko 198
Keller, Hans 109
Kerby, Paul 39
Kern, Jerome 119, 125, 221
Kessel, Barney 166

Index of Names

Kimbal, Reverend 198
Kirk, Elise K. 232
Kleinsinger, George 125
Klemperer, Otto 188, 192-194
Knight, Felix 42
Kobayashi, Takiji 204
Koechlin, Charles 212
Koegler, Horst 209
Koga, Masao 194
Konoe, Hidemaro 194
Korngold, Erich Wolfgang 41
Kostelanetz, Andre 140
Koussevitzky, Serge 121
Kowalke, Kim H. vii-viii, x, 84, 117, 152, 167, 170, 210, 212, 214, 233-234, 236, 247
Kracauer, Siegfried 26, 29
Krenek, Ernst 155-156
Kuhl, Cal 135
Kundera, Milan 253-254
Kurnitz, Harry 89
Kuroda, Susumu 194
Kuroda, Yuzuru 200

L

Lander, Jack 175
Lang, Fritz [Friedrich Lang] 9-10, 16-17, 81
Lanset, Andy 136
Latham, Edward D. 239
Lawrence, Gertrude 117
Lazar, Irving Paul 12, 83, 88, 89
Lecoq, Charles 38
Lehár, Franz 38-39, 41, 102
Lenya, Lotte 37, 49, 103-106, 111, 117, 120-122, 125-126, 128-130, 134, 141, 167, 170, 172, 174, 250-251, 256, 260
Lerner, Alan Jay 248, 256-257
Leslie, Joan 51
Lewis, John 177
Lewis, William B. 126, 128, 130-131, 135, 139
Leydi, Roberto 178-179
Lichtenberg, Bernard 57, 62
Lincoln, Abraham 58, 138
Lindbergh, Charles 61, 148
Litvak, Anatole 126, 134

Lomax, Alan 60, 64, 169, 181
Lomax, John 60, 64
Lorentz, Pare 61-62, 75
Lorre, Peter [László Löwenstein] 138
Losch, Tilly [Ottilie Ethel Losch] 104
Louis, James 174
Luce, Henry 62
Luttazzi, Lelio 167

M

MacArthur, Charles 122, 125
MacDonald, Jeanette 130
Macero, Teo 176
MacKay, Robert 108
MacLeish, Archibald 117-122, 126-136, 139, 141
MacMurray, Fred 11, 50
Maderna, Bruno x, 178-180
Mamoulian, Rouben 226, 248
Mandel, Frank 40
Maré, Rolf de 212
Martin, Tony [Alvin Morris] 166
Maruyama, Sadao 198
Marx, Groucho [Julius Henry Marx] 125
Masuyama, Takashi 186
Mataroku, Kumazawa 200
Mauceri, John 225
Maurrant, Frank 255
Mayer, Edwin Justus 38, 43, 45-46
McClinton, H. L. 131
McGee, Kristin 165
McIlvenna, Una 169
Mead, George 39
Meehan, John 39-40
Mehring, Walter 141
Meisel, Edmund 22, 25-26
Mellett, Lowell 127-128
Meredith, Burgess 119-120, 122
Mero-Irian, Yolanda 39
Meservey, Douglas 126, 134
Milhaud, Darius 133, 191, 212, 214
Miller, James S. 62
Mingus, Charles 167, 176
Mitchell, Thomas 138
Mitropoulos, Dimitri 174

275

Index of Names

Monk, Thelonious 175
Moravia, Alberto 179
Morgan, Bill 50
Morgan, Dennis 51
Mori, Masato 194
Morishige, Hisaya 203
Moroi, Saburo 198
Morton, Jelly Roll [Ferdinand Joseph LaMothe] 169, 181
Mozart, Wolfgang Amadeus 99, 191, 256, 258
Murayama, Tomoyoshi 197, 203
Murphy, Gerald 212
Murphy, Turk [Melvin Edward Alton Murphy] 169
Mussolini, Benito 136

N

Nagayama, Tomoyuki 185
Nakane, Hiroshi 194-195
Nakano, Masaaki 200-201
Nanbu, Takane 200
Nash, Ogden 86, 147, 256
Nazimova, Alia 138
Neher, Caspar 257
Neher, Erika 257
Nestroy, Johann 186
Niederauer, Henriette Margareta 104
Ninomiya, Shu 189-190
Norton, Frederick 102
Norvo, Red [Kenneth Norville] 167
Novello, Ivor [David Ivor Davies] 102

O

O'Connell, Charles 141
Offenbach, Jacques 38-41, 46, 107, 111, 256
Ohta, Misako x, 185
Oja, Carol J. 185
O'Neill, Eugene viii, 256
Otaguro, Motoo 192
Ouspenskaya, Maria 138
Overton, Hall 175-176

P

Pabst, Georg Wilhelm 4, 6, 9, 30-31, 188, 196, 198, 201
Page, Ruth 121, 125, 128
Parker, Frank 140
Partington, Jack 132
Pasolini, Pier Paolo 179
Paton, Alan 248
Pavlova, Anna 104
Pennington, Ann 213
Perelman, S. J. 256
Perret, Jeanne 140
Petrillo, James C. 139
Pickford, Mary 213
Piston, Walter 84
Polignac, Edmond de 212
Pollock, Arthur 39
Porter, Cole x, 38, 102, 106, 109, 167, 209-215, 217-221, 251
Preminger, Otto 53
Presley, Elvis 171
Pringsheim, Klaus 190
Puccini, Giacomo 227, 234, 247, 259-260

Q

Quinn, Anthony [Manuel Antonio Rodolfo Quinn-Oaxaca] 51
Quinn, Arianne Johnson x, 99

R

Rady, Simon 125
Raft, George 9
Ramirez, Carlos 53
Randel, Don Michael 211
Ratoff, Gregory 11
Ravel, Maurice 212
Redlich, Hans 251-252
Reger, Max 248
Reich, Steve 176
Reinhardt, Gottfried 39-40
Reinhardt, Max 121
Reisman, David viii
Reno, Teddy [Ferruccio Merk Ricordi] 167
Reuther, Walter 62
Riccardi, Ricky 169
Rice, Elmer 67, 124, 226, 256-257
Richter, Hans 27-28
Rilke, Rainer 256

Index of Names

Rittmann, Trude 94-95
Rizzuti, Marida ix, xi, 79
Robbins, Jerome 234
Roberts, Ben 39
Robeson, Eslanda 74
Robeson, Paul 127, 134-135
Robinson, Bill [William Luther Robinson] 125
Rodgers, Richard 38, 119, 132, 221
Rohde, Bryce 175
Rollins, Sonny [Theodore Walter Rollins] 172
Romberg, Sigmund 38, 40-41, 45, 51, 84, 102, 119, 125, 130
Rome, Harold 140
Ronell, Ann x, 79, 83-96
Roosevelt, Eleanor 119-120, 132
Roosevelt, Franklin 58
Roosevelt, Theodore 128-129, 131, 135-136
Rosen, Lucie Bigelow 124
Ross, Adrian 39
Ross, Lanny [Lancelot Patrick Ross] 248
Rosten, Leo 127
Russell, George 176
Ruttmann, Walter 24-26
Ryskind, Morrie 50

S

Sala, Massimiliano xi
Salisbury, Leah 83-84
Salten, Felix 45
Sandburg, Carl 64
Sansone, Brady xi
Sapiro, Ian 79
Satie, Erik 213-214
Sato, Akiko 200
Savory, Whitelaw 147
Scarborough, Dorothy 64, 73
Schebera, Jürgen vii
Schiffer, Marcellus 187
Schindler, Hans 168
Schmid, Rebecca x, 225
Schmidt, Jakob 148
Schmidt-Boelcke, Werner 24
Schoenberg, Arnold 52

Schröder, Kurt 29
Schubert, Franz 45
Schubert, Giselher 210
Schuller, Gunther 174-175, 180
Schwab, Laurence 40
Segal, Jerry [Gerald Segal] 175
Segal, Vivienne 50
Seiter, William 89
Selassie, Haile 136
Senda, Koreya 196-199, 201, 204
Senda, Yoshiro Ito 198
Shaftel, Matthew 211, 215
Shakespeare, William 174
Shaw, Artie [Arthur Arshawsky] 166
Shawn, Allan 228
Sheldon, Gene [Eugene Hume] 50
Sheldon, Sidney 39
Sherwood, Robert 123-124, 141
Shimizu, Keiichi 198
Shimoyagawa, Keisuke 200
Shinohara, Masao 200
Shioiri, Kamesuke 191-192, 194-196, 198, 200
Short, Hassard 125
Shorter, Wayne 172
Shostakovich, Dmitri 140-141
Sidney, Silvia 9
Simeone, Nigel 226, 230, 234
Sinatra, Frank [Francis Sinatra] 167, 250
Smith, Bessie 165, 170
Smith, Helen 232, 240
Smith, Kate 127, 131, 134
Smith, Paul 173
Sommerfeld, Paul 67
Sondheim, Stephen 234, 256
Sousa, John Philip 216
Spaulding, George 67
Spewack, Bella 89
Stalling, Carl W. 8
Stanford, Leland 67
Starewicz, Władysław 24
Stegmann, G. F. 258
Stein, Dave xi, 117, 247
Steinbeck, John 123, 256

Index of Names

STEINER, Max 67
STICKLES, William 133
STOKOWSKI, Leopold 141
STOLZ, Robert 39
STOTT, William 60
STRAUS, Josef 227
STRAUSS, Johann Jr 38-39, 41, 45, 111, 216
STRAUSS, Oscar 106
STRAVINSKY, Igor 191, 212, 227-229, 253-254
STRAYHORN, Billy [William Strayhorn] 174
STREHLER, Giorgio 178
STROBEL, Heinirch 28
SULLIVAN, Arthur 11, 16, 38, 40-41, 102, 106, 110
SUMIKAWA, Hisashi 198
SUPPÉ, Franz von 38
SUTRO, John 103
SWAIN, Joseph 230, 232
SYMONETTE, Lys 50, 84, 225

T

TAILOV, Alexander 191
TAKAHASHI, Toyoko 198-199, 202
TAKEDA, Rintaro 190-191
TAMURA, Akiko 198
TANI, Kenichi 185
TARUSKIN, Richard 252
TAYLOR-JAY, Claire ix
TERRY, David 140
THIELE, Wilhelm 7
THOMSON, Virgil 58, 61, 65-66, 75, 122-123, 251-252
THORPE, Richard 171
TIBBETT, Lawrence 127, 135
TOCH, Ernst 84
TOKUGAWA, Musei 200
TOLSTOY, Lev 253
TRIVAS, Victor 31
TROUT, Robert [Robert Albert Blondheim] 133
TYLER, Beverly 49-50
TYNAN, Kenneth 227

U

UCHIDA, Yoichi 194
UNSELD, Melanie 154

V

VALDAMBRINI, Oscar 179
VAMBERY, Robert 37, 105
VARÉSE, Edgard 176
VAUGHAN, Sarah 167, 174
VERDI, Giuseppe 181, 260
VERNEUIL, Louis 39
VERTOV, Dziga [David Abelevič Kaufman] 24, 28
VILLON, François [François de Montcorbier] 42

W

WAGNER, Richard 13-14, 23, 99, 188, 228, 230, 236, 238, 242
WALLACE, Henry 135
WEILL, Albert 249
WEILL, Emma 249
WEILL, Hans 256
WEILL, Ruth 255
WELLES, Orson 123
WELLS, Elizabeth 226, 228, 242
WESS, Richard 170
WHALEN, Grover 61
WHITE, Eric 100
WHITMAN, Walt [Walter Whitman] 118, 125, 130
WILDER, Alec [Alexander Lafayette Chew Wilder] 215-216, 220
WILSON, Teddy [Theodore Wilson] 167
WINDING, Ole 156
WOLFF, Nat 135
WOLPE, Stefan 94-95
WOUK, Herman 256
WRIGHT, Martha 248
WRIGHTSON, Earl 47, 49-50

Y

YAMADA, Kosaku 191, 197
YOSHI, Hijikata 198

Z

ZWERIN, Michael 177